THE
SOFT
WHISPER
OF
Roses

THE
SOFT
WHISPER
OF
Roses

MYRA JOHNSON

www.FawnRidgePress.com

Inquiries concerning rights should be addressed to:
William Morris Endeavor Entertainment, LLC
11 Madison Avenue, 18th Floor
New York, New York 10010
Attn: **Derek Zasky**

PUBLISHER'S CATALOGING-IN-PUBLICATION DATA
Name: Johnson, Myra, author, 1951-
Title: The soft whisper of roses / Myra Johnson
Description: First trade paperback original edition | Fawn Ridge Press, Georgetown, TX
Identifiers: LCCN 2020915554 | ISBN 978-1-7356107-0-2 (pbk.) | ISBN 978-1-7356107-1-9 (ebk.)

Cover Design © Fawn Ridge Press
Photos by Annie Spratt on Unsplash

Author represented by Natasha Kern Literary Agency

DEDICATION

For my loving husband, our beautiful daughters and their godly husbands, our amazing grandchildren, and all our extended family. I hold each of you close in my heart.

In fond remembrance of Mrs. Constance Haugarth and the cast and crew of the 1967 Mission High School production of I Remember Mama, including my cuddly old cat Tippy in the role of "Uncle Elizabeth." I cherish the memories!

1

Cell phone jammed against her ear, Rebecca Townsend paced before the windows of her room at the InterContinental Frankfurt Hotel. *Pick up, Gary. Please pick up.*

"Thank you for calling DataTech," announced the tinny recording. "Gary Townsend is out of the office at this time. Please record your name and—"

She stabbed the END button. The ten-hour overseas flight from Dallas had left her with a throbbing head and swollen ankles, and heading straight from the hotel into meetings hadn't helped. She kicked off her beige pumps and collapsed upon the downy white duvet. Staring at the ceiling, she mentally double-checked the time difference. Gary should have arrived at his office an hour ago, and his conference wasn't scheduled until later in the morning. And where was Jean? At least his administrative assistant should have picked up.

"Why aren't you answering, Gary?" Rebecca's stomach churned. Her husband hadn't been the same since they'd learned his ex-wife had terminal cancer, and the stress was taking a mighty toll on their marriage. They'd argued more than once about what would happen to Noelle, Gary and Kate's fifteen-year-old daughter, after her mother died.

Perhaps it was only a superficial solution, but she couldn't shake the idea that if only Gary would give up the chic, high-rent condo he'd been living in when they married and let them buy a real home in the suburbs—a stately Tudor or a rambling ranch-style, just anything with a lawn and trees and maybe a white picket fence, somewhere far removed from the confusing, congested Dallas freeways—then maybe they could make this blended family thing work. She had to think of her own son, too, didn't she? Though Kevin seemed to take things in stride more easily than most eleven-year-olds, he was quickly growing attached to Gary as his stepdad and deserved some stability in his young life.

More than anything, Rebecca needed to believe that after a year or two or ten, she wouldn't find herself alone again, sifting through the debris of another broken marriage.

The bedside phone warbled. Probably her boss, Matt Garrison, phoning from his suite down the hall. She forced herself upright and heard the weariness in her voice as she answered. "Rebecca Townsend."

"Hey, it's me." *Gary.* "Just making sure you got to the hotel okay."

Tension flowed out of her limbs. She closed her eyes and sent up a prayer of thanks. "I tried to call you, but your voicemail kept picking up."

"Sorry, Jean's coming in late because of a dental appointment, and I forgot to turn off the auto-responder. How was your flight?"

"Too long. I ache all over." She propped a pillow against the headboard and snuggled into its softness as she pictured her husband's strong, lean face. "How are things there?"

"Crazy. This presentation's had me tied up in knots." Papers shuffled in the background, followed by computer clicks and beeps.

"You'll do fine. You always do." Gary's sharp head for business and confidence under pressure were among the qualities she most admired about him. Except over the past several weeks his confidence had grown shaky. She rubbed her ankles and braved the question she dreaded to ask. "Have you heard any more about Kate?"

"Her mother caught me before I left for the office." More computer noises. "Kate's failing fast. A few more days, a week at the most."

"Oh, Gary."

He responded with silence, leaving her to wonder once more about what she could do to help him—help *all* of them—through this devastating situation. She prayed daily for Kate, but even more for Noelle. Losing a parent at such a vulnerable age? Rebecca shuddered. She remembered the anguish over her father's death all too well.

As for Gary, Rebecca grew more and more concerned that he'd never fully dealt with his feelings toward Kate, much less the effect of their divorce on Noelle. He grew more distant every day, refusing to even discuss what would happen to Noelle after her mother died. The most he'd ever said was that the likelihood of Noelle agreeing to move in with him was about as strong as DataTech instituting casual Fridays. Which meant never.

Gary cleared his throat. "Can we talk later? I need to put the finishing touches on my report."

"Maybe you should let someone else handle it. You should be with—"

"I've put way too much work into this project to pass it off to one of Charles Sharp's boot-licking cronies. You've worked at DataTech long enough to know the drill. This could be my career on the line."

His declaration struck a nerve, and her next words flew out before she could stop them. "So your career means more to you than your own family? Maybe that's why your first marriage ended so badly—"

Silence as dark as the Atlantic Ocean flooded the distance between them. Rebecca pressed a trembling fist to her mouth and wished she could snatch back the last twenty seconds. "Honey, I'm so sorry. That was cruel and insensitive of me."

"We're both maxed out on stress, okay? When you get home, we'll go out for dinner. Somewhere special. You pick the place."

"I'd rather—"

"Just a second, babe." A scratchy sound and then muffled voices. He came back on the line. "Gotta get ready for the meeting. Call me later."

"I will. I"—the phone clicked in her ear—"love you."

"Townsend, are you with us?"

Gary scrubbed a hand over his eyes and blinked several times. His colleagues' impatient stares scissored through him. By force of will he'd managed to put family matters out of his thoughts for the past hour and focus on business. But listening to his boss drone on about the company's latest financial forecasts and the increasing possibility of layoffs left him brain-dead.

He straightened and adjusted his tie. "Sorry, Mr. Sharp." It was always *Mr.* Sharp with his boss, a relic from the old school of corporate management. Nothing about the crusty old goat invited familiarity.

Sharp signaled his assistant to bring him fresh coffee. "I repeat, Gary, are you prepared to begin your Tokyo presentation, or shall we move on to Andrew and his Toronto report?"

"I'm ready, sir." Corralling his thoughts, Gary strode to the end of the conference room and connected his notebook computer to the projector cable outlet. Moments later, the opening page of his PowerPoint presentation flashed onto a screen. He directed the red beam of a laser pointer at figures on a graph as he updated the group on his current project, a major computer network upgrade for their sister corporation in Tokyo.

"As you can see, we've managed so far to stay well under budget . . ." Out of the corner of his eye, Gary glimpsed Jean Calhoun slip through the door. Hands clasped behind her, she cast him an apologetic glance.

"One moment, please." His gut tightened as he sidled over to his prim, gray-haired administrative assistant. "Jean, this had better be important."

Her gaze fell. "Mrs. Whitney called. I thought you'd want to know right away."

His shirt collar suddenly felt three sizes too small. He'd spoken with Irene Whitney, Kate's mother, only a few hours ago. She'd never bother him at work, unless—

Not now. Please, not now!

Keeping his eyes trained on the mole above Jean's right eyebrow, he forced himself to speak over the ache in his throat. "Kate?"

Jean nodded, her eyes moist.

Detach, detach. He sensed Sharp's knifelike glare and coughed softly into his fist. "Thank you. Please return Mrs. Whitney's call and extend my condolences."

The woman's forehead creased. "Sir?"

Okay, maybe he'd become slightly *too* adept at separating the personal and professional aspects of his life. Not much he could do about it right now, what with the rustling of papers and his colleagues' restless silence screaming for his attention.

"Tell her I'll be calling soon." With a firm hand, he ushered Jean through the massive oak door, then turned with a bland smile. "Please excuse the interruption." He clicked on his laser pointer and continued the presentation.

When the meeting ended forty-five minutes later, he marched straight to his office and collapsed into the plush comfort of his leather desk chair. Jean had gone to lunch by then but had left a note on a pink message form stuck to his telephone receiver: *My deepest sympathies to you and your daughter. Please call Mrs. Whitney ASAP.*

"Oh, God . . ." He mentally trashed the pointless beginnings of a prayer. Faith had always been Kate's crutch, and lately Rebecca's, but Gary had lost his a long time ago. Who could continue believing in a God who allowed this kind of suffering and grief, a God who beat people down, destroyed their hopes, and then systematically snatched them away?

No, he could do just fine without God's help. Whether he succeeded or failed, he did it on his own terms.

He lifted the receiver and inhaled a couple of steadying breaths before punching in the number at Kate's house. Two rings later, his ex-mother-in-law answered. "Oh, Gary, I'd hoped you'd call."

"I've been in a meeting." He twined the phone cord around his fingers until it hurt. His throat felt like the Sahara. "So Kate's . . . gone?"

"She went peacefully, just drifted off to sleep." Irene gave a sniffle.

"How's Noelle holding up?"

"I don't think she's fully accepted it yet." A pause and a muffled sob. "I know how important your work is, but could you try to spend some time with her today? You're her father, Gary. She may not admit it, but she needs you."

He extricated his bloodless fingers from the phone cord as his gaze slid to his lower left desk drawer. Heart thudding, he pulled out the framed photo he'd tucked away there after his marriage to Rebecca. Taken on the ski slopes at Aspen the winter before he and Kate separated, the picture showed Kate and Noelle bundled in fur-trimmed parkas. The willowy, long-haired girl, barely thirteen at the time, shot a brilliant smile toward the camera lens, her cheeks pink from the cold. Kate's eyes, however, shone with unspoken questions, to which he'd given all the wrong answers.

He laid the photo face down on his desk. "You haven't forgiven me either, have you, Irene?"

A long pause. "It isn't my place."

A gold-plated pen engraved with his name and title, Gary Townsend, Senior Systems Manager, lay at a precise 45-degree angle across the top right corner of his desk calendar. He rolled the pen forward until the words were obscured. "I'll come by later this afternoon. I need to wrap up some things here."

He'd scarcely replaced the receiver when his assistant, apparently back from lunch, buzzed him on the intercom. "What is it, Jean?"

"Sir, Mrs. Townsend is on line two."

Kate?

He slammed his palm against his skull. *Of course not, you idiot.*

He shoved aside his memories of the tall, dark-haired Kate, waif-thin the last time he'd seen her yet beautiful as ever, and shifted his focus to the current Mrs. Townsend, his petite, auburn-haired wife of six months. He reached for the phone. "Rebecca?"

"Hi, honey. Matt and I are leaving in a few minutes to meet our client for dinner, but I wanted to call while I had a moment. Is your presentation over? How'd it go?"

Gary shrank into the cold comfort of the leather upholstery and squeezed his eyes shut. "Kate's dead."

Rebecca tore about her hotel room tossing clothes into her suitcase and gathering up the makeup and toiletries she'd only hours earlier arranged on the bathroom counter. She had just over two hours to get to the airport, pass through security, and board her hastily arranged flight to Dallas. Already she felt the whiplash of jet lag.

But Gary needed her, even if he couldn't bring himself to say so, and her heart ached with the urgency to be with him. Vowing that no amount of Matt Garrison's pleading, cajoling, or threats would keep her in Frankfurt, she waited until she'd caught a taxi to the airport before calling Matt on her cell.

"Think about what you're doing, Rebecca." Matt's disappointment cut deep. "If you desert me now, it won't look good for the promotion we've been talking about."

Her stomach heaved. "I can't even think about the promotion right now."

"Then at least have a thought for your job security. You've heard the downsizing rumors."

Despite Germany's expanded anti-smoking laws, a faint odor of stale tobacco lingered in the taxi. Already nauseated from nerves and hunger, Rebecca tried to block the smell with a hand to her face. "Didn't you hear what I said? Gary's ex-wife just died. He's grieving. I need to be with him."

Matt released a harsh laugh. "This isn't the Rebecca I know. Your career used to be top priority. What's with you these days?"

"Nothing's *with me*. And for your information, my family has *always* come first." Guilt choking her, Rebecca wondered whom she most needed to convince—Matt or herself? She grabbed the front-seat headrest as the taxi lurched to a halt at the terminal entrance. "I have to go, Matt. I'll call you from Dallas tomorrow."

She jammed the phone into her purse and prayed she hadn't just sounded the death knell on her future with DataTech. The job had started out mainly as a means to an end. As a single mom, she'd needed steady income with insurance benefits. She'd never expected to gain so much satisfaction from determining her clients' computer programming needs, creating innovative software solutions, and training companies' in-house IT reps.

She loved her job, yes. But real meaning came from raising

her son, Kevin, the center of her universe, and it was torture being away from him so much. Her foremost goal was to gain enough seniority at DataTech that she could cut back on the travel and stay closer to home.

The weight of her suitcase threatened to pull her arm out of its socket. Inside the terminal, she paused near a bank of informational TV screens to catch her breath and watched a young mother scurry past with two fair-haired boys in tow. The smaller child tripped and fell, and the mother shouted something in German before swooping the boy into her arms and hurrying on her way. Planes didn't wait for anyone.

Neither did fast-paced careers or growing sons.

Rebecca scanned the overhead signs until she spotted the counter where she needed to check in. It was too late to book passage on a commercial airline, but her savvy travel agent had secured a seat on another company's corporate charter jet leaving for the States tonight. She muscled her suitcase and carryon toward the counter and shoved her passport toward the agent.

The dark-haired woman beamed a tired smile. "Good evening, Mrs. Townsend. We have been expecting you. *Bitte*, you have just the one large bag?"

"That's right." Rebecca rested her forearm on the counter as the agent entered information into a computer terminal. She noticed the woman's simple gold wedding ring. "You have family?"

"*Ja*, three daughters, one a teenager." The agent gave a meaningful roll of her eyes. "You?"

"A son. He's eleven." And a fifteen-year-old stepdaughter she hardly knew. *Dear God, help!* Would the girl ever be able to accept Rebecca as her stepmother?

The desk agent handed Rebecca a claim check for her luggage and explained how to find the departure gate once she passed through security. Rebecca jerked up the handle on her carryon and tramped through the terminal, almost looking forward to several hours of cramped, restless sleep in an airplane seat. The bags under her eyes must be the size of steamer trunks by now.

Her cell phone sang to her from the depths of her purse, the jazz riff tone she'd assigned to Matt. No doubt he wanted to regale her with more doom and gloom about how she was throwing her career away. She let it go to voicemail and kept walking.

Noelle hung back as her grandmother and the hospice nurse spoke with the quiet man in the dark suit who had come to take her mother away. After his assistant helped him move the body onto a gurney, Noelle rushed forward to seize his arm before he could zip up the stiff blue bag. "Please don't cover her face."

"Of course." The little man nodded and left the bag partway open.

She followed them as far as the front walk. But one look at the hearse parked in the driveway and she bolted, straight for the airy, pink bedroom where her mother had spent the final weeks of her life. Snatching up a white crocheted throw, she strained for some sense of Mom's presence, but only the subtle whisper of her mother's English Rose cologne remained.

Gran leaned in the doorway, her eyes puffy and red. "They're gone, honey. Are you all right?"

"I'm . . . okay." *I'll never be okay again.* Noelle curled one leg under her on the edge of the empty bed. Her huge black-and-white cat, Laurence, mewed and rubbed against her foot. She bent to scoop him into her arms.

Helen, the hospice nurse, slipped into the room. "Your mother was a lovely and brave woman, Noelle. Always remember her that way."

Angry words lodged like a chunk of ice in Noelle's throat.

After all Helen had done for Mom—for all of them—she'd not hurt the gentle, soft-spoken nurse for anything.

Gran dabbed her nose with a crumpled tissue. "Yes, yes, thank you, Helen."

"I'm sure y'all need some time to yourselves, to talk about arrangements and such." Helen started toward the bed. "I'll just change the linens and be on my way."

"Wait—not yet." Noelle could still see the impression of her mother's head upon the pink satin pillow. She strained to picture Mom's face from before, when she was healthy and strong, but the sickly pallor of her mother's last days would likely haunt her forever. She buried her nose in Laurence's fur and inhaled deeply. If only she could let go and cry like Gran.

Maybe she'd already used up all her tears—first when Mom was diagnosed, and then day after day watching her mother endure those horrible chemotherapy and radiation treatments. At the end of March, at a follow-up visit with the oncologist, the doctor had suggested Noelle should wait in the outer office. Fear snaked through her, and she'd refused to leave the room.

Compassion laced the doctor's normally professional tone as he addressed Noelle's mother. "We can continue the chemo and hope for a miracle, or we can stop everything except pain medication, and you can live the next few months in fairly good health, considering."

Mom had taken only a moment to decide. "I'll take the second option."

"Mom, no! *Please!*"

She'd quietly patted Noelle's hand until the sobbing had subsided, then faced the doctor with a determined smile. "It isn't that I don't believe in miracles, but I already know where I'm spending eternity. If God chooses to take me home, I'll go with courage and dignity."

So on this warm, breezy August morning, Mom had died

exactly as she'd planned, in her own home, in her own bed, with only Noelle, Gran, and the hospice nurse in attendance.

And Noelle would never, ever, ever in a million years forgive her father for not being there.

The doorbell chimed over the intercom. Helen excused herself to answer it.

Gran wiped her eyes. "It's probably Pastor Harper. I called to let him know."

"I don't feel like seeing anyone. I'm going outside." Noelle carried Laurence through the curtained French doors to the adjoining sunroom and then out to the pool deck.

The air smelled of moist earth, freshly cut grass, and hot Texas sunshine—life-smells that insulted Noelle's senses like a vicious slap. She strode with the cat down the sloping backyard to the shallow, rippling creek. Leaning against the bark of a tree, she tilted her head toward the sunlight glinting off the quivering leaves . . . and hoped heaven was up there somewhere.

At the sound of footsteps padding across the lawn, she clamped her eyes shut. No way could she listen to their minister's empty words of comfort. Nothing anyone could say—

"Noelle?"

"Warren!" She dropped Laurence and fell into the arms of the sandy-haired boy from next door. He rocked her in his solid, big-brother embrace.

"I saw the hearse leave. I'm sorry. I'm so, so sorry."

"I can't believe she's gone."

"I know, I know." Warren stroked her hair. "Your mom was an amazing lady."

"Right to the end, she worried more about me than herself." Noelle's voice became a harsh squeak. "She kept talking about her faith, how she wanted to face death with courage and dignity. She told me that . . . afterward . . . she needed me to be brave and carry on."

Something inside snapped. Jerking away, Noelle flailed her

arms at the sky. "But what's so dignified or courageous about wasting away to a skeleton? Peeing into a catheter bag? Getting high on morphine so you won't feel pain? And faith—forget it! Where was God when we really needed Him? Why did He let Mom die?"

When Warren didn't answer, she scooped up a handful of stones from the mossy creek bank. She slung them into the water with all her strength, careless of the splashes that soaked her shorts and sandals and sent Laurence skittering away. Her chest burning, she sank to the damp grass. She wrapped her arms around her knees and rocked furiously. The anger felt good, something real and solid to cling to.

Warren knelt beside her, but when he tried to draw her into a hug, she resisted. "How will I ever go on living without my mom?"

2

Warren sat beside Noelle on the creek bank in silence, for how long she couldn't say. After a while, she allowed herself to settle into his hug.

His breath warmed her temple. "You know I'm always here for you, right?"

She heaved a shaky sigh. "I know. And thank you for not preaching at me. I don't need one more person telling me this was part of God's plan."

Warren cast her a sidelong glance. "Tell me who said that and I'll punch 'em out."

She scoffed. "Gran, Helen, our pastor . . . they're always talking about God's will and how we're supposed to grow through trials."

"I'm pretty sure nobody meant to say cancer was God's will for your mom." He stroked her arm. "It's just . . . some things we'll never know the answers to this side of heaven."

Noelle twisted around to glare at him. "Now you're sounding preachy."

"Sorry, just saying what I believe is true."

One thing about Warren, he always shot straight with her,

whether she wanted to hear it or not. But right now, he was the only one who made her feel listened to. The only one who made her feel safe.

After a long pause, he murmured, "I'm worried about you, Noelle."

She wouldn't admit how worried and scared she was for herself. Instead, she hiked her chin. "I survived my dad bailing on us. Somehow I'll survive this—like I ever had a choice." To stave off further discussion of a subject she'd been purposely avoiding, she straightened and stood. Maybe by now the pastor would have finished his business and left. "It's hot. Want to go inside?"

"Good idea." Warren pushed himself off the ground and draped an arm around her shoulder as they started for the house. "I'll fix you a cold drink. You need to take care of yourself."

Like it even mattered. Like anything mattered anymore.

Stepping into the sunroom, Noelle froze at the sight of a houseful of visitors on the other side of the glass doors. *Where had all these people come from?* She retreated a step and hugged her stomach. "I can't go in there. I can't deal with this."

Warren squeezed her shoulder. "It's okay. I've got your back."

She shook her head and turned away, just as Gran opened one of the French doors from the den. "There you are, honey. Warren, thank you for coming over to be with her." Gran blew her nose and then stuffed the tissue into the pocket of the plain gray dress she'd changed into.

Noelle clamped her teeth together and trudged inside. She'd have to face everyone sooner or later. Might as well get it over with. Then maybe they'd go away and leave her in peace.

Warren's mother hurried over and hugged her. "Oh, sugar, I'm so, so sorry." Her soft Texas drawl poured over Noelle like warm honey. "You've been like one of our own kids ever since you moved here, and it hurts my heart knowing how much you've gone through."

Pastor Harper joined Mrs. Ames and took Noelle's hand. "Yes,

I remember when you were this high." He made a motion at waist level. "What were you, about five or six, when your family moved to Arden Heights?"

"Yeah . . . I think so."

"Your dad had just gotten another promotion, right? Arden Heights was real blessed to get your mom as a teacher that year."

Noelle's breath froze in her lungs. "Excuse me. I can't—" She let her perspiring hand slide from the minister's grasp and fled back outside, sucking huge gulps of air. Kneeling at the edge of the pool, she splashed cool water on her face and let it trickle down her neck and forearms.

"Noelle?"

At the sound of the familiar husky voice, her body went rigid. *Dad.*

She caught the woodsy aroma of his cologne. He'd changed to something more expensive since marrying Rebecca. Noelle had grown up with two favorite scents, her mother's classic English Rose and her father's British Sterling. Two years ago, when her father announced he was moving out, she'd gone to his bathroom cabinet and poured every last drop of his aftershave and cologne down the drain.

Anger simmered behind her breastbone, boiling up her throat like lava. If he hadn't moved out, hadn't signed the divorce papers, hadn't married Rebecca—if his whole life didn't revolve around his career and money and success—

"What are you doing here?" She asked without turning around. "Surely you have a meeting or something?"

She held herself rigid and hoped he'd leave. That's what he was best at, after all.

Gary thought about simply walking away, but something inside wouldn't let him. *Not this time.* He moved closer, his leather-soled shoes scraping against the aggregate. "I know how you feel about me . . . but under the circumstances can't we . . ." He was no good at this fatherhood business, never had been. "I wish I'd been here more for you these past two years. I wanted to be, but—"

Uncoiling long, tanned legs, Noelle dabbed her face with her T-shirt sleeve and turned toward him. Man, she'd grown up fast —where had the years gone? And she looked so much like Kate, it was a stab to his heart.

"Then what's the point of coming today?" she snapped. "Mom's gone now, and you've still got Rebecca and her spoiled-rotten kid—"

"That's enough!" Gary's hand shot out, his index finger halting inches from his daughter's nose before he made a fist and lowered his arm to his side. He couldn't remember the last time he'd shouted at his daughter, and the sudden outburst stunned him as much as it likely had Noelle. His voice shook. "Hate me all you want, but leave Rebecca and Kevin out of it."

The girl shrank back, a flicker of remorse in her eyes. "I—I just don't know why you're wasting your time here. It's too late. We don't need you now."

Her words hit him like a punch to the gut. "I'm still your dad. I —" *I love you*, he wanted to say, but after all the ways he'd let her down, why should she believe him? "I want to make sure you're okay."

Avoiding his eyes, Noelle ran a hand through the tangles in her straight brown hair that hung nearly to her waist. "Gran is taking care of the funeral arrangements. Uncle David and Aunt Susan are flying in this afternoon." She coiled a strand of hair around her finger. "Everything's under control."

"Is it?"

"Give it up, Dad. It's not like Mom's death was unexpected."

"I know, but . . ." He deserved her anger, even her hatred. But it still hurt, more than he ever imagined possible. He took a halting step closer and tried to put his arm around her shoulder, but she sidestepped him with a half-turn.

He shoved his hands into the pockets of his suit pants. "All right, I'll leave you alone . . . if that's what you really want."

Noelle folded her arms and stared into the pool. "It's what I really want."

It was nearly 2:00 a.m. when Gary maneuvered his hulking SUV into the garage next to Rebecca's blue BMW. Something seemed out of place about her car being there, but with his thoughts muddled by several Scotches, neat—and no appetite for a decent supper—he didn't have the brain power to figure out why. Giving his head a shake, he heaved himself out of the car and hit the wall button to close the garage door. As the electric motor hummed, he stumbled into his condo through the chrome-and-glass kitchen. He squinted beneath the glaring LED can lights and wished for another drink.

"Gary?" Heels clicked across the Spanish-tile entryway. Across the dining room, Rebecca appeared in a rumpled pantsuit. "What are you doing out this time of night? And where's Kevin?"

Wait, Rebecca was supposed to be in Frankfurt. She was home already? "Kevin? Oh, uh, he stayed over at Mrs. Gaylord's." Good thing the sitter was flexible. No way he'd inflict his inebriated state of melancholy upon the stepson he'd come to care about more than he could have imagined.

"Good. I'm glad you thought to ask her." Rebecca met him in front of the dining-room windows. "I left a message on your cell as soon as my plane landed. I thought you might be staying with Noelle."

"No . . . no . . ." While his sluggish brain tried to put the pieces together, he accepted her consoling embrace. Breathing in, he caught the herbal scent of her hairspray. Convenient how she fit so neatly under his chin. "Hey, how'd you get home so fast?" He couldn't mask his intoxicated slur.

"Long story—don't ask." She snuggled closer. "I've spent so much time on planes or in airports lately that I'm not even sure what day it is."

"Mmmm." He staggered slightly.

She stepped back and frowned. "You're drunk."

He raked his fingers through his hair and looked away. "Maybe a little."

"But you drove yourself home? You could have—"

"I made it just fine, okay? Give me a break. My wife just died —" Rebecca's stricken look temporarily sobered him. He lifted his hands to his eyes and rubbed them with a vengeance. "I mean Kate."

"It's all right," Rebecca said, her voice tight. "Please, let's go sit down and you can tell me all about it."

He let her drag him to the sofa, where he collapsed in a heap of misery. What good would talking do? How could it change the fact that his daughter despised him, probably even blamed him in some twisted way for her mother's death? He searched Rebecca's face hoping for answers, but for a disconcerting moment he saw only Kate—her soft brown curls, her warm eyes, her delicate nose and playful smile. He lurched to his feet and strode to the picture window. A shaft of moonlight severed the commons and sliced across their front lawn. It felt as if the beam cut clean through the glass and stabbed him in the chest—or was it only his grief that hurt so much?

"I don't get it," he said. "I'm at the top of my field. I've achieved an enviable standard of living. I've worked like crazy to ensure my family will never want for anything." Swiveling toward Rebecca, he spread his arms. "Tell me, how did things get so messed up?"

Hurt and confusion clouded Rebecca's eyes. She massaged her forehead. "It's late. You and I are both exhausted." She stood wearily. "Maybe things will be clearer in the morning."

So suddenly she didn't want to talk? He pressed his arm against the window and buried his face in his sleeve. "Go to bed if you want to. I'm too strung out to sleep."

"Then let me make us some decaf. I don't want to leave you alone like this." Her footsteps scuffed on the carpet behind him.

"Forget the coffee. I need something stronger." He lurched across to the wet bar in the dining room and filled a glass with ice from the small refrigerator, then splashed in a generous serving of Scotch.

"You've already had too much." Rebecca reached out as if to stop him.

"Don't lecture me on the evils of alcohol. Just because you've quit drinking doesn't mean I have to be a teetotaler." He tossed back a large gulp and grimaced as he swallowed. Before she could protest, he refilled his glass and carried it to the window, turning his back to her.

Rebecca's throat clenched. Gary was shutting her out again. *Oh, God, don't let me lose him, too!*

Why did she have to fall for another man who couldn't be true to her? She could accept that Gary and Kate had a history, but when he'd referred to Kate as his *wife*—as if the last six months he'd been married to Rebecca had never happened—it was all she could do to swallow the pain and try to understand what Gary was going through.

Numb with fatigue, she retreated to the breakfast nook. Sinking into one of the white cane chairs, she kicked off her shoes. She loved Gary—loved him as she'd thought she could never love again, not after Rob Marshall had broken her heart nine years ago and left her with a toddler to raise alone.

But had she made a mistake by marrying a man with so much baggage? These past few weeks, Gary certainly hadn't been acting like the man she'd fallen in love with. When they'd first started dating, it seemed they had so much in common. They were both career oriented with clear goals in life, not to mention working for the same company had given them plenty to talk about over dinner. And since they'd both been married before, there was a shared sense of needing to get it right this time.

Except lately, Gary hadn't been sharing much of anything with her.

Even more concerning was the fact that her son was already deeply attached to his new dad. At the rate things were going, Kevin could find himself abandoned all over again.

Dear Kevin, what a trooper! His resilient spirit made being a mother pure joy. For most of his eleven years, Rebecca had done her utmost to be Super-Mom. Then a few months ago, shortly after marrying Gary, she'd experienced a small epiphany. It had happened in the middle of a sleepless night as she hung over a commode in a strange hotel room. Stress and stomach acid had burned her insides raw, and as she'd wretched up bile and blood, she'd known something had to give.

Stumbling footsteps and the clink of ice interrupted her thoughts. Gary had obviously poured himself another drink. He'd definitely earned the hangover he was bound to wake up with tomorrow morning. She snorted a harsh laugh—it was already tomorrow! Her whole body cried out for sleep, and yet she struggled as much as Gary to shut down her churning thoughts. In a moment of weakness, she considered uncorking the chardonnay that friends from work had brought over for dinner a couple of weeks ago.

But no, she'd learned long ago that numbing her brain with alcohol only masked the issues. The only true Source of comfort and peace was God. Her Bible lay on the table across from her, where she'd left it after her early-morning devotions. She pulled it closer and thumbed through the pages for the passage from

Haggai that had spoken to her so vividly that life-changing night in the hotel room:

> *"You have planted much, but harvested little. You eat, but never have enough. You drink, but never have your fill. You put on clothes, but are not warm. You earn wages, only to put them in a purse with holes in it."*

Wake up, Rebecca, an inner voice had spoken that night. *Wake up and see what you're missing before you lose it completely.*

Step by hesitant step, she'd been rethinking her priorities—number one, to build a strong, lasting marriage and a stable home life for Kevin. A life that *didn't* include one or both of his parents away on business trips several weeks out of the year. She longed for Gary to commit to those same goals, to realize family was so much more important than the success-driven lifestyle they'd both bought into.

Not that Rebecca had it all figured out yet—this delicate balance between motherhood, career, and now remarriage. But women did so all the time these days, didn't they? Even the venerable Kate Townsend had maintained a successful teaching career while married to Gary and raising their daughter.

Oh, but that's what it came down to, wasn't it? Women like Kate always made it look so easy.

And life had never been easy for Rebecca.

If one more person showed up with a casserole and a sympathy card, Noelle would scream. She'd been able to avoid most of the visitors by staying outside by the pool with Warren. Under the blistering midday sun they kicked off their flipflops and dangled their feet in the cool water while Noelle pretended it was just another ordinary day. For all the good pretending did. At least it kept her from thinking about the uncertain future—a future she suspected would somehow involve bringing her father back into her life, and *that* she would gladly do without.

Gran stepped out from the sunroom, shielding her eyes from the glare. "I'm warming up something for lunch." She gave a sad chuckle. "We certainly won't starve for the next few weeks. Can you believe all the food people have brought over?"

"I'm not hungry." Noelle flicked a bug out of the pool and slanted a weak smile toward Gran. "You go ahead, though."

Her grandmother's lips trembled. "You need to eat."

It broke Noelle's heart to see the grief and fatigue in Gran's eyes. She groaned and pushed to her feet. "Okay, I'll try if you will. You come, too, Warren."

"Yes, do." Gran dabbed her cheeks. "The house seems so empty now."

Noelle and Warren followed Gran to the kitchen and took chairs at the round pedestal table. Sunlight streamed through the front windows, silhouetting hanging planters of scraggly ferns, wilted begonias, and an English ivy with crispy brown leaves. Noelle's heart clenched. Mom had made her promise to take care of the plants, but Noelle had neglected them for weeks. The greenery seemed to have withered and died right along with Mom.

Warren started the cheesy broccoli-and-chicken casserole around. Noelle's grandmother served herself a tiny spoonful and then fingered her blue flowered placemat. "I gave these to Kate two Christmases ago."

"I remember. She loved them." Noelle watched a blue jay swoop down from an oak tree, retrieve some tidbit from the lawn, then swing up to his perch in a wide loop. "The funeral—when will it be?"

Gran picked up her fork, laid it down again, and then dropped her hands into her lap. Always a tiny woman, she seemed somehow smaller. "Pastor Harper suggested Friday evening."

"I don't know why we even need a funeral." Noelle pushed out her chair and stalked to the window. "Mom's gone, and she's never coming back. So what's the point?"

Her grandmother's choked cry reminded Noelle once again that she wasn't the only one hurting. She slunk to the table and gripped the back of her grandmother's chair. "Sorry, I know the service is important to you."

Gran patted her hand. "It's our last chance to say goodbye, and friends will want to pay their respects."

Friends . . . and Dad and his *other* family, probably. Or would they have the decency to stay away?

Seeing a shiny red sedan turn into the driveway, Noelle shook off her bitter thoughts. "Must be Uncle David and Aunt Susan."

"My goodness, is it that time already?" Gran hurried to the front door and ran out to meet them.

Noelle followed, pausing to paste a smile on her face before greeting the uncle and aunt she adored.

"Hey, kiddo," Uncle David opened his arm to include her in the embrace he shared with Gran.

Gran kissed him on the cheek. "I see you still haven't gotten rid of that beard," she teased, though her voice quivered. "Come inside. The guest room is all made up for you."

Uncle David hesitated. "What about you, Mom? I thought you'd be using the spare bedroom."

"Gran's staying in my room while you're here," Noelle explained. They had only the one guest room, so Noelle had volunteered to sleep on the sofa bed in the game room. It was too soon to even think of anyone else using Mom's bedroom. "Come on, I'll help carry your stuff."

Pausing near the trunk, Uncle David took Noelle's hands and fixed her with red-rimmed eyes. "Yesterday was the saddest day of my life. I lost my only sister, and now my favorite niece is without her mother." He hugged her to him, his dark, bushy beard tickling her cheek.

"Favorite niece? How about your *only* niece?" Noelle squeezed him tightly. An unbearable pain sliced upward from her heart into her throat, and she ached to cry with her uncle and make the pain go away.

3

Gary's head swam. Yeah, he had too much to drink last night. But he hadn't been able to stop himself, not even when Rebecca returned to the living room with a scalding cup of coffee and begged him to lay off the booze. His harsh retort had sent her back to the kitchen in tears.

He wriggled deeper into the plush white sofa cushions, where he and Rebecca had both succumbed to sleep sometime in the wee hours of the morning. His tie lay in a tangle on the floor next to his discarded wingtips. His suit coat hung across the arm of a chair. Blow-dryer sounds from the master bedroom told him Rebecca must have showered and washed her hair. He needed to do the same—and toss this shirt into the hamper, or maybe the trash. Between stale body odor and spilled booze, he smelled like a sewer rat. Kate would never have let him into the house in this condition.

Kate, oh my Katy-girl. What happened to us?

She'd told him about the cancer only days before the divorce became final. Shaken more than he'd ever expected to be, he'd offered to postpone the proceedings until after Kate recovered.

"Absolutely not. You need to get on with your life," Kate had insisted. "Noelle and I will be fine. Your work took you away from us so many times over the years that we learned to face crises without you."

Kate's words had been spoken without malice, but the truth stabbed Gary to his soul. Those early years with DataTech and the series of technical schools they'd sent him to had begun his endless chronicle of absences. He'd missed wedding anniversaries, holidays, even Noelle's birth—the latter through no fault of his own, thanks to an ice storm that stranded him at Chicago's O'Hare. Through it all, he'd tried—or thought he had—to give his family the best life possible. Everything he ever did was for them, because no way would they ever know hardships like he'd grown up with, not if he could help it.

So began his calculated ascent to the higher echelons of DataTech management. On top of the long hours he put in each week, each successive promotion required more frequent and often lengthy business trips. He'd lost count of how many of Noelle's "firsts" he'd missed—first steps, first spoken words, a piano recital, horseback riding lessons, her first role in a play. Not only had he missed the celebrations but the tragedies, small and large—lost teeth, a broken arm, Grandpa Whitney's death.

The absentee father. No wonder she hates me so much. He tossed back the dregs from the last glass of Scotch he'd poured sometime around 4:00 a.m.

"It's not your fault Kate died." Rebecca stood over him, wearing fresh makeup and a teal-green pantsuit. Her makeup couldn't fully hide the dark shadows beneath her eyes. "It would have happened whether you'd stayed with her or not."

Gary sat upright. "You think I don't know that?" Mentally cursing his sharp tone, he hung his head. "I'm sorry. You don't deserve this—any of it."

"No, I don't. But I'm trying to understand—"

"I don't think you can. Your son loves you, and at least you know your ex-husband's life goes on, wherever he is. But I don't even have that now. And my daughter can barely stand the sight of me. She thinks I deserted them at the worst possible time in their lives."

Rebecca set her coffee cup on the end table. The lipstick stain on the rim formed a mocking smile that contrasted with the tender tone of her voice. "We were already married when Kate learned her cancer was terminal. What could you have done?"

He let out a long, grating sigh. "I could have been there." Not just during Kate's illness, but before. Long, long before. "I *should* have been there."

For the next couple of days, Rebecca tried to give Gary the space he needed to work through his emotions. She was dealing with too many confusing emotions of her own, and her marriage was shaky enough without inviting more arguments. What terrified her more than anything was the possibility that Gary didn't love her anymore—had never really loved her. That he'd have given anything to save Kate and put their family back together.

Not that Rebecca could begrudge him such thoughts, because in a perfect world, Rob would have remained faithful, and she'd have lived happily forever after, possibly without ever having met Gary.

This was no fairy tale, though. Even with prayer and faith, life got messy. Marriages failed, people died, families splintered.

And exasperating stepdaughters had to be dealt with. As Rebecca put together a turkey sandwich to have for lunch at her desk later, her thoughts lingered on Gary and whatever plans had been made for Noelle's future. Surely he and Kate must have discussed it at some point, but if so, he'd never said anything—not that his silence should surprise her these days.

Eventually, though, he'd have to step up to the parenting plate and make some decisions. The unspoken solution seemed to be for Noelle to live with her grandmother in Nebraska, which would certainly ease Rebecca's worries. On the other hand, with Noelle so far away, Gary could probably give up any hopes he had of repairing his broken relationship with his daughter.

Rebecca's heart went out to Noelle. No child should have to face the loss of one parent, let alone two. She shivered as memories percolated—two police officers standing on the front porch, her mother's anguished cry, her own wail of disbelief. *"No! Not my daddy!"*

She shoved the past aside and focused on fitting the sandwich and an apple into her insulated lunch bag. "Kevin, hurry up or you'll make me late for work."

Her skinny, towheaded son slurped the milk at the bottom of his cereal bowl and dragged his hand across his mouth. "Can we do something fun this weekend? You aren't going out of town again, are you?"

"No, your dad and I will both be around."

"Oh, yeah." His mouth slanted into a worried frown. "I guess Dad will want to be with Noelle since her mom died."

"Yes, I'm sure." Though she wasn't sure at all.

Kevin bent to retie his shoelace. "I wish we could go to the water park again before school starts."

"I'll find out what your dad's plans are. Maybe Sunday afternoon, if nothing else comes up." Certainly all of them could use a break from the recent stress, if only for a couple of hours.

Gary strode into the kitchen, the hard plastic wheels of his suitcase rattling across the tile floor. He reached for the coffee carafe and filled a black-and-silver travel mug bearing the DataTech logo.

Rebecca stared at the suitcase, then at her husband. She lifted an eyebrow. "What's this?"

"I need to check on some things at the Chicago office. I'll be back early next week."

"But Kate's funeral is tonight."

"Can't make it." He found a package of string cheese in the refrigerator, peeled away the wrapper, and bit off a chunk. "Sorry, hon, gotta catch my flight. Kev, you be good for your mom, okay?" He gave the boy a gentle cuff on the chin. Then, almost as an afterthought, he dropped a kiss on Rebecca's cheek before striding out to the garage.

As the door banged shut behind him, Rebecca pressed her knuckles to her lips and breathed out slowly. *It doesn't work to keep running away, Gary.* Not from his daughter, and not from this marriage.

Kevin carried his bowl to the sink and slipped his arm around his mother's waist. "It's okay, Mom. You and me can go to the water park by ourselves."

She smiled and tousled his shaggy, white-blond hair. The boy had shot up like a cornstalk this past year. He'd grown almost as tall as she. "Sure we can, tiger. How about tomorrow, just the two of us? We'll have a great day."

"I feel bad for Noelle, though. Are you going to her mom's funeral? I could go with you since Dad can't."

She'd been wrestling with the dilemma for two days now, and had decided Gary should go alone. Noelle didn't need more reminders that her father had another family now, even if technically it was Noelle's family, too, though she'd never admit it. In any case, no matter how Rebecca felt about her stepdaughter's coldness toward them, the girl didn't deserve this latest episode of Gary's "absent father" routine.

"Go brush your teeth, kiddo." She gave her son an affectionate pop on his backside. "We need to get a move on."

On her way to the office, she dropped Kevin at Mrs. Gaylord's, where he stayed during the summers and after school while Rebecca worked. Eleven now, he'd been pestering her to let him stay home alone after he turned twelve in January, but the idea of her son becoming a "latchkey kid" tied her stomach in knots. Life as a working mom was hard enough, and quality time spent with Kevin had become a precious commodity.

Quality time. Such a cliché. Could you ever invest enough of yourself in your child?

Sipping ginger tea at her desk later, Rebecca considered phoning Noelle's house. Someone should let the family know Gary wouldn't be attending the funeral, and she suspected he hadn't bothered calling them himself. Retrieving her cell phone, she scrolled through her address book. She found Kate Townsend's number and pressed the call button, praying all the while that anyone but Noelle would answer.

When Irene Whitney's voice greeted her, she sighed inwardly. "Hello, Mrs. Whitney. It's Rebecca Mar—er, Townsend." Was it merely the newness of her marriage, or the fact that lately she sometimes didn't feel like Gary's wife at all?

The woman replied stiffly, "How are you, Rebecca?"

"Excuse me for disturbing you, but I wanted to make sure you were aware that Gary won't be at the service tonight. I was afraid he wouldn't have time to call you."

"I don't understand . . ."

Rebecca massaged her temple. "He had to leave town this morning on some unexpected business." Unexpected for her and everyone else, anyway.

Silence. "I appreciate your consideration."

"Mrs. Whitney, I'm so deeply sorry about your daughter. I've kept all of you in my prayers through this whole ordeal."

"How kind of you." The woman exhaled audibly. "Forgive me if I sound ungracious. I don't mean to. You're an innocent party to all of this. It's just . . . so hard."

The understatement of the century. Rebecca forced a swallow and tried to keep her voice steady. "I'm sure Gary will be in touch with Noelle when he gets back from his trip."

"Yes, of course. Thank you for calling." The woman said goodbye.

Why do I feel so guilty? Gary was the one ducking out of his responsibilities. Rebecca swiveled her chair to gaze out the eighteenth-story window across downtown Dallas. Between the tall buildings, she glimpsed the slate and bronze mansard roof of the historic Hotel Adolphus, the metalwork weathered to a moss-green patina. Though dwarfed by towering modern skyscrapers, the old hotel claimed its right to be there with a kind of stubborn pride. If only some of that confidence would rub off on Rebecca.

Nibbling her lip, she retrieved another telephone number and placed a call.

"Brenda's Gifts and Flowers."

"Good morning. I'd like to order a floral arrangement for a funeral."

As the clerk described selections in several price ranges, Rebecca's mind drifted to the first time she'd met Kate. It had been entirely by accident, a full year before Rebecca and Gary had started seeing each other. Leaving the DataTech building to meet with a client, she passed one of the first-floor conference rooms, where a party was in progress for someone's recent promotion. A slender brunette stood outside the door, a weary look on her face. As Rebecca drew near, the woman smiled and nodded toward the open doorway. "It was getting a bit too crowded for me."

"I know what you mean." Rebecca admired the woman's stylish forest-green dress, her glance falling upon a striking corsage of pale pink roses pinned to her shoulder. "I didn't realize they gave out such gorgeous flowers for these events. You must be pretty high up in the company."

"Actually, the party is for my husband, Gary Townsend. And yes, at this rate he will soon be *very* high up in the company." Her smile flattened. "The corsage is my husband's way of marking his territory."

Rebecca had taken an invisible step backward, realizing she'd unwittingly initiated a conversation she had no business taking part in. Gary Townsend's reputation as the ascendant superstar of DataTech's management ranks was known throughout the company. Rumors that his career success had taken a toll on his marriage also abounded.

"Please forgive me," Mrs. Townsend said, her tone sincere. "I don't usually indulge in public pity parties. It's just that I hardly know a soul in there, and I'm feeling out of place."

"Well, you certainly don't look it." Rebecca extended her hand. "It's nice to meet you, Mrs. Townsend. I'm Rebecca Marshall."

"Kate, please. Happy to meet you, too, Rebecca, and thanks for being so gracious about my utterly *ungracious* moment." Kate tilted her head and touched her nose to one of the pink rosebuds adorning her shoulder. An ethereal smile creased her cheeks as she softly inhaled. "What can I say? Gary may be married to his career, but he always remembers my favorite flowers."

"Ma'am?" The florist's nasal twang shattered Rebecca's memory. "Have you decided?"

"Yes, pink roses, one of those sprays you described in the two-hundred-dollar range." Rebecca provided her charge card number along with the time and location of the funeral. "And sign the card, *In loving memory, Gary.*"

Standing before her full-length mirror, Noelle adjusted the teal-and-fuchsia retro-print skirt. She loved the drape of the slanted hem—so trendy. Snapping a silver belt at the waist, she turned from side to side, studying the effect.

A soft knock sounded on her bedroom door. "Noelle?"

"Come in, Gran." She brought her long braid forward, placing it just so across the shoulder of her fuchsia peasant blouse.

Her grandmother sucked in a breath. "You aren't wearing that to the funeral, are you?"

"What's wrong with it?"

Gran folded her arms across her plain black dress. "Don't you have something less . . . colorful?"

Noelle smoothed the lines of the skirt. "Mom helped me choose this outfit. It was the last thing we shopped for before—" She stared hard at the toes of her suede platform pumps, remembering that day at the department store. When she'd stepped from the dressing room to model the skirt and blouse, Mom's eyes had sparkled—not quite a happy smile, not quite a sad one. Maybe she already knew her time was running out.

Aunt Susan tiptoed in behind Gran. "I think she looks marvelous, Mom. Kate would approve, I'm sure."

Gran's expression softened. She fingered Noelle's sleeve. "The outfit is fine, sweetheart."

The church parking lot had filled to overflowing by the time they arrived. Uncle David parked the red rental car in the spot reserved for family. When Noelle shoved the rear door open and stepped onto the pavement, a sultry evening breeze whipped at her skirt. She brushed a loose strand of hair out of her eyes, her throat closing when she saw how heavily Gran leaned upon Uncle David's arm as he escorted her up the narrow sidewalk.

"Coming, Noelle?" Aunt Susan reached for her hand.

She gave a nod and followed her aunt through a side door and down a short hallway leading to the sacristy, where Gran and Uncle David had taken straight-backed chairs. Through the closed door to the sanctuary, Noelle listened to the organ wheeze out the chords to some dreary, plodding hymn. She chewed the end of her braid. "Mom would absolutely hate this music. It's so depressing."

Gran lifted her chin. "But it's approp— "

"I don't care if it's appropriate. It's not one of the songs Mom picked out. Didn't anybody tell the organist?"

"Noelle . . ." Uncle David's tone carried a warning note. He glanced pointedly at Gran, who silently dabbed away tears.

Biting the inside of her cheek, Noelle paced the narrow room. If only she could be anywhere but here, on this night, for this reason.

Pastor Harper, robed in black, stepped into the room and offered a sad smile. "It's time."

Uncle David helped Gran to her feet. Noelle paused in the doorway, her gaze fixed on the closed coffin at the front of the church. A lavish spray of pale pink roses graced the top. At least someone had remembered her mother's favorite flower.

"Let's go, sweetie," Aunt Susan whispered, nudging her.

Noelle averted her eyes as she walked past the coffin and lowered herself onto the hard wooden pew between Gran and Uncle David. Naturally, Dad was nowhere to be seen. As usual, business came first—nothing new there. Her fingers curled around the edge of the seat as she pushed her father from her thoughts. He wasn't worth the effort.

Instead, she struggled to listen to Pastor Harper's words. She sang Mom's favorite hymns with the rest of the congregation. She tried to pray silently along with the minister's petitions. And she hoped, deep within her heart, that somehow all of it would make a difference.

But God felt so very far away, and in the end nothing had changed. Her mother was still dead, and the crushing emptiness around Noelle's heart made her gasp for air. She could not imagine her mother in that gray box, could not accept that soon the funeral director would place the coffin in the hearse and carry her mother's body to the crematorium. She could not imagine Mom reduced to the contents of a small urn resting on a shelf in some cold marble mausoleum.

Uncle David touched her arm. "It's over, honey."

Noelle squared her shoulders and led her family down the aisle behind the six dark-suited pallbearers escorting the coffin. She kept her gaze just above the heads of the guests, exactly as she'd learned to do in her drama classes to conquer stage fright.

It's an act, after all. I'm not here. This isn't happening—can't be happening.

In the narthex, she let out the breath she'd been holding. The pallbearers, including Warren and his father, waited for instructions from the funeral director. Warren caught her eye briefly, but Noelle glanced away before his tender gaze undid her. She plucked a pale rosebud and inhaled its fragrance, closing her eyes against the sight of the coffin.

She didn't open them again until she heard the groan of the wooden church doors swinging shut.

Rebecca sat cross-legged on the gray brocade comforter atop her king-size bed, a frosty glass of diet cola in one hand and the Sunday paper spread around her. After church, she and Kevin had gone to their favorite restaurant for brunch, then she'd dropped him at his friend's for the afternoon.

She studied the real-estate classifieds through tortoise-shell reading glasses. Rockwall might be nice, somewhere near the lake. Kevin enjoyed swimming and water skiing. It would be fun to have a boat.

A door slammed, and she glanced up. "Kev? Is that you?"

"Just me." Gary's tired face appeared at the bedroom door. He parked his suitcase in front of the closet and sank onto the foot of the bed.

Rebecca set her drink and reading glasses on the nightstand and crawled over to him. "I didn't know you were coming home today." She planted a quick kiss on his lips. A faint taste of alcohol lingered. She surmised he'd had a couple of drinks on the plane—and prayed he hadn't stopped for a couple more on the way home. The idea of his driving Dallas freeways in such a condition did not bear thinking about.

She knelt behind him and massaged his shoulders through

the nubby cotton of his monogrammed polo shirt. "You look like you haven't slept all weekend."

His jaw tightened. "Maybe because I haven't."

"You shouldn't have gone away in the first place, and you know it." She slipped her legs over the side of the bed and scooted in beside him.

"Can we not argue about this? I feel bad enough as it is." He draped an arm around her shoulder and brushed a brief kiss across her forehead.

Cherishing even this small show of affection, she snuggled closer. "I sent flowers."

"Thanks."

"Gary," she began hesitantly, "we need to talk about this. Decisions have to be made." He couldn't give up on his daughter. For both his and Noelle's sakes, they had to find a way to reconnect, to be a family again—even if the thought of bringing a resentful teenager into their home made Rebecca want to down a handful of antacids.

"Just . . . not now, okay?" Gary rose and strode from the room. Moments later came the clink of ice and the opening and closing of the liquor cabinet.

Against her better judgment, she followed him to the living room, her bare feet padding across the cool, white carpet. Gary sprawled in an armchair, swirling a highball glass filled to the rim with the dark amber liquid that could only be his usual Glenfiddich Scotch Whisky. "Kevin will be home any minute," she stated, hands on hips. "He shouldn't see you like this."

"You're right." Was that a flicker of guilt in his expression? "Don't worry, I'll leave." He drained his glass in one gulp and slammed it on the end table before standing on unsteady legs.

A furious, desperate panic strangled her plea for him to stay. Before she found her voice, a key rasped in the front latch. The door swung open, and Kevin loped in.

"Yo, Mom. Hey, Dad, you're back." The tanned, lanky boy

stuck out his arm for a fist bump, which Gary awkwardly returned. "You shoulda been at the water park with us yesterday. I finally talked Mom into going down the giant slide. She screamed all the way."

Rebecca locked her fingers together to stop them from shaking as she glared at her husband over the top of Kevin's head. Gary's eyes spoke a silent apology. He raked a hand through his disheveled hair and then squeezed his stepson's shoulder. "Sorry I missed it."

"Boy, Dad, your eyes are really bloodshot," Kevin stated. "Hey, I gotta call Bryan. I think I left my computer game in his mom's car." He jogged toward the kitchen.

Gary reached for Rebecca and gathered her into his arms. "I know, I know. I've been really messed up lately. I don't know why you put up with me."

"Because I love you, that's why."

"I love you, too, hon, even though I've done a terrible job of showing it lately." He released a tired groan. "Give me a couple more days, and I promise I'll pull myself together and figure all this out."

Slowly, slowly, her fear and anger subsided, and she clung to her husband with all her might. "I hope so, Gary, because our family needs you. *I* need you." She lifted her chin to search his face. "And I need you to promise me you'll stop drinking."

Doubt clouded his shifting gaze, but he muttered a tentative, "I'll try."

4

On Thursday morning, Gary nicked himself twice while shaving, his only goal to finish getting dressed and hightail it to the office. There, at least, he could pour all his concentration into his work, the panacea for all things troubling. Especially a daughter he had no clue how to handle.

Handle? He handled delayed flights, programming bugs, testy bosses, overeager underlings. Those things he was good at. Parenting? Not so much.

Since last Sunday, Rebecca had tried several times to draw him into a discussion about his daughter—discussions he avoided like economy-class airline seats. He could only imagine how much deeper Noelle's resentment would be if he stepped into her life at this late date and started acting like a father again.

Again? Tell it like it is, Townsend—when did you ever really act like a father?

Maybe in the beginning, before the job completely consumed him. What he wouldn't give to return to the days when Noelle was a bright-eyed toddler racing into his arms when he returned from a business trip. Or the kindergarten program where Noelle proudly recited the poem she'd memorized. He hadn't missed *all* the important events . . . at least not at first.

Was it too late to make up for lost time? Could he, even if he tried?

He'd purposely stayed late at the office yesterday, then slept an extra hour this morning. By the time he'd dragged himself out of bed, Rebecca and Kevin had already left—which was also part of his argument avoidance strategy. He downed a glass of juice and a slice of toast before heading out to his car. As the garage door rumbled open, he looked up to see Rebecca's BMW pull into the driveway. She parked in the garage and strolled around the back of his SUV.

Wait—khaki shorts and sandals? "What's this? You taking the day off?"

"I am. And so are you." She linked her arm through his and shepherded him back into the kitchen. "Kevin's spending the day at Bryan's, so you and I have the place to ourselves."

Okay . . . he was guessing she didn't have romance on her mind. It didn't take a rocket scientist to figure out the reason for her return involved a certain teenager with long brown hair and the temper of a cornered grizzly. "But I have appointments. I—"

"Already phoned Jean. She's rescheduling them for tomorrow." Rebecca firmly closed the door behind them. "Coffee? I'll brew a fresh pot."

Jaw clenched, he glanced from his wife to the door. "I can't do this today, okay? I need more time—"

"Gary, you're out of time." She spun around, aiming the coffee scoop at his chest. "You're not leaving this house until you sit down with me and figure out what we're going to do about your daughter."

Their gazes locked. Gary swallowed. "We?"

"Yes, *we*. We're in this together." Her words carried much more certainty than her tremulous tone implied. With stiff, precise movements, she finished measuring the coffee and filled the reservoir with water.

As the coffeepot burbled, Gary trudged to the counter and braced his elbows on the edge. He stared at the dark liquid drip-drip-dripping into the carafe. "I made a total mess of the last fifteen years. Now I don't know where to start."

"Then you'd better figure it out quick." Speaking with firm but gentle assurance, she touched his arm. "She's the kid, you're the parent. It's time you started acting like one."

He bristled and pulled away. "So making a good living and providing for my family's every need doesn't count as responsible parenthood?"

The sad, hurting look in Rebecca's eyes clearly communicated her reply. "*Every* need, Gary?"

He lowered his head. "Okay, okay, I get the point. But my career, this lifestyle"—his broad gesture took in their entire luxury condo and all its expensive furnishings—"it's who I am. It's who you married, in case you forgot," he added with a sideways glare.

"And I still love you with all my heart. But *this lifestyle,*" Rebecca said, imitating his sweeping arm motions, "isn't what makes us family. You, me, Kevin, Noelle—we're a family now. Everything else aside, you can't escape the fact that you are the parent of a hurting and confused teenage daughter. She needs her father, Gary." Her breath snagged. "She needs to know you'll be there for her when it counts."

Way to nail him to the wall. He stared at her and shook his head. "You expect me to change into the perfect father overnight? It's not that easy."

"Easy? I *know* it isn't easy." Rebecca closed her eyes for a moment as if fighting off some private pain. She removed two black ceramic mugs from the cupboard and filled them with the pungent Kona brew. "It will never be easy. But you *have* to decide on something—anything—and follow through."

He wrapped his hands around the mug. Too bad it wasn't a crystal ball. He could use some supernatural answers right about now.

Rebecca sighed and took a cautious sip of her coffee. "Have you given any thought at all to what you want for Noelle? Do you really want her living in Nebraska with Irene?"

Time for honesty, Gary. Fess up. Everything Rebecca said was true. No matter how intimidated—no, *terrified*—his own daughter made him feel, he couldn't keep dodging his fatherly responsibilities. He squeezed his eyes shut. "What I want is for her to love me again. I want . . ."

"What, Gary?"

His gaze met hers. "I wish I could start over with Noelle. I wish . . . somehow . . . we really could all be together, like you said. Like a real family."

Rebecca drew in a long, shuddering breath, and the hard lines of her face began to ease. "Then somehow we'll make it work." She set her coffee on the counter and reached for the phone. "Here, call her right now. Tell her the plan."

His eyes widened. "Plan?" When had they made a plan? It wasn't like they had a spare room here at the condo for Noelle.

Of course. All that pressure from Rebecca to meet with a real estate agent, start looking for a house. He'd assumed she was just getting "nesty," but maybe she'd anticipated all along they might need to make room for Noelle after Kate died.

He pressed the heel of one hand into his eye socket and cursed. "How could I be so oblivious?"

Rebecca's mouth flattened in an accusing frown "Didn't you and Kate ever talk about Noelle's future?"

"I think she tried, but I kept brushing her off. Guess I never wanted to believe she'd really die."

"But she did. And what happens next is up to you." Rebecca thrust the phone into his hand. "We'll figure out the details later. Just make the call."

Noelle wrapped a towel around her hips and led Warren into the sunroom. Their early-morning swim helped sweep out the cobwebs from too many restless nights. "How about some orange juice?"

"Sounds great." Warren toweled off his wet hair. "Need help?"

"Nope, stay here. One of us dripping water through the house is enough."

In the kitchen, she found her grandmother hunched over the breakfast bar, ear pressed to the telephone receiver. "Yes, I agree, we've put this off too long already. It's time we talk this through, find the best way—" Gran saw Noelle and immediately went silent.

Taking the hint, Noelle quickly poured two glasses of orange juice and carried them to the sunroom. She handed Warren his juice and plopped into one of the yellow padded chairs, and they sipped in comfortable silence. If she didn't think too hard about things, she could almost imagine it was a summer day like any other.

Then Gran appeared in the doorway. Her glance shifted uneasily.

"What's wrong?" Noelle set her glass on the side table. "Who was on the phone?"

"It was your father." Gran sank into the chair across from her.

Noelle adjusted the strap of her magenta bikini top and tried to ignore the sudden twist beneath her breastbone. "So he finally decided to check in, huh? Probably feeling guilty for skipping the funeral." She reached for a chunky purple comb and jerked it through her wet hair. "That's my dad. When the going gets tough, the wimp leaves town."

Casting Warren an embarrassed frown, Gran touched two fingers to her temple. "You need to stop being so hard on your father."

"How can you defend him?" Noelle stared open-mouthed at her grandmother. "Mom was your daughter, and *he left her.*"

"There are two sides to every divorce." Gran gripped the armrests, her voice tight with control. "Your mother knew when she married Gary that he had lofty ambitions."

"They were teenagers. Fresh out of high school. Why didn't you and Grandpa stop her?"

"As if we could have." Gran quirked her lips in a sad smile. "Someday, when you fall in love, maybe you'll understand."

"I could never love anybody like him." Noelle pursed her lips. "Mom deserved better." *I deserved better.*

Gran closed her eyes briefly. "We can't change the past. Hard as it may be, Noelle, we have to look ahead now."

Warren rose and draped his towel around his neck. "I should go. Y'all need to talk some stuff out."

Noelle grabbed his hand, sudden dread squeezing her chest. "Wait for me outside, okay?"

He gave a shrug, his gaze softening. "Yeah, sure."

As soon as the sliding door closed, Noelle turned to her grandmother and steeled herself for the worst. "Obviously you and Dad were talking about more than the weather. Just spit it out, okay?"

Her grandmother's eyes filled with regret. "I know you don't want to think about this, but avoiding the subject won't make it go away. Honey, we need to discuss what you're going to do when I leave."

"Leave?" The purple comb hit the glass-top side table with a clatter. "Gran, you can't—"

"I can't stay here indefinitely, sweetheart. I have a farm to run back in Nebraska, remember?"

Noelle's heart pounded. She scooted to the edge of her chair. "But what am I going to do, Gran? You're all I have now."

"No, dear, I'm not." She stood and stared over Noelle's head toward the pool, hands tucked into the pockets of her denim dress. "You have your father. You'll be living with him now."

"You're kidding, right?" A tremor began in the pit of Noelle's stomach, writhing up into her throat. She tried to breathe, but her lungs wouldn't cooperate. She scrambled to her feet and fled outside.

Warren leapt from a deck chair by the pool. "Hey, slow down. What'd your grandmother say?"

She almost screamed her reply. "She says I have to live with my father now. She's crazy."

"Hey, hey, it's okay." He guided her into the chair and stood behind her, kneading her shoulders.

She inhaled long and painfully while Warren's firm touch massaged the harsh edges off her anger. "It's not okay," she murmured. "It's never going to be okay."

Warren came around and knelt in front of her. "I know you've got your problems with him, but he's still your dad."

She cast him a sidelong glance. Warren was doing his know-it-all big-brother routine, as usual. But what would she do without him, especially now? She shoved past him and paced to the other side of the pool, then sank into the sun-warmed grass beside the decking. "Okay, I admit it, I hate him for divorcing Mom. I hate him for leaving us and marrying somebody else and ignoring Mom and me like we never even mattered to him. Which is exactly why I could never see myself living with him now."

"So what are your other choices?" Warren plopped down beside her. "Could you go live with your grandmother?"

She stifled a harsh laugh. "Can you honestly see me living on a farm? I'd be bored silly in Shickley, Nebraska."

"How about Phoenix with your aunt and uncle?"

The possibility had crossed her mind, but . . . "Uncle David and Aunt Susan want to start their own family soon. I'd only be in the way." Sighing, she plucked at a blade of grass. "Anyway, all my friends are here. And the drama club—that's practically my whole life."

"Then what do you want?"

"What I want is to have my mother back." Her voice cracked, and she couldn't speak the rest of her thoughts: *And have my father living here and doing things with me like a real dad is supposed to, and never, ever going away again. A real family, like we were always meant to be.*

Warren remained silent, his eyes filling with sympathy she almost couldn't bear. She pushed herself up from the ground with a moan. "I know, I know. I'm being a jerk. I'd better go apologize to Gran."

Hugging herself against an inner chill, Rebecca paced the small expanse of her gleaming white kitchen. Gary had been ensconced in the bedroom for over half an hour. The red "extension in use" light on the kitchen phone had flickered off a good ten minutes ago. Why didn't he come out? Had his conversation with Noelle gone that badly?

She couldn't wait a moment longer to find out.

"Gary?" She leaned against the frame of the partially open door and tried to appear casual, though every nerve prickled.

He sat on the edge of the bed, elbows braced on his knees. When he lifted his head, he could barely meet her eyes. What was it she saw there—despair, desperation, dread?

"Well? Are you going to tell me or not?"

"You don't want to know." He released a humorless laugh as he rose. "Believe me, you do not want to know."

"Don't tell me. Noelle pulled her defiant act on you and you backed down." She strode toward him, fists clenched. "You can tackle a roomful of testy executives, but you can't stand up to one teenage girl?"

Gary briskly shook his head. "Not the same thing at all. Anyway, I didn't even talk to Noelle. I talked to Irene." He swept past her, and she followed his long strides to the dining room.

"Oh, no, you don't." She stepped between him and the liquor cabinet, daring him to push her aside.

Arms raised in surrender, Gary plodded to the living room and collapsed into a chair. He pressed his knuckles to his forehead and groaned. "Okay," he said, dropping his hands to the armrests, "you'll have to hear this sooner or later. Try to remember, this was *not* my idea. It was Kate's."

A chill corkscrewed up Rebecca's spine. "Tell me."

His jaw worked. He closed his eyes. "Kate's plan—which, unfortunately, I never gave her the chance to tell me, so, yes, you can put all the blame on me—was that after she died, we'd all move into her house with Noelle."

"Move into—" Rebecca staggered to the chair opposite Gary and fell into it before her knees gave way. She looked with longing toward the wet bar, sorely tempted to fix herself the stiff drink she had just denied her husband.

Dear Lord, is this Your idea of a joke?

But the only laughter she heard was the maniacal kind in her own head, along with the bitter reminder to be careful what you prayed for, because you just might get it.

"Rebecca and Kevin living *here*?" Noelle's effort to apologize to her grandmother had somehow led to this bizarre announcement. The very idea of Rebecca bringing her things— her ultra-modern, career-centered lifestyle—into this house that Mom had filled with such warmth and love and beauty— "Is this *The Twilight Zone*? Have we all gone wacko? Somebody pinch me and tell me you didn't just say that."

"Noelle—"

"No. Don't even *try* to talk me into this!" Casting her grandmother a look of utter disbelief, she slung her towel over her shoulder and stormed to her room.

A vigorous shampoo and a long soak under the pounding shower spray barely put a dent in her rage. Her damp hair secured in a braid, she dressed in faded denim shorts and an oversized T-shirt. No way could she face her grandmother, who'd only try to reason with her. Instead, she slipped out the patio door from her bedroom and marched over to Warren's. If anyone would stand with her as an ally against this insanity, surely Warren would.

She wasted no time filling him in on this latest development, but his only response was a thoughtful nod and a quiet, "Interesting."

"Is that all you can say?"

His mother, who'd obviously overheard, peeked in from the kitchen. Her smile warmed with sympathy. "You know, honey, it does kind of make sense."

"Yeah," Warren chimed in, "in a weird sort of way."

Noelle stared at both of them in disbelief. "You're as crazy as Gran. You're all crazy if you think I can—" She broke off with a shudder.

"You already said you'd go bananas living on a farm," Warren said.

Mrs. Ames stepped closer and rested her arm around Noelle's shoulder. "Think about it, honey. At least this way you get to stay in the house you grew up in."

"Right," Warren added. "You can keep living right next door. No changing schools or anything."

"No, just changing parents." Easing out of Mrs. Ames's embrace, Noelle flipped her head sideways and faked a grin. "Gee, when y'all put it that way—"

"That's it—the complaint department is closed. Time to do

something fun." Warren grabbed her by the wrists and tugged her toward the game room.

"Good idea, kids. Chill out for a while." With a tender smile directed at Noelle, Mrs. Ames said, "It'll all work out, honey. Trust me. Trust God."

Noelle didn't put much trust in God or anyone else lately, but she gave a meek nod while trying to rein in her runaway tongue. Battling for supremacy in one of Warren's convoluted video games might be just what she needed to vent her frustration. For the next couple of hours, she took immense pleasure in picturing her father's face atop the cave troll's body as she skewered the beast with poisoned-tipped arrows.

Later, Mrs. Ames popped in to say Noelle's grandmother needed her at home. She trudged across the lawn and into the kitchen, where she found Gran taking two chickens out of the oven to baste. A large glass baking dish containing some kind of vegetable casserole sat on a lower oven shelf. "Looks like enough food for an army. We'll never be able to eat all that." She glanced at the empty table. "Shall I set?"

"I've already laid everything out in the dining room." Gran straightened, her hands swathed in daisy-print oven mitts. "We're having guests this evening. Your father is bringing Rebecca and Kevin over for dinner."

Noelle staggered backwards as though she'd been hit in the stomach. "No way."

"Yes, *way*." Gran rolled her eyes and propped the chicken baster on a spoon rest. "It's time we all talked face to face."

"But, Gran—" Noelle sidled toward the dining room. Her throat closed at the sight of her mother's best china and silver, the heirloom lace tablecloth, the glistening crystal. Her eyes burned, but the tears held back.

"Now you listen to me, young lady." Gran jerked off the oven mitts and strode toward her with a raised finger. "If you can't sit at this table like the dignified young lady your mother would expect you to be, then don't come to dinner at all." Her voice trembled as she continued. "It hurt me more than you can imagine to see my only daughter's marriage break up. But what's done is done. Your mother never let what happened between her and your father destroy her life, and you can't let it destroy yours."

Gran rarely raised her voice, and Noelle shrank beneath the sharp words. She hung her head. "Okay. I'll try to be polite, and I'll act *dignified* . . . for Mom's sake." She glanced up at her grandmother, unable to control the defiance narrowing her eyes. "But I don't have to like it."

"I don't like this." Rebecca swallowed against the acid inferno flaming up her esophagus.

"I'm not asking you to like it." Gary swung the SUV into the driveway of his deceased ex-wife's home. Kate's home. Noelle's home. "Just be patient until we figure out how we can make this situation work."

Kevin leaned up from the backseat. "Awesome—look how big the yard is. Maybe we could get a dog someday. Do they have a pool?"

"Yep, and a game room, too." Gary shut off the engine and opened his door. "You'll have your own pool table."

Rebecca clamped her lips together and felt for the ground with the toe of her right foot. They didn't make SUVs for short people. And why did Gary have to sound as if the whole moving-in-with-Noelle plan had been settled? Surely there were other options? She couldn't imagine Noelle accepting the idea of her father's new wife and stepson moving into Kate's house. No, they'd talk this out and come up with a more workable solution, a new house in a new neighborhood where they could all have a fresh beginning.

Of course. It was the only solution that made sense.

Resting a hand on Kevin's shoulder, Rebecca followed her husband to the front door. One foot missed the narrow walk, and her four-inch heel sank deep into lush grass. Perhaps she'd overdressed for the occasion, but it didn't help that Noelle had a good six inches on her. Rebecca needed every advantage she could get.

Gary rang the bell. Moments later his tall, slender daughter appeared, dressed in torn jeans and no shoes. Now Rebecca felt certain she had overdressed.

"Hi, Noelle," Gary said stiffly. "Good to see you again."

"Gran just went to freshen up. She'll be right back." The girl's rigid mouth belied the artificial politeness in her tone. She held the door wider so they could step inside.

Rebecca placed her gray snakeskin handbag on the hall table and forced a smile. Through the archway to her right, she glimpsed a dining room looking as if it were set for royalty. Kitchen aromas tickled her nostrils, and her stomach shifted as if it couldn't decide between nervousness and hunger. She hugged one arm across her abdomen. "Something smells delicious."

"Gran's roasting a couple of chickens. You can have a seat in the living room. Or help yourself to drinks. Dad knows where we keep stuff." With a barely disguised sneer, Noelle backpedaled through the dining room and disappeared through the far door.

Kevin tugged on the sleeve of Rebecca's linen jacket. "Hey, Mom, can I check out the backyard?"

She glanced at Gary, but his flat-lipped expression showed he hadn't heard the request. "I don't think anyone would mind, but we should probably ask first." Seeing no sign of Irene yet, she hesitantly followed after Noelle and found her in the kitchen. "Excuse me," she began, clearing her throat.

The leggy teen spun around, almost dropping a platter of hors d'oeuvres. Rebecca thrust out a hand to steady the wobbling tray. "Didn't mean to startle you. Is it all right if Kevin goes out back?"

Noelle smiled coldly and nodded toward the doorway behind her. "Be my guest."

"I don't think she likes us being here," Kevin muttered as they found their way through the den and sunroom.

"We have to be understanding. She's been through a lot." Wishing her husband would show a little more understanding of her own awkward status, Rebecca slid open the glass doors, letting in a gust of warm summer air. It bore the light, fresh scent of chlorinated water. "Well, there's the yard and pool."

"Cool. Can I stay out here while you guys talk?" The boy had already kicked off his Doc Martens and was rolling up the legs of his khakis.

Rebecca frowned. "All right, but stay nearby and don't get your clothes wet, okay?" She followed the sound of voices back to the living room.

Noelle had set the hors d'oeuvres on the mahogany coffee table. Rebecca took her seat next to Gary as he reached for a canapé. "These look tasty," he said in a strained imitation of small talk. "Did you make them, Noelle?"

"Me? You've got to be kidding." The girl curled one leg beneath her in a salmon-pink velvet armchair. "Anyway, I just found out about five seconds ago that you were coming."

Gary cast Rebecca a quick glance, then flicked his gaze back to Noelle. "I talked to your grandmother hours ago. She didn't tell you she'd invited us?"

"She knew I wouldn't like the idea. But don't worry. I promised I'd try to be civil." Noelle bit into a stuffed olive and glared at Rebecca.

Irene Whitney glided into the living room, a mauve shirtdress complementing her gray-blond hair. "Good evening, Gary, Rebecca. I'm glad you could arrange to come on such short notice." She took the matching chair across from Noelle. "Dinner should be ready soon. Has Noelle offered you something to drink?"

"Yes, thanks, Irene. We're just enjoying the appetizers." Gary selected a rye cracker with seasoned cream-cheese spread and nearly dropped it. In the stiff silence, Rebecca could hear his slow, deliberate chewing.

"Perhaps I should check on dinner." Irene rose with a gracious smile and went to the kitchen.

Noelle sat forward and tapped her fingers on her knees. "Sure I can't get you something? Maybe Kevin would like a Coke."

"That would be nice," Rebecca said. "Thank you."

Edginess to match her own radiated off Gary. He started to rise. "Is there any Scotch in the house?"

Rebecca's heart lurched. She placed a restraining hand on his arm. "Gary..."

"Sorry, Dad. Did you forget you took the hard stuff with you when you moved out?" Noelle cast a cruel smirk over her shoulder and started for the kitchen.

Irene appeared just then, announcing dinner, and Rebecca breathed a silent sigh of relief. The meal served as a temporary distraction from the purpose of their visit, although Rebecca barely picked at the scant amount of food she'd taken. Every swallow raised fears of rushing to the bathroom to throw up. It didn't help that she had no idea where the bathroom was.

Half an hour later, Gary crumpled his napkin next to his empty plate and eased his chair away from the table. "Thank you, Irene. Haven't had a home-cooked meal like this in ages." Jaw muscles bunching, he lowered his eyes. "I mean, with Rebecca and me both working and traveling so much..."

Irene offered Rebecca a feeble smile. "Shall we have coffee in the living room? Perhaps Kevin would like to watch TV in the den while we talk."

Rebecca crumpled her napkin beside her plate. "Noelle, let me help you clear the table."

"I can handle it." Flipping her braid across one shoulder, the girl started stacking plates faster than a diner waitress hustling for tips. "Why don't I do the dishes while y'all talk?"

"Just put them in the sink for now." Irene pushed her chair out and stood. "We have more important matters to deal with."

Important indeed, and long overdue. Rebecca only wished she and Kevin could have been excused from this summit meeting. Noelle was certainly doing her dead-level best to stall. Maybe if they let Gary and Irene discuss things in private, they'd both come to their senses. *Please, God, let them see the insanity of this ludicrous plan.*

Doing a little stalling herself, Rebecca took Kevin to the den. As he plopped onto the floor in front of the massive entertainment center, she looked around for the remote, then went into minute detail making sure he knew how to operate the system.

"I got it, Mom." Kevin yanked the remote out of her hands.

"Okay, sorry." Wiping perspiring palms against her skirt, she exhaled sharply and strode to the living room.

"Rebecca, would you care for coffee?" Irene stirred cream into a dainty china cup.

Each click of the silver spoon shrieked Kate's exquisite taste. Rebecca declined Irene's offer and wished she could disappear into the sofa cushions. She hadn't seen much of Kate's home yet, but it all looked so comfortably elegant in warm and welcoming earth tones accented with muted splashes of color—nothing like the modern stark-white decor of Rebecca and Gary's condo. She couldn't stop picturing Gary's life here with Kate, couldn't stop comparing it to all the things she missed in her own life.

"Very well, then," Irene said. "It's time we talk about Noelle's future."

Noelle chewed on the end of her braid. "I thought my future had already been decided."

Gary gave a nervous cough. "Look, I know none of this is easy for you, but . . ." He spread his hands, then let them slap against his thighs.

"According to Gran, I don't have much choice." Noelle stared pointedly at her father. "Do I?"

He sighed. "What do you want from me, Noelle? There's nothing I can do to bring your mother back. Just because we got divorced doesn't mean I stopped caring, either about her or you. You're still my daughter."

"Yes, but you stopped being my father a long time ago." She turned her head away, hugging one knee to her chest.

The look on Gary's face tore at Rebecca's heart, eclipsing the pointless comparison game she'd been playing. She slipped her hand into his, willing him courage, praying for her own. When he didn't say anything, she broke the silence. "Noelle, this situation is not what any of us would have asked for, least of all the death of your mother. But if we work together, maybe we can find some way to . . ."

Her words trailed off as she studied the subtle nuances in Noelle's expression. Beneath the girl's façade of bitterness lay a broken, bewildered heart—feelings Rebecca could identify with all too well. Kate Townsend must have realized that after her death, more than anything else, Noelle would need a solid, stable foundation from which to grieve and heal. If it meant staying in the home she'd grown up in, how could Rebecca refuse? She'd survived worse than this, and with God's help, she'd survive this too. Somehow they'd make it work.

Because if they didn't . . .

Tightening her grip on Gary's hand, she willed strength into her voice and held Noelle's gaze. "I admit, I had serious reservations at first, but—for now, anyway—your mother's idea does seem like the most practical solution. Maybe we should give it a chance."

She felt Gary squeeze her hand in silent gratitude. He heaved out a breath and angled his daughter a pleading glance. "If

Rebecca and Kevin are willing to give this arrangement a try, certainly you can do the same."

Noelle gave an exaggerated shrug. "Seeing as how I have no say in the matter." She faced her father squarely. "But I have two conditions. Number one, you will not have Mom's bedroom. It will be left exactly the way it is."

Her father rubbed the back of his neck. "Rebecca and I can take the guest room, but what about Kevin?"

"He gets the sofa bed in the game room."

Gary glanced at Rebecca, and she nodded her assent. She hoped her expression didn't give away her immense relief. The situation was bizarre enough. Occupying the same bedroom Gary had once shared with his ex-wife would have been the ultimate impossibility.

Gary turned to Noelle. "And your other condition?"

"Nothing—*not one thing*—in this house is to be changed. Not the furniture, not the dishes, not the curtains in the windows. Nothing. Got it?"

Rebecca sat back heavily and closed her eyes. Five minutes ago she'd been envying all Kate's beautiful things. Now that they'd been forced upon her, she wanted to run screaming back to their stark, functional condo. *Oh, God, help me!*

"Please, Noelle," Gary said, his voice strained. "Rebecca is my wife now, and she has her own tastes and needs. You can't expect her to—"

Noelle lifted an eyebrow. "Those are my terms. Take them or leave them."

5

They drove back to the condominium under an orange-and-lavender Texas sky. After merging onto the expressway, Gary dared a glance toward his wife. The heat had abated only a few degrees after sunset, but the atmosphere in the car had become downright frigid.

"How will we ever make this work?" Sniffling, Rebecca wagged her head. "I'd honestly convinced myself we were doing the right thing, but I'm not sure I can survive Noelle's resentment."

His grip tightened on the steering wheel. "It'll have to work. What other choice is there?" He could kick himself now for ducking out every time Kate had tried to talk to him about Noelle's future—but he'd grown even more adept than his daughter at living in denial.

Following his phone conversation with Irene, however, he'd gradually come to terms with Kate's idea. It would provide Noelle a semblance of continuity while also giving him a much needed opportunity to get to know his daughter all over again—and in surroundings familiar to them both.

Rebecca adjusted her air conditioner vent and sat back with a jerk. "I admit I agreed to this arrangement, and I'll do my best to support you in this decision." Her voice held none of the courage and conviction she'd displayed earlier. "But everything in that house shouts of the life you shared with Kate."

Gary took his eyes off the highway long enough to cast her an incredulous glance. "You're *jealous*? Of my dead ex-wife?"

"I don't know—maybe I am." She ripped open her handbag and extracted a wad of tissues. "And I'm afraid if we consent to Noelle's conditions, she'll never even give me a chance. Not as her stepmother, not as her friend."

He wanted to reach out to her, but if he let emotions get in the way, he'd chicken out himself. "I admit it's going to be hard—for all of us. But for now, I need to do what's best for Noelle."

"What about what's best for Kevin? Do you suppose for a minute Noelle will even pretend to make him feel welcome?"

"Come on, Mom, it'll be okay," Kevin piped up from the rear seat. "We'll finally have a big backyard and our own pool. And it'll be fun sleeping in the game room. Hey, and since Noelle will be home with me after school, you don't have to make me stay at Mrs. Gaylord's anymore."

Rebecca released an audible sigh, doubtless because of her son's not-so-subtle hint that he was getting too big for a babysitter. At least Kevin seemed excited about the plan. The kid was probably the most resilient of all of them. Gary wished he could reassure Rebecca somehow, but he'd run out of words. Maybe if he focused on the logistics, which was what he was best at. Outline the strategy, then institute the action steps—the formula had never failed him on the job, and he couldn't afford for it to fail him now.

Step one seemed obvious. "We'd better plan on moving next weekend."

The statement elicited a gasp from his wife. "So soon? But there's so much to think about."

"I'll clear my schedule. We'll get it done." He began a mental checklist—putting furniture in storage, packing their clothes and personal items, getting the mail forwarded . . . "I'll contact a real estate agent first thing in the morning and get the condo on the market."

"But what if this plan doesn't work out?" Another sniffle. "Maybe we shouldn't sell the condo right away."

Quite a turnaround from a couple of weeks ago, when Rebecca had been bugging him about house hunting. "Okay then, we'll keep the condo and leave everything there just the way it is. If things get too sticky for you with Noelle, you'll always have a place to escape to."

In the darkened car, he listened to his wife's soft whimpering. A rush of protectiveness surged through him, along with guilt over how insensitive he'd been to her feelings. He loved Rebecca. Tender, fascinating, self-assured, she'd come into his life when he'd given up hope of ever finding anyone who really understood him and the world he operated in. He reached for her hand and pressed it to his lips. "Hang in there, honey. We'll get through this, I promise."

She blew out a long, tremulous breath. "I hope you're right."

Gary turned into their driveway and parked the SUV in the garage. "Straight to bed, young man," he told the yawning Kevin on their way through the kitchen. He ruffled the boy's hair. "'Night, kiddo. And thanks for being such a good sport about this."

"'Night, Dad." When Kevin grinned up at him, then turned to accept Rebecca's kiss on the cheek, Gary swallowed over the catch in his throat. Kevin had been calling him "Dad" since before the wedding, as if he couldn't wait for Gary to fill the shoes of the father Kevin had barely known. And Gary had stepped willingly into the role, savoring the boy's affection so freely given. Over the past few months, he'd become more of a father to Rebecca's son than he'd been to his own daughter in years.

What's different? How many times lately had he asked himself that question? He still put in ten- and twelve-hour days and made business trips as often as ever. Maybe because Rebecca also traveled so much, she and Kevin had both learned to make the most of the time they had together.

It sounded too simple, though. Following Rebecca to their bedroom, he felt there had to be more to it, a better answer. If he didn't discover it soon, it might be too late to salvage what was left of his relationship with Noelle.

While he emptied his pockets into the ebony tray on his dresser, Rebecca emerged from the bathroom, her face freshly washed. She slipped between the gray satin-trimmed sheets. "Are you coming to bed?"

"In a minute." Giving himself a mental shake, he shrugged off his blazer and draped it over a polished wooden hanger, then hung it in the closet between two other blazers of similar color. After wedging shoe trees into his tasseled loafers, he set them side-by-side on a lower shelf. On his way to the bathroom, he spotted his briefcase by the door and nudged it half an inch to the left.

He froze. *What do you think you're doing, man?* Organization, focus, a clear plan of attack—something told him the skills he'd relied on throughout his career would be of little use when it came to actually relating to his daughter.

A few minutes later, clad in maroon silk pajamas, he stretched out on top of the bedcovers and stared at the ceiling. His hand crept toward Rebecca, but she shifted and rolled away. In the hushed darkness, a sea of loneliness washed over him. He ached to pull his wife into his arms and bury his face against the curve of her neck, taste the salty-sweetness of her lips, and silence the clamoring voices in his head with the reassurance of their love. But Rebecca wouldn't be a willing partner tonight, not while her own feelings were still raw.

He gazed at his wife's curving silhouette and inhaled the

delicate scent of her perfume. If he were forced to choose between their marriage and his daughter . . .

No, in the midst of all this, he couldn't lose Rebecca, too. There had to be a way to hold his family together—all of them.

If only he could figure out how.

Noelle slid into an empty desk at the back of the geometry classroom. It would be just her luck if the teacher liked to seat everyone alphabetically and she happened to end up on the front row. Teachers always called on students in the front row—not a good spot for a C student in math skills.

"Noelle, hi." Trisha Phillips took the desk across the aisle. "I'm real sorry about your mom."

"Thanks." Noelle gave a half-smile. She was getting good at this now. Trisha must have been the fiftieth person today to say something about Mom, and it was only second period. She saw pity in their eyes, and she hated it.

How dumb she'd been, thinking she could drift through the first day of school as though nothing had happened—as though her entire life hadn't been battered and shattered and tossed in the dumpster. Too many people knew her, and even more had known Mom, one of the most popular teachers at Arden Heights High School.

Cassie McCormick, Noelle's best friend after Warren, bounced into the room in cotton-candy-pink denim overalls. She claimed the seat in front of Noelle's and raised her palm for a high-five. "All right! We get to suffer through Polygon Potter's geometry class together."

Noelle grimaced and rubbed her stinging hand against her thigh. "I can't believe they really call him that."

"Hey, let me see your schedule." Cassie's blond curls framed her pixie-like smile. "Maybe this year we'll have more classes together."

The tardy bell sounded, and Mr. Potter strode into the room. One of Mom's pallbearers. Lean and mean, his wiry hair standing on end, he silenced the chatter with his icy glare, then flipped open his roll book and began taking attendance. When he reached Noelle's name, he paused. "Noelle," he said softly, "I'm glad to have you in my class."

She murmured a quick thank-you and broke eye contact. *Please, God, get me through this day.*

Too many hours later, she trudged out of her last class and stepped into the steamy late-August afternoon.

Cassie caught up with her on the front sidewalk. "How are you getting home from school?"

Noelle stopped short. Her stomach rebounded a millisecond later. She'd been heading toward the faculty parking lot, where she would have met her mother at the car. "I almost forgot. I rode with Warren today."

"Rats. I was hoping you could come home with me so we could help each other with that killer geometry assignment. Did you get what he was saying about protractors and angles and everything?"

She focused on her friend's bubbly chatter—anything to escape all the painful reminders today had brought. "Oh, Cass, we learned most of that in junior high."

"Like, that was a couple of years ago already? Seriously, can you come over and help me?"

"I'd sure rather go to your house than mine. Kevin's supposed to ride the bus home from middle school." She rolled her eyes. "Can you believe this? They're not sending him to his old babysitter's after school anymore. What do they think I am, free childcare service?"

"Bummer." Cassie flicked at a stray leaf that had fallen onto her notebook. "He could stay by himself for an hour or two, couldn't he?"

"You'd think. Rebecca's *so* overprotective." Noelle pretended to gag.

"So how about it? Is it too late to change your plans with Warren?"

Warren appeared out of a knot of students and sidled up next to Noelle. "I heard my name. What's up?"

"Cassie just asked me to go study at her house."

He made a face. "Guess that means you can't help me write my very first junior English theme: 'What It Means to Be a Texas Citizen.'"

"Yikes. How boring." Cassie hugged her notebook and looked heavenward. "Makes me glad I'm still a soph. All we have to do for English homework is conjugate a few verbs."

Warren nudged Noelle with his elbow. "Hey, you write my theme, and I'll conjugate your verbs. Whaddya say?"

"I don't know. . . . I think I'd rather go over to Cassie's for a while."

"But what about Kevin?" Warren's brows drew together. "I mean, weren't you supposed to—"

"I'm sure he'll be okay. The truth is," Noelle added with a downward glance, "I really don't want to go home yet."

He cast her an understanding glance. "That bad, huh?"

"It was bad enough after everyone moved in last weekend, even with Gran still there to run interference. But since she went back to Nebraska . . ." Noelle huffed and moved a few paces away.

Cassie shaded her eyes and looked toward the drive-through. "There's my mom now. You coming, Noelle?"

She hesitated. Seriously, how much trouble could an eleven-year-old get into at home alone for an hour or so? "Sure, I guess."

Warren tugged on Noelle's braid. "I'll keep an ear out for Kevin for you. And I'll be home all evening if things get rough later."

"Thanks." She shot him a quirky smile and followed Cassie to Mrs. McCormick's car.

Later, with their geometry assignments spread across Cassie's bedroom floor, Noelle stifled a yawn. "I've had it. I don't care if I never see another triangle."

"My sentiments exactly." Cassie slammed her textbook shut and shoved it across the carpet, where it collided with her purple vinyl notebook. She snatched one of about a zillion teen heartthrob magazines piled on her nightstand and began paging through the photos. "Have you seen this article about Nick Jonas? Man, he's cute!"

Hiding an eye roll, Noelle crossed her ankles. "Uh, no, Cassie. I've had a few other things on my mind."

"Oh, wow, Noelle, you sure have." Cassie laid the magazine aside. "I really admire the way you're handling your mom's . . . well, you know."

"It's okay to say *death*, Cassie. People die all the time." Noelle rested her arm on the edge of the bed. She couldn't take it if her friend got all mushy on her.

"I just mean you don't have to put up a front with me. I know how hard it must be."

"Don't start." Noelle's jaw tightened. "All I've heard for weeks now is people urging me to express my grief. Would everyone feel better if I broke down and sobbed hysterically?"

Cassie lowered her eyes. "That's not what I meant."

Noelle caught the hurt look on her friend's face. Her shoulders drooped. "Sorry. I've been chewing everyone's head off lately."

"It's not like you don't have a right to be upset."

"I just want to get over it and get on with my life." An aching lump settled at the base of Noelle's throat. She gathered up her books and moved toward the door. "I should get home."

Twenty minutes later, Cassie's mother dropped her off. The pulsating beat of a rock song on the stereo greeted her as she plodded up the front walk. *Not again.* Kevin was obsessed with those cheesy Christian rock bands. And how could he stand the music so loud? The kid seriously needed to get himself a decent set of headphones.

"TURN THAT STEREO"—she burst through the front door —"off," she concluded in the immediate silence.

"Sorry." Kevin stood in the den, his hands clasped behind his back.

"Thank you." She strode past him and dropped her books on the piano bench.

"Hey, Noelle, wanna play pool with me? I've been practicing."

She eyed him coolly. "If there are any rips in that table ..."

"No way. I'm real careful." The kid gave her a can't-resist-me smile. "Pleeeeeze."

She stared down her nose at him, wishing he would stop trying so hard to be friends. That's all he'd done since he moved in. Noelle this, and Noelle that, like a pesky little puppy.

"Since your mother isn't home, I'd better see about supper." She turned on her heel.

In the kitchen she found a note on the refrigerator: *Casserole in freezer. See microwave & oven directions on box—should take about 40 minutes total. Lettuce and veggies in fridge for salad. Baguette on counter—warm in oven for ten minutes. Home by 6:30. R.*

Shrugging off her irritation, Noelle started the casserole thawing in the microwave, then turned on the oven. As she reached for the lettuce in the refrigerator drawer, Kevin came up behind her. "Can I help?"

"Here." She handed him a crisp, green head of Romaine. If the kid was determined to hang out with her, might as well put him to work. "It needs to be washed, and take the core out." Watching him from the corner of her eye, she rinsed three ripe tomatoes and placed them on a cutting board. "Salad bowl's in the cupboard next to the dishwasher."

Kevin removed the lettuce from the cellophane bag. With

expert motions, he gave the core a twist, yanked it out, and shoved it down the disposal. After pulling the lettuce apart, he rinsed the leaves under the faucet and patted them dry between paper towels. Then he tore the leaves into bite-sized pieces and dropped them into the salad bowl.

Noelle raised an eyebrow. "Where'd you learn to do that?"

"Mom taught me some, but mostly I just figure stuff out. I help out a lot since Mom's so busy with her job." Kevin smirked. "I love my mom and all—she's terrific—but she can't cook worth a flip."

Noelle remembered Sunday's burnt-hamburger fiasco when they'd returned from taking Gran to the airport. She held the cutting board over the salad bowl and pushed the chopped tomatoes onto Kevin's nicely prepared lettuce.

Watch it, girl, or you may actually start to like this kid.

Rebecca drummed her silver pen on the cover of her portfolio. The once-a-month interdepartmental staff meeting dragged on with all the appeal of watching paint dry. She was still fuming over Kevin's phone call earlier. Apparently, Warren from next door had stopped by to tell him Noelle was doing homework with a friend and would not be coming straight home from school. It was reassuring to know someone with a sense of responsibility was looking out for Kevin, but Noelle had no business changing her plans without checking with Rebecca first.

Unfortunately, she couldn't discuss the problem with Gary. He'd left early this morning for London on another of his business trips—this one for legitimate reasons, at least—and told her he wouldn't have a chance to phone or email until tomorrow.

An unwanted thought nudged its way into her brain, a pesky little voice that had grown progressively louder in recent weeks: *What do you suppose your husband is really doing when he's away on these trips? Do you honestly believe he's any more trustworthy than two-timing Rob?*

She bit the inside of her cheek hard enough to taste blood. How could such doubts still haunt her after all these years? Gary was *not* Rob. Whatever else came between them, she wouldn't let herself believe him unfaithful.

"All right, people." Charles Sharp shoved away from the conference table with a decisive flourish. "You have your marching orders for the next few weeks. Let's get cracking."

Matt Garrison, seated beside Rebecca, glared at her as he snapped his laptop closed. "My office, now."

Had her inattention been that obvious? Or was it because she'd left gaping holes in her progress report on the Stewart Industries account? Either way, Matt wasn't happy with her. Rising slowly, she paused long enough to fish a roll of antacids from the pocket of her pumpkin-colored blazer. The mint-flavored tablet left her mouth feeling dry and chalky. She stopped at a water fountain for a quick drink on the way to Matt's office.

"Have a seat," Matt instructed without making eye contact. He snapped his laptop into the docking station, punched some keys, and studied something on his monitor for several long moments before turning to face Rebecca.

"Matt, I'm sorry my report was incomplete. I need to make some follow-up phone calls, but I'll have the final figures on your desk by nine tomorrow at the latest." She hugged her portfolio as if it could shield her from the disapproval she read in his gaze. "Please, you can't imagine what I've been going through lately. My mind has been a million miles away."

Matt rubbed a hand across his narrow, graying moustache. "You know there's a reason DataTech doesn't condone interoffice relationships."

She squared her shoulders. "Gary and I have both been extremely careful not to let our relationship interfere with work issues. It's all these . . . other things causing us problems right now."

"Yeah, I know." The small-built man folded his hands on the desktop. "But it puts me in a bad position. You're one of my top account managers, and this department can't afford for you to be working at any less than your best." He grimaced. "What makes it even worse is that I'm getting flak from higher up. Apparently, Gary has been as distracted lately as you have, and Sharp wants an end to it."

She winced. Despite the fact that Charles Sharp helped run a cutting-edge technology corporation, he didn't seem able to move his management style into the twenty-first century. The man was the quintessential caricature of a dictatorial, workaholic executive headed for a stress-induced heart attack. She could only pity his family, or rather, what was left of it. Alimony and child support were a poor substitute for a husband and father—a lesson Gary was also learning the hard way, and she only hoped it wasn't too late for him—or for their marriage.

Matt spoke, interrupting her thoughts. "I understand how tough things are at home, but it doesn't alter your work obligations." He ran the edge of his thumb along the desktop. "Maybe I should set you up with the company psychologist. It might appease the big bosses."

Tears welled. No doubt counseling would be a wise choice for both her and Gary. Even if Gary resisted, she could go on her own, but the idea of talking over such personal issues with a psychologist on DataTech's payroll made her cringe. "I appreciate the advice, but if I decide it's necessary, I'd rather see someone not affiliated with the company."

"Have it your way. But I'm serious. If your job performance doesn't improve, I may have to resort to more drastic measures." He dismissed her with a wave of his hand and turned back to his computer.

Drastic measures? She didn't even want to think about what those might be.

The drive through stop-and-go traffic from downtown Dallas to Arden Heights only worsened Rebecca's mood. Arriving at the house, she took advantage of the vacant space in the garage while Gary's car was parked at the airport. As she stepped from her very practical BMW sedan, she paused to admire Kate Townsend's luxurious white Lexus convertible and allowed herself a moment of envy at the lavish gift Gary had once purchased for his former wife.

Clearly, she was more jealous of Kate than she wanted to admit. She envied everything the woman represented—a comfortable home in the suburbs, a fulfilling career that left plenty of time for both mothering and homemaking, the love and respect of neighbors and friends, and most of all, an unshakable faith even in the face of suffering and death.

She paused, one hand on the doorknob. *Lord, help me stop comparing myself with Kate and envying the life she had. Help me to somehow find contentment in this difficult situation and trust You to see us all through.*

As she laid her briefcase on the dryer in the laundry room, a rich, cheesy aroma from the warming tuna casserole wafted from the kitchen. She kicked off the three-inch power heels she wore to give herself a little more edge at the office and rubbed a sore spot on her toe. The cool tile against her feet brought welcome relief. She stepped through to the kitchen as Noelle carried the casserole dish to the table, and annoyance surged again. Was it asking too much for the girl to be around to keep an eye on Kevin after school? Apparently so. She wished she'd kept her heels on for the inevitable confrontation.

"Yo, Mom." Kevin looked up from the table, where he dished salad onto individual serving plates. "Supper's almost ready. I did the lettuce."

Her heart softened at the boyish pride in Kevin's eyes. "Nice job, tiger." She turned to Noelle and swallowed the angry words she'd been about to spew. "Everything looks great. Thank you."

"No problem." The tall teen swung her braid over her shoulder and pulled out a chair.

As Noelle started the casserole around, a furry tail brushed Rebecca's leg. She jumped, sending her napkin fluttering to the floor. Retrieving it, she looked across the table to see Noelle's black-and-white cat, Laurence, peering at her from Gary's empty chair.

She gasped. "Noelle, please don't tell me you allow the cat at the table."

"It's the tuna. Laurence loves the stuff." Laughing, Noelle fetched a saucer from the cupboard and dished out a spoonful of the casserole. After stirring the food until it cooled, she set the saucer on the table in front of the cat. He placed his paws on either side and nibbled delicately. Noelle cast Rebecca a self-satisfied smile. "You may as well get used to it. Laurence is family."

The unspoken *and you are not* rang in Rebecca's ears, and she closed her eyes briefly against the sting. Then, unwilling to allow Noelle the satisfaction, she sat up straighter and cleared her throat. "I completely understand. However, I do hope Laurence won't be offended if the rest of the family pause a moment to say grace."

Noelle had just taken a huge forkful of casserole. She made a choking sound, and her fork hit the plate with a clatter. She meekly bowed her head.

"Gracious Lord," Rebecca began, "thank You for all Your wonderful gifts. Bless this food for the nourishment of our bodies, and nourish our spirits with Your eternal love." *And please forgive me for relishing this brief moment of triumph over Noelle's attempt to undermine me.* "In Jesus' name, amen."

6

Noelle frowned as she stuffed wads of stringy lettuce and gooey cheese back into her grease-soaked taco shell. "I wish my father would hurry up and get home."

Cassie jerked her head up. "What did you say?"

Warren reached across the lunchroom table and felt Noelle's forehead. "You're not getting sick, are you?"

She swatted his hand away. "What I'm sick of is being super-polite to Rebecca and Kevin. If Dad were around, maybe they'd spend their evenings bugging him and leave me alone."

Warren grimaced. "Are they that hard to live with?"

"Kevin's constantly after me to play pool or a video game or help him with his homework. And all Rebecca does is march around in those ridiculous spiked heels and complain about Laurence."

"Laurence?" Cassie tucked in her chin. "Does your wicked stepmother have something against cats?"

"She gripes about cat fur getting on her clothes, and she says I don't clean out his litter box often enough." Noelle glanced down. "And the other night I let him eat at the table."

Cassie burst out laughing. "You didn't! Your *mom* wouldn't even let—I mean—oh, rats, Noelle, I'm sorry."

The horrible burning sensation started around her eyelids again. A shaky laugh escaped. "Mom always let Laurence lick her empty ice cream bowl."

But she definitely drew the line at having him at the table.

Warren gave Noelle's shin a playful jab with the toe of his sneaker. "So what happened with Rebecca? Did she banish Laurence from the kitchen forever?"

Noelle grimaced. "She said grace, and we went on with supper . . . Laurence included."

"Wow." Cassie stirred her fork through a puddle of refried beans. "Sounds like she's at least *trying* to get along with you."

"Well, it's not working." If Rebecca thought she could worm her way into Noelle's life by making friends with Laurence, she was dead wrong.

At the sound of the bell, Warren gulped the rest of his fruit drink. He pushed out his lower lip in a mocking frown. "Oh, darn. No time to finish my taco."

"What a crime." Cassie dumped the remains of her meal into the nearest trash can.

"You two don't know how to appreciate a good meal." Noelle poked the last bite of taco into her mouth and chewed with relish. "You should be forced to eat Rebecca's cooking. Raw squid would be more appetizing."

After school, Noelle met Warren and Cassie in one of the lecture halls for the Drama Club meeting. Noelle had been waiting all day to find out what Mrs. Sanchez, the club sponsor, had chosen for the fall production. Calling the group to order, Mrs. Sanchez introduced the president, Lynn Larson.

The slender, fair-haired senior stepped to the front of the lecture hall. "The play we're doing is called *I Remember Mama*. It has lots of parts, so everyone will get a chance to act, even you first-timers." Lynn turned to Cassie, the club secretary. "Would you pass around the copies, please?"

Noelle glanced through one of the playbooks. She'd caught part of the movie on TV a couple of years ago, a classic black-and-white film about a Norwegian immigrant family. Noelle remembered little of the story, only that it featured a girl who wanted to become a writer, but her family and all their problems kept distracting her. In the end, however, the girl finally sold a story about her mother.

I Remember Mama. Swallowing hard, Noelle closed the book and pushed it to the edge of the desktop. Maybe she should skip this production and wait until the spring play.

"Let's have an impromptu read-through," Mrs. Sanchez suggested. "Noelle, I'd like you to read the part of Katrin. And Lynn, you be Mama." Before Noelle could find her voice to decline, the teacher had assigned all the parts in act one.

With trembling hands, Noelle turned to the opening scene, willing everything from her mind except the words on the page. The actress in her took over, and she worked to capture just the right inflection as she read Katrin's lines, pausing only briefly to skim the stage directions interrupting her first speech. Page by page, the character grew on her. Before they finished, she made up her mind to ask Mrs. Sanchez for the role.

"You're perfect for Katrin," Cassie told Noelle when the meeting ended. "I'd like to be Dagmar, the little sister. She gets to carry the cat around."

"It'll probably be a stuffed cat," Warren said. "Unless . . ." Turning to Noelle, he wiggled his eyebrows.

"You mean Laurence?" Her eyes widened as she pictured her cuddly old cat on stage. "What if he panicked and escaped? What if he meowed at the wrong time?"

"It would add some realism to the show." Cassie tugged on Noelle's arm. "Think about it, okay? Laurence is such a sweet kitty. He wouldn't be any trouble at all."

Noelle chewed her lip. "I suppose we could try him at rehearsals, if Mrs. Sanchez says it's okay."

On the ride home with Warren, Noelle decided having Laurence in the play would make it even more fun. In fact, the whole idea of immersing herself in the drama production might be exactly what she needed. Anything that gave her a little more distance from her so-called family was worth it.

Loosening his tie, Gary stretched his legs across the hotel bed and leaned against the headboard. He'd been away over a week now, and though DataTech almost always put him up in a five-star hotel, he missed the comforts of home, especially his pillow-top king-size mattress. Unfortunately, the bed was at the condo, and the queen-size guest bed at Kate's house—he still thought of it as Kate's house—made a poor substitute.

With a tired sigh, he reached for his cell phone to call Rebecca, dialing the landline at the house for better reception. Kevin finally answered.

"Hey, Kev. How's everything in Big D?"

"Hi, Dad! When are you coming home?"

Gary smiled at the excitement in the boy's tone. "A few more days. Still have some loose ends to tie up."

"Wish I could go to England. It'd be so cool to see the Tower, and Buckingham Palace, and those guards in the big fuzzy hats."

"Someday, kiddo. Where's your mom? Can I talk to her?"

"Hang on. She's finishing up the dishes."

Seconds later Rebecca came on the line. "Hi, honey. How's foggy old England?"

"A little cool and rainy today, but the sun came out this afternoon." Hearing the sound of her voice was the warmest he'd felt all day. He unlaced his Italian wing-tips and kicked them onto the floor. "How are things there?"

A brief silence hung between them. "Nothing I can't handle."

"You mean Noelle." He blew out a long breath. Like he even had to ask.

"She's been agreeable enough," Rebecca said slowly, "in a patronizing sort of way. The truth is, I hardly see her except at dinner."

"She still feeding Laurence at the table?" He couldn't suppress a chuckle. Rebecca had emailed him about the tuna casserole incident.

"No, just that once—thank goodness."

"That old cat has been around a long time, honey. He's like part of the family."

"So Noelle keeps telling me."

Time to change the subject. "How's work?"

"Tense." She gave a rueful laugh. "I think Matt's punishing me for being distracted the past few weeks."

"Yeah, I know the feeling. Sharp's been on my case, too. Rebecca, I . . ." He scraped a hand through his hair as guilt strangled him. He'd failed as a parent, and if he didn't watch his step, he'd end up a two-time loser at marriage. "I wish I could promise you the worst will be over soon."

She heaved a noisy sigh. "Don't worry, I'm hanging in there."

"I'll be home Tuesday." He imagined her in his arms again, the scent of her perfume arising from the soft, warm hollow behind her earlobe. If only he could hold her until all their troubles evaporated. "My flight gets in around five."

"Wonderful." Her tone suggested anything but. "You can kiss me hello and goodbye at the same time."

"Huh?"

"I'm booked on a flight to Chicago Tuesday evening. McDonough Technologies has problems with the accounting software we designed for them. Matt's sending me to check it out. I'm glad you'll be back, because Mrs. Gaylord is expecting house guests and I don't feel comfortable asking Noelle to be responsible for Kevin overnight."

"With the Ameses right next door, I'm sure they would have managed," Gary said, but considering how Noelle had treated her new stepbrother so far, he didn't feel convinced. "How long will you be away?"

"Only a few days, I hope. But these things have a way of turning out to be more complicated than you expect."

"Right." He slid lower onto his pillow, succumbing to exhaustion. It was nearly two in the morning London time, and he'd been up since the previous dawn overseeing the installation and testing of a new computer network, encountering one glitch after another. He didn't feel like getting involved in a detailed discussion of computer workings. "I'm bushed," he said, yawning. "Give Kevin a hug for me. I'd ask you to do the same for Noelle, but we both know how that would go over."

"She's not home anyway."

"It's after eight there, isn't it? What's she doing out this late on a school night?"

"They're having some kind of play tryouts. She told me not to hold supper for her."

He grimaced. School plays—one more of his daughter's interests he'd failed to make time for. "Tell her I asked about her, okay? And text me your flight info. I'll look for you at the airport Tuesday when my flight gets in."

"Will you?" Hopefulness rose in her voice. "I'd love it if we could have at least a few minutes together before I leave."

"I'll do my best, hon, I promise." They said their goodbyes, and Gary switched off the light. Too tired to change out of his clothes, he pushed aside the bedspread and tried to get comfortable.

Thirty minutes later he turned onto his back and stared into the darkness. He'd been in London almost the whole time since they'd moved in with his daughter. How were the two of them supposed to get reacquainted this way?

When are you going to get it, Townsend? Your career aspirations are what came between you and your family in the first place.

Maybe so, but his job hadn't created a problem for him and Rebecca. Okay, at least until now. She may have consented to the idea of living in Kate's house, and she'd certainly taken the high road where Noelle was concerned. But how long could Gary honestly expect his marriage to last if he and Rebecca kept passing each other like the proverbial ships in the night? He should have learned by now the pitfalls of long-distance marriages.

And long-distance parenthood.

"Daddy, why can't you be at my play? It's my first one. I'm going to be Little Red Riding Hood. Please, please, don't go away!"

Loneliness engulfed him, threatening to swallow him alive. A long time ago he'd imagined growing old with Kate—his lover, his wife, the mother of his child. Something told him he was only just beginning to grasp everything he'd lost, everything he risked losing now if things didn't change.

A drop of moisture slipped down his temple. He swallowed and closed his eyes. This time he fell asleep immediately.

Rebecca's gaze darted up and down the airport terminal, skimming past any number of tall, tawny-haired men, none of whom turned out to be her husband. Just a quick hug and kiss before she boarded her flight to Chicago was all she asked. She checked her cell phone. No incoming calls. No missed calls. No voicemail.

No Gary.

Her stomach on fire, she waited until the last possible second before falling in line to go through security. She barely made it to the gate before boarding was called. Finding her seat in business class, she struggled to hoist her roll-aboard into the already jammed overhead. It came crashing down on her right shoulder. She cried out and let the bag fall onto the seat.

"Here, let me." A fifty-something man in a gray pinstriped suit came to her aid. After stowing her bag, he took his seat across the aisle and shot her a pleasant smile. "Headed to Chicago?" At her nod, he asked, "Business or pleasure?"

"Business, if I can survive the trip." She rubbed her throbbing shoulder. "Thanks for the help."

The man nodded and settled into his seat. He withdrew the in-flight magazine from the seat pocket, then looked over at her with concern. "That's gotta hurt. You should ask the flight attendant for some ice."

"I'll be okay." She retrieved her phone once more and willed it to ring before flight regulations required her to turn it off.

It buzzed in her hand, and she almost fumbled it to the floor. She didn't even pause to check the Caller ID before answering. "Hello? Gary?"

"Hey, Becky, it's me. I can't believe I finally tracked you down."

Nine years receded in the space of one gut-wrenching second. *Rob.*

7

"**R**ob?" Rebecca gripped the phone with a shaking hand. "How did you get this number?"

"I remembered you'd gone to work for DataTech. It took some convincing, but your administrative assistant finally gave me your cell." Her long-lost ex-husband released a nervous laugh. "Guess I could have just called your mom, but I figured she wouldn't be too keen on hearing from me."

Like I am? She squeezed her eyes shut. What could Rob possibly want? His child support checks landed with regularity in her bank account, but the man hadn't phoned, hadn't written, hadn't so much as sent his son a birthday card since sailing out of their lives nine years ago in pursuit of his latest shipboard romance. Rob Marshall, cruise ship entertainer extraordinaire, always hoping to be discovered by a record-company mogul and make it big. Nobody could sing "Feelings" with more feeling than Rob.

"Where are you?" It was all she could think to ask.

"Dallas. Arlington, actually. Just moved into my new apartment."

"You—you're here to *stay*?" Rebecca fumbled through her

purse until she found the package of antacids. She popped three into her mouth and chewed like crazy.

Rob sighed. "I have a lot to tell you, Becky, and a lot to apologize for. I know you're on your way out of town, but—"

"I'm sitting on the plane right now," she mumbled over her antacid tablets. She swallowed and ran her tongue over her teeth. The *call waiting* beep sounded in her ear, but she ignored it. "Just get to the point. Why, after all these years, are you calling me *now?*"

Another sigh. "It's a long story. Like I said, we need to talk."

She felt a tap on her shoulder. "We're preparing for takeoff, ma'am. Please end your call and turn off your phone."

"Rob, I have to go. My flight—"

"When can I call you back?"

She rubbed her forehead. "Try me again in the morning."

Moments after she disconnected, the words *Missed Call* appeared on the display, followed by Gary's name and cell number. The flight attendant cast Rebecca another warning glance. She nodded and set the phone to airplane mode. Thanks to Rob's untimely reappearance in her life, her husband would have to wait.

When the alarm clock buzzed Wednesday morning at six thirty, Noelle's eyes shot open, then instantly squinted shut. The white-hot glare of her reading lamp sliced through her muddled brain. How long had she stayed up studying her script?

Way too late, you moron. She stumbled out of bed and tripped on her playbook. It must have slid to the floor when she'd finally drifted off to sleep.

After a long, steamy shower to ease the crick in her neck, she plaited her damp hair in two long braids and wrapped them around her head, securing them with hairpins. She studied the effect and smiled. "Verrry Norrrvegian," she said to her reflection, mimicking a Scandinavian lilt. "Ya-ah."

She stalled a few minutes longer to be sure her father had already left for the office, then hurried to the kitchen to grab some breakfast, almost plowing over Kevin on her way through the den. Grabbing his backpack, he slung it onto one shoulder. "Better hurry or you're gonna be late." He darted out the front door seconds before the school bus arrived at the corner.

Groaning, Noelle jammed two slices of whole-wheat bread into the toaster. Bad enough she had to put up with Rebecca ordering her around. Why did her pesky little stepbrother have to be so cheerfully annoying? She gulped a glass of orange juice, smeared some jam across her toast, and scarfed it down as she jogged next door.

Warren waited in the car, revving the engine. He shoved open the passenger door. "I was beginning to wonder if you were coming."

Noelle plopped into the bucket seat. "Sorry, I fell asleep studying and had a hard time getting myself in gear this morning."

"Cramming for your first geometry quiz?"

Her stomach plummeted. She slapped a palm against her forehead. "Oh, no, I completely forgot! How did you know about it?"

"Cassie bugged me to help her study at rehearsal yesterday while you and Mrs. Sanchez were going over your part."

Noelle slunk lower in the seat. "Great. I'm going to flunk for sure."

Rebecca checked in at the McDonough Technologies security desk and then found her way to the accounting department. She introduced herself to the person at the nearest computer terminal.

"Hi, Mrs. Townsend." The clean-cut young man adjusted thick glasses and offered his hand. "Paul Cho, department chief. Glad you could get here so fast. This bug's about to drive us all insane."

"Show me to a workstation and I'll see if I can get you up and running."

The accountant led her down a broad, tiled corridor that smelled of industrial-strength pine cleaner from last night's mopping. He unlocked the door to an unoccupied office and flipped the light switch. "This terminal has access to the entire system." He handed her his business card. "I've jotted down the admin login on the back. Can I bring you some coffee?"

She almost said yes. Then her first cup of the day, brewed in the small coffeemaker in her hotel room, answered for her with a ribbon of stomach acid snaking up her esophagus. "No, thanks. Could I have some bottled water?"

"Sure thing. Buzz me if you need anything else."

"I'm sure I'll be fine."

After an hour of studying program code, she stood to stretch and rubbed her bleary eyes. Before she could sit down again, her cell phone rang. Recognizing Gary's assigned ringtone, she went weak with relief. She'd lost too many hours of sleep last night agonizing over what Rob Marshall could possibly want after all this time. Much as she needed answers, she needed to hear her husband's voice even more. "Hi, honey. I'm so glad you called."

"Sorry we missed connections at the airport. My flight landed over an hour late. Did you get my message?"

"Yes, but I knew you'd be exhausted. I opted for an early night too." If she counted actual time spent *trying* to get to sleep.

"Yeah, these trips can be killers." He exhaled long and slow. "I miss you."

Those words comforted her in ways he couldn't even imagine.

"I miss you, too, honey." A sip from the bottle of water Paul had brought helped wash away the quaver in her voice. "Did you get to spend some time with Kevin and Noelle after you got home?"

"Kevin gave me a big hug when I walked in the door. Noelle grunted and went to her room."

She felt his disappointment and searched for something encouraging to say. She came up empty.

"I'd hoped she'd tell me about her play," Gary continued, "maybe break the ice between us. Instead, I ended up playing a quick game of pool with Kevin." A snort. "At least he appreciates me."

"I hope you didn't let him stay up too late."

"He was tucked into the sofa bed at nine thirty on the dot. Very convenient when his bedroom is also the game room."

Rebecca bit back a snide comment. Noelle's "house rules" continued to grate on her. If this arrangement continued much longer, maybe they could at least refurnish the game room with a real bed and dresser for Kevin. Although she felt certain he'd never give up the pool table.

"So how's McDonough?" Gary asked. "Find the software problem yet?"

"I'm narrowing it down." She tapped the polished nail of her index finger on the edge of the keyboard. "Gary, something happened."

He released a harsh sigh. "If it's about Noelle ..."

She almost wished it were. Giving Gary another lecture about sticking his head in the sand where his daughter was concerned would be a hundred times easier than telling him about Rob's unnerving call. She pursed her lips. "No, this time it's about me ... if you have time to listen." Her last words seeped out with an edge of sarcasm.

"Rebecca—"

"Sorry, I'm really shaken up over this, not to mention confused." A tremor rippled through her. "Rob called last night."

Gary didn't respond for a full three seconds. "Rob. As in Rob Marshall, Kevin's father?"

"One and the same. We didn't talk long because my plane was about to take off. I've been on pins and needles all morning waiting for him to call back."

"Then you don't know what he wanted?"

"Not a clue. Unless . . . Gary, I don't even want to think about it, but"—she pressed a hand to her hammering heart—"after all this time, what if he wants Kevin?"

Kevin forked up a cheesy mouthful of the prepackaged lasagna Gary had heated for their supper. "Dad, can we play some more pool after supper?"

"We'll see, after you finish your homework." Gary bit off a chunk of impromptu garlic bread—Kevin's unique concoction consisting of a slice of regular whole wheat smeared with butter, sprinkled with garlic powder and Parmesan cheese, and browned in the toaster oven. Too bad Noelle wasn't around to enjoy this gourmet meal. She'd made it clear her play rehearsals took priority and informed Gary not to expect her home in the evenings before nine at the earliest. Where—or what—she was eating for dinner these days was anybody's guess. At least for the time being Mrs. Ames next door had offered to check in on Kevin after school.

Gary's frustration with Noelle only made him more appreciative of his closeness with Kevin. He'd hate to see the boy's life turned upside down by the sudden reappearance of his AWOL father. A man who had never even tried to form a bond with his son, who'd walked out on him and his mother nine years ago without even a backward glance.

Like you've got room to talk? He hadn't worked nearly as hard as he should have to maintain ties with Noelle. What gave him the right to force himself into her world now?

"Dad?" Kevin jabbed his arm. "You flaked out there for a sec."

Gary shook his head and speared a slippery lasagna noodle with his fork. "Just thinking."

He had to admit, it was tons easier relating to Kevin. The boy was agreeable and open-hearted, if sometimes painfully honest, whereas Noelle could seem as distant as the moon and more turbulent than the stock market. If only he could write his daughter into a computer program, instruct it to analyze the data, then sit back and wait for it to spit out the solution.

Not much chance.

He stuffed a burnt bread crust into his mouth and shifted his thoughts to Rebecca. She'd promised to let him know as soon as she heard from her ex again. He grimaced. It would hurt him almost as much as it did Rebecca if Kevin's father tried to claim him.

He pushed his plate aside and rested his forearm on the edge of the table. Framing his question as nonchalantly as possible, he asked, "Hey, Kev, ever think much about your real dad?"

The boy chewed his lip. "Yeah, sometimes. But I don't even remember him, and you're my dad now, so it doesn't really matter."

Gary's heart clenched. What had he ever done to deserve such affection?

And why couldn't he earn a smidgen of it from Noelle?

Wrapped in a plush terry robe, Rebecca curled her legs under her on the hotel bed and pressed a damp cloth to her burning eyes. She'd ordered room service for dinner, selecting broiled fish and steamed green beans, the most elaborate meal her abused stomach could manage.

All day she'd scrutinized computer code, looking for the elusive cause of McDonough's problems. Each discovery and subsequent reprogramming resulted in a chain reaction of additional errors. Heads would roll in her department when she returned to Dallas. Probably her own if she wasn't careful. She may not have done the bulk of the programming herself, but she'd signed off on the final version. Now it was her responsibility to fix the problem.

It didn't help that a sizable part of her brain had devoted itself to fretting over Rob. Would he ever call back and explain?

Until she had met Gary, it was just her and Kevin, the two of them against the world, like the refrain from a classic Helen Reddy song. If Rob tried to take her son from her now—*please, God, no!*

Logic told her not a judge in the state would remove Kevin from her custody and turn him over to a father who had remained conspicuously absent all these years. But what about joint custody, or visitation rights? She would do everything in her power to avoid subjecting Kevin, or herself, to an arbitrary division of holidays and vacations, especially with a father he had no memory of.

Her cell phone chirped, the generic ascending chime indicating the caller was not in her directory. She scrambled across the bed to retrieve the phone from the nightstand. The display indicated a number with an 817 area code, which included Arlington, Texas.

Her voice shook as she answered. "Hello?"

"Hi, Becky." Rob—finally. "I was in a conference that ended up lasting all day. Hope you haven't been stewing."

"*Stewing?*" Flames licked her neck. "I get nothing from you but checks in the bank for nine long years. Then you phone me out of the blue and say we need to talk. I wait all day for you to call back. *Stewing? Please!*"

"I get it. Really, I'm sorry. I didn't mean to worry you." He groaned. "If I had any sense, I'd have put this off until you got home from your business trip."

Her free hand crushed the damp washcloth in a death grip. "Too late. So are you going to tell me what this is about? Or are you going to make me *stew* some more?"

"Man, so much has happened. Where do I start?" She could almost see him laying a hand to the back of his sandy hair in a gesture she had long ago memorized—and wished she'd forgotten.

She turned her stinging eyes toward the ceiling. "Start at the beginning. The middle. Anywhere."

"Okay, okay." Rob sighed, his tone softening. "I know this is coming out of left field, but I've been thinking about a lot of things . . . especially about Kevin."

Her stomach did a nosedive before hurtling its contents up into her throat. She jammed the washcloth against her mouth until the nausea subsided. "No. He's mine. You didn't want anything to do with him before, and you're not getting him now."

She stabbed the *end call* button and powered off the phone before Rob could call her back.

8

Noelle raced through the supper dishes Sunday evening and scurried to her room. If pesky little Kevin cornered her for one more game of pool, she'd scream. Thank goodness for the play rehearsals, which gave her an excuse to be out of the house on weeknights. Her family didn't need to know she wasn't exactly rehearsing the whole time. The after-school practices normally ended by six, after which she'd grab something from Wendy's or Chick-fil-A and then hang out with Warren or Cassie doing homework.

Okay, to be perfectly honest, while her friends studied, Noelle was usually running her lines.

She tried not to think about the geometry test, which she'd undoubtedly failed. How soon before her father found out about her poor grades and did something parental like ground her for life? How could she explain to him or anyone else that she didn't care about school or studying or much of anything anymore? Since Mom died, nothing mattered.

Except the play.

On Monday morning, second period, she cringed as "Polygon" Potter strode into the classroom and slapped a stack of papers onto his desk. "Good morning, class. I hope all of you had a wonderful weekend, because for many of you, I am about to ruin the rest of your day."

Noelle crossed her arms and sank lower in her seat. *Here it comes.*

Mr. Potter lifted a paper from the stack. "When I call your name, please come forward and pick up your test. Will Wright . . . Dianne Springer . . . Cassie McCormick . . ."

"Eighty-one—yes!" Punching the air, Cassie waltzed back to her seat, yellow curls bouncing. She waved her paper under Noelle's nose. "Can you believe it?"

Noelle mumbled her congratulations. "I heard Warren helped you study."

"Couldn't have done it without him." Cassie settled into her seat, swinging her gray poodle skirt under her legs. This week, the incurable drama queen was into the '50s look.

"Noelle Townsend."

Cringing, she trudged up to the desk.

"I'm sorry, Noelle," Mr. Potter murmured. The now painfully familiar expression of pity shadowed his eyes. "I know you're going through a hard time. If you need tutoring after school, I'd be happy to help."

Muttering a terse "Thank you," she rolled the test paper into a tube and tapped it against her palm. At her desk, she unrolled the page just far enough to see the grade—46. She sucked air through her teeth.

Cassie turned sideways, trying to glimpse Noelle's paper. "Oooh! What happened?"

"I forgot to study." Noelle slapped her hand over the bold red number. "But I have time to bring my grades up before reports come out."

By lunchtime, she couldn't stomach the idea of facing either Warren's brotherly support or Cassie's exhausting cheerfulness. Reaching the cafeteria, she found a seat in one of the corner booths, away from the table her friends normally shared. She gnawed on a piece of rubbery grilled chicken while she studied her dog-eared playbook.

"What's the deal?" Warren stood over her, gripping his lunch tray.

She tried for a nonchalant smile. "I decided to eat by myself so I could study my lines. I've got a big part to memorize."

"So you'd rather I didn't join you?" His offended tone stabbed her heart.

"No, it's okay. Have a seat." She made room for him to set his tray across from hers.

"Good. For a minute there, I thought maybe you were avoiding me." He settled onto the seat and bit into his patty melt. "Didn't do so hot on your geometry test, huh?"

Her face burned. Out of the corner of her eye, she glimpsed Cassie sitting at their regular table chatting with three other friends, including the cute guy from the drama club who usually did the lighting. Cassie'd been flirting with him since last year's spring play. "I can guess who blabbed that bit of information."

"Cassie's worried about you. I am too."

Noelle pushed her tray away, orange drink spilling onto the remains of her lunch. "I can take care of myself. I wish everybody'd get off my case."

"Excuse me. I didn't realize I was *on* your case." He snatched up his tray.

"Warren, wait—"

Sliding from the booth, he cast her a disappointed frown, then marched over to join some guys at a table across the room.

An aching lump rose in Noelle's throat. They'd had disagreements before, but Warren had never turned his back on her, never let her bad moods come between them. Surely by the end of the day he'd cool off and forgive her. He had to. She needed him too much.

Except why would anybody in their right mind want to be

anywhere near her? Lately she didn't even like her own company, another reason why immersing herself in the play—being somebody else for a while—felt like a much safer place.

Katrin once again, she forced her gaze back to the playbook. *"For as long as I could remember, the house on Steiner Street had been home...."*

"'...I remember that every Saturday night Mama would sit down by the kitchen table and count out the money Papa had brought home in the little envelope.'"

"Very good, Noelle." Mrs. Sanchez applauded. "I can't believe you've memorized so much of your part already."

Noelle's chest warmed. "I worked on it all weekend."

"Terrific. Let's continue." Mrs. Sanchez gestured to Lynn Larson. "Go ahead, 'Mama.'"

Throughout the rehearsal, Noelle imagined each character in costume, performing onstage in front of Warren's beautifully crafted sets. She could even see Cassie playing Dagmar, carrying sweet old Laurence as the battle-scarred alley cat, Uncle Elizabeth. Laurence was perfect for the part. He'd certainly survived his share of cat fights in his younger days. Thank goodness he stayed inside most of the time now—fat, lazy, and out of harm's way.

Lately the old cat had become Noelle's one true friend. Laurence didn't smother her with sympathy, didn't lecture, didn't prod her to share feelings she wasn't ready to face. If only the humans in her life could be so understanding.

Or maybe she just needed to give them a chance, because by the time rehearsal ended, the way she'd treated both Cassie and Warren earlier was eating a hole in her gut. She approached her friends with a pleading gaze. "Can a failure at geometry apologize?"

Cassie turned and smiled her answer. "Only if you'll accept an apology from this nosy buttinsky." She extended her arms for a hug.

Warren shouldered between them. "Hey, can I get in on some of this action?"

Noelle welcomed the forgiveness in his eyes, her heart racing with feelings she couldn't name. She would never stop needing her friends, no matter how hard she tried to pretend otherwise. "I'm sorry, you guys. I've been awful lately. How can you stand me?"

Cassie gave her an extra squeeze. "Because you're Noelle Townsend, our very best friend. Don't forget."

She gulped and nodded her thanks. The trio drifted apart, and Noelle went to gather her books. As she followed her friends toward the exit, she felt a hand on her shoulder and turned to look into Mrs. Sanchez's kind brown eyes.

"Noelle, I just wanted to say again what a fine job you're doing."

"Thank you. I love playing Katrin."

"I'm glad you've taken so well to the part." Mrs. Sanchez smiled sadly. "You may not realize this, but the play was your mother's idea. She would be so proud of you."

"Mom's idea?" Noelle's eyebrows bunched.

"Your mother was not only a wise and insightful teacher but a very dear friend. Did you know she used to help me evaluate play scripts?"

"I sort of remember that."

The dark-haired woman swallowed and blinked back a tear. "Early last summer, when I was visiting her one day, the subject of the fall play came up. She suggested *I Remember Mama*. She hoped somehow the story would help you bring things into focus, to remember the good things after she died."

Noelle's chest tightened. *Good things?* Images of Mom wasting away in her last days of cancer were still too close to the surface.

She tried to think of something polite to say, but words wouldn't come. "I'd better go. Warren's waiting to take me home."

Before they reached the parking lot, she was already mentally running through her lines.

After checking Kevin's homework and sending him to get ready for bed and lay out his school clothes for tomorrow, Rebecca carried a frosty tumbler of iced tea out to the backyard and slipped into the pool. The water temperature was just cool enough to be comfortable on this sultry September evening. Settling onto the built-in bench, she rested her head against the coping, still warm from the afternoon sun.

After working through the weekend, she'd finally wrapped up the McDonough Technologies situation, then snagged the first available flight back to Dallas. Matt Garrison had been none too happy to learn the extent of the software bugs, and even less thrilled when he'd tried to call her cell phone and found it turned off.

But she hadn't been able to bear the idea of Rob calling again. Immediately after their last conversation, she'd called Craig, her assistant, and informed him that under no circumstances was her ex-husband to be provided with any further contact information. What if he'd phoned Noelle's house and Kevin answered? She had to protect her son at all costs.

A loud, rhythmic rumble sounded next to Rebecca's ear. She opened her eyes and stared into two jade-green marbles. "Hey, kitty." She reached up to scratch Laurence's chin. His purr deepened, and he moved his head to get a better angle on the scratching. "If you ever tell Noelle we're friends, you're dog food, you hear me?"

Laurence mewed and draped one white-stockinged paw over

the coping. His breath reeked of whitefish-and-tuna gourmet cat cuisine.

The door to the sunroom slid open, and Gary strode out in shorts and a T-shirt. He kicked off his loafers and plopped down next to Laurence, dangling his feet in the water. He stole a sip of Rebecca's iced tea. "Wondered where you'd gone off to."

"I needed some air. I thought you were working in the study." She reached around the cat and retrieved her glass. "I have to admit, it is kind of nice having a pool right outside my back door."

"When it gets cooler, you'll enjoy the hot tub, too."

Rebecca pressed her lips together. Hard as she tried, she couldn't help resenting Gary's easy familiarity with the home he once shared with Kate. "It must be almost nine." Dripping water, she stepped out of the pool. "I need to get Kevin tucked into bed."

Gary stood and shook the water from his feet. "Let me. Stay out here awhile longer if you want."

"Thanks, but I can take care of my son." The words came out a little snippier than she'd intended. She snatched up her towel from a nearby chaise and briskly rubbed herself dry.

Gary reached for her arm. "Becky, what's—"

She jerked away. "I've told you before, I hate that name."

"Is this about Rob? Did he call again?"

She wrapped the towel around the waist of her navy batik tank suit. "No, and I hope he never does."

"What makes you so sure he wants custody of Kevin?" Gary stepped in front of her. "If you don't talk it out with him, this thing will never go away, and neither will he. Call him. Call him right now."

So now Gary was lecturing *her* on family matters? Well, this time he was right. She lowered her head. "Okay, okay. I know I'm only delaying the inevitable." Sighing, she started for the house. "Let me get Kevin to bed first. I don't want him asking questions."

Gary reached for her hand. "How about we say good night to him together?"

In the game room, they found Kevin sitting cross-legged in his pajamas on the open sofa bed. Hair still wet and spiky from the shower, he stared at the TV screen while maniacally working thumb controls. "Ooooh no you don't! Take that, Mega-Vortex!"

Gary stepped between Kevin and the screen. "Game over, big fella. Time for lights out."

"Aw, Dad. I was about to top my highest score ever."

"Too bad. Mega-Vortex will live to fight another day." Gary took the game remote and pressed the off button.

Rebecca fluffed one of Kevin's pillows. "Have you brushed your teeth, young man?"

With a groan, Kevin scooted off the mattress and trudged into the adjoining bathroom. A few minutes later, Rebecca bent over him for a good-night kiss, avoiding his toothpaste-smeared chin. She rubbed the mint-green spot with her thumb and suppressed a shiver of apprehension.

Gary lightly touched her shoulder before reaching down to tousle Kevin's hair. "Good night, kiddo. Sleep tight."

With Kevin tucked in for the night and Gary channel-surfing on the den TV, Rebecca postponed the dreaded phone call a bit longer by changing out of her swimsuit and washing her hair. Dressed in a beige satin gown and matching robe, she closed the study door and sank into the desk chair, cell phone in hand. Rob's number was still in her recent calls list. She pressed the redial button and held her breath.

"Becky? I've been trying to reach you for days. Didn't you get my messages?"

"It's *Rebecca*, and it's been a hectic week." She wouldn't mention she'd deleted all his voicemails without listening to them. "Just get to the point. What exactly do you want?"

"I tried to tell you the last time we talked, but it didn't come out right over the phone." He gave a snort. "As usual, I'm good at singing. Not so good at communicating."

That much was true. She pressed a palm to her forehead. "I can only assume you've experienced a drastic change of heart and now want back into Kevin's life. Well, it's not going to be so easy."

"Change of heart?" Rob's gentle laughter rippled against her ear. "Yeah, that about says it all. Look, maybe a phone conversation isn't the best way to handle this."

"Handle what?" Her pulse thundered. "Just *tell me*."

Giving a huff, he fell silent for a moment. "This is harder than I thought. Do you think we could do this in person, maybe meet for lunch tomorrow?"

Against her better judgment, she agreed. "There's a TGI Friday's in Arlington near I-30 on Collins. Let's make it one thirty and we can avoid most of the lunch crowd."

"Perfect. I drive right by there on my way to and from work."

So he had both an apartment and a job. *Rob Marshall, what in heaven's name are you up to?*

9

When Mrs. Ames tactfully suggested it was getting late and that Noelle should go home, Warren walked her out. "See you in the morning," he said from his front porch, then shook a chiding finger in her face. "And *don't* stay up too late studying your lines, okay?"

She replied with a roll of her eyes.

The house stood eerily silent as she stepped through the front door. In the den, she dropped her school books on the piano bench and glanced around. Surely everyone hadn't gone to bed already? Through the patio doors she glimpsed her father's dark profile, where he sat alone in a patio chair out by the pool. No sign of Rebecca, thank goodness.

Heading for the kitchen, she tiptoed past the game room. The door stood open a crack, and Kevin's snuffling snores whispered through the darkness.

Every time Kevin called her father "Dad," the word zapped her like a paperclip stuck in a light socket. Kevin had his own dad . . . somewhere. Noelle may not be crazy about her father, but she didn't feel like sharing. Hadn't she given up enough already?

Snooping in the refrigerator, she found a package of pepper

loaf and some provolone that was getting dry around the edges. She fixed herself a sandwich and poured a salty pile of potato chips onto her plate. Taking the food and a frosty can of Coke to her room, she sat on the bed and nibbled while she studied her script. So what if she was staying up a little later than usual these days? Warren didn't need to know.

Shortly after ten, her cell phone chirped. Shoving her empty plate across the bed, she snatched up the phone. "Hello?"

"I bet you were reading the play again," came Cassie's bubbly voice. "Did you remember to do your book report? They're due in English class tomorrow, don't forget."

Noelle slapped the playbook against her thigh. "What? Why didn't you remind me sooner, you creep? I could have worked on it over the weekend."

"I finished mine days ago and didn't think about it again until just now when I was printing it out." A pause. "You *have* been reading a book, haven't you?"

"What do you think?" How could she have forgotten? She'd gone to the library with the rest of the class and had even checked out a book, *The Pearl*, by John Steinbeck. She'd picked it for one reason only: it was *short*.

And there it lay, right where she'd left it, unopened on her nightstand.

Cassie snickered. "Looks like you'll be pulling an all-nighter. Better put that script away and get cracking."

Noelle clicked off her phone and glared at the novel. She picked up the slim volume and flipped through the yellowed pages. Small print, no pictures, not like the good old days in elementary school. Not such a quick read after all.

After an eternity of staring blankly at the first page, she slammed the book shut. She'd never get through it in one night, let alone write a report. Only one thing to do. Not an idea she was proud of, but she couldn't afford another failing grade.

Supposedly there were all kinds of essays, reports, and research papers online, all prewritten, all there for the copying.

Guilt soured her stomach. *Just this once, okay?* She didn't know whom the apology was meant for—God? Mom? Herself?

Rolling onto her stomach, she fumbled for her laptop, shoved halfway under the bed. With the computer propped on a pillow, she opened her browser and then did a web search for Steinbeck's book. Within seconds she'd located several complete book reports.

Okay, so technically she was cheating, but out-and-out plagiarism? Nope, not her style. Fingers trembling and with frequent glances toward her closed bedroom door, she selected portions of the best three reports and performed repeated copy-and-paste operations into a document file. After some careful manipulating and rewording, she'd created what she felt was a superbly composed book report. With a self-satisfied smirk, she sent the document to the wireless printer in the study.

Feet stuffed into bear-claw slippers, she crept down the hall. When she slipped into the darkened study, the cloying scent of Rebecca's perfume tickled her nose. Fanning the air in front of her face, she crossed to the printer to retrieve her report. After a quick perusal to make sure everything printed correctly, she gave it a thump of approval.

"Noelle?" Her father peeked in through the partially closed door. "Thought you'd already gone to bed. It's late. You've got school tomorrow."

Like she needed reminding. Like she needed a father. Tucking the report against her chest, she scooted past him. "Just finishing my homework."

"Did you get something to eat?"

"I'm a big girl, Dad. I can fend for myself." She marched to her room and laid the report on top of her notebook, then decided not to give her father the parental satisfaction of sending his child off to bed. She spun around and headed back out to the kitchen, almost colliding with her dad.

"Now what?" He sidestepped out of her way.

"Grabbing a snack. I'm craving a glass of milk and some of Mom's chocolate chip—"

Her throat muscles clamped down. Milk and homemade cookies in the quiet kitchen with her mother—their favorite bedtime ritual.

Her father shoved his hands into his shorts pockets. "Your mother's cookies were the best."

"Yeah, well . . ." Refusing to let her father see the pain ripping her insides apart, she continued to the kitchen. "Maybe I'll just have some hot chocolate."

Dad's incredulous voice followed her. "Hot chocolate? It's still over eighty degrees outside."

"If I want hot chocolate, I'll make hot chocolate!" She scoured the pantry in search of the tall glass apothecary jar, the one her mother used for the special blend of cocoa mix she made each fall.

The jar stood empty.

The ache in Noelle's chest sliced up into her throat. She shut the pantry door with a bang and barged past her father. She nearly tripped over his briefcase, sticking partway out beneath the built-in desk in the den—would he never learn a safer place to keep that thing?—and stormed down the hall to her room.

Slamming the door, she went to her adjoining bathroom and splashed cold water on her face. She pressed her fingertips to the mirror, touching the reflection of her red, burning eyes.

Cry! Why can't you cry?

With the sound of Noelle's door banging shut still echoing in his ears, Gary winced. He'd noticed a light under the guest room door earlier and figured Rebecca had finished her call to Rob and gone to bed. Maybe he should check on her and ask how the conversation had gone. Except doing so would require emotional energy he wasn't convinced he could dredge up at the moment.

"Dad?"

He turned to see Kevin standing in the middle of the den. "Everything's okay, kiddo. Go back to bed."

Instead, the sleepy-eyed boy wandered over and stopped next to Gary. He squinted down the darkened hallway. "Why is Noelle always so mad about everything?"

Gary jammed a hand against his forehead, but nothing could dull the agony of seeing the betrayal in his daughter's face. "She's still sad about her mom." *And angry with me.* "Come on, you need to get to sleep, young man."

Kevin traipsed after Gary to the sofa bed and climbed under the covers, then instantly bounced up and reached for something on the end table. "Did you see this, Dad? It's what Mom brought me from her trip."

Gary sat on the edge of the creaking mattress. "A watch. Cool."

Kevin strapped the tan leather watchband to his wrist. He turned his arm to examine the crystal as it reflected the soft light drifting in from the kitchen.

Gary held Kevin's wrist for a better look. "Your mom picks good presents."

"Mom's the greatest."

In the semi-darkness, he studied the boy's face. "Kevin, can I ask you a question?"

"Sure, Dad. Shoot."

"Is it hard for you that your mother has to be away so much?"

The boy's expression turned solemn. "A little. But she can't help it. It's her work."

"But do you ever wish maybe she had a different job, one where she could stay home more?"

"Sometimes. I miss her a lot when she's gone."

"Do you ever get mad at her when she goes away?"

"Hey, that's three questions."

Gary blinked. "Sorry."

"That's okay." Kevin shrugged. "Well, I used to get really sad, when I was little. I didn't understand why Mom had to be gone so much. But now it's not so bad. She calls me almost every night. She even helps me with my homework over Skype sometimes. And sends me funny e-cards and links to websites that tell about where she is. Like the time she went to Nairobi. I had fun checking out all those sites about Kenya." He admired his watch again. "And when she comes home, she always brings me neat stuff."

Kevin's response shamed Gary for not trying harder to stay in touch with Noelle and Kate when he'd been away on business. He could have done better—a lot better. But complicated schedules and unreliable internet or poor cell connections caused too many problems. Besides, he'd assumed his wife and daughter wouldn't be interested in his work life. Not to mention his job kept him so preoccupied that he rarely thought to ask about their day.

He shook his head. How selfish could a guy get? Rebecca never failed to call or email regularly during a business trip. If he neglected to phone her, he'd pick up his cell to find a series of text messages and voicemails. More than once, she'd given him a verbal dressing-down for forgetting how important it was for them to stay in touch.

Kevin poked Gary's arm. "Something bugging you, Dad?"

"Nothing for you to worry about." As he rose to tuck the sheets around the boy, a thought occurred to him. "Get some sleep, kiddo. I'm going to run out to the grocery store for a minute."

"Mom got stuff on the way home from the airport."

"I know, but I need to get something special."

Kevin gave him a knowing look. "If you get cherry cheesecake, save me a slice."

"Don't worry. Now good night already."

In the cupboard over the spice rack, Gary found Kate's cookbooks, and next to them her recipe file. He took the hand-stenciled wooden box to the counter. Sliding onto a bar stool, he flipped through the dividers. Under BEVERAGES he found the card labeled "Irene Whitney's Cocoa Mix." He ripped a sheet of paper from the note pad by the kitchen phone and jotted down the ingredients.

Thirty-five minutes later he was back from the supermarket, lining up boxes and containers along the counter. He found the apothecary jar in the pantry. One by one he measured the proper amounts of powdered milk, cocoa, confectioner's sugar, and coffee creamer into the jar. Snapping on the lid, he tilted the jar up and down, side to side, watching the layers shift and blend like one of those sand paintings under glass.

"Well, Kate, I hope I did this right." He heated a mug of water in the microwave, then stirred in a heaping scoop of the cocoa mix.

Instantly the heavenly chocolate aroma filled the kitchen. Ignoring the powdered-sugar handprints decorating the front of his shorts, he sat at the kitchen table under the golden glow of the chandelier. Slowly he sipped the cocoa, closing his eyes and remembering the first time he'd tasted it. Must have been close to twenty-five years ago, sitting at Irene Whitney's kitchen table back in Shickley, Nebraska. He was a lanky high-school kid then and falling for the Whitneys' beautiful brown-eyed daughter. He'd been so naïve—restless and cocky and brimming with audacious career goals.

He recalled another night of sipping cocoa, at this very table, the night he and Kate first spoke of separation. Noelle had already gone to bed, and Kate made them both a cup, plopping a handful of miniature marshmallows into each steaming mug.

Sitting across from him, her voice high and tight, Kate had said, "I don't want to live like this anymore, Gary. Something has to change."

"You've already changed." He'd stared at the marshmallows melting into a white foam around the rim of the mug. "You had to go back to teaching, get your master's degree. Now all your time's taken up by school and Noelle. You're not here for me like you used to be."

"Maybe I just got tired of waiting for you." He started to protest, but she silenced him with her schoolteacher glare. "Face it, Gary. Success has always been your top priority."

He bristled. "Why do you think I work so hard? I do it for you. For Noelle."

"Can you honestly tell me Noelle and I mean more to you than that new Mercedes parked in the garage, or the 'Outstanding Manager' award above your desk?" Kate shook her head. "No, Gary. We're just two more items crossed off your life goals to-do list. Get married, *check*. Start a family, *check*."

"What are you trying to tell me, Kate? Do you want out of this marriage?"

"No!" She reached for his hand, but he pulled away. "Gary, I love you, always have. I just need you to be *present*, at least emotionally, even if you can't always be here physically."

He'd tried again to convince her he'd dedicated himself to his career for their sakes, to give them the secure future that had eluded his own parents. Was he so wrong to want to make something of his life? Growing up in rural Nebraska had been a daily struggle, and by the time he'd finished high school, he knew he had to escape. No matter what it took, he swore he'd provide a better life for his own family. They'd never want for anything.

He'd married Kate two weeks after graduation, and with scholarships and hard work they made it through college. Kate earned her teaching degree, and Gary's major in business information technology set him up for an entry-level management position with DataTech.

But when his mother suffered a fatal stroke while flipping burgers at Cindy's Diner, Gary was at a company seminar on policies and procedures. When his daughter entered the world on Christmas Eve, he was stuck at O'Hare waiting out an ice storm. And by the time Kate learned her illness was terminal, Gary had moved out of her life, moved on with his, moved into remarriage with Rebecca.

Well, I'm home now. He drained the last swallow of cocoa and spoke to his reflection in the dark glass of the bay window. "And I swear, this time things are going to be different. I'll be the best husband and father I know how, and I'll make things up to Noelle if it's the last thing I do."

After rinsing his mug, he pawed through a cabinet for Kate's stash of gift wrapping supplies. Selecting a roll of colored ribbon, he carried it to the kitchen and cut off a length of shiny pastel blue. With fumbling fingers he tied a lopsided bow around the neck of the cocoa jar. He cleared a spot in the center of the table and set the jar where Noelle would be sure to see it at breakfast.

A smile played at the corners of his mouth, and he sent Kevin a silent thank-you for the reminder about Rebecca's thoughtful gifts. Maybe the cocoa mix could somehow break through Noelle's barriers, show her he really did care. Turning off the lights, he padded down the hall to the guest bathroom and changed into his pajamas. Ten minutes later, he crawled between the sheets and cocooned his body against Rebecca's.

Her warmth seeping into him, he ran his hand along her arm and pressed soft kisses against the back of her neck. When she didn't respond, he edged away, rolled onto his back, and blew out a frustrated sigh. He couldn't blame her, though. After a week of hotel beds and trying to track down software bugs, who wouldn't be exhausted? Not to mention the stress of dealing with a cranky stepdaughter and a prodigal ex-husband.

Add it all up and their lovemaking became one more casualty of their out-of-control lives.

Rebecca pretended not to notice when Gary slipped into the bed and snuggled up behind her. Making love was the last thing on her mind. Her nerves still jangled following the phone conversation with Rob earlier, and afterward, she'd been eager for a little reassurance in her husband's arms. But when she finished the call and found Gary brooding by the pool, something in his expression made her retreat to the bedroom alone.

Later, she'd heard Noelle moving about, and then Gary talking to his daughter in the hallway. Maybe he'd only been waiting up to say good night to Noelle. Still, he didn't come to bed. The garage door rumbled, followed by a swath of headlights across the front windows. The minutes ticked slowly by on the clock radio beside the bed. Hearing Gary's car return, she'd crept through the dark house and watched unnoticed as her husband tore through packages, measured ingredients, and prepared an aromatic cup of hot chocolate.

Hot chocolate on a night like this, when the air conditioner ran full blast?

And then the colorful ribbons. As she watched her husband tie a crooked bow around the apothecary jar, hot tears—selfish tears—pricked the backs of her eyelids. She couldn't fault him for doing whatever it took to win back his daughter's love. But didn't their marriage deserve equal effort? Despite Gary's attempts at reassurance, Rebecca sensed her personal concerns were edging farther down her husband's list of priorities.

With one look at the apothecary jar the next morning, Noelle scooped up her books and stormed out the front door. Warren met her at his car, where she plopped into the passenger seat and yanked the door shut.

He cast her a sidelong glare as he started the engine. "You're in rare form today."

"Just drop it."

"Yes, *ma'am*." Warren rammed the gear shift into reverse, tires squealing.

Frenzied honking filled the air. Halfway into the street, Warren stomped on the brakes. Noelle's books slammed into her diaphragm, forcing the air from her lungs. She whipped her head around to see the driver of a sanitation truck flashing obscene gestures. At least with the windows closed she didn't have to hear the ugly words spewing from his mouth.

The garbage truck chugged toward the next house, and Warren cautiously backed into the street.

Noelle adjusted the stack of books on her lap. "I'm sorry. It was my fault." She vented a few ugly words of her own. "All I ever do anymore is apologize. And take it for granted that you and Cassie will understand and forgive me."

Warren didn't say anything until they reached the stop sign at the end of the next block. He whooshed out a breath. "You can't stay mad at the world forever. Other people have feelings, too, and even a friend can get tired of being yelled at all the time."

Ashamed to look at Warren, she twisted a strand of hair. When had she turned into such a bitter, spiteful person? "I really am sorry."

"And, as usual, I forgive you. Now, want to tell me what's eating you?"

Staring out the window as they continued on toward school, Noelle told him about the cocoa mix. "He just doesn't get it. All the things he gave me and Mom over the years never made up for his not being there. I wish he'd stop trying."

10

Rebecca parked her BMW in the lot behind TGI Friday's at precisely 1:34 p.m., according to the dashboard clock. Fashionably late? Or merely a feeble attempt to maintain the upper hand in a situation that had her feeling terrifyingly out of control? Leaving the engine running, she checked her makeup in the visor mirror and tucked a stray curl into place. Another useless stalling tactic, since the relentless North Texas wind would rip her style to shreds the moment she stepped from the car.

Besides, why should it matter what she looked like? She certainly didn't need to impress Rob. He meant nothing to her. It was over the day he'd walked out of her life.

And that's a crock. It had taken years before she even considered dating again. And she wouldn't have if not for literally bumping into Gary one day during a business trip to see a New York client. Realizing they both worked for DataTech, Gary had invited her to join his team for dinner. Two hours later, it was just the two of them getting to know each other over decafs in the hotel coffee shop. Two weeks later, Rebecca had begun to believe again in true love.

Today, though? She wasn't nearly as confident.

Noticing a couple walking toward the car next to hers, she pretended to check messages on her phone until they got in and drove away. The dashboard clock ticked over to 1:37, and still she couldn't scrape up the nerve to enter the restaurant. Why, oh why, had Rob Marshall chosen now to waltz back into her life and dredge up the past?

Giving a snort, she stuffed her phone into her purse and shut off the engine. Her life was . . . tolerable now, if not ideal. She had the house in the suburbs she'd always dreamed of, and she'd even picked up a small potted plant at the supermarket a couple of weeks ago—something green and pretty and hers alone. She might not be a regular at PTA meetings, but she had visited Kevin's new school so she could meet his teachers. Thank goodness for Kevin's easy-going nature, which had helped him adjust quickly to the unexpected changes in their lives.

But how would he handle the sudden reappearance of his real father? How would any of them?

Holding her hair in place as best she could against the wind, she stepped from the car and made her way past the red-and-white striped awnings toward the entrance.

A bubbly brunette hostess greeted her at the front desk. "Table for one?"

"Actually, I'm meeting someone." Would she even recognize Rob after all these years?

Then she did, at a table near the windows. He rose and waved, his expression tentative. He appeared a bit broader around the middle, but not unattractively so. The faintest dusting of silver graced the temples of his sandy-blond hair. His eyes, so much like Kevin's, held their familiar teasing sparkle—a look that twelve years ago would have made her go weak in the knees and send her heart into spasms.

Well, not today. No way those baby blues would laser through her defenses. She steeled herself and wove among the diners, both hands clutching the straps of her taupe designer-label handbag. As she neared Rob's table, he gave her a nervous smile.

"Rob . . ." Her mouth twitched, and she gave a quick nod. How did one greet an ex-husband, after all? Especially one she'd never expected—much less *wanted*—to see again in this lifetime?

"You look great, Becky." He pulled out a chair for her. "Success becomes you."

She sat stiffly. A young man in a red T-shirt appeared with a menu. "Something to drink, ma'am?"

"Water, please, with lemon." She paged through the menu without seeing it. "Have you ordered yet?" she asked Rob.

"I waited for you. Think I'll just have a salad. I need to cut back a bit." With a soft chuckle, he patted his stomach. Then his voice took on a pensive tone. "Funny how being happy with your life puts the pounds on."

She laid the menu aside and studied him, really seeing him for the first time since she'd walked into the restaurant. He did look happy. Content. More at ease with himself than she could ever recall. Her gaze fell upon the tiny gold pin tacked to the collar of his olive-green polo shirt. *A cross?*

He must have noticed her staring. He glanced down and fingered the cross. "This is partly what I wanted to talk to you about."

"I don't understand." The Rob Marshall Rebecca remembered had kept himself as far as humanly possible from anything resembling religion.

Rob gave his head a small shake. "Never thought I'd meet the Lord in a Jamaican bar over a piña colada. But two years ago there He was, saying, 'Rob, you've really messed things up. Time to clean up your act.' I looked around at the other losers sitting at the bar and decided it was time to listen."

Rebecca squeezed the lemon wedge into the water their waiter had dropped off and poked the ice with a straw. Years of Rob's irresponsibility, infidelity, and his ultimate desertion could not be blotted out by one little gold cross. After all the ways he'd hurt her and ignored their son, why should she trust anything he said?

Rob reached for her hand, his touch like a thousand hot needles. "I realize you have no reason to believe me, but even though I greatly oversimplified how it happened, it's true. I knew I'd never turn my life around if I stayed with the cruise line, so I quit and went home to Houston. I was directionless for a while, but I wandered into a church one Sunday and realized the praise music spoke to me." Gazing out the window, he added quietly, "More than that, it convicted me."

Either he was telling the truth, or he'd become a very good actor. Rebecca studied his profile, trying to reconcile the man sitting across from her with the glib and charming Rob Marshall she'd fallen in love with all those years ago. Withdrawing her hand, she tucked it into her lap and waited silently for him to continue.

With a slow, deep breath, he turned his gaze to hers. "Becky—Rebecca—I'm here today to ask your forgiveness. Somehow, some way, I want to make up for what I did to you. What I did to our son."

Rebecca took a sip of water while she framed her reply. Her voice came out high and tight. "Nine years, Rob. *Nine years*, and nothing from you but those meager child support checks." She thunked her glass down, sloshing water and crushed ice over the rim. Nervously she dabbed at the mess with her napkin. "So why now? Why do you think after all this time I would willingly relinquish my son to you?"

Rob sat back, his brows meeting in the middle like two surprised caterpillars. "Relinquish?"

"That's what this is about, isn't it? You want Kevin." She couldn't disguise the panic in her tone.

Looking confused and offended, he rubbed his temples. "I

have no intention of forcing myself into Kevin's life. That wouldn't be fair to either of you."

"Then why—" Her voice broke. She forced a swallow. "Why are you here?"

"Haven't you been listening?" Patience filled Rob's tone as he leaned closer, one hand extended toward her across the table. "I'm ashamed of what I did to you and how I neglected our son. You have every right to hate me, and nothing I say or do will ever make up for my mistakes. But I needed to tell you in person how sorry I am. How truly, deeply sorry."

Rebecca stared at her ex-husband as if he were a stranger—which he was, it seemed. Certainly this was not the same man she'd fallen for in college, the man whose love songs and irresistible blue eyes had charmed her into dropping out of school to get married and start the family of her dreams. The man who'd promised her and their new baby son the world, then walked away to follow his own dreams as if all those promises meant nothing.

Slowly the truth dawned. All Rob wanted was forgiveness.

She moistened her lips. "I shouldn't have jumped to conclusions. It's just . . . your phone call coming out of the blue like that . . . it scared me."

"I can see now how it would. I'm sorry. I just needed so badly to make amends that I didn't think this all the way through." A smile turned up the corners of Rob's mouth. "So is it okay to ask about Kevin? He's eleven now, right?"

"Twelve in January." But of course Rob should know his own son's birthday.

He laughed softly, a hint of sadness in his eyes. "Where did the years go?"

"He just started middle school and he's the best, just the best." Silence fell between them for a few moments. Then Rebecca inhaled a shaky breath. "God's been working on me, too, Rob. If forgiveness is what you need from me, it's yours."

He blew out through pursed lips. "Thank you. That means more than you'll ever know."

"Guess we've both had some growing up to do." Swallowing the lump in her throat, she confessed her humbling experience in the hotel bathroom when God first began speaking to her about priorities. "It's an ongoing struggle, especially married to a man with lofty career goals of his own, but I'm working on it."

"I'd heard you'd remarried." Rob glanced away briefly, his smile wavering.

"Gary's a good man. Sure, we have our problems," she began, the weight of them pressing heavily upon her. "But he loves Kevin very much. They're great together."

"I'm glad." Rob nudged his fork a fraction of an inch to the left, then moved it back. "Strange, but it really helps to know that."

The waiter sidled up to the table. "Have y'all decided?"

Her worries dispelled, Rebecca suddenly felt famished. They ordered lunch and spent the next hour alternately laughing and crying as they caught up on the past nine years.

Following her last class of the day, Noelle made a quick trip home with Warren to fetch Laurence for the afterschool play rehearsal. Mrs. Sanchez recommended they give the cat plenty of chances to get used to all the noise and confusion so there would be no surprises on opening night. Noelle brought along Laurence's dome-shaped wicker basket and set it in a quiet corner of the lecture hall. If things got too crazy for him, at least he'd have a familiar hiding place.

But leave it to Laurence to ham it up like an old pro. Basking in the attention, he lolled like a miniature king of beasts atop Noelle's geometry book. The cast immediately dubbed him the drama club mascot, and Noelle warmed with pride.

Warren came up beside her and squeezed her arm. "He's a hit."

"Yeah, I wish Mom—" Her fists knotted at her sides.

"Let's get busy." Mrs. Sanchez clapped her hands. "We'll work on act two today, from the top. Places, everyone."

Noelle seated herself in the chair at stage right and chewed her lip as she pondered her character's mood and motivation in the upcoming scene. Concentrating on the script, she tried to get the inflection just right for each line of dialogue.

When they came to the scene where the cat, "Uncle Elizabeth," was supposed to howl in pain, the action stopped. "How are we going to get Laurence to howl?" asked Justin Higgins, who played Papa. "Stick him with a pin?"

Everyone laughed, except for Noelle. "How about we stick *you* with a pin, Justin?"

"Hey, I was only kidding."

"All right, all right, kids." Mrs. Sanchez tapped her chin. "Warren, you're not in this scene. Do you think you could howl like an injured cat?"

Warren let out a long, wailing "Meeeoooowwww!"

Laying his ears back, Laurence leapt from the desk and darted into his basket. From inside, two iridescent green marbles scanned the room.

Mrs. Sanchez chortled. "Warren, I believe you have discovered a new talent."

He grinned and winked at Noelle. The rehearsal continued, but the cast members could barely stay in character each time Warren let go with one of his howls.

Later in the scene, Cassie, as Dagmar, had to retrieve the injured pet from the pantry, where he'd spent a night of recovery under the effects of chloroform. Mama and Papa thought the cat had died, but his twitching tail said otherwise. When Cassie rushed out to center stage with Laurence, Lynn as Mama began to chide Dagmar.

Laurence, snuggling up under Cassie's chin, twitched his tail and purred—right on cue, to everyone's delight and applause.

When rehearsal ended, Noelle curled up with Laurence in the passenger seat of Warren's car. "That was the most fun I've had in ages. Wasn't Laurence great?"

"Oscar material for sure."

"Your 'injured kitty' howl was pretty spectacular, too."

Warren squeezed her hand before starting the car. "Anything to make you laugh again."

"Yeah, feels like forever." A fuzzy, fizzy feeling bubbled up in her chest until it burst out in the beginnings of a chuckle. "Right now, I could almost let myself laugh at Kevin's corny jokes. He told a cute one this morning over breakfast—wish I could remember the punch line."

Warren's mouth fell open. "Don't tell me you're actually starting to like the kid?"

"Not sure I'd go *that* far. But considering I never asked for a stepbrother in the first place, he's . . . not so bad." She tucked Laurence's head beneath her chin. Poor Kevin—all his big-hearted attempts to make friends. She definitely had to give the boy brownie points for trying.

As Warren steered the car out of the school parking lot, he murmured, "Sounds like God's answering my prayers."

Noelle slanted him a doubtful glance. "What prayers?"

"That you and your new stepfamily would find a way to get along."

"Don't get your hopes up. We're still a *long* way from getting along." Her lighthearted mood evaporating, Noelle faced forward. "And I wish you and Kevin would both cut the God talk. I don't even believe in God anymore, not after how He let my mom suffer. Not after the mess He left my life in."

"Hmm, sounds like you do believe in God. You're blaming Him for all your problems."

Heat rose in her cheeks. "Would you just stop?"

Warren reached for a knob on the console to lower the stereo volume. "So what exactly has Kevin been saying to you about God?"

She huffed. "Oh, stuff like, 'Aren't you glad your mom's in heaven with Jesus now, where she's not sick anymore?'"

"I know it's trite, but aren't you?"

"No. I want her here with me." Her lips trembled. Her eyes burned. "I want things back the way they were."

Before Warren could tell her to quit wishing for the impossible and get real, she twisted the volume knob until the music blasting from the speakers drowned out her own thoughts.

All except one. *Mommy, I miss you!*

At the sound of the front door slamming, Gary's head shot up. It could only be his daughter. He turned from the kitchen sink and glanced at the clock on the oven control panel—7:56. Early for Noelle.

She stormed into the kitchen, then stopped short, eyeing him suspiciously. "My father is doing dishes? Will wonders never cease!"

His neck muscles cramped. He rinsed another plate and tried to keep the irritation out of his voice. "Didn't know you'd be home so soon. We just finished dinner. There's some leftover meatloaf in the fridge."

She turned up her nose. "If Rebecca made it, no thanks."

For the millionth time, Gary wondered what had happened to the sweet, loving child his daughter used to be. He snuck a glance at Noelle while scraping food scraps into the garbage disposal.

She opened the refrigerator door and studied the contents. The door whispered shut, and she turned empty-handed to the pantry. Moments later, she stuck a can of chicken noodle soup under the can opener and then dumped the contents into a microwavable bowl. After heating it, she grabbed a spoon and a Diet Coke and disappeared in the direction of her room.

With a silent moan, Gary set the last plate in the dishwasher and dried his hands. His gaze drifted to the table, where the apothecary jar of cocoa mix sat untouched. So much for good intentions.

He found Rebecca in the den, fresh from an evening swim and a quick shower. Her damp auburn curls and green eyes seemed brighter somehow against the paleness of her makeup-free complexion. She sat curled up in a plush easy chair, a women's magazine in her hand and reading glasses perched on the end of her nose.

She glanced up and smiled. "Thanks for doing the dishes, honey."

"What can I say? You've trained me well." He settled on the end of the sofa nearest her chair and scrubbed a hand over his eyes.

"What's Noelle angry about tonight, other than my atrocious cooking?"

He gave an exaggerated shrug. "Who knows?"

"She's home earlier than usual. Do you think something happened?"

Fatigue catching up with him, Gary slid lower onto the sofa. "As usual, she's not talking. And I've given up asking."

From the game room came the sound of a cue ball slamming into the rack, then Kevin's "Yes!"

Rebecca nodded toward the sounds. "You've created a monster." She laid the magazine aside and removed her glasses. "Now that our children are otherwise occupied, do you have time to talk? A lot happened today and I—"

"Yeah, I know. Rob." Guilt corkscrewed up Gary's spine. He should have asked hours ago how things went at lunch, but did he really want to know? The battle to hold on to his daughter was exhausting enough. If he had to compete for Kevin's affection, too...

Or what if Rob's agenda included winning back both his son and his ex-wife? Where would that leave Gary?

Too tired and too twisted up inside to think rationally, he blurted out an excuse. "We'll talk later, okay? I promised Kevin a game of pool before bedtime."

11

When English class ended Friday afternoon, Mrs. Eckles called Noelle up to her desk.

This could *not* be good.

Noelle hugged her notebook and stood beside the woman's chair. "Yes, ma'am?"

"About your book report." The teacher pinched the paper-clipped pages in her right hand. "I have cause to wonder if you actually read the book."

Noelle winced at the bold red F emblazoned across the title page. "I . . . ran out of time."

"I have access to the internet, too, not to mention some extremely useful plagiarism detection programs." Mrs. Eckles shook her head. "Honestly, Noelle, I expected much more of you, considering—"

"Considering who my mother was." She squeezed her eyes shut. "Give me a break, okay? That's all I've been getting from every teacher in this school." As if she hadn't come down hard enough on herself the last few days. Mom would have gone ballistic.

Mrs. Eckles rose, fingertips pressing into the desktop. "I was going to say, considering you found your way into an honors English class, obviously because of your excellent grades prior to this year."

Noelle turned away. She could hardly breathe. *Mom, I'm sorry. I'm failing at everything.*

Mrs. Eckles perched on the edge of the desk. "What is it, Noelle? You seem awfully distracted lately, and I'm worried about you. Have you been able to talk to anyone about . . . about the loss of your mother?"

She drew up her shoulders and fought for control. What was there to talk about? Mom was dead. Noelle had accepted it. It was everyone else who refused to give it a rest. She took a few steps toward the door before turning to face her teacher. "The truth is, all I can think about lately is the Drama Club play. I've got a major role, pages of lines to learn."

"Then perhaps I should speak with Mrs. Sanchez."

"No, don't! I promise I'll do better. Do you want me to redo the book report?"

"Only if you intend to read the book."

"I will. I'll do it this weekend and bring you my report—my *real* report—on Monday."

Mrs. Eckles creased her lips. "Very well, I'll grant you an extension. In deference to your mother's memory, we'll pretend this never happened." She ripped the plagiarized report into four neat pieces and dropped the crumpled pages into the wastebasket. "But I'll have to take an automatic ten points off for turning your paper in late."

Noelle lowered her head and trudged out of the classroom. So much for getting out for a little fun this weekend. At least she had a legitimate excuse for hiding away in her room for two solid days. She'd grown tired of even pretending to be civil to her dad and his *other* family.

Rebecca looked up as Matt Garrison strode into her office. He dropped a stack of computer printouts on her desk. "Merry Christmas."

"For me? It's a little early, but thank you." Rebecca shot him a cheery smirk.

"Nice to see you in a better mood these days." Groaning, Matt plopped into the chair across from her and loosened his tie. "DataTech must be the last major corporation that hasn't succumbed to the 'casual Friday' movement."

"And it'll never happen as long as Charles Sharp has anything to say about it." Rebecca riffled through the first several pages of the printout, recognizing the status reports from her Chicago trip. Thank goodness everything seemed to be operating within normal parameters.

"So to what do we owe your attitude adjustment?" Matt propped one ankle across the opposite knee. "Did Gary finally see the light and tell his daughter to shape up or ship out?"

Rebecca's good humor fizzled. "Not funny, Matt."

"Yow. Sore subject, eh?"

"So let's change it, okay?" She reached into a lower drawer for a water bottle and popped the cap. "If I do seem less edgy these days, it's thanks to the good news I just got from my ex-husband."

"I heard rumors floating around that he'd shown up out of the blue." Matt fished a small Swiss Army knife from his pocket, tugged out the nail file, and set to work on a jagged fingernail. "So what's up?"

Taking a sip of water, she confessed her fears that Rob had intended to take Kevin away from her. "Turns out all my worries were groundless." She gave her head a quick shake. "Rob just wanted forgiveness."

Giving her an odd look, Matt shoved the knife back in his

pocket and rubbed his jaw. "How does Gary feel about having your ex-husband back in town?"

"He's too preoccupied with his insolent daughter to bother with what's going on in my life." Her reply surprised her with its sharpness. She flipped to another page of the printout—not that any of it made sense to her just now.

"Maybe I shouldn't bring this up again," Matt began slowly, "but it sure sounds like you could stand some counseling. Maybe you and Gary both. Have you given it any more thought?"

Frowning, Rebecca swiveled her chair toward the window. "You know Gary—a totally self-made man. I can just imagine how he'd respond to the idea. Yes, I know I could go on my own . . . and maybe I will, if things don't improve soon."

Matt stood and slid the knot of his tie back into place. "Good, because a marriage can only take so much strain before it cracks, and from where I'm standing, it looks like yours is getting pretty close to the limit."

As if she weren't already well aware.

Wrapped in a pink chenille bathrobe, Noelle closed the cover on *The Pearl* and gazed out her bedroom window across the sunlit backyard. With the book report redo hanging over her head, she'd hardly slept last night. When she finally did doze off, it was short-lived, her eyes popping open in the wee hours before dawn. Deciding to get a head start—okay, a very late start—on her reading assignment, she'd been glued to the pages ever since. The story gripped her, touching her in ways she never expected—a fisherman and his quest for happiness, the pearl he hoped would purchase that dream. But he discovered only heartbreak, realizing too late that riches can never replace love.

Maybe she should leave the book on Dad's nightstand. Maybe then he'd get the message.

With the reading done, she decided to reward herself with a break. Already, ideas for the report bombarded her brain—ideas a thousand times better than any she'd copied off the internet. If she gave her thoughts a little time to germinate, she could come back later this afternoon and write a winner of a report, at least good enough to earn a B after Mrs. Eckles deducted the ten-point penalty.

In the meantime, it was too nice a Saturday for hanging around the house, especially if it meant another round of her father's favorite game lately—"Let's Play Family." Stretched across her bed, she reached for her cell phone and called Cassie. "Hey, Cass, I just finished reading my book for English—"

"You mean the one you *didn't* read before?"

"Don't rub it in. Anyway, I just gotta get out of this house for a while. You busy?"

"Nope. Unlike *some* people, I am totally caught up on all my homework. Hey, maybe I can get my mom to take us shopping."

"Super. Dad dropped a wad of cash on my dresser last night— my weekly allowance."

Cassie groaned. "Wish I had a rich dad to bankroll my 'compulsive shopper' habit."

"Your dad makes plenty." Noelle adjusted the pillows behind her back. "I haven't seen you flipping burgers at Mickey D's just to earn some spending money."

"Oh, yeah, and like you have?"

"Believe me, I'm entitled to every penny my father gives me." And she'd return it all in a second, flip burgers, even clean toilets in the boys' locker room, if only she could have her mother back.

She swallowed the bitter taste that had risen into her throat. "So you think your mom will take us shopping or not?"

A whooshing roar started up on Cassie's end of the line. "Oh, great, scratch that. Our housecleaner had to switch days this week, and my control-freak mom always has to personally make sure Loretta gets every last crumb off the carpet and every fingerprint off her precious stainless-steel fridge."

"Rats." Noelle clamped the phone against her shoulder, freeing her hands to tear at a split end. "Then how about I come over there."

"Are you kidding? *I* don't even want to be here."

"Any other ideas, then? Come on, Cass, I've just *got* to get out of this house!"

"Hmmm." Cassie grew silent, and Noelle could almost hear the wheels turning in her friend's mind. "Hey, maybe Warren would drive us to the mall. We can shop, grab some lunch, maybe take in a movie."

Noelle suppressed a shiver. She loved spending time with Warren, but lately she'd been too snappish for her own good. It tore her up inside every time her mouth betrayed her and something she said hurt his feelings.

She faked a wry laugh. "What makes you think Warren Ames would be caught dead escorting a couple of fashionista mall rats?"

"You did say you were desperate. And right now he's our only hope. I'd, um . . ." Cassie's tone became soft, almost shy. "I'd be happy to call and ask him."

"Okay, if you want to. Let me know the plan."

They hung up, then Cassie called back a few minutes later. "He said yes!" Honestly, the girl acted like she was on a permanent sugar high. "Meet him at his car in thirty minutes."

Noelle slipped out of her bathrobe and draped it on the hook inside her closet door. After dressing in jeans and a favorite T-shirt, she eyed her reflection in the dresser mirror. "Come on, smile like you mean it."

The attempt failed miserably. *You're an actress, for crying out loud. If you want to convince the world you're okay, you'll have to do way better than that.*

Through her curtained French patio doors came the sound of

rushing water. Peeking out, she saw Rebecca and Dad using the spa. Better play by the rules and inform them of her plans. Slinging her purse over her shoulder, she sauntered outside.

"I'm going to the mall with Warren and Cassie," she shouted over the rumble of the water jets. Without waiting for an answer, she spun around and trotted across the backyard to the Ameses'.

Through the steam that swirled above the churning waters, Gary watched his daughter disappear around a stand of ornamental shrubbery. Sinking lower into the spa, he reached for his glass of orange juice and wished he could have gotten away with lacing it with vodka. But he'd promised Rebecca he'd cut back on the drinking, and he'd really been trying.

"You're letting her just walk away like that?" Rebecca faced him, her jaw dropping in disbelief. "She didn't even ask permission."

He slowly sipped his juice. "You want me to go chase her down and tell her she can't go?"

"You could have said something—anything!"

"She's nearly sixteen. After all these years, how can I expect her to suddenly accept my authority?"

"She has to, Gary. You're her father."

"In name only, dear, in name only." Swamped with discouragement lately, he rested his head against the coping and let his eyelids fall shut. "Sorry, it's just that things seem to be getting worse instead of better, and I'm not feeling very optimistic at the moment." A burbling jet pounded against his back. He shifted until it hit right between his shoulder blades, the one spot that always stiffened after too many hours at his desk.

All week his mind had lingered over Noelle and the cocoa mix. Or rather her total lack of interest in the cocoa mix or anything else family related. The jar had remained untouched on the kitchen table for three days. He'd finally removed it himself, tossed out the scraggly bow, and tucked the jar out of sight on the pantry shelf.

Steam rose around Rebecca's shoulders. With an annoyed huff, she pushed damp bangs off her forehead. "The girl is begging for a firm hand, Gary. Surely Kate didn't let her get away with acting like this?"

"Leave Kate out of it." Couldn't Rebecca see he was doing the best he knew how? Now she had to hold up to him what a perfect parent Kate had been, meaning what a lousy one he was.

True, he'd never been the disciplinarian, never had to be. And Kate never seemed to find it necessary. Noelle worshiped her mother. Which made Gary . . . what? A figurehead? The breadwinner? More like the infrequent and embarrassingly inconvenient intruder upon their happy twosome.

Rebecca squeezed his knee, her tone pleading. "Gary, will you please talk to me about this?"

He forced himself to look at her. "Do I need to stiffen my drink first?"

"Gary."

"I was kidding." *Sort of.* He reached for the spa controls and shut off the jets. In the sudden silence someone's lawnmower started up. A kid across the creek shouted for his dog. A mockingbird chattered from a branch in the oak tree. Crazy how loud the world was when you weren't trying to block it out. "Okay. Let's talk."

Rebecca flicked a droplet of moisture off her cheek, and Gary couldn't tell whether it was a tear or a splash of water from the spa. "I hate how these problems with Noelle are coming between us. And it's obvious she's enjoying every minute of it."

That much Gary could believe, which complicated this whole mess even more. "I know you're right, but what do you want me to do? Spank her? Ground her for a month? Yeah, it's my fault, but punishing her won't make her love and respect me."

"Even so, you can't continue ignoring her defiant attitude. Letting her do whatever she wants isn't the way to win her over, either."

He rubbed his eyes. Somewhere in the house the Bloody Mary mix and a bottle of Grey Goose were calling his name.

"I'm just so tired of being disrespected," she continued in a shaky voice. "I'm tired of bending over backwards to make this arrangement work, only to be continually treated like an unwelcome houseguest."

Gary's abs tensed. Was he closer to losing Rebecca than he even imagined? He cast her a worried glance. "Are you thinking about moving back to the condo?"

"No, of course not. I'm not trying to *escape* the problems here. I'm trying to find a way to work through them." She looked away and gave a small, pained laugh. "I know I shouldn't be complaining. This is my dream house, for crying out loud. For years I imagined Kevin and me moving out of the city, settling into a friendly suburban neighborhood, doing ordinary family things like having backyard barbecues or . . . or even playing pool in our own game room."

He smirked. "Just not under these circumstances. I get it."

She gave a helpless shrug. "I thought I could do this. I hoped in time Noelle would come around, but—" A sob caught in her throat. "I want *my own room*. I want *my things* in *my house*, arranged the way I want them. *I'm* your wife now, Gary. Is that too much to ask?"

He fingered his empty glass. Between agonizing over his daughter and trying to placate his wife, he felt like he was being ripped in two. "We promised Kate's things would remain untouched."

Rebecca swung around to face him. "Honey, don't you see what's happening here? Claiming she wants to keep her mother's memory alive may be her rationale, but the real reason Noelle is holding us to that promise is because she wants to be in control.

Because she wants to make living here as hard on us as she possibly can."

He stood and slammed his palm against the coping, feeling the sting all the way into his shoulder. "Admit it, why don't you? Noelle's not the real issue. It's your resentment toward me for dragging you into this situation. Toward my abysmal failure as a husband and father. Sorry I've disappointed you so badly."

Reaching for his terry robe, he clambered out of the spa. He dripped puddles through the sunroom and into the den, where he halted at the sight of Kevin sprawled on the floor watching a Saturday-morning nature program.

Kevin looked up with a frown. "Uh-oh, you and Mom had another fight."

Gary froze and stared at his stepson. A harsh exhalation ripped from his throat. "You don't miss anything, do you, Kev?"

"I know the signs."

"Signs?"

"You get all stiff-legged and sort of lean over with your shoulders hunched." Kevin stood to demonstrate. "And you squeeze your hands into fists until they turn white."

Gary shook out his knotted fists and stuffed them into the pockets of his robe. He gave a halfhearted chuckle. "You make me sound like Frankenstein's monster."

Kevin grabbed the remote and muted the TV. "What did you fight about this time?"

Shrugging, Gary cast his stepson a helpless look. "I guess you know your mom isn't very happy living here."

"She just wishes Noelle would be friendly. But Noelle's mad all the time too. She stomps around the house just like you."

"Yeah, I guess she does." Like father, like daughter? Noelle would love to hear that.

Kevin enveloped Gary in a rough bear hug. "There. Feel better?"

"Lots. Thanks, kid." He gave the boy's shoulder a brisk rub.

How'd Kevin get so smart? Eleven years old and already wiser than Solomon. The boy was a study in contrasts. His eagerness for affection and closeness was something most boys his age were already outgrowing, or pretending to. Gary wished he could transfer some of that love-hunger to Noelle.

On his way down the hall, something made him pause outside the closed door to Kate's room, the room he'd shared with her until their separation. Hesitantly he reached for the knob and gave it a turn. The door swung open onto the bright, sunlit space. With an intake of breath, Gary felt himself transported back in time.

The lace curtains were drawn back, offering an expansive view of the lawn and tree-lined creek, where deep green leaves reflected the sun with early-fall touches of copper, russet, and gold. The bed was made, the gold-and-pink comforter tucked crisply under pillows in matching shams. In the dresser mirror Gary caught the reflection of the pink velveteen chaise behind him, and for a tingling moment he thought he glimpsed Kate reclining there. Before bedtime, after her papers were graded and her lesson plans ready for the next day, she used to relax in the chaise with a good book, while he sat up in bed with his laptop working on . . . whatever.

He pressed his knuckles into his eye sockets before pivoting to stare at the empty chaise. What had first seemed like Kate's ghost in the mirror had merely been the reflection of her portrait hanging on the wall.

Aw, Katy-girl, I never thought I could miss you so much! Gary stood before the picture and gazed into the tender brown eyes of his first love. Kate was the one he'd wanted to do everything for, be everything for, win the world for. How hard he'd tried, and how badly he had failed! Now it felt as though she were looking at him, seeing right through to his misguided soul. The sensation was so real, the accusations so strong in his mind, he almost expected Kate to speak.

"Gary?"

His heart skipped about four beats, then played marimba on his ribcage. "Rebecca. I didn't hear you come in."

"What are you doing?"

He gave a weak shrug. "I haven't been in this room since I moved out, except for the few times I came to see Kate after she got sick."

Rebecca, wrapped in a thick velour robe, glided over to Gary's side and linked her arm through his. "I'm sorry we argued. I know you loved her."

Turning toward the portrait, he whispered, "I guess a part of me still does." He glanced at Rebecca. "I'm sorry if that hurts you."

"I can't deny a twinge of envy. Kate was so beautiful, so capable and self-assured." Rebecca's voice faltered. "Countless times I've asked myself how you could fall in love with me after being married to someone so perfect."

Gary studied his wife through narrowed eyes. He'd always seen Rebecca as the perfectionist—diligent, driven, just like him. A feeling of protectiveness filled him, and he drew her close. "You don't ever have to be jealous of what Kate and I had. Whatever it was, it wasn't strong enough to hold our marriage together."

Rebecca peered up at him. "Is what we have strong enough?"

He wished he could assure her it was, but he no longer felt sure of anything. His whole world seemed to be crumbling beneath him. He was more frightened than he'd ever been in his life.

Parked in front of Cassie's house, Warren had to tap the horn three times before Cassie finally bounded down the sidewalk. Noelle moaned from the passenger seat. "Oh, no, she's gone cowboy."

Cassie wore skin-tight Levis tucked into red Roper boots, a plaid shirt with pearlized snaps, and a tan felt cowboy hat perched atop her blond curls.

Warren got out so Cassie could slide into the rear seat. "Hope you won't be too cramped back there. Sorry about the mess."

"I'll survive." Cassie nudged aside an old T-shirt and some CD cases. She poked Noelle's shoulder. "Dibs on shotgun on the way home!"

As they headed toward the freeway, Cassie passed a CD up to Warren. "Play this one, okay?"

Carrie Underwood's velvety voice filled the car, and Cassie belted out her own harmonization while Noelle resisted the urge to plug her ears. Cassie was definitely not *American Idol* material. When the song ended, Cassie reached between the seats and turned down the volume. "Did y'all hear the student council is sponsoring a country-western dance after the football game next Friday night?"

Noelle bit the inside of her lip and kept quiet. It didn't take Dr. Phil to notice Cassie was fishing for a date to the dance.

Warren eased his Mazda into a parking space near the entrance to Macy's and shut off the engine. "Saw the posters but hadn't decided about going. How about you, Noelle?"

"I'm not much into dances these days." She threw open her door and stepped out. Heat from the sun-baked pavement slapped her in the face and filled her nostrils with the biting odor of asphalt.

"Oh, come on, y'all." Cassie clamped her hat on her head as she maneuvered out of the backseat. "You wouldn't make me go alone, would you? It'll be so fun."

Warren gave his door a shove and locked the car with the remote. He lifted a shoulder. "Noelle?"

She'd recently begun to suspect Cassie might be developing a crush on Warren. If the girl wanted to go out with him, here was her chance. "Count me out. But you two should go."

Suddenly Cassie didn't look so confident. "Are you sure?"

"Of course I'm sure." Which she really wasn't after all, now that she thought about it. But she had no claim on Warren beyond friendship, and things on that front were shaky enough these days. "Come on, let's go shopping."

Reaching the entrance to Macy's, Noelle pushed through the heavy glass doors several steps ahead of her friends. Rounding a display, she ran headlong into a perfume counter.

"May I help you with a fragrance?" A woman in a slim black dress came around the counter with a sample bottle. "Donna Karan is offering a special Cashmere Mist collection this month —eau de toilette, body lotion, and a lovely tote. Care to try some? "

Noelle pulled up short, her stomach convulsing. "I wouldn't be caught dead wearing Cashmere Mist." She shot the girl an icy glare before stalking toward the exit to the mall.

"Will you slow down?" Gasping, Warren snagged her arm.

She jerked to a halt and fixed her gaze on a winsome scarecrow in the Hallmark window display. Blazing resentment burned within her. The last thing she needed was some salesgirl waving Rebecca's fragrance under her nose. She inhaled a long, deep breath and blew it out slowly. "Guess I kind of freaked out back there."

Cassie touched her hand. "Something remind you of your mom?"

"Something like that." She had to stop acting so weird in front of her two best friends. If she didn't chill out, it wouldn't be long until she drove them both away. "I skipped breakfast this morning and I'm starved. Can we get an early lunch? I heard there's a new gourmet burrito place in the food court."

"Fine with me." Warren hooked his thumbs in his belt loops.

"Me too. I like the veggie kind, with lots of sour cream and salsa." Cassie sidled between Noelle and Warren as they started down the mall.

After picking up their food orders, they found an empty table. While Noelle stuffed herself with a monstrous black-bean burrito, she tried to shake off her chronic grouchiness. Life would be so much better if she could be as bubbly and bouncy as Cassie instead of acting like a depressed, neurotic, self-centered creep.

A terrifying thought gripped her. How could she live with herself if her two best friends only stuck by her out of pity? Especially Warren—the guy deserved a life, after all. It would be perfectly normal for him to start getting interested in someone— a real girlfriend, not the pathetic kid sister type who lived next door.

And why shouldn't it be Cassie? Maybe the "opposites attract" thing could actually work with them. If Warren gave Cassie half a chance, maybe he'd grow to like her in a new way. And maybe that way, Noelle could hang on to both of them.

After lunch, they checked out the movie listings at the mall theater. Spying a new Chris Hemsworth movie, Noelle insisted they had to see it. Getting lost in an action flick sounded like the ideal antidote for her lousy mood. Even better, the movie could be just the thing to nudge Warren and Cassie closer together.

Cassie clung to her arm and whined like a two-year-old. "But you *know* I get creeped out by evil villains and fight scenes. Let's pick a romantic comedy instead."

"You can close your eyes during the scary parts. Besides, Cassie"—Noelle shot her friend a meaningful eyebrow lift —"*Chris Hemsworth*? Come on!"

"Well . . . he is really cute . . ." A grin worked its way across Cassie's face. "Okay, okay." She let Noelle drag her toward the ticket booth.

They followed the ticket taker's directions to theater number five. Noelle took the lead, groping her way up the dimly lit steps. Choosing the third seat in their row, she pulled Cassie into the second seat, which forced Warren to sit next to Cassie, who finally took off the ridiculous cowboy hat and held it in her lap.

Smiling into the darkness, Noelle hit the recliner button and stretched out her long legs. Moments later, the feature presentation flashed onto the screen. *Perfect.* The moment the creepy villain appeared on the scene, Cassie would be hiding her face behind that ten-gallon hat and gripping Warren's arm for dear life.

12

R ebecca hadn't planned to return to the condo. It just sort of happened. Since they'd moved in with Noelle, she'd done her best to resist the impulse, refusing to give in to the same avoidance measures Gary habitually practiced. He'd cut back somewhat on his physical absences, but as he put more effort into his relationship with Noelle, the emotional distance between him and Rebecca seemed to widen.

Their encounter in Kate's room had been less than reassuring. After changing out of her swimsuit, she'd decided to get out of the house for a few hours and give them both some space. Kevin wanted to spend the day with one of his new school friends, so she dropped him off and then headed toward Highland Park Village, where a new boutique had recently opened.

But instead of stopping, she drove right by, and the next thing she knew, she was pulling into the driveway at the condo, as if her trusty BMW had a mind of its own.

Stale air greeted her when she let herself in from the garage. The day they'd moved out, she'd set the A/C to hold at 79 degrees—no sense letting their furnishings bake. She cracked the kitchen window and turned on the ceiling fan, then lowered the thermostat to 74. Pacing from room to room, she'd expected a sense of comfort and familiarity, but she felt only loneliness.

This isn't your home anymore, Rebecca.

Maybe not, but neither was Kate's house.

It could be, if you'd let it.

"Even if I tried, Noelle won't allow it." Halting mid-step, Rebecca clamped a hand to her cheek. "Talking out loud to an empty condo? Now I've really gone over the edge."

With a hopeless moan, she trudged to the kitchen and opened the refrigerator. Yes, a six-pack of diet colas, exactly where she'd left them. She popped the top on one and drank from the can. For a few blissful moments, the cool metal rim against her lips and the rush of fizz across her tongue made her forget everything else. Then, as she leaned against the counter, her gaze fell on the answering machine. The blinking red display indicated fourteen messages.

"How dumb can you get, Rebecca?" Why hadn't she thought to have their calls forwarded? A teensy bit preoccupied, maybe? Surely, anyone who mattered would know to try their office or cell phones.

Pressing the PLAY button, she whisked through the calls. The first was a wrong number, the next two callers hung up without leaving a message. Then came a series of calls from Rob. The machine's date/time stamp indicated he'd tried to call this number before finally reaching her on her cell. When the last of her ex's messages came to an end, she hit the rewind button and replayed it. *"Becky, it's me. Please call if you get this message. I promise you I don't intend to make trouble. I just want to talk."*

She hadn't spoken with him since their Tuesday lunch. Both had agreed they needed time to think about how and when to introduce Rob back into their son's life. She still had no idea how to tell Kevin his father now lived in the Dallas area, but sooner or later she'd have to. Kevin had a right to know his father, and Rob truly seemed like a new man.

After listening to Rob state his phone number at the end of each of his five messages, she had it memorized. As unsettled as things stood between her and Gary, maybe allowing Kevin's father the chance to know his son could be at least one positive step she could take. She lifted the cordless phone and keyed in the number.

"Hello, Rob, it's Rebecca." She laughed nervously. "I wasn't sure you'd be at home on this gorgeous Saturday afternoon."

"You just caught me. I was on my way out to the jogging trail."

"Oh, then don't let me keep you."

"No hurry. What's on your mind?"

"I . . . thought we should talk more about Kevin."

He remained silent for a moment. "Are you sure you're ready? I told you, no pressure."

She glanced down at her green Chaco sport sandals. Better suited for leisurely nature hikes than running, but she should be able to make a mile or so before blisters set in. "How about I join you for a jog and we can talk on the way?"

"Did you say this is Rebecca Marshall?" Rob released a soft chuckle. "Sorry, but the woman I know by that name thought *jogging* was a four-letter word."

"Rob, my name is Townsend now, remember? And believe me, after sitting at a computer terminal day after day, I need to be jogging."

His voice mellowed. "I mean it, Becky, when I saw you in TGI Friday's the other day, you looked as fantastic as the night I first laid eyes on you in the campus coffee shop."

Her thoughts flew back to that night, when a silky voice she hadn't heard before had drifted over the coffee shop sound system. She'd turned toward the small stage to see who was singing her favorite 'N Sync song, "This I Promise You," and found herself gazing into the most tantalizing blue eyes she'd ever seen. Oh, how she'd wanted to believe every one of Rob's promises.

She shifted the phone to her other hand and wiped her damp palm on her Bermudas. This was no time to go skipping through sugarcoated versions of the past. "Will you give me directions to your place?"

Forty-five minutes later she parked in a visitor's space beside Rob's Arlington apartment building. He lived on the top floor of a three-story unit, and she arrived at his door winded from the climb.

He greeted her wearing red running shorts and a T-shirt proclaiming "He Chose Nails" superimposed upon an image of Jesus. "Should have warned you about the stairs. You're panting like you've already jogged five miles."

"Just give me a minute to catch my breath." She entered uncertainly, stifling the warning voice in her head. She was committed to Gary. But did that mean she couldn't be friends with her son's father?

"We can skip the jog if you'd rather." He stepped into the narrow kitchen and filled a glass with ice water. "Here, looks like you could use this. I can always go for a run later this evening. It'll be cooler then anyway."

"If you're sure you don't mind." She gratefully accepted the glass and took a long drink. "Considering how out of shape I am, I doubt I could hold up my end of the conversation past the first ten yards."

Rob showed her to the sofa, then eased into the Danish-style leather recliner across from her. "I'm glad you called. Haven't had time to make many friends here yet, and my pals from the old days aren't exactly the type of people I need to be hanging out with."

She pressed the cool glass between her palms and stared at him. "I'm still incredulous over the changes in you. So you're really a church praise team leader now?"

His boyishly endearing smile made her glance away. "You mean you can't picture me singing Christian music?"

"Not exactly. For as long as I knew you, church was never your thing."

"My loss. It's good to know you're raising Kevin in the faith. Where does your family worship?"

She named their small, friendly church on Marsh Lane. "But it's just Kevin and me. Gary isn't interested." Her chest ached at the reminder. "I've tried to talk to Gary about God, but he tunes me out." *And not just about God*, she wanted to add.

"Sounds like there's something else going on." Rob sat forward, his gaze searching hers. "What aren't you telling me?"

How could she begin to explain about her problems with Gary, about his self-centered, headstrong daughter, about the deceased ex-wife whose memory haunted them like a B-movie phantom? "Gary was married before, too," she began stiffly. "He has a teenage daughter, and his ex recently died of cancer. We're all trying to adjust."

"Wow. When we talked at the restaurant, you never let on how much you were dealing with."

"Guess I didn't want you to know what a mess my life is in." She tried to laugh, but it sounded hollow. "Anyway, maybe now you can understand a little better why your showing up when you did threw me into a tailspin."

Nodding slowly, Rob braced his hands on his knees. "I'm so sorry. If I'd known—"

"You couldn't have. And what's done is done. It's just—I mean, with everything else going on—" Her lower lip began to tremble. The last thing she wanted was to break down in front of her ex-husband.

Rob crossed the space between them and sat beside her. He started to reach for her hand, then pulled back and cleared his throat. "Are you getting some help? Talking to your pastor or a family counselor?"

"No . . . not yet. I'm afraid I'd just end up going by myself . . . again," she added under her breath. Hadn't she tried and failed to get Rob to go with her to a marriage counselor when he'd first asked for the divorce?

He glanced away with a guilty sigh. "Yeah, I blew it—another of my many regrets. But you shouldn't have to carry this load alone. You need to talk to someone."

She'd tried talking to Gary, for all the good it had done so far. And now Rob was here and Gary wasn't, and the chance to unburden herself was so tempting. Why shouldn't she confide in someone with whom she shared a history . . . shared a son?

"My life's falling apart," she began haltingly, unable to hold back a rush of tears. "I love Gary so much, but I'm terrified our marriage won't survive all these changes."

In the next moment, she found herself weeping against his shoulder, the warm, cottony smell of his T-shirt blending with the lingering menthol scent of shaving cream. A disarmingly familiar sensation swept through her, sending tingles down her limbs.

He gently pushed her away, then found a tissue somewhere and pressed it into her hand. "It's okay. It'll be okay."

Stabbed with sudden guilt, she sucked in a breath and pushed to her feet. "I'm so sorry. This was wrong. I should never have come—"

"Becky, you didn't do anything wrong." He followed her to the door.

She drew a deep breath and turned to face him—and had to lift her gaze another foot to keep from staring into the eyes of Jesus looking back at her from Rob's T-shirt. What she wouldn't give for a pair of heels right now! Stiffening her shoulders, she stated firmly, "I told you before, I go by Rebecca now." She reached for the doorknob. "I'll talk to Kevin about you soon."

It was Friday night and here Noelle sat, home alone.

Again.

Stepping out of her pleated skirt, she drop-kicked it across the room, where it slumped against her closet door. One by one she kicked off her ankle boots, sending them sailing into the air and landing with a soft thud on top of the skirt. She slam-dunked her cotton cowl-neck sweater onto the pile and trilled, "Two points."

After pulling on a baggy red T-shirt and teddy-bear-print boxers, she dropped onto her unmade bed. She yanked the elastic band from the end of her braid and tossed it in the direction of the nightstand. She nearly barfed as she watched the band sink slowly through a layer of curdled milk in the glass she'd left there two nights ago—right next to a half-eaten ham sandwich. Nothing left but the bread, with tiny teeth marks indicating Laurence had been scavenging. She shoved the dishes to the far edge of the nightstand with a mental reminder to take them to the kitchen later, preferably when everyone else had gone to bed.

Things had grown way too quiet over the past week. Dad and his perfectionist little wife hardly spoke lately, especially after Rebecca had returned from wherever she'd taken off to last Saturday. At least Kevin had made several friends at his new school, which helped keep him out of Noelle's hair. Still, the relative calm made her nervous, like living in the eye of a hurricane.

On the positive side, she'd been doing a pretty decent job of controlling her emotions in front of Warren and Cassie, even managed to talk her way out of complaints from her teachers about the schoolwork that occasionally fell by the wayside. Most important, she'd memorized almost all her lines for the play. She had two new mantras: *Stay on an even keel,* and *Don't let anyone rock your boat.* A sad chuckle tickled her throat. How Mom would cringe at the clichés!

She loosened her braid with the fingers of one hand and

reached for the play script, flipping it open to act two. One more night and she'd have the whole thing down pat. Good thing she'd weaseled out of going with Warren and Cassie to the football game and dance tonight.

She glanced at her bedside clock. Seven twenty. Warren and Cassie were probably sitting in the stands right now, watching the pre-game activities. She pictured Cassie in the new outfit she'd bragged about all week—boot-cut jeans over tan faux-alligator boots, hand-tooled leather belt with her name across the back, turquoise-and-yellow paisley shirt with rhinestone trim, and a snakeskin headband for her Stetson. Fashion sense? Cassie had none. A flair for the dramatic? Oh, yeah.

And Warren? He'd most likely be wearing his old brown scuffed boots, the ones he wore when he went hunting with his dad. He'd wear his favorite blue plaid western shirt tucked neatly into faded Lees. Nothing fancy or pretentious about Warren.

Good old dependable Warren.

Nice, sweet Cassie.

They'll thank me for this someday. Just wait and see.

She flopped onto her stomach, a tangle of hair cascading across her shoulders and onto the edges of the playbook. Images of Warren and Cassie faded as she visualized herself on stage as Katrin, playing to a full house.

The rest of the weekend brought more of the same. Noelle spent most of it in her room, not even bothering to dress. And any excuse to avoid family mealtimes—*ugh!* Instead, she carried plates of food back to her room, where it mostly went uneaten. Her father and his *other* family didn't seem to notice her absence, or maybe they did and were grateful she was shutting her personal black cloud away behind closed doors.

Late Sunday afternoon, she glanced out her window to see Warren jogging along the path by the creek. Kneeling at the window, she rested her chin on the sill and admired his long, graceful strides. There was a time when he would have stopped by to tap at her back door and invite her to come along. She felt more alone and forgotten than ever.

When her friend disappeared from view, she crawled onto the bed and curled up with a huge stuffed bear, the one Warren had given her for her birthday two years ago. She couldn't seriously expect him to stay her best friend forever, especially not the way she'd been acting. She could feel it—she and Warren were drifting apart.

Maybe she needed a boyfriend of her own. He'd be tall and oh-so-handsome. He'd be smart and devoted and love her forever, and he'd never, ever leave—

"Noelle?" A soft knock sounded on her door. "It's Dad. Could I talk to you?"

So *Dad* wanted to talk to her, just when she'd conjured up her faceless admirer. Oh well, what was one more shattered fantasy? Brushing a strand of hair from her eyes, she trudged to the door and opened it a crack, hoping he couldn't see past her to the mess of her room. "What?"

Her father stood there shuffling his feet, hands stuffed into his jeans pockets. "Look, I know you'd rather not, but it would mean a lot to . . . to the family . . . if you would join us at the table for supper."

She set one hand firmly on her hip before her dad could notice the tremor of gratitude sweeping through her—her own heart turned traitor! She strove for the coolest tone she could muster. "Whose family are we talking about? Mine, or yours?"

"Ours, Noelle. Ours. Whether you want to admit it or not, the four of us are a family now. Even if you don't like the idea, would you at least grant us some common courtesy?"

The desperate, pleading look on her father's face made Noelle glance away. She heaved an exaggerated shrug. "Okay. I'll be out in a few minutes."

She shut the door in his face, afraid the expression in her eyes would betray her. How could she feel this happy and relieved that her family hadn't forgotten her, when she'd been trying so hard to push them away? Had to be her loneliness talking. And possibly wishing she could have gone to the game and dance with Warren and Cassie?

Yeah, that had to be it. Well, she'd just have to work a little harder on keeping up her defenses.

Rebecca closed the oven door and set the timer for another five minutes. "Well? Is her royal majesty joining the common folk for supper or not?"

Gary leaned against the refrigerator and crossed his arms. "I tried, okay? You don't have to cop an attitude."

A knot of remorse clogged Rebecca's throat. "It's just my frustration talking. So . . . what did she say?"

"She's coming." He picked up two of the iced tea glasses sitting on the counter and carried them to the table, then glanced in the direction of Noelle's room, his expression a battle between hope and futility. "At least she said she was."

Rebecca had to give her husband credit for taking the initiative, but she couldn't keep from muttering, "I'll believe it when I see it." She yanked a serving spoon from the drawer and slammed it shut. "Honestly, I don't know how much more of this I can take."

Gary swung around. "What—her, or me?"

"Both of you, I guess. If only you'd—"

"Well, if you weren't so—"

"Mom, Dad." Kevin thumped the end of his knife on the table. "You guys need to cool it and stop being mad at each other all the time."

Flinching under Kevin's reproachful glare, Rebecca released a repentant sigh. "You're right, Kev. It's just . . . things are really tense right now."

She cast Gary an apologetic smile and then succumbed to a different kind of guilt. She still hadn't told her son about his real father. Worse, she hadn't been able to put aside the disorienting mix of emotions she'd experienced in Rob's apartment. The idea of counseling might deserve more serious consideration before this whole situation exploded into something irreparable—if it hadn't already.

Noelle trudged into the kitchen. She wore a pair of wrinkled jeans and an oversized oxford shirt, both looking like she'd dug them from the bottom of the laundry hamper. Laurence followed, pacing back and forth around Rebecca's feet as she removed her quickly thrown together chicken à la king from the oven.

Nearly tripping, Rebecca nudged the cat to one side with her ankle. "Laurence, do you mind?"

Noelle let out an abrasive chuckle. "At least Laurence likes your cooking."

A snicker escaped Gary's throat—was he laughing at her, too?

It was suddenly more than Rebecca could take. She slammed the casserole dish in the middle of the table and bolted from the room, angry tears threatening. She had tried so hard to be patient with Noelle's moods, to empathize with the girl's grief. But would Noelle even attempt to be polite? And Gary hadn't uttered a word in Rebecca's defense.

Halting halfway through the den, she took several deep breaths. This madness had gone on long enough, and she would not let them get the best of her. She stormed back into the kitchen, finding Gary, Kevin, and Noelle quietly taking their seats around the table and exchanging uncertain glances. "Okay, so I'm not the greatest cook in the world. You should all be as appreciative as Laurence."

She shuffled place settings around, brought another chair from the dining room, and took a bowl from the cupboard. With a large serving spoon she scooped out a generous portion of casserole, then fished an ice cube from her tea glass and stirred it through the mixture until the steam subsided. She plopped the heavy black-and-white cat into the empty chair and placed the bowl before him. He set his paws on either side of the bowl and dove in, chewing and swallowing over a vibrating purr loud enough to shake the whole house.

With a satisfied nod, Rebecca took her seat. "Kevin, as usual, Laurence has started without us, but would you ask the blessing?"

"I'll help with the dishes," Noelle said, stacking plates.

Rebecca breathed a small sigh of gratitude. "Thank you."

The dinner hour hadn't exactly been filled with pleasant conversation, but something had definitely shifted. Her critics had even managed to polish off respectable servings of her boring chicken casserole.

"Kevin," she said, tousling her son's blond hair, "let's go outside. I have something to tell you."

Gary's gaze grew tender. Beneath the table, he squeezed her hand. "I'll stay and help Noelle."

"Bonding time. Oh, boy," Noelle quipped, and yet her tone didn't carry quite the bite it usually did.

Rebecca and Kevin strolled down to the creek and found places to sit on the gnarled roots of an oak tree. The boy tossed a stone into the burbling water. "That was totally awesome, Mom."

She wrapped her arms around her knees. "What?"

"Making Laurence a place at the table. Did you see the look on Noelle's face?"

She grimaced. "I did, but I'm not sure what it meant."

"It was like she decided you were a pretty cool person after all."

"You think so?" A minor breakthrough, if it were true. How did her son get to be so observant?

"So what did you want to tell me?" Kevin turned his narrowed gaze upon her. "Mom, are you going out of town again?"

"No, this has nothing to do with my work." She moistened her lips. "Kevin, it's about your dad. Your real dad."

She watched his spine stiffen under his thin cotton T-shirt. "He didn't die, did he? Because even though I don't know him, I like to think he's alive somewhere and maybe thinking about me sometimes." He ran a finger under his nose and sniffed. "Not like Noelle's mom. I feel bad for her."

"I do too." If only she could find a way to get close to the girl. She pushed aside those concerns for now and rubbed her son's shoulder. "How would you feel if I told you your dad is living nearby? That he wants to meet you?"

Another suspicious glance. "Mom, you wouldn't joke with me about something like this?"

"It's true, honey. Your dad has moved back to Texas. He's living in Arlington. He has a job leading the praise team for a church."

The boy's steely blue eyes softened. "Seriously? Have you talked to him? Have you seen him?"

"A couple of times, yes. Since he left us, he's changed a lot . . . for the better." She gazed across the creek toward the yard behind theirs, where a gray-haired man tossed a Frisbee for a galumphing golden retriever. "Your father and I have been talking about giving you two a chance to get acquainted."

Kevin glanced over his shoulder toward the house. "Does Dad —I mean, does Noelle's dad know?"

"Yes."

"Do you think it would hurt his feelings if I wanted to meet my real dad? I mean, he treats me like his own kid, and he's the only dad I've ever had."

"I think he'd understand." She fingered a dead leaf. "He loves you a lot, but right now he really wants things to be better between him and Noelle. If you got to know your own dad again, it might help Noelle, too, if she didn't feel she had to compete with you for her father's time and affection."

Kevin studied her face. "What if I liked my real dad and wanted to be with him sometimes? Would you be sad?"

She struggled to answer honestly. "You and your father have a right to know each other, and if it means I have to share you . . . well, it'll be hard, but I'll get used to the idea."

Kevin leaned sideways to give her a quick hug. "You'll always be my mom, no matter what."

Later, as she prepared for bed, her own words came back to accuse her. *Gary and Noelle have a right to know each other too. Are you as willing to share your husband with his daughter as you claim to be?*

13

The weekend had pushed Noelle deeper into some heavy soul-searching, and the drive to school Monday morning was her chance to deliver the carefully rehearsed speech she'd been polishing since last night. "Warren, I've been thinking."

He glanced her way. "About what?"

"You shouldn't have to give up so much of your time for me, like . . . like driving me to school and rehearsals and all."

Warren stopped at a traffic signal and gawked at her. "What planet did this nonsense come from?"

"It isn't nonsense." She forced a smile. "I know how selfish I've been lately, and you deserve some freedom to live your own life."

The light turned green. Warren gunned the engine, jamming Noelle's head against the headrest. "I don't see it that way at all. I'm sorry if you do."

She'd blown it again. Nothing she said or did around Warren seemed right anymore. "I was only trying to—"

"Drop it, okay?" Warren's tires screeched around the next corner. "There's no reason for me not to give you rides. We live next door, for crying out loud."

"I know, but—"

"I said, it's no big deal."

"Well, if you're sure. Because I don't want to take advantage of you."

"If it ever feels that way, I'll be the first to let you know."

Swallowing, she cast him an anxious frown. "Promise?"

"Promise." Warren heaved a lengthy sigh, his annoyed expression mellowing into a smirk. "Besides, if it will make you feel better, come December, you can return the favor by driving *me* around."

Her thoughts shot ahead to her sixteenth birthday. She'd looked forward to getting her driver's license for so long, waited for the day when she'd finally get to sit behind the wheel of her mother's shimmering white convertible. Except Mom was supposed to be the one teaching her how to drive, and now, with her whole life in the toilet, Noelle hadn't even thought about signing up for driver's ed.

A terrible, choking tightness throbbed in her chest. On top of saying the wrong thing to Warren—again—this stupid, going-nowhere conversation had sent her thoughts to places where she wasn't ready to go.

And the day only got worse. Three of Noelle's teachers handed her failing notices, in history, geometry, and biology—not her best subjects, but she'd never come anywhere close to failing a class before. She stuffed the notices in her purse. How could she ever show these to her dad and ask for the required parental signatures?

Then at lunch, all Cassie could talk about was the "terrifically awesome" time she'd had with Warren Friday night.

"Warren had to explain every football play to me," Cassie said between cheesy bites of pizza. "I've never understood why those guys in the striped shirts are always throwing out their little yellow handkerchiefs. You can barely see them anyway from way up there in the stands. And by the time the players notice, they're usually halfway to the other end of the field."

Noelle was more interested in watching Warren's expression than listening to Cassie's babbling. Amusement flickered in his eyes, something like when his three-year-old cousin came to visit and sat on Warren's lap describing every last detail about his trip to the Dallas Zoo.

"Oh, and the dance was awesome." Cassie reached across the table to jiggle Noelle's elbow, almost making her drop her fork. "You really should have been there."

And I'm really glad I wasn't. Not that she wasn't happy to see how well her plan was working—getting Cassie and Warren together was her idea, after all. But seeing it up close and personal like this? She suppressed a twinge of discomfort and pasted on a smile. "So what are you guys planning for next Friday night?"

"The football game's out of town, so that's out." Cassie hooked her arm through Warren's and rested her chin on his shoulder. "Any ideas?"

Noelle tried to keep from staring as that uncomfortable twinge swelled into something ugly and green. *Jealous? No way!*

"Cassie, come on." With an uneasy chuckle, Warren gently but firmly extracted his arm and reached for a handful of Fritos. "No special plans for me." He looked expectantly at Noelle. "How about you?"

He'd clearly said *me*—singular—not *Cassie and me*. Were things not going as well between them as Noelle had thought? Still puzzling over both her own reaction and Warren's, she shook her head. "I, um, thought I'd give my uncle a call, maybe see about flying to Phoenix for the weekend."

Warren perked up. "Fun. Wish I could tag along. I didn't get much chance to talk to David when he was here for the . . ." He shifted and took a swig from his soft drink. "Anyway, he promised he'd give me some advice about architectural schools."

Cassie made a long face. "What? You wouldn't both leave me totally alone for the whole weekend?"

"Don't panic," Warren said with a roll of his eyes. "I'm already committed for Saturday morning with the set crew. Lynn's dad is letting us use his pickup to move a desk and chair and a couple of other things over to the auditorium."

"Katrin's desk?" Noelle brightened. "I can hardly wait till next week when we start rehearsing onstage."

Warren's mouth spread into a proud grin. "I think you're going to like what we've done with the sets."

"Your sets are always great." Noelle smiled back.

"So." Licking a drop of pizza sauce off her thumb, Cassie bumped shoulders with Warren. "We still haven't decided on Friday night plans. How about a movie?"

"Yeah, I guess." Warren's lips twitched in a brief smile. "Figure out what you'd like to see and let me know."

Noelle's chest tightened again. Better not to analyze the Warren-and-Cassie thing too closely—even worse, her suddenly bewildering feelings about them dating each other. Didn't she have plenty of stuff to deal with on the home front?

She glanced at her tray, realizing she'd barely touched her salmon patty and green beans. Lately everything was tasteless anyway. She laughed to herself. How else could she have forced down Rebecca's insufferable chicken casserole last night?

Funny how things had seemed almost normal for a while as she'd sat down to a meal with her . . . her *family*. And Rebecca, giving Laurence his own bowl, right there at the table. It was . . . kinda cool.

She clenched her fists and squeezed her eyes shut. *It's weird enough you've started making friends with Kevin. But liking Rebecca? That would be just too much.*

When the Monday-afternoon staff meeting ended, Matt Garrison walked Rebecca to her office. "Nice to have you back on board," he said. "I hope this is a permanent change."

What else could he be referring to but her mental attitude? "I'm doing my best, Matt, all things considered."

"And what exactly is 'all things' this week?" He dropped into a chair and propped his feet on the corner of her desk.

She laid her portfolio on the desk and crossed to the window. A light rain had begun, and the roof of the Hotel Adolphus glistened under a sun struggling through patchy clouds.

"Let's see." She began ticking off items on her fingers. "I've moved into my husband's late ex-wife's home, I'm being snubbed by my stepdaughter, and my long-lost ex-husband showed up out of the blue expecting me to welcome him with open arms back into our son's life. How much worse can it get?"

Matt grimaced. "You're making me sorry I asked."

Giving an eye roll, she sank into her chair. "I might be exaggerating about Rob, but yes, he would like to meet Kevin." She steepled her fingertips. "And I've decided to let him."

"Wow. You're brave."

"Brave? Not hardly. Resigned, maybe." She shook her head. "He is Kevin's father, after all. He's convinced me he'd never do anything to hurt his son."

Matt lowered his feet to the floor and sat forward. "Well, I'm glad things are looking better on that front, anyway, because I'd like you in a good mood when I present my offer."

She pressed a hand to her stomach. "Offer?"

"I've been talking with the expansion committee, and I recommended you to head up the Corporate Software Accounts department in our new branch office." He smiled magnanimously, as if he'd just presented her with a key to the executive lounge.

She swallowed and contemplated reaching into her drawer for antacids. "Where?"

"Austin."

"*Austin?* Matt, you know I can't move to Austin."

He lifted his shoulders. "It's only a couple hundred miles down the road. You can commute home on weekends. It's perfect for you. Nothing has to change."

She couldn't speak for several moments. Her gaze darted across her desktop, pausing upon Kevin's latest school photo, then a snapshot of her and Gary at their wedding reception, and finally her computer monitor, where the screensaver scrolled through her favorite Bible verse, Jesus' words in Matthew 6:33: "*But seek first his kingdom and his righteousness, and all these things will be given to you as well.*"

Matt's voice interrupted her jumbled thoughts. "You'll need some time to think about it. I understand."

She blinked several times, and their eyes met. "No, Matt. I can give you my decision right now. The answer is an absolute no."

"Don't be hasty, Rebecca. I'm talking a sizable raise, expense budget, the works. In today's economy, you do realize what that means?"

She did. It meant job security when DataTech's latest restructuring moves had already eliminated at least a dozen management positions. It meant the company valued her contributions, her expertise, her experience.

It meant being on the road and away from her family five days a week.

"I'm sorry, Matt. I just can't do it."

He slanted her a disbelieving look. "We've been grooming you for this position for the past couple of years. I thought you'd be thrilled."

She fell into her chair and massaged her temples. "I'm grateful, I really am. But you never hinted the promotion you had in mind would mean leaving Dallas." She shook her head. "Matt, I thought you understood. Where my priorities are concerned, my family is second only to God. What you're asking is impossible."

He rose and shrugged. "This kind of opportunity doesn't come around twice. I hope you realize you've effectively shut yourself out of any future advancement."

The door slammed behind him.

A full week with no business travel? Hard to believe nothing pressing had come up, but for Gary it was a welcome change of pace. He was actually growing to appreciate getting home from work at a reasonable hour and sitting down to supper with his family. Well, most of them anyway. Noelle still couldn't seem to come straight home after play rehearsals.

And then Wednesday evening she did, surprising them all when she breezed in just as they sat down for the Chinese takeout Rebecca had brought home.

"Golden Dragon? My favorite!" Grinning, Noelle dropped her backpack at the end of the counter. "Is that cashew chicken I smell?"

With a stunned glance at Gary, Rebecca pushed back her chair. "We didn't expect you till later. I'll set another place."

Kevin scooped fried rice onto his plate. "Mom, do we have more soy sauce?"

"Keep your seat, Kev. I'll get it." Noelle was already grabbing a plate and flatware. "Anyone need anything else while I'm up?"

"We're good, but thanks." Returning his wife's stare, Gary mouthed, *Who is this girl?*

Noelle was the picture of politeness and affability all through the meal. By the time she popped up to clear the table after everyone finished, Gary had begun to suspect an ulterior motive. With the clatter of dishes in the sink muffling his words, he leaned closer to Rebecca. "She wants something."

"You think?" Lips in a twist, Rebecca motioned Kevin toward the game room. "Time to start on homework, tiger. Didn't you say you needed help studying for your science quiz?"

Great, abandoning him to his fate. Gary drew a long, slow breath and ambled over to where Noelle was loading the dishwasher. He grabbed a dishcloth and began wiping the counter. "Sounds like the play's coming along. I know it's a lot of work, and I—I'm really proud of you, Noelle."

"Uh . . . thanks." She dropped a handful of forks into the utensil basket, then straightened and crossed her arms. Her smile seemed more strained than ever. "So, Dad, I was thinking. I mean, as much time as I've been putting in at rehearsals, plus, um, schoolwork and all . . . it sure would be nice to get away for the weekend."

His brows shot up. "Yeah, I guess we could do something. Hot Springs should be pretty this time of year. We could rent a boat, do some fishing—"

"I wasn't meaning all of us. Anyway, fishing?" She rolled her eyes and snickered. It wasn't a pretty sound. "What I meant is, I'd like to fly to Phoenix. By myself. To see Uncle David and Aunt Susan."

Caught off guard, Gary paused a beat. On the upside, a quiet weekend with zero teenage daughter drama held massive appeal. Besides, saying yes could significantly raise his "good dad" quotient in Noelle's eyes.

But Rebecca? She'd most likely see it as another major fail by a perpetually ineffective parent. And she'd be right, because Gary knew good and well his daughter hadn't earned this kind of privilege, but he could feel himself caving anyway. Still, what could it hurt? Couldn't they all use a break from the tension, if only for a couple of days?

"Okay," he heard himself say.

She narrowed one eye. "You mean I can go?"

He nodded. "I've got plenty of frequent flyer miles. I'll set it up."

"Really? Wow, thanks, Dad!" She looked almost ready to hug him, then quickly backed toward the family room. "Well, I, uh, should probably start some laundry. Plus I've got a reading assignment for history and, uh . . ."

"Right. Go on. I'll work on those flight reservations."

As he went to retrieve his laptop, Rebecca came up beside him, her expression grim. "I couldn't help overhearing. Are you sure this is such a good idea? Because it sounds more like avoidance—on both your parts."

"You're not entirely wrong." He set his laptop on the breakfast bar and opened his web browser. "But I've always had a lot of respect for David and Susan. They're a good influence on Noelle, and I'm thinking a weekend with them might be good for her." He met her doubtful gaze with a hopeful one of his own. "And for us."

She studied him, one corner of her mouth slowly turning up. "I like the sound of that. I hope you're right."

So did he. More than he wanted to admit.

14

N oelle set her travel bag on a bench near an antique maple highboy. She loved Aunt Susan's guest room, so cheery in shades of yellow and pale blue. And such a relief to put a thousand miles between her and all her problems back in Arden Heights.

Getting Dad to agree to the trip had been crazy easy. Too easy, in fact. Like he was jumping at the chance to have her out of his hair for a few days. Guess she couldn't blame him, but a tiny part of her—okay, maybe not all that tiny—almost wished he'd said no.

Aunt Susan came in to say good night. "You've been in our thoughts so much lately. I'm glad your dad let you come."

"Me, too." Noelle unfolded her robe and nightshirt. "Weekends around my house are pretty tough. I needed a break."

"Not getting along any better with your father?"

"Mmm." That sounded noncommittal enough. It grew harder and harder to tell exactly where she stood with Dad. She could tell he was trying, and she wanted to believe he was sincere. But could she simply ignore all he'd done . . . or hadn't done?

Aunt Susan turned down the bedspread. "Dave and I have

had some long talks with your grandmother. She's pretty worried about you."

"Nobody needs to worry." Her fingers toyed with the zipper on her tote. "Besides, it's just a couple more years until I'll be going off to college, and then it won't matter anyway."

"Of course it matters, sweetie. Family always matters." Aunt Susan frowned and started for the door. "I'll let you get some sleep. We can talk more in the morning."

On Saturday, Aunt Susan put together a picnic lunch while Uncle David went next door to borrow a spare tennis racket for Noelle. They claimed an empty court at a nearby city park, and David took on the two of them, still beating them soundly—not surprising since he'd played on his college tennis team.

"No fair." Aunt Susan faked a pout. "I think you should give us a thirty-point handicap."

"I'm not that much of a good sport." He shoved his racket into its leather case. "Who's ready for lunch?"

They moved to a picnic table near a small pond. Susan opened the wicker basket and laid out cold rotisserie chicken, four-bean salad, and wheat rolls. Noelle poured three cups of iced tea and brought out the paper plates and plastic utensils.

"So how's life in Big D?" Uncle David asked, gnawing on a chicken leg.

She told him all about the play and how much she loved her part as Katrin. "Laurence even has a role. I wish you could come. Opening night is the second Friday of November."

David glanced at Susan, and she nodded. "I think we could arrange it. But would you have room at the house for us?"

Noelle grimaced. The only unoccupied bedroom was her mother's.

Aunt Susan must have caught her look. She tore a wheat roll apart and spread it with butter. "We can always stay at a motel."

"But *you're* my real family, not—"

"Stop right there." Mouth firm, Uncle David wiped his fingers on a napkin. "Your dad and Rebecca and Kevin—*they* are your family, the ones you need to be counting on, day in and day out. Susan and I are more than glad you wanted to come for a visit this weekend, but if this was only a means to put off dealing with issues at home—"

"No, I really wanted to see you." Her throat ached. She drew a quick breath. "I know I need to get straight with my dad. I'm working on it, okay?"

"I hope you mean that." Uncle David speared a kidney bean with his fork. "We would love to be there for your play. And we'll worry about sleeping arrangements when the time comes."

Noelle released a silent sigh of relief. Maybe by then, Dad would finally see this living arrangement was doomed.

Except . . . then where would she be?

On Sunday, with Rebecca and Kevin still asleep and Noelle in Phoenix, the house stood silent. In the golden glow of the late-September morning, Gary relaxed in a sunroom lounge chair while sipping his first steaming cup of coffee and savoring the view of the creek and trees at sunrise.

Too bad this otherwise pleasant moment had to be marred by what lay in his lap. Setting his mug on the glass table, Gary studied again the three failing notices he'd found when he'd ventured into Noelle's room yesterday on his rounds emptying wastebaskets. Hers had been filled to overflowing with scraps of paper, tissues, pencil shavings, and snack crumbs. The failing notices weren't even in the basket but crumpled on the floor next to it.

He wracked his brain. This wasn't like Noelle at all, at least the daughter he used to know—bright, studious, always at the top of her class. She'd never had a failing grade in her life that he was aware of, until now. Surely Kate would have informed him if there had been problems anywhere near this serious.

If the failing notices weren't enough, Gary could hardly believe the state of Noelle's room. Never had he known her to be anything but meticulous and organized, traits he'd always proudly claimed she'd inherited from him. She'd made her bed every morning before school, always put her clothes neatly away. No toothpaste in the sink, no wet towels on the bathroom floor. Even as a little girl, she used to fuss at him on the rare occasions he dropped a newspaper beside his chair or walked away leaving a glass or cup on the coffee table.

Bewildered, Gary could think of only one thing to do. Carrying his coffee and the notices, he plodded to the kitchen phone.

At his former mother-in-law's bright hello, he said, "Irene, it's Gary. There's something I need to talk to you about."

Irene sighed. "Oh, dear. Noelle?"

"She's failing three classes." He slapped the smoothed-out papers against his leg. "And she didn't even tell me. I found out by accident."

"I see," Irene said slowly. "Last time we talked, I thought things had improved slightly."

"I thought so too. At least I'd hoped so." Gary laid aside the papers and pinched the bridge of his nose. "I admit I didn't know her as well as I should have before, but even so, she's not the same girl. I'm at my wit's end."

"She's been through a real trauma, Gary. Losing a mother is —" Irene released a muffled sob and then cleared her throat. "I suppose I could talk to her, but she'll wonder how I found out."

"And I'll be accused of snooping." He explained how he'd found the notices and went on to describe the horrible condition of Noelle's room.

"Maybe I can tactfully say something in one of my emails," Irene suggested. "In the meantime, Gary, you're going to have to take charge. You have no one to blame but yourself if you keep letting her get away with these things."

"I know, I know." Gary swirled the dregs around the bottom of his coffee mug. Hadn't he suffered through the same lecture innumerable times from Rebecca? "But Noelle already hates me."

"Nowhere is it written that a child must like her parents."

"I just wish I could get through to her."

"There's only one way that will ever happen," Irene told him. "You were absent from Noelle's life for so long that the only way she can trust you again is for you to convince her you'll be there for her no matter what. Stop worrying so much about gaining her acceptance and just be the father you were meant to be."

Dressed for church in a beige linen suit, Rebecca went to the game room to rouse Kevin from sleep. "Get a move on, kiddo. We need to leave in forty-five minutes."

In the kitchen she found Gary staring at the empty coffeepot. "It usually works best if you add water and ground coffee."

He looked up as if he hadn't heard her. "'Morning, hon. Want me to brew a fresh pot? I just polished this one off."

"I'll get some at Sunday school. Don't bother." She took the orange juice carton from the refrigerator and poured herself a glass. Downing her multivitamins with a gulp of juice, she noticed the wad of papers crushed in Gary's fist. She set down her glass and touched his arm. "What are those? Is something wrong?"

He held them out to her, and her mouth slackened as she read Noelle's failing notices. Somehow she wasn't surprised. "How long have you known about this?"

"Happened on them while collecting trash yesterday. I just called Irene. Thought she could give me some advice about how to handle it."

He chose to call his ex-mother-in-law before talking to *her*? Rebecca stifled a surge of resentment. "And did Irene have any words of wisdom?"

He leaned against the counter and leveled his gaze at her. "She gave me the same spiel I'm always getting from you about how I need to take responsibility and act like a father."

"Wow. Imagine that." Holding back a smug smile, she filled a bowl with raisin bran.

Kevin sauntered into the kitchen, his blond hair slicked back from the shower. He glanced at the notices lying near Rebecca's hand. "Uh-oh, secret's out." He chuckled and poured himself a bowl of granola.

Rebecca stared at her son. "You knew about these?"

"Oh, yeah." Milk splashed from his bowl onto the counter, and he grabbed a dishcloth to mop it up. "There were only about seventeen million messages from her teachers on the answering machine when I got home from school Friday." He shoveled several spoonfuls of cereal into his mouth on his way to the table. "I told her when she got home, and she said if I told either one of you, she'd throw all my video games in the creek and shove cat food down my throat."

As if on cue, Laurence ambled into the kitchen and wound himself between Rebecca's ankles. She gave the cat a gentle nudge and leaned against the breakfast bar to eat her cereal. "Kevin, I hope you understand that for something this serious, Noelle had no right to demand your silence."

"Aw, she didn't scare me. Figured she was just waiting for a good time to tell you."

Like there would ever be a good time. Seeing Gary's distracted look and furrowed brow, Rebecca couldn't help feeling sorry for him. "Gary, honey, maybe if you . . . prayed about it."

He shot her a disgruntled frown. "If I thought it would help, I would."

She set her bowl on the counter and tucked both her arms

under his, pulling him close. "Do it anyway. You might be surprised."

His chin settled atop her head, but his body remained stiff. "I don't think I know how."

"Then I'll keep praying for you." *For all of us.*

Half an hour later, Rebecca stopped by his chair on her way through the den and kissed him on the forehead. "Remember, Kevin and I won't be home until later in the afternoon."

He looked up from the business section of the *Dallas Morning News.* "Huh? I thought we were going to do something together while Noelle's away."

The pleading note in his voice brought a tremor of guilt. Yesterday had been nice. Even though they'd spent the day catching up on things around the house, they hadn't argued once.

Then she realized why. Gary had emptied wastebaskets shortly after lunch yesterday, so he'd had all afternoon and evening to bring up Noelle's failing notices—and she was just finding out about them this morning, *after* he'd phoned Irene for advice.

Dear God, what's happening to us? Why can't we talk anymore?

She pressed two fingers to the bridge of her nose. "Perhaps if we actually communicated like a husband and wife are supposed to, you'd remember I'm taking Kevin to meet Rob today."

Without waiting for a reply, she called Kevin from the game room and marched out the front door.

15

Ignoring a driver's angry honking, Rebecca executed a last-minute lane change and shot down the exit ramp off I-35. She circled under the freeway and headed south toward I-30.

"Mom, church is the other way." Kevin whooshed out a breath and released his death grip on the armrest.

"Change of plans." She shot her son a bright smile. "I thought we'd visit your father's church this morning. That way you could see him from a distance before you two actually meet."

He lifted an eyebrow and settled back. "Whatever you say."

One Hope Community Church was abuzz with the gathering crowd. Rebecca and Kevin made their way along a side aisle and found seats about halfway up from the chancel. At ten fifty-five, a group of praise singers strolled out and found their places at a keyboard, drum set, and a row of microphones. Rob was among them, carrying a guitar. Rebecca's heart fluttered. She didn't even know Rob could play guitar. Under the rosy stage lights, he looked amazingly handsome and youthful, so much like her first glimpse of him in the college coffee shop that her head swam.

Recovering herself, she nudged her son. "That's him, in the middle. Recognize him from your baby book photos?"

Kevin released a shaky breath. "My real dad . . . wow."

When the service ended, Rebecca led Kevin to the foyer and stood on tiptoe to peer through the crowd in hopes of catching Rob when he emerged. She spotted him carrying a black guitar case and chatting with other members of the praise team. She steered Kevin in Rob's direction and stopped three feet away, waiting for a break in the conversation.

"Rob, you are the greatest." The very pregnant lead singer gave him an awkward hug. "One Hope is so blessed to have you."

A red-haired man who appeared to be the woman's husband patted Rob on the shoulder. "We're headed to Chili's for lunch. Can you join us?"

"Please do," the woman said. "My single sister's coming, too." She shot Rob a conspiratorial grin.

Rob's cheeks reddened. "Sounds like fun, but I've got other plans." Just then he glanced up and caught Rebecca's eye. His gaze drifted to his son's face, and his surprised expression turned to a look of happy recognition. He took a faltering step toward them.

Rebecca swallowed down the horde of butterflies threatening to choke her. "Rob, I'd like you to meet your son."

Kevin extended his hand in manly politeness. "Hi . . . um . . ." He looked to Rebecca as if unsure how to address the father he'd never had a chance to know.

Rob filled the uncomfortable moment. "Wow. I wasn't expecting to see you until later." He gripped his son's hand, but his moisture-filled eyes suggested he wanted to do much more.

"It was a spur-of-the-moment thing," Rebecca said. "I thought Kevin might like to see you in your new job."

"Getting paid to do something I enjoy this much?" Rob ducked his head. "It's a blessing and an honor."

"Mom said you used to sing on a cruise ship."

Rob's jaw froze in an embarrassed grin. "Not exactly the same thing."

Kevin reached out to touch his father's guitar case. "Can you teach me how to play?"

"I'd love to. But . . ." He angled Rebecca a hesitant smile. "That's kind of up to your mom."

She squeezed her son's shoulder. "Why don't we talk about it over lunch?"

Rob offered to drive them to the restaurant, then return for Rebecca's car later.

She hesitated. "Maybe it would be better if we drove separately."

"If you'd rather." Rob nodded his understanding, but his tone held a hint of disappointment. He offered Kevin a hopeful smile. "Would you mind riding over with me? We could start getting reacquainted."

Mother bear instincts kicking in, Rebecca decided she wasn't ready to let Kevin out of her sight. Not that Rob had given her any reason not to trust him, but he hadn't been back in their lives long enough to risk taking chances. "I changed my mind," she said, ushering her son toward the exit. "We'd both be happy to ride with you to the restaurant."

Grin widening, Rob showed them to his silver Honda Accord, but then came the whole problem of who sat where. As he opened the front passenger door, it would have seemed perfectly natural for Rebecca to slide into the seat. *Too* perfectly natural, and thus not wise. Instead, she nudged Kevin forward. "Climb in, honey, so you and your dad can talk. I'll sit in back."

Despite her good intentions, the fifteen-minute drive through Arlington's Sunday noon traffic kept conversation to a minimum. Unfortunately, it also gave Rebecca time to reflect on how strangely awkward this whole situation was. She wondered how Gary was coping with his afternoon alone. Maybe it would have made more sense to reschedule today's visit with Rob so she and Gary could have spent a few hours of quality time working on their marriage.

Too late, though. She'd committed to making this father-son reunion happen, whatever it cost her emotionally.

At the restaurant, Rob asked the hostess to seat them somewhere with a little less noise. She showed them to a booth near the back, well away from the busy entrance and kitchen area.

Before Rebecca had even picked up her menu, Rob and Kevin began talking a mile a minute, as if neither could wait to start making up for lost time.

"So you like sports?" Rob was saying. "What's your favorite?"

"Basketball, mostly. A lot of my friends play soccer, but I'm not too good at it." Kevin scanned the menu. "Can I get a cheeseburger and onion rings?"

"Sure, anything you want. I mean, if your mom says it's okay." Rob cast Rebecca a hesitant glance.

"No, that's fine." Nice of him to acknowledge she was still the parent in charge. She raised a brow in Kevin's direction. "Just don't order more than you think you can eat."

The server came to take their order, barely causing a blip in their conversation. Talk slowed only slightly after the food came, Rob and Kevin mumbling over bites of their burgers, while Rebecca mostly listened as she nibbled on her chicken Caesar salad.

They were back to talking about Rob's new job, and Kevin said, "I always thought it'd be so cool to be in a band."

"Yeah, it's fun. And seriously, if you'd like to learn guitar—"

"Drums would be even cooler. I wished I could have signed up for school band, but then we moved . . ." Kevin lowered his chin.

Fork halfway to her mouth, Rebecca froze. "I didn't realize you wanted to learn an instrument. Why didn't you say anything?"

He shrugged as he broke apart an onion ring. "The

afterschool practices and stuff would have been too hard with your work and all."

"But, honey, we could have figured something out."

"It's okay, Mom. Maybe next year."

The reassurance did little to assuage Rebecca's embarrassment. After she'd ripped Rob apart for ignoring his son all these years, now she'd been caught in her own failure as a parent. How could she not know her son was interested in music?

Like father, like son? The thought jolted her, and for a moment she couldn't breathe.

Breaking the awkward silence, Rob dabbed his lips and asked, "Anyone leave room for dessert?"

With most of her salad wilting on her plate, Rebecca shook her head.

Kevin swallowed his last couple of bites of burger, then said he could really go for a brownie sundae. "Is that okay, Mom?"

"Sure, honey," she said all too quickly. Considering her increasing load of guilt, she'd have gladly let him order one of everything on the dessert menu—except then in addition to being an uninformed parent, she'd also qualify as dangerously overindulgent. And perhaps too quick to pass judgment on Gary's permissiveness with Noelle?

"A brownie sundae looks good to me, too," Rob said. He signaled their server and placed the order.

The server returned shortly with their desserts, and a wide-eyed Kevin began spooning in mouthfuls of the rich, chocolatey brownie topped with vanilla ice cream.

Taking a bite of his own dessert, Rob turned to Rebecca, his voice softening. "I'm sorry if today has been uncomfortable for you."

"It was bound to be, at least a little." Forcing a smile, she sipped her iced tea. "But we had to start somewhere, and it can only get easier, right?"

"Let's hope." An amazed grin spread across his face as he

returned his gaze to Kevin. "I can't thank you enough for allowing me to spend this time with our son. He's an awesome kid."

She tugged affectionately on her son's collar. "I think so, too."

"I don't want to press my luck here," Rob said, "but is there a chance we could do this again soon? Or maybe Kevin and I could take in a Cowboys game some weekend."

Kevin turned a chocolate-smeared smile toward his mother. "Awesome. Can we, Mom?"

She used her napkin to dab his chin. "It's a distinct possibility."

"You'd always be welcome to come along," Rob added softly. "With your husband, of course."

Reminded she'd left Gary alone this afternoon, she nodded. "Thank you. And thanks for lunch, too, but we should probably be getting home."

"Right." Releasing a muted sigh, Rob signaled their server for the check. "I'll take you back to your car."

Breathing hard, Gary heaved himself from the pool and brushed water from his eyes. He'd hoped a long, hard swim would take the edge off his restlessness. Bad enough he still fretted over how to handle Noelle and her failing grades. Worse, Rebecca was off gallivanting around Arlington with her ex-husband. He wasn't sure how he was supposed to feel about that. Sure, Kevin needed to meet his father, but the timing couldn't be worse.

"I need you, Rebecca," Gary said to the cloudless sky. "I need you to help me know what to do about Noelle."

Like you've listened to any advice she's given you so far.

Like pray? She made it sound so easy. Just tell God your problems and He'll make it all better. Like God had made it better for Gary's parents. Like He'd made it better for Kate. And please.

What kind of God would snatch away a vulnerable teenager's mother and leave her hurting and angry at the entire world?

He fought the urge to march inside and make himself a drink. The last thing he needed was for Rebecca to come home and find him plastered, which would be all too likely if he gave in to his present state of mind.

Get a grip, Gary.

Anyway, he had to pick up Noelle at the airport later, and he'd already taken some pretty serious risks in the past few months by driving under the influence. *You're just lucky you haven't killed yourself yet . . . or someone else.*

After showering and changing into a fresh polo shirt and khaki shorts, he ambled into the kitchen and stared into the refrigerator. Toward the rear of a middle shelf he spotted half a six-pack of Shiner Bock. Surely he could handle one beer. It wouldn't have quite the numbing effect of Scotch on the rocks, his usual drink of choice, but if he didn't find something to calm his screaming nerves, he would explode.

As he reached for one of the dark amber bottles, he heard a car in the driveway and then a key in the front door. Grabbing a Diet Coke instead, he turned in time to see Rebecca and Kevin step into the kitchen.

"You're back," he said, popping the top with nervous fingers. "I was just getting a soda. Want one?"

"No, thanks." Rebecca's narrowed gaze spoke suspicion. "Drinking that straight, I assume?"

"What? Of course." He faked a nonchalant grin and took a long swig. Sidestepping his wife, he strode into the den, flopped into the recliner, and started riffling through the Sunday paper. He seized the sports page and made a pretense of studying football stats. Crazy to suddenly feel so nervous around his own wife. And it wasn't only because she'd almost caught him grabbing a beer.

No, it was knowing she'd just spent the last few hours in the company of her ex. If the thought of his inevitable confrontation with Noelle weren't enough to drive him to drink, all he had to do was picture Rebecca and Rob getting all cozy while they bonded over their son.

Jealous much? And he'd accused Rebecca of being jealous of Kate.

Rebecca nudged Kevin toward the game room. "Change out of your Sunday clothes before you do anything else, okay?" She slipped off her heels and planted herself in front of Gary's chair, her spiked pumps held at hip level like loaded pistols. In a low voice she said, "Would it have cost you so much to forget your own problems for one minute and ask him how it went with his father?"

Guilt flooded him. He laid the paper aside. "Great, I screwed up again. Of course I care how it went. I just—" Groaning, he massaged his temples. "Sorry, but I kept imagining you with Rob and thinking of all the ways I'd like to hurt the guy."

"Gary—"

"I know, I'm being stupid. But I can't help it—I was mad that you chose him over me and left me here by myself all afternoon. So yes, I was feeling sorry for myself. It just feels like I can't do anything right in your eyes anymore."

Her lower lids brimmed with tears, but he didn't know what he could say to make things better. She expected too much of him, everyone did. How, for God's sake, was he supposed to manage a demanding career, an angry teenage daughter, a wife with ex-husband issues, and a preadolescent stepson all at the same time?

For God's sake. There he went with the God stuff again. He certainly wasn't praying . . . or maybe deep down, he was, for all the good it would do.

And now he'd made his wife cry. Again. How much more of a loser could he be?

The phone rang. Flicking a tired glance toward Rebecca, he grabbed the cordless extension from the end table.

"Mr. Townsend, hi, it's Warren. Just wondering when Noelle's flight gets in."

Gary rerouted his train of thought. "Her itinerary's in my phone. I'll have to look it up for you. Five-something, I think." He checked his watch. Already after four. He'd need to leave pretty soon to make it to D/FW on time.

A girlish twitter sounded on Warren's end of the line, and Warren excused himself while he murmured a reply to someone else. Coming back on the line, he said, "Sir, if you wouldn't mind, could Cassie and I meet Noelle's flight?"

A flood of relief washed over him. He'd been trying all day to work out in his head what he'd say to Noelle when he picked her up. On the other hand, a long drive through congested Dallas traffic would not be the ideal time to bring up the failing notices. Better to wait until they could sit down face to face with no distractions. "Actually, it would help me out a lot. Thanks, Warren. Hold on and I'll get you the flight information."

Flicking away the moisture on her cheeks, Rebecca marched to the bedroom and flung her shoes in the general direction of the closet. After Warren's phone call, and knowing Gary didn't have to make the drive to the airport, they might actually have been able to sit down together and talk through the feelings they were each struggling with. This time, though, it was all on her, because after what she'd been through today, she had no energy left to deal with emotions.

And was it even worth trying anymore? Considering their ongoing struggles, was there any hope at all Gary could become the husband she needed him to be? *Give it up. Cut your losses and get out.*

Dangerous thoughts. The Bible stated emphatically that God hates divorce. Was that the root of her problems? She and Gary had both been married to other people, both divorced once already. Maybe this marriage was destined to fail. Their punishment for former sins.

She needed to talk to someone, someone who would really listen and help her sort through this clash of emotions. But did she have even one true friend she could call on at a time like this? It suddenly hit her how few close friends she had . . . and why. Between work and trying to maintain home and family, she'd given herself little time to cultivate other relationships.

Yes, she knew scores of people at DataTech—acquaintances at best. Matt Garrison, her boss, knew her better than most, but any personal advice he offered would be tainted by his loyalty to the corporation. As for church, she did well to make it to Sunday morning worship and the occasional adult Sunday-school class— when she was in town. Business travel made it impossible to commit to ladies' groups, evening Bible studies, or committee involvement. She couldn't even bring herself to call her own mother, who had enough worries of her own after bringing Rebecca's aging grandfather into her home.

Then in her mind she pictured Rob, his broad forehead and strong jaw, the easy smile that once took her breath away. Rob . . . still the same, but so enticingly different. No matter how he'd hurt her in the past with his one-night stands and ultimately his desertion, finding God had clearly changed him. She was still learning to trust this new Rob, but so far, she liked what she saw.

Could his return to Texas somehow be providential? Knowing the obstacles Rebecca and Gary would face, had God been planning this reunion all along? Rob was Kevin's father, after all, and the three of them had once been a family, as short-lived as it may have been. Could God possibly be trying to tell her He wanted that family restored?

Her cell phone was still in her purse where she'd left it in the den, but an ivory designer extension phone sat on the nightstand. Her hand hovered over the receiver. She lifted it, then dialed the first four digits of Rob's number. A guilty tremor ran through her, and she broke the connection. Moments later she held the phone to her ear as she entered another series of numbers. Matt Garrison's voicemail answered, and she asked him to return her call ASAP.

She'd barely hung up her linen suit and changed into jeans when the phone rang. She grabbed it up before Gary or Kevin could get to it first.

"Rebecca? What's up?"

"Hi, Matt, sorry to bother you on a Sunday afternoon."

"No problem. I'm at the office anyway. "

She should have guessed as much. She chewed her lip. "About the promotion . . ."

Gary knew he should have hung up when he realized the call was for Rebecca, but hearing Matt Garrison's voice, and then the word *promotion*, his curiosity got the better of him. One hand covering the mouthpiece, he sat stiffly and listened.

"You mean the Austin assignment?" Matt laughed in a way that could only be described as triumphant. "I knew you'd change your mind."

"Not exactly, but I may have been hasty in saying no. Is it too late?"

"Don't worry, I held off passing along your original response." Another satisfied chuckle. "I know you too well. Rebecca Marshall, queen of the glass-ceiling smashers."

The fine hairs rose on the back of Gary's neck. *Townsend. Her name is Townsend now, you jerk.*

"I have to be honest, Matt," Rebecca replied. "If I do accept, my motives are based more on personal reasons than career goals."

"Either one works for me, but care to elaborate?"

A pained sigh. "The way things are going, putting a little distance between me and my family problems might be best for everyone concerned."

Gary's stomach knotted. He moved his thumb to the disconnect button and let the phone drop into his lap.

Moments later, Rebecca appeared beside his chair, her green eyes smoldering. "You were listening, weren't you? I heard the click."

"So what if I was? You should have told me Matt offered you a promotion. And what's this about Austin? Are you planning on moving there? Without me?"

"As if you haven't made your share of decisions lately without caring how I was affected."

Gary shoved himself out of the recliner and towered over her. "We at least discussed things first. I never sideswiped you with anything that would so obviously change our lives."

"Sideswiped?" She stepped closer, wagging a finger in his face. "Feels more like I've been hit by a semi, flattened by a steamroller, and run through a shredder."

"Fine, then. Go to Austin." He spun away from her, one hand lifted in futility. "Go back"—his voice cracked—"go back to Rob, for all I care."

"Mom? Dad?"

Wishing he could snatch back his last words, Gary swiveled his head toward the game room door, his gaze landing on Kevin's bewildered face.

"What's wrong, you guys? Why are you fighting this time?"

"Kev, honey, it's okay." Rebecca held out her hand to her son.

He came to her and slid under her arm. "I heard you say something about moving. Mom, are you gonna make me change schools again?"

"Oh, honey, nothing's settled yet." Her voice shook. She stroked a wispy blond strand off Kevin's forehead. "Your dad—I mean, Gary and I have some issues to discuss."

So now he was just plain Gary again. Was it because Kevin's real father had re-entered the picture, or because Rebecca had decided to systematically write Gary out of their lives, starting with this move to Austin?

"All you guys do is fight anymore." Kevin's gaze filled with worry. "Are you getting a divorce?"

The word severed the air between them like a falling ice shard. No one spoke for several seconds.

Finally Gary answered, his gaze holding Rebecca's. "Your mom and I may be arguing a lot, but it doesn't mean we don't love each other." At least he hoped that held true for her. "We're still a family. We'll figure this out." Though he'd tried to sound convincing, for his own sake as well as for Kevin's, inside he was terrified. One more misstep and he could lose both them and his daughter forever.

"Your dad's right, Kevin," Rebecca said. *Your dad.* A small concession but a welcome one. "It's true, we have some serious things to talk out, but please keep trusting us, because we're trying to make the best decision for everyone."

A sob caught in the boy's throat. "Just don't split up, okay?"

16

When Noelle spotted Warren and Cassie waiting for her in the baggage claim area, her knees nearly buckled. She'd been dreading the long drive home with her dad while she tried not to gag at his lame attempts at fatherly conversation.

On the other hand . . . Warren and Cassie. Seeing them together should make her happy. So why didn't it?

She adjusted the shoulder strap of her tote, pasted on a huge grin, and marched toward them. "Hey, y'all, what are you doing here?"

"Picking you up, of course." Cassie slipped her hand into Warren's.

With a weird kind of laugh—somewhere between embarrassed and annoyed?—Warren freed himself from Cassie's grip, then relieved Noelle of the tote. "I told your dad we could save him the trip. Didn't think you'd mind."

"No, that's great!" Except now she faced a forty-minute drive having to watch Cassie openly flirting with Warren. Maybe having Dad pick her up would have been more tolerable after all.

On the way to the parking lot, Cassie hooked her arm through Warren's. "Oh, Noelle, you *have* to see that movie Warren and I went to Friday night." She described it in excruciating detail, sounding so much like Alvin the Chipmunk that Noelle had to grit her teeth to keep from shouting, *Shut up!*

In the car, she wedged herself into Warren's cramped backseat and closed her eyes, shutting everything else out. *"For as long as I could remember, the house on Steiner Street had been home. . . ."*

"Hey, you asleep back there?"

Noelle sat up with a start, surprised to see they'd arrived in her driveway. She crawled from the backseat and stretched while Warren got her luggage out of the trunk. "Thanks again for picking me up," she said as he walked her to the door. "See you in the morning as usual?"

"Same time, same place." Warren nodded toward the car. "Say, Cassie has some kind of surprise picnic thing we're doing at the park. You, uh, wouldn't want to come along, would you?"

"What, and spoil your romantic evening?"

Warren flinched. "It's not—"

"Anyway, I'm exhausted. I'm planning to make it an early night." A bitter taste, like something green and moldy, clung to the back of her tongue. "Have fun. And thanks again for bringing me home." With the cheeriest smile she could muster, she waved and closed the door.

Entering the den, she found her father staring out the back door, hands jammed into his pockets. Rebecca sat stiffly on the edge of the sofa, a damp tissue crushed between her clasped hands. The door to the game room was closed, and from beyond it came a now excruciatingly familiar chorus from one of Kevin's favorite Christian rock bands, punctuated regularly by the thwack of billiard balls.

What new family crisis had she walked in on? Or was this just more of the same?

"Uh, I'm home." She started for the hall. "Gotta go unpack."

"Wait a minute." Seeming to draw himself from somewhere far, far away, her father moved to the lamp table.

At the coldness in his tone, her stomach clenched. She didn't want any part of whatever was going on here. "I should really, um..."

"Excuse me." Rebecca ducked around Noelle and darted down the hall toward the guest room.

When her father snatched up several sheets of paper from the table and held them out to her, she froze—the failing notices. "Where did you get those?"

"Not that it matters, but I was emptying wastebaskets and found them in your room."

She wanted to lash out at him for snooping—he deserved it, after all—but hadn't she known all along these failing notices would eventually come back to bite her? She couldn't stop seeing her mother's face, disappointment etched in every line of her expression.

Dropping her bags, she crossed her arms and stalked to the fireplace. "Let's just get this over with. I'm tired."

"So am I." Her father let out a long, slow breath, his shoulders curving in around his chest and making him look a hundred years old. "These forms plainly state you're to have them signed by a parent. They're dated almost a week ago, Noelle. When, if ever, were you planning to show them to me?"

She ran a finger along the mantel. "I don't know." *Maybe never.*

"You realize you're living dangerously. Your grades could exclude you from performing in that play that's so important to you. If I'm not too far out of the scholastic loop, I believe failing students aren't allowed to participate in extracurricular activities."

The pretzels she'd eaten on the plane writhed up the back of her throat. How could she have been so stupid? She strode to the end table, fumbled through the drawer for a pen, and thrust it at her father. "I'll study harder from now on, I promise. Could you sign the papers now? Please?"

Dad's eyes glazed over with a distant look as he took the pen.

Leaning over the table, he scrawled his signature three times. He folded the papers and laid them in her outstretched palm.

No lecture? No punishment? Chin trembling, she mumbled, "Thank you." She started for the hallway, then paused. Somehow she had to make amends, before he decided she deserved something much worse. "Is there, um, anything I can do to help with supper?"

Her father shrugged and shook his head. Once again he stood staring into the backyard, as if he'd already forgotten all about her and the failing notices.

Something was wrong . . . really, really wrong. And it had to be something between Dad and Rebecca. What if that meant Rebecca and Kevin might not be living here much longer? Such news should make her happy, because then this ludicrous charade of a family could end.

But what if Rebecca did move out? It wouldn't be as if Mom could return and take her place. No matter what happened now, nothing would ever be the same.

"Rebecca, you look terrible."

"Why, thank you, Matt. I so appreciate your honesty." Jaw clenched, she angled her chair away from her boss and shuffled through some papers on her desk.

Matt settled into the chair across from her. "I know you had reservations about accepting the promotion, but after your call yesterday, I thought you were working through them. Why do I have the impression that's not the case?"

She drew a hand across her forehead. "Let me see. . . . Could it be the bloodshot eyes, the gray hairs that sprouted overnight, the half-empty bottle of Tums sitting open on my desk?"

"So what's the problem? Gary? Your son? Your ex? Or are you just getting cold feet?"

Matt's last comment stung her professional pride. "You and I both know there's no one more qualified for the Austin position than I am."

"Then do you want the job or not?"

"Yes—no—" She bit her lip to keep from sobbing but couldn't blink fast enough to keep silent tears from spilling over.

Matt handed her a tissue from the box on the corner of her desk. "Talk to me, Rebecca."

She dried her eyes and took a shaky breath. "Just before I phoned you yesterday, Gary and I were arguing, and the idea of putting space between us tempted me."

"But now you're not so sure?"

She sighed. "Gary heard the phone ring and was listening on the extension."

"Uh-oh."

"We had another nasty blowup, and Kevin overheard us. Now he's afraid Gary and I are going to get divorced."

Matt folded his arms. "Is that a possibility?"

She clasped her hands in her lap and closed her eyes. "I was so upset last night, I couldn't even stay in the same house with Gary, so I went to the condo. If things don't change pretty quickly, then yes, divorce is a distinct possibility."

The finality of her words echoed in the silence, the cold truth of them settling like an iceberg in her chest.

Matt rose and moved to the window. "How long have we known each other, five years now?"

She swallowed and dabbed at her eyes. "Closer to six, I think."

"Long enough to shoot straight with each other, anyway." Pushing some papers out of the way, he sat on the edge of her desk. "I know I've given you an earful about the pitfalls of marrying within the company. Even so, I've always thought you and Gary had a good thing going. I'd hate to see you two split up."

"Why?" Rebecca snapped, her voice raspy. "Wouldn't it solve everyone's problems? I'd no longer have to put up with Noelle's rudeness, and Gary would have no choice but to deal with his daughter. More importantly, Kevin wouldn't be subjected to the never-ending emotional chaos. And maybe . . ."

Maybe what? Did she really think there was a chance of reuniting with Rob? Once upon a time they'd taken solemn vows before God to love, honor, and cherish each other. Yes, she'd been young and naïve. And yes, Rob had broken those vows more than once, then removed any chance of reconciling when he'd walked out on her and Kevin. It had taken years to get over the desolation his betrayal had caused—years to let herself believe in love again.

Until she met Gary.

"I want you to go home," Matt stated.

She jerked her head up. "What?"

He moved to the other side of her desk and picked up the file folders he'd carried in with him, obviously something he'd intended to cover with her. "Take the rest of the day off. Tomorrow, too, if necessary." He nailed her with a pointed gaze. "I don't want you back in this office until you are one hundred percent certain about your decision, whatever it is. Anything less, and you're worthless to me, worthless to DataTech. *Do you understand?*"

The office door slammed behind him, and Rebecca sat in mute shock for several long minutes. Quietly she shut down her computer and gathered up her handbag and briefcase. Stepping into the outer office, she paused at her assistant's desk. "Craig, could you please cancel those teleconferences I'd scheduled for this afternoon?"

"Sure, ma'am." The young man looked up with concern.

"You can call my cell phone if anything urgent comes up."

"Is everything okay? I noticed you didn't seem yourself when you came in this morning."

"It's a private family matter, but thank you for asking." She started for the corridor.

"Whatever it is, I'll be praying for you," Craig called after her.

She paused and offered him a quick nod of gratitude. Craig had become her administrative assistant only a few months ago, and she hadn't had many opportunities to get to know him on a personal level. Now his offer of prayer, completely unexpected, was a welcome reminder that no matter how alone she felt, God still cared.

Dressed in T-shirt, jeans, and sneakers, Rebecca felt strangely exhilarated driving to Kevin's school to pick him up. She parked in the drive-through, joining the queue of other waiting parents, and watched for Kevin to exit the building. Spotting him, she stepped from the car and waved. When his quick smile of recognition changed to bewilderment, she felt a prick of motherly delight at being able to surprise him.

Kevin slid into the passenger seat. "Why aren't you at work, Mom?" Before she could answer, a terrified look came over him. "Oh, man, it's bad news, isn't it? After you left last night, I was so scared."

Before leaving for the condo yesterday, she'd told Kevin about Matt's offer, saying she needed some time alone to think things over. She should have known her showing up at school like this might cause him to assume the worst. "It's okay, honey. Nothing bad like what you're thinking."

"Then why aren't you at work?"

"Would you believe I got 'expelled' for the day?"

He cast her a puzzled look. "Huh?"

"My boss is worried about me. He doesn't want me making any snap decisions." She pulled away from the curb and headed onto the street.

Kevin hugged his books to his chest and stared straight ahead. "I thought maybe you'd already decided."

"No, honey, there's too much at stake." Rebecca let a long

breath slip out as she pulled up to a stop sign. "I definitely don't want to make you change schools again, but I can't bear the idea of commuting to Austin every week and leaving you here while your dad and Noelle are still fighting so much." She gave her head a quick shake. "Your dad—Gary—I don't know how to refer to him anymore where you're concerned."

"Yeah, I know. It's weirding me out, too. I love Dad—Gary. I hardly even know my real dad."

"Another point of concern." Rebecca waited for an opening and then turned left into the after-school traffic. "If I did take you to Austin with me, it would be harder for you to spend time with your father."

"But I like my new school, and being away from Dad—Gary —" He made a choking noise and drew his shirt sleeve across his eyes. "I'm sorry, Mom, but Gary *is* my dad. He's the only dad I've ever known."

"I know, I know." She turned off the busy street and wound through a neighborhood park. Though she and Gary had only been married a few months, Kevin had latched on to him from the start, eating up the fatherly attention he never had the chance to receive from Rob. Stopping in the shade of an elm tree near some picnic tables, she shut off the ignition. "Let's take a walk."

Fall color came slowly to Texas, but a few trees showed early signs of gold and orange. Rebecca's sneakers stirred up tiny clouds of dust as she and Kevin walked along the shaded path.

With a sigh, she began, "No one is more confused than I am about what's happening in our lives. I've prayed and prayed about what to do, how to cope with all these changes and surprises." She rested a hand on his bony shoulder. "I can only imagine how hard it is for you. I wish I could make it easier for both of us."

"Sometimes I wish we could just move back to the condo. Noelle doesn't like having me around, and it makes me mad how she treats you. And she walks all over Dad like he's dirt." Kevin kicked a stone. "Why can't things be like they used to be?"

Chest aching, Rebecca sadly shook her head. "Things will never be like they used to be. All we can do is try our best to accept the changes and ask God to help us grow through them."

They strolled in thoughtful silence for a while, and then Kevin spoke. "So are you taking the job in Austin or not?"

She stopped walking and pulled her son into her arms. It astonished her all over again that she could no longer easily rest her chin on his silky blond head. He'd be a teenager soon, then driving, graduating, heading off to college. How quickly time passed, how fleeting the chance to make a difference in her own child's life, to do right by him, to give him the best possible start in a terribly mixed-up world.

"Oh, Kevin," she said, tears welling, "I love you so much. I never, ever wanted to drag you into this mess."

"I know, Mom." He sniffled. "Hey, remember when I was little, before you met Dad, and you used to play that old song you like and we'd sing it together?"

"'You and Me Against the World.' I was just thinking about it the other day." The melody echoed in her mind, and she hummed the first few notes.

"So don't be sad, Mom," Kevin said. "It'll always be you and me. And just like in the song, no matter how bad things get, God's on our side."

She swallowed over the boulder-sized lump in her throat. "Yeah, I know. But it's always nice to be reminded." She gave his neck an affectionate squeeze and they walked a little farther. "Well, you've helped me settle one important issue today. Taking the Austin job definitely feels wrong. There are too many reasons to say no, and you're right there at the top of the list."

"I know what I said about not wanting to move and all," Kevin began, slowing his stride, "but I'd feel really bad if you turned down a job you want because of me."

"It's more than that. Just like in the song, loving someone means you stick up for each other, even in the bad times.

Running away from problems doesn't help." Which was exactly what accepting the Austin job would have amounted to.

Kevin's voice grew timid. "Then . . . you and Dad . . . you're staying together?"

She paused under a chinaberry tree and fingered a red-tinged leaf. "I don't know yet, Kev. If Gary and I can't reconcile our differences, then I honestly don't see how our staying together would be good for us—much less for you and Noelle."

Gary hadn't been able to concentrate on anything all day. At least Charles Sharp hadn't been in town to witness his abysmal meltdown during the morning staff meeting. Attempting to update his colleagues on the Tokyo project, he'd forgotten names, misquoted statistics, and generally displayed utter incompetence.

After the staff meeting fiasco, he found himself outside Rebecca's office. If only she'd give him a chance to make up for how horribly wrong things had gone yesterday. If only he could undo all the mistakes he'd made as a husband and father.

Craig, her assistant, greeted him with an apologetic frown. "Sir, she's not in."

"Not . . . in?" Disappointment curdled in the pit of his stomach.

"No, sir, she left for the day. She . . . didn't tell you?"

Without answering, he turned slowly and walked away. The rest of the afternoon he couldn't shake the terrifying sense that his marriage was very nearly over, and surely would be if he didn't act soon.

Sitting behind his desk, he pressed his knuckles into his eye sockets. Drinking on the job was one temptation he'd managed to resist so far, but days like this sorely tested his resolve.

Besides, he'd promised Rebecca more than once he'd stay sober—although he wasn't sure a promise made under duress amounted to much. They'd talked endlessly yesterday afternoon yet still found themselves miles from resolving the conflict between them. As stunned as he'd been to learn Rebecca was seriously considering the Austin position, it cut him to the marrow when she admitted her primary motivation—the fact that she felt so out of touch with her own husband.

"But you can't leave me," he'd argued. "I need you. I depend on you."

"For what? Advice about Noelle that you won't even follow? Someone to play 'bad cop' to your 'good cop' when discipline is in order? Well, I'm tired of the game. I'm tired of always being the strong, dependable one. What about *my* needs? When do I get to lean on you for support and understanding?"

And then Noelle had arrived home from her weekend trip, and he'd had no choice but to break off their discussion and deal with his daughter's failing notices. The next thing he knew, Rebecca had packed an overnight bag and announced she was spending the night at the condo.

"You can't. What about Kevin? He won't understand—"

"He already doesn't understand. I've already talked to him. He can get himself on the school bus in the morning. He'll be fine."

"Are you leaving me?" The question had torn through his throat, but she'd walked out without giving him an answer.

Now, as he stared at his honeymoon photo next to the desk phone, the question crashed around in his mind all the more.

Are you leaving me?

"Oh, God—" Returning to the present, he opened his eyes, leaned forward, and clasped his hands. *Was he praying?* No. No, he wasn't ready to take that step yet.

On the other hand, help from on high might well be his only hope out of this mess. "If You're there, God—if You even care— then You know I've failed in every way possible. I love Rebecca, and I can't lose her. I've made a mess of my marriage, of my entire life, *and I need help.*"

17

Returning home after their stop at the park, Rebecca sent Kevin to the game room, then collapsed onto the sofa, her thoughts still in turmoil. Maybe she should pack a few more of her things and return to the condo. How could she spend another day in this house where she felt so unwelcome? Another night in the same bed with Gary?

She could take Kevin with her, leave a little earlier in the mornings to drive him back to Arden Heights Middle School. If her marriage really was over, maybe she could eventually buy a little house in the community, not too big but with a nice backyard and the white picket fence she'd always dreamed of. In any case, she absolutely refused to uproot her son again.

Thwack!

Heaving a sigh, Rebecca meandered to the game room doorway and watched her son line up another shot. They'd definitely need a house with space enough for a pool table.

"Wanna play me, Mom?"

She shook her head and angled him a crooked smile. "Maybe another time."

The doorbell rang, and she turned to answer it. Through the

peephole she recognized Warren's mother, from next door. Debby Ames shifted from foot to foot, glancing toward her own house every few seconds as if she couldn't decide whether to go or stay.

Though they'd spoken a few times in passing, their conversations had always been awkward, shadowed by unspoken reminders of how close the Ames family had been with Kate.

She hauled in a lungful of air, stiffened her shoulders, and pulled open the door. "Hi, Debby. Can I help you?"

The woman flipped her head around and shot Rebecca a shaky grin. "Hi, Rebecca. I saw your car pull up and . . . well . . . I don't mean to intrude, but you're not usually at home this time of day, so I wondered . . . I mean, there's nothing wrong, I hope?"

"We're fine." *Not by a long shot.* "I'm just taking the rare afternoon off. I picked up Kevin from school and we stopped for a walk in the park."

"Perfect day for it, isn't it? Well, I'm sure glad everything's okay. Oh, here, this is for you." She thrust a foil-wrapped loaf into Rebecca's hands. "I made banana bread today and thought I'd share."

The bread was still warm, the nutty-fruity aroma tempting Rebecca's taste buds. "How very kind of you. It smells wonderful."

"Well, I should let you get on with whatever you were doing." Debby turned to leave.

An unexpected urgency filled Rebecca, perhaps the aching need for another woman's friendship. This was the life she'd always longed for, wasn't it—the life she remembered from her childhood? Neighbors visiting back and forth, exchanging baked goods, chatting over coffee.

She burst out, "This banana bread would sure taste good with a cup of English breakfast tea. Would you have some with me?"

Debby paused, her smile softening. "That would be real nice. Thank you."

Rebecca showed her to the kitchen, although the longtime neighbor no doubt knew the house better than Rebecca did.

While Debby served them each two hefty slices of banana bread, Rebecca started the electric teakettle and brought cups, saucers, and the box of teabags to the table. "Sugar or sweetener? And would you like milk?"

"Just sugar, please."

The teakettle clicked off, and Rebecca poured boiling water into their cups. While the tea steeped, they munched silently on the banana bread.

Debby sipped her tea and cast an appraising glance around the room. "Everything looks just like it always did." Her eyes met Rebecca's for a split second before she dropped her gaze to her plate.

Rebecca's neighborly thoughts cooled slightly. "Yes, well . . . it helps Noelle." As if anything did. She'd long ago surmised this was less about Noelle's comfort than the girl exercising her power over the household.

Debby clicked her tongue. "Kate told me last summer how she'd come up with the idea that Gary and y'all should move in here after she died. I've been hoping for the chance to tell you how much I admire you for making this decision."

Rebecca stirred her tea. "I took quite a bit of convincing."

"I'm sure, and believe me, I know it must be hard."

"Hard? That's an understatement."

Debby's mouth quirked. "Honey, I've known Noelle long enough to understand exactly what a handful she can be. You're a saint to be putting up with her."

If the woman only knew how close Rebecca was to giving up and walking away. She leaned back, hands upraised. "I am no saint!"

"Hey, Mom." Kevin loped into the kitchen. "Hi, Mrs. Ames."

"How're you doing, Kevin?" Debby went to the counter and cut off a slice of banana bread for Kevin, then smiled over her shoulder at Rebecca. "Quite a gentleman you raised here. One day when the school bus dropped him off, he noticed I was trying to lift a big box the UPS driver left, and he came over to help. We had a nice long chat that day, didn't we, Kev?"

"Warren has some neat video games, Mom. Mrs. Ames said I can come over after school and play sometimes." Kevin stuffed half the slice of bread into his mouth and grabbed a juice box from the fridge.

Slightly envious her son had already made such good friends with the neighbors, Rebecca tried to keep her voice level. "Don't spoil your supper, Kevin."

"Yes, ma'am." He spun around, waved at them over his shoulder, and jogged back to the game room.

"Such a polite young man." Debby added more hot water to her teacup and offered some to Rebecca before reclaiming her chair. "I think he's a good influence on Noelle."

Hiking a brow, Rebecca dunked her teabag. "Really?"

"It's good for her to have a little brother. It's teaching her patience and kindness, makes her think of somebody besides herself."

"I hadn't noticed."

Debby gave a sad chuckle. "Yes, she hides it well." She sipped her tea. "It's good for Noelle having you in her life too."

Rebecca shoved her chair back and carried her dishes to the sink. "I'm the *last* person Noelle wants in her life."

"Sorry if I spoke out of turn." Debby appeared at her side and set her own dishes on the counter. "It's just that I know how badly the girl needs a mother figure. Not to take her real mother's place, but as a friend, a constant."

"Noelle spends so much time with Warren at your house that I thought you were filling the role."

"I do what I can, but it isn't the same. You're her family now."

"Not if Noelle has anything to say about it. In fact, I have serious doubts about how long this arrangement can continue." Rebecca shot a glance toward the game room and lowered her voice. "Before you came over, I was on the verge of packing up and moving back to our condo."

Debby studied Rebecca's face. "You mean just you and your son. Without Gary." When Rebecca answered with one silent nod, Debby swiveled away and thrust a hand to her forehead. "Why, I could wring that stubborn child's neck. I'll have a talk with her. I'll—"

"No, don't. Don't make matters worse than they are." Rebecca hugged herself. "Besides, it's not entirely her fault. Things between Gary and me have been tense for a while now. We have our own problems to work out, things that have nothing to do with Noelle." Well, *almost* nothing.

No, the issues with Noelle were only symptoms of a much deeper problem, one that Rebecca no longer felt she had the strength to fight.

Debby crossed to the breakfast bar and busied herself rewrapping the foil around the remaining banana bread. "I won't presume to tell you how to deal with your marital situation, but I pray, for Noelle's sake and for yours, that you can work things out. The last thing that girl needs is the breakup of the only family she has left."

Debby's words echoed in Rebecca's thoughts long after they said goodbye at the front door. Returning to the kitchen, she made herself another cup of tea and carried it to the guest room. Time for some serious soul-searching.

As if she hadn't been doing plenty already.

She crawled onto the bed and propped pillows against the headboard, then balanced her cup and saucer on her drawn-up knees. Maybe it wasn't fair to knock one more prop from beneath Noelle's shaky foundation. Even so, Rebecca couldn't quite believe the truth of Debby's words—that Noelle *needed* her. The girl didn't act as if she needed *anyone!*

And yet . . . Noelle's pain seemed achingly familiar. How could Rebecca so easily forget her own stewpot of emotions after her father died? She'd been angry and confused, swinging between an overwhelming sense of desertion and the absolute certainty that the medical examiner had identified the wrong man. Then Mom went to work full-time, which piled on Rebecca's responsibilities at home. It hadn't been easy, but she'd learned valuable lessons about initiative and self-reliance.

At least Rebecca's mother hadn't abandoned her emotionally, as Gary had with Noelle. Even working eight or ten hours a day, Mom had never lost track of what was happening in her daughter's life, never allowed herself to become unavailable when Rebecca most needed her. When Rob's desertion forced her to join the ranks of single mothers in the workforce, she'd tried her best to follow her mother's example.

But sometimes it was hard. So very, very hard. What made her believe that once she and Gary were married, things would get easier? She certainly hadn't married him for the sole purpose of bringing a father figure into Kevin's life, but creating a stable, two-parent home had definitely held its appeal.

On the other hand, there was nothing *stable* about their current situation.

And just because she could empathize with Noelle didn't mean the problems between them would magically disappear. Was she crazy for contemplating sticking it out a while longer? Would moving out only make things worse, for all of them?

The diamond on her left ring finger flickered in a slanting sunbeam. All right, she'd stay. For now. But only because she wouldn't be the one to tip over this already rocking boat.

But I'm telling You, God, if You don't fix things soon, don't be surprised if I abandon ship.

Rebecca lifted her cup to her lips only to find the tea had grown cold. Just like her marriage.

Just like her heart.

One by one, Noelle returned the signed failing notices to her teachers, each time having to explain why she'd held them for an entire week. By the third time, she had her excuse memorized: "My father is a very busy person and I didn't get a chance to talk to him until yesterday."

It wasn't exactly a lie. She simply left out the part about how hard it was to care about grades these days—much less give her father any more control over her life than he already had. Too bad she hadn't given more consideration to the consequences.

As for keeping up with her studies, she could no longer use the excuse of having to memorize her lines since she now knew them perfectly—and everybody else's as well. By the following Friday she'd brought her daily work averages in the three problem classes up to a passing seventy. Now, if only she could keep her grades up through exams.

The weekend was ushered in by the first cold front and an autumn thunderstorm. Torrents of rain and lightning bolts sliced through thick, black clouds. Watching swaths of rain sweep down the sunroom windows, Noelle let out a frustrated groan. There would be no escaping the house today. Probably just as well, considering all the studying she needed to do. She pulled her fuzzy bathrobe tighter around her waist and shoved her hands into its deep pockets.

"Breakfast," Rebecca called from the kitchen.

Noelle shuffled through the den, turning up her nose at the pungent aroma of brewing coffee. Dad liked it so strong the smell was almost nauseating.

Kevin laughed and pointed at Noelle as she sat down at the table. "Your hair!"

"If you don't want to look at me, go eat somewhere else." She flicked a snarled lock away from her face and took the chair across from her father. Eyes lowered, she spooned a serving of rubbery scrambled eggs onto her plate.

"There's water in the teakettle if you'd like some hot chocolate." Rebecca sat down and buttered a slice of toast.

Noelle's heart clenched at the sight of her mother's apothecary jar sitting on the counter, now almost half empty. Apparently someone in the house had been enjoying Mom's cocoa mix recipe.

The roar of the thunderstorm gave way to a loud, steady clatter. Kevin swiveled his head toward the bay window. "What's that awful noise?"

Marble-sized hail pelted the lawn and driveway. From her place at the table, Noelle could just see the trunk section of Rebecca's blue BMW as ice chunks bombarded it.

Rebecca's chair scraped across the tile as she flew to the window. "Oh, no, my car! Gary—" She turned to him with a stricken look.

"There's no room in the garage. There's nothing we can do." He went to stand beside Rebecca, both of them staring into the storm.

A pang of empathy caught Noelle by surprise. "Oh, wow, your poor car." Then she pictured her father's silver Lincoln Navigator parked in the garage next to Mom's convertible, the way it should be, the way it should always have been. All kind thoughts toward Rebecca evaporated. She forked up a mouthful of eggs. "Hope you got insurance."

Rebecca whirled around, eyes shooting daggers. "You don't care one whit about my car, or about anything that concerns me. You only care about yourself, and apparently not all that much. Your room's a mess, your laundry's piling up—" Disgust contorted her expression. She opened her mouth as if she had plenty more to say, then clenched her jaw and bolted from the room.

Scrambled eggs stuck in Noelle's throat. She cast a stunned look at her father. "I wasn't trying to be rude. I just meant—"

His cold stare unnerved her. "Sorry, kid, I've defended you to Rebecca for the last time."

"Dad?" The word froze on her lips, like in one of those special-effects movies where suddenly everything stretches out, like time and space being ripped apart.

Exactly like her life.

Dad strode to the breakfast bar and spread his hands across the granite surface. Exhaling sharply, he turned with a glare. "Your mother used to talk about you with such pride, how you were growing up to be a caring, kind, loving young woman." His penetrating gaze cut deep. "What happened to that girl?"

She let her hands fall into her lap and gazed at her plate. "When did Mom ever talk to you about me?"

"Oh, let's see." When she glanced up, Dad had extended his arms like one of those TV preachers about to call down judgment. "How about when I phoned to see how your mom was doing, to ask if there was anything she needed? Or the times you hung up on me and made your grandmother answer the phone the next time it rang."

"You hardly ever called."

His arms fell to his sides. "True. I could have done more, done better, and I'll never be able to make up for it. But even if I could, you're intent on never letting me forget it. You're hurting me, you're hurting Rebecca, and even Kevin, who had no part in any of this." Grimacing, he sadly shook his head. "You're living on anger, and you're blaming your problems on everyone but yourself."

"Shut up!" She pressed her hands to her ears. "Shut up, shut up, *shut up!*" Her chair fell backwards against the wall as she scrambled away from the table and tore down the hall to her room.

Panting, she slammed the door and fell against it, hugging her ribcage. "It's not true! It's not, it's *not! Mother!*"

She slid to the floor. Her chest heaved and her lips trembled, but her only answer was the rain beating against the windows and thunder echoing in the distance. It was as if the whole sky were crying for her, crying the tears she couldn't release, even now.

Dignity, Noelle . . . I'm counting on you.

"I'm sorry, Mom," she said on a rasping moan. "I don't have any dignity left."

Gary sank into his chair, his hand trembling as he lifted his coffee mug to his lips. The pungent brew had long since cooled, but he barely noticed. He gulped, blinked, tried to marshal his thoughts. Had he really said those things to his daughter? Were they the *right* things?

Yes. Yes, he'd spoken the truth to her at last. And to himself.

"Dad?"

Setting his coffee mug aside, he glanced at Kevin. The boy stared at him as if he were a stranger.

He whistled softly, a small semblance of calm returning. "I'm sorry you had to witness that."

Kevin heaved a one-shoulder shrug, then frowned toward the den. "Do you think Mom's okay? She looked really upset."

"Yeah, I should go check on her." He rose and ruffled Kevin's hair, then impulsively bent over the boy's head and planted a kiss on those tousled locks.

On his way through the den, he glimpsed Rebecca shivering in the sunroom. She stared through the rain-sheeted outer glass as the downpour splashed into the pool and washed across the patio. He had so much he needed to say to her, but he couldn't just walk in there and take her in his arms and comfort her. Somehow, he felt as if he'd lost that right. Finally he opened the door and stepped beside her. "Honey, I'm really sorry about your car."

Her shoulders tensed, and she moved a step away. "As Noelle so thoughtfully pointed out, the insurance will take care of it."

His anger surged again. How had he ever allowed a rebellious teenager to dictate how his family would function? He closed his eyes, ran his hand across his forehead. "Starting today, it's over. Noelle's stranglehold on us is finished."

Rebecca glanced at him briefly, a flicker of doubt in her eyes. "What do you mean?"

"You didn't hear the heated exchange I just had with her?"

"The door was closed. All I heard was yelling."

"Just as well. It wasn't pretty." He moved closer, shyly stretching his arm around her. When she didn't pull away, he closed his eyes in gratitude. "I'm going to do better, I promise."

Rebecca spoke with a tremor in her voice. "I know you want to—at least I want to believe it. But the way you've allowed Noelle to come between us—it's hurt me deeply, Gary."

"I realize that now. And you've got to believe me when I say I'm going to change."

"Words come cheap," she replied, and he sensed the subtle tensing of her body before she shrugged off his embrace. "I should get some chores done."

He should have known she wouldn't quickly forgive him, let alone trust him again. How could he blame her? Somehow he'd have to prove he intended to change. He rested his forehead on the cool glass of the sunroom door and muttered the only prayer he could muster: "God, help."

This prayer thing was becoming a habit—but did he really believe it could make a difference? What was it about the human psyche that needed to believe in a higher power? Why this compulsion to entrust one's life, one's very being, into the hands of the Invisible? No matter how hard he tried to make things work, time and again, fate—God, karma, whatever people chose to call it—stepped in and drastically altered his best laid plans.

Then again, his relationship failures were certainly not God's doing—he'd succeeded in destroying those just fine on his own.

Rebecca had once said that if God chose to allow problems

and heartbreak, He could be trusted to redeem the experience by bringing something good out of it—a lesson to be learned, a truth to be grasped, a character trait to be developed.

If that's true, God, You've got my attention.

At the next roll of thunder, he backed away from the glass and turned to go inside. Just then, Noelle crossed the den, her arms laden with dirty plates and glasses, and he stepped back before she noticed him. Had his words gotten through to her? At least she'd dressed and combed her hair. He waited silently as she returned from the kitchen and trudged back down the hall.

With an exhausted moan, he went inside. He followed the sounds of billiard balls and found Kevin in the game room. "Where's your mom?"

"She left to run some errands." *Thwack.* The nine-ball sent the four-ball spinning before rolling cleanly into the corner pocket.

"You're getting pretty good at this game."

Kevin grinned and handed him a cue stick. "Best two out of three?"

Noelle felt numb all over, except for her head, which throbbed unmercifully. She'd cleared out the dirty dishes. Time to tackle the piles of discarded clothing. Bending stiffly, she began to sort through the mess in front of her closet, pairing up shoes and boots, separating the clothes into batches for the washer. As she hefted an overflowing laundry basket, she glimpsed a glass she'd missed on her nightstand—the one containing the putrid-smelling, milk-coated ponytail band. She dumped it, glass and all, into the trash. "Noelle Townsend, you truly are disgusting."

She spent the rest of the day making trips to and from the laundry room, this time carefully folding or hanging up each item as it came from the dryer. She brushed and polished her scuffed boots and shoes and placed them neatly onto the shoe rack. She changed her sheets and made her bed, then took a dust cloth to her furniture and vacuumed the carpet. By mid-afternoon, the room looked normal again, everything in its place, exactly as she'd always kept things . . . until last summer.

To finish off her day's work, she climbed into the shower for an all-over scrubbing. If only she could wash deep enough to get rid of the ugliness inside herself! *Oh, God, what's wrong with me? Will I ever feel right again? Will this pain ever go away?*

Later, dressed in a clean pair of jeans and a sweatshirt, she braided her damp hair, then scraped up her courage to deal with this morning's aftermath. Rebecca's sudden outburst at breakfast had been a shock, and though the scared and scarred little girl inside Noelle wanted with all her being to deny she'd deserved such anger, she couldn't escape the truth. Now, like it or not, she owed Rebecca an apology—and for a lot more than her insensitive remark about the car insurance.

Traipsing through the house, she found her father in the game room with Kevin, lining up a shot on the pool table. She gave a small cough. "Excuse me."

Her father's cue slid off the white ball and almost tore a hole in the felt. "Noelle. You startled me."

She took a step nearer, lowering her gaze. "I . . . um . . . I know I've been awful lately. To Rebecca and Kevin . . . and to you." Her throat closed, but she lifted her chin and forced herself to continue. "Before Mom died, she talked a lot about how I needed to live with courage and dignity. I'm sorry I don't live up to her expectations." She turned to leave.

"Wait," her father said. "I'm sorry, too. It's taken way too long, but I understand now how much I've let you down over the years. It would mean a lot to me if . . . if we could have a fresh start."

Her eyes burned. She pushed a strand of damp hair away from her face. "I think I saw some pizzas in the freezer. Unless y'all had other plans, I could heat them up and make a salad for supper."

"Rebecca's out running some errands, but I'm sure she'd appreciate it. Thank you."

Starting for the kitchen, Noelle pressed a hand against her fluttering stomach. This truce thing wouldn't be easy, but she had to try, because she was so, so tired of being angry all the time.

"Why are you here, Rebecca?" Rob's tone was gentle, his narrowed gaze unnervingly perceptive.

She blinked. How could she reply, when there was no simple answer? She'd been sitting on his sofa for the past ten minutes, saying little, pondering much, and utterly overwhelmed by an avalanche of complicated emotions. A trip to the grocery store had turned into another pilgrimage to the empty condo. She'd wandered through the stark white rooms and the ultra-modern furnishings, decor that was more Gary's than hers but beautiful for its clean simplicity. Perhaps it was subconscious at the time, but maybe she'd left everything as it was because she'd needed to remind herself that she was an urban, career-centered woman. Her dream of life as a contented suburban wife and mother was simply that—a dream.

"Rebecca?" Again, Rob's voice drew her back to the present.

She mentally shook herself. "I'm sorry. I've taken terrible advantage, dropping in unannounced like this. I'm not sure why, except—I guess I just needed to ... to ..."

He rested his hands on his knees. "Why don't you quit stalling and tell me what's going on."

With images of her suburban fantasy life dancing across her mind's eye, she tried to picture sharing it first with Rob and then with Gary. Oddly, neither of them fit.

She rose abruptly. "It was wrong for me to come here. I don't know what I was thinking."

As she snatched up her purse and started for the door, Rob caught her wrist. "Stop running, Becky. I need you to be honest with me and yourself about why you came here today."

Her gaze locked with his. With a frightening loss of control over both her brain and her vocal chords, her next words flew out before she could stop them. "Do you still love me? Is there any chance you and I—"

"Whoa, hold on." He backed up two steps and lifted his hands. A regretful laugh escaped his lips. "Yeah, I admit, the thought crossed my mind when I first moved back to town, but it was obvious you'd moved on with Gary. And besides, you and I aren't the same people we were back in college."

Hot shame singed her neck and cheeks. Her breath quickened, and she hid her face behind her hands. "Forget I said anything, please. How could I have been so stupid?"

Tenderly Rob guided her hands to her sides. "Rebecca Marshall Townsend, you are anything but stupid. You are a wonderful and amazing woman, and I am so proud to share a son with you. But am I still in love with you? No, not in that way. Like I said, we've both changed."

Her face still burned, and she could not bring herself to meet his gaze. "I know. You're right. I'm sorry."

Hesitantly, Rob asked, "Do you still have feelings for me?"

Slowly, she shook her head. "I honestly don't know what I feel anymore."

"Then sit back down and let's talk this out." He eased her into the nearest chair. "Besides, you're in no frame of mind to be driving."

A stifled sob escaped as she dropped her purse onto the floor beside her. Eyes closed, she heaved a few shaky breaths until she felt calm enough to speak. With a sigh, she began, "Things have gotten so much more complicated since we moved in with Noelle.

Gary and I are arguing entirely too often, and I can't stop wondering if marrying him was a huge mistake."

Brow creased, Rob settled onto the ottoman in front of her but maintained a respectful distance between them. "Are you thinking of leaving him?"

"I almost did, until our next-door neighbor convinced me how much worse it would make things for Noelle." Her fists knotted. "Lately *everything* is about Noelle. I have tried so hard to be accommodating and patient, to give Gary time to work things out with his daughter, to give Noelle time to accept me. But lately it feels like living on the slope of a volcano about to erupt."

She stared at her wedding band and told Rob about being offered the DataTech promotion and then turning it down. Then her conversation with Debby Ames and a long week of trying her best simply to endure. "Everything came to a head this morning. I stopped just short of giving Noelle a huge piece of my mind, but then Gary blew up at her, and afterward he promised me things are going to change—that *he* is going to change. I can see signs that he wants to, but I don't think I have the strength to trust him and wait it out." The tears flowed, and she buried her face in her hands. "I keep asking God if all these problems are my punishment for divorcing and remarrying in the first place."

Rob knelt beside her chair, taking her in his strong arms. As before, the familiar masculine smells of spices and warm skin threatened to undo her. Just as quickly, the physical attraction subsided, and she allowed herself to accept the tender concern of a trusted friend.

"Ah, now things are starting to make more sense." He sat back on the ottoman and took her hands. "Sounds like we need a refresher course on a few things. Number one, I'm the one who walked out on you. You would have worked like crazy to keep us together, for Kevin's sake if nothing else, if I hadn't been such a self-centered jerk and pushed you for the divorce. Number two, two wrongs don't make a right. You're married to Gary now, for better or for worse—or weren't those words part of your wedding vows?"

She nodded. "But I didn't realize there would end up being a lot more 'worse' than 'better.'"

"Point number three. One of the first things I learned after God took hold of me is that the past is the past. Whatever mistakes we've made, including messing up at marriage, God's already forgiven us. We may face consequences for our poor choices, but Jesus has already taken our punishment."

"You're right, I know." Rebecca found a tissue in her purse and dabbed the wetness from her cheeks. "When I married Gary, I married him for a lifetime. I can't give up. Not yet."

"That's the Rebecca I know." Rob tweaked her chin. "Trust me, God will see you through this."

She glanced at Rob and bit her lip. "You're right about one thing. You are definitely not the same man I remember."

"And why did it take me so long to change?" He gave a rueful laugh. "If I knew back then what I know today . . . I don't dare let myself imagine how differently things might have turned out."

She nodded, unable to find her voice. Something had changed inside, a door closed, a corner turned, a glimmer of hope that hadn't been there an hour ago. Standing tiredly, she pocketed her damp tissue and retrieved her car keys. "I should go. My family's waiting."

18

The savory aromas of tomato sauce, garlic, melting cheese, and yeasty dough met Rebecca as she stepped into the foyer. The family must have started supper without her. How had it grown so late? She set her purse on the hall table and turned hesitantly toward the kitchen.

"Just in time." Gary set a steaming, bubbling pizza on a trivet in the center of the table.

"Hi, Rebecca," came a shy voice from behind Gary. *Noelle?* "What would you like to drink? I just made a fresh pitcher of iced tea—decaf, the way you like it." She peered into the refrigerator. "Or we have Diet Coke, Seven-Up, root beer . . ."

"I, uh . . ." *Am I in the right house?* "Iced tea is fine."

"Coming right up. Dad? Kevin?"

While Noelle filled drink requests, Rebecca freshened up in the bathroom and then took her seat at the table. She glanced toward Gary but kept her eyes lowered. "Sorry I was out so long. Thanks for getting supper ready."

Gary served her a slice of pizza. "Noelle gets the credit. Kevin and I just followed orders."

Rebecca tried to keep the shock out of her voice. "That's . . . that's really nice of you, Noelle. Thanks."

The girl rolled her eyes. "It's just frozen pizza. Any idiot can turn the oven on." She gave a small gasp. "I mean, it was something easy to fix and I thought—"

"It's okay, I understand." Rebecca unfolded her napkin across her lap. "Kevin, would you pass the salad dressing?"

He nudged the bottle of Italian toward her. "Where were you all afternoon, Mom? You were gone, like, forever!"

"Yeah, hon." Under the table, Gary's hand found her knee. He gave it a timid squeeze. "We missed you."

"I had . . . some things to sort out." She took a bite of pizza, but it stuck like a hunk of glue halfway down her throat. She reached for her tea glass and swallowed two quick sips. Best to change the subject before this day of roller-coaster emotions threw her off balance again. "It must be getting close to your play performance, Noelle. How are rehearsals going?"

Noelle glanced up as if startled. A string of mozzarella stretched like a spider web from the pizza slice she held. "The play? It's going great. Just great."

"Great. I can't wait to see it."

Conversation continued in the same hesitant vein for the rest of the meal, but at least no verbal brawls broke out. Gary seemed especially subdued, and also noticeably more attentive. Without being asked, he got up to refill Rebecca's glass, even remembered to bring her another lemon wedge and sweetener packet.

And there sat Kevin wearing a Cheshire-cat smile. Obviously, the boy thought they'd reached some sort of turning point.

"Thanks again for making supper, Noelle." Rebecca crumpled her napkin beside her plate.

"Really, it was nothing." Noelle rose to clear the table.

No, Rebecca thought, her throat constricting, *it was everything.*

First thing every morning for the next week, Noelle gave herself a little pep talk: "I won't sass my dad. I won't be rude to Rebecca. And I won't snap at Kevin. I'll pay attention in class. I'll study hard and turn my homework in on time. I'll smile at Cassie and ask her how it's going with Warren. And I won't unload my problems on them. I can do it. I can make it through the day . . . one day at a time."

Thanks to Saturday's confrontation with Rebecca and then Dad laying it on the line, she'd been forced to admit how badly she'd messed up. But maybe she wasn't completely hopeless. If she could only get control of her attitude! She had a lot of changes to make—and a lot of forgiving to do. No matter how hard Dad tried to make up for the past, it still hurt remembering the many times he'd failed her.

Now it was Thursday evening of the third week in October. Grade reports had come out today, and Noelle breathed a little easier with her C-plus scores in biology, history, and geometry. She showed her grades to her father at supper without saying a word.

"This is good, Noelle. I knew you could do it." Taking his Cross pen from his monogrammed shirt pocket, Dad signed the paper and handed it back.

In her room later, finishing up a geometry assignment, she jumped when her cell phone threatened to vibrate itself right off her nightstand.

It was her grandmother. Noelle pushed her hair behind her ear. "Hey, Gran!"

"Hi, honey! How are things with you? Did you get my last email?"

"Sorry I haven't written back." She chewed on her pencil eraser. "I've just been so busy."

"I figured as much. I've talked with your father a couple of times." Gran paused. "He's been quite concerned about you."

Noelle stared out the window at the moonlit expanse of lawn. "I've been behaving, I promise. I know I was awful in the beginning, but I apologized to Dad and Rebecca. Even Kevin."

"Don't worry, I'm not calling to lecture you." Gran cleared her throat. "In fact, I wanted to tell you I'm thinking about flying out to visit soon. I was hoping to catch opening night of your play."

Noelle brightened. "Really? That's terrific. Did I tell you Laurence even has a part?" As if recognizing his name, the cat leapt onto the bed, rubbing his head against her arm.

"I'll make flight reservations and plan to stay through the weekend."

"Super. Uncle David and Aunt Susan said they'd come too."

A pause. "Noelle, there's something else we need to talk about."

The serious tone of her grandmother's voice made her stiffen. "What is it, Gran?"

"While I'm there, we should go through your mother's things."

"Go through—" An oppressive black shadow closed in. Noelle gasped for breath. "Why?"

Gran heaved a sigh. "Because it's time. Your mother lives on in your heart, not in the possessions she left behind."

"But her things—they're all I have now."

"You have your memories, honey. They're what's important."

Hot knives sliced through Noelle's abdomen. "It's Dad, isn't it? He asked you to help him talk me into this so they could have Mom's room."

"Absolutely not. I haven't even mentioned this to your father." Her tone mellowed. "It's simply time to move on, to stop living in the past. Eventually you've got to face your grief, work through it, and go forward."

"But—"

"I really must go now, honey, but we'll talk more about it

when I visit. And please don't blame your father. This is my idea, not his."

Noelle jabbed the disconnect button and tossed her phone across the bed. Didn't matter whose idea it was. No way could she part with her mother's things. Getting rid of them would mean Mom was really, truly gone.

She slipped down the hall and into Mom's room as she did many a night when sleep wouldn't come. She lay across the pink damask spread and hid her face in her mother's pillow, her eyes aflame and yet dry as dust.

Please, God, don't make me say goodbye, not yet!

"Good afternoon, folks." Matt Garrison strode into the conference room. A murmur of tense greetings, Rebecca's among them, came in response. Matt unbuttoned his blazer, plopped his briefcase on the table, and sank into a chair. "I know you've all been anxiously awaiting the board's decision about who'll be heading up the Austin office." His gaze settled briefly on Rebecca, and she tried not to squirm. "We thought we had our top candidate ready to sign on the dotted line, but when that fell through, the board had to start from scratch."

As he continued his explanation of the selection process, Rebecca mentally tuned him out. He'd remained friendly on a personal level since she'd firmly declined the Austin job, but on a professional level Rebecca could sense his withdrawal. The premier assignments he once funneled directly to her now went to others in the department, men and women fresh out of college, hungrier, more ready to sacrifice their personal lives in pursuit of higher salaries and corner offices.

If they only knew what that kind of single-minded ambition could cost them in the long run.

"So, without further delay," Matt said, "I am pleased to

introduce our new Austin Corporate Software Accounts Director, Colette Kincaide."

The tall, poised Black woman rose to a conservative patter of applause. A tangible pall of envy chilled the atmosphere in the conference room. Despite her own conflicting feelings, Rebecca nodded in silent approval. Colette was the penultimate professional: competent, personable—and unattached. Rebecca stood and leaned across the table, offering her hand. "Let me be the first to congratulate you, Colette. The board made an excellent choice."

Colette gripped Rebecca's hand firmly, her wide brown eyes sending a silent message of understanding. "Thank you, Rebecca. Coming from you, that means a lot."

As soon as the meeting ended, Rebecca retreated to her office. She checked her interoffice email and downloaded the latest mediocre and tediously uncomplicated project Matt had assigned to her—in front of everyone in the staff meeting. Talk about rubbing salt in the wound! Every nerve sang, a restless energy simmering in the pit of her stomach. *I deserve better than this. The promotion should have been mine, not Colette's.*

A long, hot breath sizzled between her lips, and she clamped her eyes shut. How fickle could she get? Not one hour ago, woolgathering as usual during the boring remainder of the staff meeting, she'd been pondering her dream life again, imagining herself as a stay-at-home mom and there to greet Kevin with milk and cookies every afternoon when he returned from school. Then why, suddenly, did she so resent Colette Kincaide's being awarded the prestigious position that rightly should have been hers?

Make up your mind, girl. You can't have it both ways.

The intercom buzzed. She took a moment to compose herself, then hit the answer button on her desk phone. "What is it, Craig?"

"Someone's here to see you, ma'am. Colette Kincaide."

She pressed a hand to her stomach. Why couldn't the woman leave well enough alone? She had the job. Did she also need to stop by to gloat? Rebecca felt tempted to say she was in the middle of something important, but Colette, along with everyone else at the meeting, had heard Matt Garrison assign her this manifestly unimportant task.

Oh, Lord, help me be gracious. She pressed the intercom button again. "Show Ms. Kincaide in."

"Forgive me for dropping by unannounced," Colette said as Craig closed the door behind her. "Do you have a few minutes to talk?"

"Of course." Rebecca rose, giving a short laugh as she waved a hand over the scant paperwork on her desk. "It's not as if I'm in the middle of pressing business."

Colette glanced at the floor. "That's partly what I wanted to talk to you about."

"Would you care for coffee, or maybe some herbal tea?" When Colette declined, Rebecca joined her on the visitor's side of the desk, and they sat facing each other with nothing in between, nothing for either to hide behind.

Colette crossed her ankles beneath the chair and fingered a wide gold bracelet on her right wrist. She seemed far less confident than she had earlier in the conference room. "I just needed to make sure there are no hard feelings between us. The whole department knows you were Matt's first choice for the promotion. I know you turned it down, but I still feel as if I've stolen something from you."

"Don't be silly. As you said, it was my choice to decline. How could I hold anything against you?"

"It's just . . . I sensed something in the meeting, especially after Matt covered the new project assignments." Colette reached across the space between them, her dark hand resting on Rebecca's pale one. She tipped her head toward Rebecca's computer screen. "Matt did that on purpose, you know."

She nodded. "I know perfectly well."

"Then why did you do it? Say no to the promotion, I mean?" Colette's pleading look was piercing. "Is there something I should know about the job, or about Matt, perhaps? Am I going to regret accepting the position?"

"No, no, of course not. My reasons were intensely personal." Rebecca gave Colette's hand a squeeze, then looked down at the bare fingers of the woman's left hand. She held up her own in comparison, nodding toward her wedding ring. "I have a husband, a son, and a very troubled stepdaughter who recently lost her mother. Taking the Austin job would have meant deserting my family during an already difficult time."

"I didn't realize. I'm so sorry."

"You're single now, with no attachments to hold you back," Rebecca went on. "But someday you'll meet someone, maybe start a family of your own, and then you'll have some hard decisions to make."

"I don't see that happening." Colette set her hands upon the armrests. Her back stiffened. "I've worked too hard on getting an education and establishing my career. DataTech is my life."

Rebecca gazed at her sadly, and every ounce of envy and resentment drained out of her. She rose and leaned against her desk, arms crossed as she faced the trim, dark-haired woman. "DataTech is *not* your life, Colette. It tries to be. People like Matt Garrison and Charles Sharp want it to be. But watch out, because one of these days you could wake up and discover that in spite of your innumerable colleagues, subordinates, and clients, you are utterly alone." She looked away, a shiver of regret rippling through her. "And believe me, it's not a fun place to be."

Opening night for Noelle's play was barely three weeks away, and rehearsals had moved to the school auditorium. Noelle took her position at the wooden writing desk at stage right, and as she spoke her lines, she let her gaze drift across the empty seats and tried to picture them filled with spectators.

"'. . . Dagmar's different. She was always the baby—so I see her as a baby.'"

She glimpsed Warren and Cassie sitting next to each other at the end of the second row. As they followed along in a playbook, Cassie reached for Warren's hand and touched her forehead to his. He sat up straighter, shifting sideways and clearing his throat. Embarrassed about being caught in a public display of affection?

Too late, Warren. Noelle's mind went blank. Heat rose in her cheeks as she fumbled for the next line.

"What is it, Noelle?" Mrs. Sanchez tapped her director's copy with a pen. "You knew this perfectly four weeks ago."

"Sorry. Let me start over." Fixing her gaze on the exit sign over the far doors, she sucked in a noisy breath and tried again.

After a successful run-through of act one, Mrs. Sanchez announced a fifteen-minute break. Noelle slipped into her bulky cardigan and carried Laurence outside to an enclosed courtyard between the school buildings. Never straying from her side, he sniffed around for a few minutes, then batted a fallen leaf. After relieving himself in some sandy soil under a cedar tree, he mewed and rubbed against Noelle's ankles. She hugged him inside her sweater and hurried toward the auditorium.

"Hey, there you are." Cassie burst through the side door and almost knocked the cat out of Noelle's arms.

"Watch it. You'll scare Laurence." Tightening her hold on the cat, she stepped around Cassie and ducked inside.

Cassie caught up and cornered her between two rows of seats. She heaved a sigh that made her shimmy from head to toe. "Guess what, Noelle! Warren's taking me to the game and homecoming dance on Friday."

"Wow, terrific. Y'all have a great time. Can you tell me about it later? Laurence could use some quiet time in his basket before we start act two." Noelle forced a quick smile and darted toward the women's dressing room, almost colliding with Warren as he ambled up the aisle.

"Noelle—?"

"Sorry. Later, okay?" Thank goodness the dressing room was empty. Noelle pushed the door shut and leaned against it, clutching Laurence into the folds of her cardigan and breathing in the cool, earthy scent of his fur.

What was wrong with her, anyway? She'd intentionally pushed Warren and Cassie together, even offered suggestions on how Cassie could capture Warren's interest. It was supposed to feel wonderful having her two best friends fall for each other. It was supposed to cinch their friendship, link them to her forever.

Then why do I feel so alone?

Someone pounded on the door. "Noelle? Are you in there?" Cassie. "Come on, let me in." The knob pushed against Noelle's back.

Moving away, she set Laurence down and shrugged out of her sweater. "The door's open."

Cassie stepped in, eyes wide. "Are you all right? You ran away so fast, I thought maybe you were feeling sick or something."

"I told you, Laurence needed to get away from all the commotion." She plucked a wisp of cat fur off her blouse.

Cassie touched her arm. "It's Warren and me, isn't it? You're upset because he's taking me to the dance."

Noelle forced a laugh. "Are you crazy? You two are great together."

Cassie leveled her gaze at her. "Look, all you have to do is say the word and I'll back off. I couldn't stand it if my crush on Warren ruined our friendship."

"No, no! That's why—" Catching herself, Noelle bent to stroke Laurence. "I mean, don't be silly. You'll always be my best friend."

"I feel the same way about you. It's just . . . I kind of always thought it would be you and Warren getting together."

"Are you kidding? Warren and I are too much like brother and sister." Noelle gave her head a rapid shake. "There's no way we could be interested in each other . . . *that* way."

Cassie stared until Noelle finally had to tear her gaze away. "I don't know what it is about you these days. Sometimes the words you say don't match up at all with what I see in your eyes."

Hearing Mrs. Sanchez calling the cast back on stage, Noelle started for the door. "You know how crazy my life's been. Sorry if I've been a little weird. It doesn't mean anything."

Cassie caught her arm. "Are you sure?"

"Sure, I'm sure. Don't pay any attention to me." She paused in the doorway but kept her gaze averted, just in case Cassie really could read the truth in her eyes. "I couldn't be happier for you and Warren. Really." She smiled as though she meant it—she was an actress, after all—and stepped up to her stage marker, slipping instantly into the character of Katrin.

Rebecca slipped off her terry robe and shivered in the chilly evening air. The swirling, steaming waters of the hot tub quickly warmed her, and she settled her back against a pulsating jet and let it pound her tense muscles.

"May I join you?"

She looked up into Gary's timid smile. "Of course."

He set two iced drinks on the coping, tossed his towel over a chair, and then felt his way down the steps. As he situated himself next to her, she eyed the drinks with a wrinkled brow.

"Don't give me that look. It's plain old ginger ale, with a twist of lime. I know you like something cool to drink after you've been soaking awhile."

She gave herself a mental talking-to for her lack of trust. She hadn't seen Gary with anything alcoholic for weeks, and she was grateful. The roar of the water jets made conversation difficult, so for the next several minutes they sat without speaking. When the timer ran down, Rebecca reached for her towel and dabbed the perspiration from her face. "Mmm, I really needed that." She took a sip of ginger ale.

"You were pretty quiet at supper." Gary edged his foot closer to hers, their little toes touching.

She sighed and set her glass down. "It's been one of those days."

"I heard Colette got the Austin job. Are you okay with it?"

"I am now. But I admit, I struggled for a while." She glanced shyly at him, touched by his thoughtful concern in a way she hadn't experienced in a long time. "Thank you for asking."

He made a noise in his throat and looked away. "You shouldn't have to thank your husband for asking how you feel."

"I know you're trying, Gary. It means a lot."

"Then you haven't given up on us?"

"I've had a lot to sort through, so many conflicting emotions. About you, about my career, about my entire life."

He spoke softly, hesitantly. "Have you made any progress?"

"Maybe." She leaned her head against the coping and stared up at a star-studded sky. A wisp of cloud marked a pink trail across a quarter-moon. "One thing I've come to realize is that my fantasy life may not be as fulfilling as I once imagined."

Gary looked askance at her. "I'm not sure I want to hear this, especially if it involves guys with names like Hugh Jackman or Matt Damon."

Rebecca couldn't suppress a chuckle. "Not *that* kind of fantasy." She gave him a playful punch on the arm before turning serious again. "I meant recreating the life of my childhood."

"You mean before your dad died."

"Mom was the typical stay-at-home mom, always there to welcome my little brother and me after school with homemade treats and tall glasses of milk. She'd help us with our homework, drive us to Scout meetings, sit with us while we practiced our piano lessons."

"But then your dad died." Gary's hand slid into hers.

"I was only fourteen. I needed both my father *and* my mother, but then Mom took a full-time job and I didn't have either one. At least, not the way I was used to. By the time I went away to college, I was ready to marry the first man who promised to fill up the empty places my dad's death left behind."

Gary inched away. His voice hardened. "Then you met Rob Marshall."

"We were both young, immature in so many ways. By the time we realized we wanted completely different things in life, we had Kevin. The next thing I knew, Rob was serving me with divorce papers."

"I hoped you and I wanted the same things. Was I wrong? Were we both wrong?"

Rebecca retrieved her glass and swirled the melting ice. "When Matt announced Colette had been chosen for the Austin job, it felt like I'd been backstabbed."

"I don't blame you. You earned the promotion." Gary heaved a ragged breath. "You shouldn't have turned it down because of me. Because of us."

"Why?" Her gaze blazed into his. "Because we're not worth fighting for?"

"I didn't mean it that way. I just meant . . ." The words fell away on a helpless shrug.

She inhaled a quick breath and tried to refocus her thoughts. "The truth is I *am* good at what I do. My management skills and technical expertise—they're as much a part of me as my size four-petite body and this mop of rust-colored hair. I've established a good reputation, not only within DataTech but with all the clients I've served. I'm proud of the fact, and I think rightly so."

One of Gary's brows notched lower. "What exactly are you saying?"

Comprehension had been long in coming, but admitting the truth, first to herself and now aloud to Gary, felt amazingly freeing. She spoke with firm assurance. "I'm saying I can't stop being a career woman any easier than I could grow ten inches. Finding personal satisfaction through my work is a God-given gift, the same as the fulfillment I experience as Kevin's mother and your wife. It's *all* part of who I am."

Gary cupped his hands and splashed water on his face, then slicked his hair back. "You've always made it look so easy, combining career and family. I envy you."

"Easy? Not by a long shot! There are so many hard choices." And not all of them so clear-cut. Some decisions, like moving into Kate's house, felt more like grossly inequitable concessions.

"Apparently I've made all the *wrong* choices," Gary said. "What we've gone through since last summer—it's forced me to see that everything I've worked for, all the sacrifices I've made—" He seized his glass and flung the ice across the surface of the water. "How could I have come this far only to wind up empty-handed?"

Rebecca's heart twisted at the abject desolation in her husband's voice, the misery in his eyes. She pulled him close and wrapped her arms around him. His arms crept up her back, and he clung to her fiercely, crushing her against his chest until he took her breath away. With a liquid sigh, she moved her mouth next to his ear. "Do your hands feel empty now?"

"Please, Rebecca," he murmured into her hair, "please don't leave me. I'd rather die than lose you."

In the fear in his voice, the savage hunger of his embrace, understanding grew in Rebecca's heart. Gary, Noelle, Kevin, herself—all any of them really wanted was to trust in the ones they loved, to believe, once and for all, that they wouldn't be abandoned yet again. Not by each other, not by God.

She pressed deeper into her husband's embrace and tasted the salt of his tears—and her own. Any remaining doubts she held about keeping her marriage intact melted away as quickly as the ice tossed from Gary's glass.

"Kev, it's almost ten. You're supposed to be sleeping." Rebecca fished the remote from beneath a pile of Kevin's schoolbooks and shut off the TV.

"I couldn't fall asleep. I was waiting for you and Dad to come in from the hot tub."

Easing onto the mattress beside him, she ran her thumb across his smooth cheek. "What's on your mind, tiger?"

"Is everything okay with you and Dad? I mean, I was just wondering..."

Rebecca bent to kiss his forehead. "It's going to be okay, Kev. I promise."

"Good." With a relieved sigh, he snuggled deeper under the covers. "'Night, Mom."

As she tiptoed from the room, she halted at the slamming of a door. Seconds later, Noelle stumbled through the den, and even in the half-light from one of the table lamps, Rebecca could clearly see the girl was upset. Anger? She'd seen plenty of that. But this look spoke another emotion. Confusion? Disillusionment? And incredible, unbearable *sadness*.

But she never cries. In all the weeks since Kate's death, Rebecca hadn't seen Noelle shed a single tear. It wasn't healthy. Something had to give, and soon. "Noelle," she tried, hoping against hope that the girl might open up to her.

Her response was a hand waved in dismissal. "It's late and I still have homework. Good night."

Gary emerged from the guest bath just as Noelle brushed past him on the way to her room. Striding toward Rebecca, he cast her a worried frown. "What just happened?"

"No idea." She pressed a hand to her cheek. "I'm scared for her, Gary. We've got to find a way to help her."

"I know, honey. I'm not giving up." He slid an arm around her waist, and his clean, masculine smell wrapped around her senses.

She snuggled into the warm softness of his bathrobe and sighed. "Me, neither."

19

"Yes, sir, be right there." Gary replaced the telephone receiver as gingerly as if it were made of nitro. What did Sharp want now? Good news, bad news? Always hard to tell with the guy.

No sense borrowing trouble. Things had been going so much better lately—at work and at home. After Rebecca had reassured him the other night that she was still willing to fight for their marriage, a huge weight had been lifted from his heart. Noelle remained withdrawn, but at least the hostility had vanished. Yet in some ways, her quiet surrender worried Gary even more.

His mind returned to the command performance in Sharp's office. With a grimace, he tugged on his suit coat and strode out the door. "I'm headed to a meeting with Mr. Sharp," he told his assistant. "Hold my calls."

"Of course, Mr. Townsend."

Adjusting his tie, Gary started toward the corridor, then spun around. He shot the prim, gray-haired woman a crooked smile. "Jean, how long have we known each other?"

She arched an eyebrow. "Sir?"

"Just wondering. What's it been, three or four years now?"

Jean nodded thoughtfully. "That sounds about right."

"I recall we recently celebrated your twenty-five-year service anniversary." He rubbed a sideburn. "Forgive me for the way this is bound to come across, but, ah, you've got a few years on me, wouldn't you say?"

Jean Calhoun tittered and laid a hand to her gray chignon. "Yes, sir, I would say so."

He stepped forward and cast her a persuasive smile. "Then either I'm going to have to start calling you Mrs. Calhoun, or you'll have to drop this Mr. Townsend business and call me Gary."

The woman gasped. "It would hardly be proper, considering our business relationship, Mr. Towns—"

He held up one hand. "I realize it's old-school company protocol, but at least when it's just you and me, do you think you could be comfortable addressing me as a friend and we could be on a first-name basis?"

Jean studied him for a long moment, then smiled. "Very well. *Gary*." Turning back to her computer screen, she paused, and the corners of her eyes wrinkled in concern. "Stay on your toes with Mr. Sharp. The rumor mill is running rampant."

Armed with this bit of insight, Gary strode down the maroon-carpeted corridor toward his boss's office. He had a sinking feeling he knew why Sharp wanted to see him. Pushing through glass doors stenciled with CHARLES E. SHARP, VICE-PRESIDENT, ENTERPRISE SERVERS AND NETWORKING, he paused at the administrative assistant's desk.

Back to formalities. "Good morning, Steven. Mr. Sharp is expecting me."

"Go right in, Mr. Townsend." Barely looking up from his computer screen, the stone-faced assistant extended a hand toward the inner office.

Easing open the broad, oak-paneled door, Gary steeled himself for the encounter. If he'd guessed right about the reason for this meeting, he'd have to do some fast talking to make things go his way, and Sharp was a tough person to reason with.

"Townsend? Come in and have a seat." The stout, balding executive leaned back in his custom-made leather chair.

Gary stepped into the plush office, similar to his own but much larger. As he took a seat across from his boss, he couldn't help admiring Sharp's expansive view of the Dallas skyline.

"Care for some coffee? It's Jamaican Blue Mountain."

"No, thanks." Gary was tense enough without pumping more caffeine into his system.

Sharp flipped open a manila folder and spread the contents across his desk. "This is the latest field report on the Tokyo project."

Gary swallowed. Just as he'd predicted.

"As you are aware, the next phase of this project will require extensive supervision. You'll be flying over at the end of the week. Plan on staying a couple of months. Steven has already booked your flight for early Thursday morning. He'll give you the details on your way out."

Leave town for two months? Gary's stomach plummeted. This was even worse than he'd prepared for.

Speak now, Townsend, or forever hold your peace.

He roughly cleared his throat. "Sir, I, uh, may have a problem."

His boss lifted an eyebrow, coffee cup poised in mid-air. "Oh?"

"Yes, um"—he sucked in a sliver of breath—"my daughter is performing in a school play. Opening night is a week from Friday."

Sharp gave a humorless chuckle. His Adam's apple jiggled above his stiff white collar. "We all have to miss things now and then. It's the nature of the beast."

Gary studied his wingtips while he garnered his self-control. Sharp had been divorced for several years. His children were grown now with families of their own and living in other states.

How could the man be expected to understand when he had given even less consideration to family life than Gary?

He rose stiffly. One hand propped loosely on his hip, he ran a knuckle along his chin. "Sir, I'll need to fly back for the weekend of the play. It'll only be for a couple of days."

Steepling his fingertips, Sharp wagged his head. "Not possible. This job is too important to be left without supervision."

"The Tokyo staff is well-qualified. They'll manage fine without me for one weekend." Gary set his jaw. His voice fell to a murmur. "My daughter may not."

Sharp released an ugly snort. "Surely by now your daughter understands these things? She's—what? Sixteen? Seventeen?"

"She's only fifteen. And thanks to my job—" Scratch that. Thanks to his former *attitude* toward his job. "What I mean is, my preoccupation with work has prevented me from being the father I need to be—a fact I'm trying to change."

Mr. Sharp swiveled to face the window. He stared out at the city for what felt like a full minute, leaving Gary to wonder if the discussion was over.

"Mr. Sharp—"

The man harrumphed and turned toward him. "Over the years you've been with DataTech, I've watched you jet your way up from first-level management to a position as one of our top executives. Certainly you realize where your success came from. It's a little too late to come in here today and tell me you're ready to throw it all away."

Gary's chin inched up. "Are you implying my job is at risk if I insist on coming home for my daughter's performance?"

Sharp eyed him with steely calm. "There are plenty of people in your department who would jump at the chance to fill your position—and at far less than what you are presently being paid."

Gary mentally reviewed the possible candidates. None of them had his level of knowledge and expertise, least of all where the Tokyo project was concerned, a fact Charles Sharp could not be blind to. The man was bluffing—had to be—and Gary was feeling just reckless enough to call him on it.

He rested his perspiring palms on the gleaming mahogany desk. "Here's the deal, Mr. Sharp. I'll go to Tokyo as planned this week. But I'm flying back the weekend of my daughter's play, and then for alternating weekends until the project is complete and the Tokyo upgrade is online."

The red-faced man gaped, his mouth working like a dying fish.

"Face it, Sharp, it would take weeks of indoctrination to get someone else ready to take my place over there. Even you are too far removed from the specifics to step in. So for now we'll handle it on my terms, okay?" He gave his dumbstruck boss a curt nod and marched out of the office.

He stopped at the assistant's desk. "Hello again, Steven. I believe you made some flight reservations for me?"

"Yes, Mr. Townsend. I just emailed you the confirmation."

"Great, thanks. Mr. Sharp has also given his okay for me to fly home every other weekend. I need you to get me on a return flight to arrive at D/FW a week from Friday by four thirty p.m. *at the absolute latest.* Jean will be in touch concerning the details."

Back in his own office, he fell into his chair and stared out across the city, the giant silver ball atop Reunion Tower sparkling in the afternoon sun. A slow smile spread across his face. *I've finally done something right.*

Only then did he realize how badly his hands shook.

"Goodbye, honey. Be safe." Rebecca leaned close and gripped his hands, while a stream of sleepy-eyed pre-dawn travelers ebbed and flowed around them in the airport terminal.

"I've never dreaded leaving town so much in my life." Gary hauled in a huge breath. "Sure you'll be okay with the kids?"

"We'll be fine." Eyes moist, she reached up to give her husband a lingering, fervent farewell kiss. Gary's two months in Tokyo would be the longest separation they'd endured so far. She didn't know how she would have survived if he hadn't assured her he'd be making regular trips home.

With one last kiss that left her breathless, blushing, and aching for more, he pulled away to join the TSA PreCheck queue. Rebecca stood watching through tear-filled eyes for as long as she could catch a glimpse of him, lifting her fingers in an encouraging wave each time he glanced back. After he'd passed through security, she waved a final goodbye and strode to the parking garage, where they'd left Gary's Lincoln Navigator.

At least Gary's travel plans made this week the ideal time to drop Rebecca's car at the body shop to have the hail damage repaired. But she'd rarely driven the huge SUV and had to play with the seat adjustments until she could see over the hood *and* reach the gas and break pedals. The vehicle felt cavernous without her husband, and yet his masculine smells emanating from the leather upholstery, the subtle imprint left by his hands on the steering wheel, brought sweet comfort.

With Gary in Tokyo, Rebecca also planned to make the most of a lengthy opportunity to get to know Noelle. She'd seen tentative indications the girl might be softening toward her father, and possibly toward Rebecca and Kevin as well. But Noelle still carried so much anguish. Would she ever fully forgive her father for the past? Could she ever make room in her life—in her heart—for a stepmother and stepbrother?

Dawn painted the horizon in shades of salmon and purple as Rebecca drove toward downtown Dallas. After the trip to the airport, she arrived at work much earlier than usual. Passing the empty desk of Matt Garrison's assistant, she noticed Matt's open door and caught his startled glance. He signaled her to enter.

"This is a pleasant surprise," he said while finishing some dexterous two-finger typing at his computer. His loosened tie hung limply down the front of his wrinkled shirt, sleeves pushed up to his elbows. He'd probably been at his desk all night.

"I just took Gary to catch his flight. No point in driving all the way home and back."

"Ah, then I assumed wrongly. Thought you might have had a change of heart about your recent career self-sabotage." He returned to his computer screen as if she were no longer present.

She dropped her briefcase on one chair and plopped down in another. Her throat contracted with a mix of anxiety and determination. "Since I'm here, perhaps we should clear the air about a few things."

Matt hit a few more keys, then sat back, his eyes narrowed. "What things are you referring to?"

"These, for one." She withdrew several thin file folders from her briefcase. "Any entry-level clerk could handle these accounts. If you're trying to tell me that's where I'm headed—"

"Those weren't my idea." Matt gave his tie a nervous flick. "I do what I'm told around here, just like everybody else."

So her recent assignments had come straight from the top. Matt's immediate supervisor was Charles Sharp's division counterpart. Clearly, the two top-level executives had been discussing their wayward underlings. She crossed her arms. "A conspiracy, is it? Why am I not surprised?"

His expression became patronizing. "What do you want me to say, Rebecca? You made your priorities perfectly clear, and DataTech was not, apparently, very high on the list."

Her temples throbbed. She refused to let them force her out of a job she not only excelled at, but that brought a strong sense of personal fulfillment. Others might not see how managing corporate software accounts fit with the commonly accepted definition of "calling," but as far as Rebecca was concerned, if she genuinely cared about finding the best and most individualized solutions for each client, no other word would suffice.

She drew a steadying breath. "Welcome to the twenty-first

century, Matt. For a cutting-edge technology corporation, I'm surprised it's taking so long for you and the other old fogies at DataTech to realize there are more effective ways of managing a successful business. Ways that *don't* include undermining family values. Believe it or not, it is possible to have a career *and* a happy, lasting marriage."

Rising, she slapped the tattered folders on Matt's desk. "Here, give these to someone more—or should I say *less*—qualified to handle them. And as soon as your assistant gets in, have her retrieve those client files you had me transfer to Max Marbach. In the meantime, I'll be on the phone explaining to my contacts in those companies that the change in account reps was an unfortunate blunder and that I'm back on the job ready to give a hundred and ten percent."

When Cassie arrived at school Friday with a horrible cold, Noelle kept her distance. She didn't dare risk catching it and coming down with laryngitis or a hacking cough before opening night. Sitting across from Cassie and Warren at lunch, she erected a barrier of textbooks around her as a shield against the barrage of germs. She twirled limp spaghetti around her fork as she peered over the barricade. "You should be home in bed, Cassie."

"No kidding." Warren inched his chair sideways. "No sense exposing the entire school to your cold."

"There's only half a day left. And I only have to stay on my feet long enough to make it to my costume fitting tomorrow. Then I can collapse for the weekend." Cassie sneezed and made a hasty dive for her purse, groping for a tissue.

Noelle flinched and waved invisible germs away with her spiral history notebook. "I can't wait to see what my dress will look like. What's your costume going to be, Warren?"

He wrinkled his nose. "I heard it's somebody's old double-breasted suit that reeks of mothballs."

"Well, I know you'll look great in it." Cassie locked her arm around his and leaned against his shoulder.

Grimacing, he freed his arm. "Sorry you're sick, Cass, but we'd all appreciate it if you kept your germs to yourself." After sliding his chair even farther away, he returned to pushing cold spaghetti around with his fork.

Noelle stabbed a piece of soggy lettuce dripping with industrial-strength Italian dressing. Pasting on a smile, she asked, "You two have plans for tonight?"

"I'm not going anywhere but home to bed." Cassie blew her nose again.

Warren cast Noelle a hopeful glance. "There's a home game tonight. Want to go?"

Noelle's heart threw in an extra beat. He was asking *her*? With Cassie sitting right there? She rushed to change the subject. "Hey, you never told me how Homecoming went."

Cassie cringed and forced a grin. "I know how it bugs you when I carry on about stuff."

Yeah, right. Never stopped her before. "I bet Lynn Larson was gorgeous as Homecoming Queen. She deserved to win."

"Oh, wow, you should have seen her!" Cassie's eyebrows shot up, and the dam broke on the enthusiasm Noelle knew she'd been holding back. "Her dress was amazing! And the dance was spectacular. Daystar played. They're fabulous!"

Noelle pinched her lips together and tried to look interested. "The drummer—isn't he Bruce Thatcher, the drum major from marching band?"

"He is such a hunk!" Cassie rolled her eyes before glancing sheepishly at Warren.

"So what about tonight?" Warren crumpled his napkin. "Want to go to the game with me, Noelle? It'll be cold, but I can bring my stadium blanket."

She peeked at Cassie, then shook her head. "Better not. Dad left for Tokyo yesterday, and Kevin made me promise I'd play pool with him." Her mouth twisted. "It's kind of a Friday-evening tradition for Kevin and my dad."

Cassie dabbed her nose. "I can't believe it. You're actually being nice to the kid."

"Kevin's okay." As stepbrothers went, he was probably better than okay. Besides, it appeared she was stuck with him. Amazingly, the thought no longer made her want to throw herself off an I-35 overpass.

Warren stacked his utensils and empty soft drink can on his tray. He pushed away from the table. "I need to stop by my locker before class."

"Warren, wait for me!" Cassie hurried to catch up.

When she reached for his hand, he yanked it away. "Cassie, would you just go home and take care of that cold?"

Shaking her head at the two of them, Noelle unearthed a bottle of hand sanitizer from the bottom of her purse and squirted a dollop onto her palm. She'd like to rub out all the bad stuff in her life as easily as she annihilated a few germs. Gathering her books, she marched down the crowded corridor, ignoring the other students brushing against her. She couldn't get the picture out of her head—Warren and Cassie at the homecoming dance, Cassie's arms wrapped around Warren's neck, his arms hugging her waist. Warren bending low to whisper something in Cassie's ear, to kiss her cheek—

Stop it! She jerked to a halt in front of her locker and let her head fall against the louvered metal door. If only this wild emotional roller-coaster would stop long enough for her to jump off! Why couldn't things be black and white for her, like the markings on her sweet old tuxedo cat? Would she ever get to a place where a friend was a friend, a father was a father, and facing the future didn't feel like a whole new kind of torture?

20

Rebecca carried a stack of supper dishes to the counter and opened the dishwasher. Her feet ached and her head throbbed. Had she been insane insisting Matt restore her client load? She'd been flattered by so many enthusiastic welcomes back on board, but while she played catch-up, they were keeping her hopping like a jackrabbit on steroids. Maybe she could get to bed early tonight.

"I'll clean up," Noelle volunteered. "Go sit down. You look beat."

"It *has* been a tiring day." Rebecca suppressed a look of astonishment at Noelle's unexpected show of compassion. Maybe the girl really was coming around. Exhausted as she felt, Rebecca couldn't ignore an opportunity to encourage conversation. "If you'll fill the dishwasher, I'll put away the leftovers and wipe off the table."

Noelle shrugged. "Sure."

Rebecca selected a couple of plastic containers and began filling them with the remains of tonight's dinner, chicken parmesan and a squash casserole, both of which were frozen entrées. She received far fewer complaints that way. "You must be getting excited about the play."

"I am." Noelle sorted knives and forks into the compartments of the utensils basket. "Can't wait to see Gran and my aunt and uncle again."

"I'm looking forward to getting to know your family." The problem would be sleeping arrangements, and Rebecca and Gary had already talked briefly about how they'd accommodate everyone. "Your dad and I thought we'd sleep at the condo while they're here and come over during the day."

"Mmm." Melting ice clattered as Noelle emptied glasses into the sink. Apparently, that line of conversation had ended.

Rebecca tried another subject. "I know you promised Kevin his Friday-night game of pool, but he'd understand if you wanted to go out with your friends instead. I heard there's a home game. Is Warren going?"

"I guess so. I mean, I don't know, since Cassie's sick." Noelle seized the pot scrubber and attacked a hardened piece of chicken stuck to a plate.

"But I thought . . ." Something was going on here. Something Noelle wasn't being honest with herself about. Rebecca backed off a moment while she set the leftover containers in the refrigerator. She joined Noelle at the sink and wet a dishcloth. "You and Warren have been friends for a long time, haven't you?"

Noelle paused scrubbing just long enough to whisper out a sigh. "Just about forever, it feels like."

"And Cassie?"

"We met in junior high when we both joined the drama club." Noelle shoved the now spotlessly clean plate into the dishwasher rack and continued her siege on the next plate.

Rebecca began wiping the counters. "Judging from what little I know about Cassie, she seems much more . . . *gregarious* than you."

Noelle slid the last plate into the rack. She gave a half-laugh as she squeezed dishwasher soap into the dispenser. "Gregarious. Yeah, that fits. I'd also use *dramatic, energetic, enthusiastic*—"

"All wonderful qualities." Rebecca leaned against the counter and studied Noelle's face. "Still, if I had a friend with such a strong personality, I'm afraid I'd feel terribly overwhelmed at times."

"She means well." Noelle's lips quirked. "But sometimes it feels like everything has to be about her."

The aching vulnerability in her voice made Rebecca want to reach out and hold her. She was just a girl, after all—a confused, hurting, messed-up teenager in need of love and understanding. *Lord, I want to love her. Help me.*

Noelle's shoulders stiffened. Her tone grew brusque. "Kevin's waiting for our game." She slammed the dishwasher door, pushed the start button, and marched out of the kitchen.

Rebecca stared after her and wished for one more minute, one more word. Maybe—just maybe—she might have broken through.

The minute Noelle walked into the game room, Kevin jumped up from the sofa and shut off the TV. "Ready to play?"

"Sure. Rack 'em up." Noelle chose her favorite cue stick and chalked the tip, but her mind lingered on some things Rebecca had said. Best friend or not, Cassie was definitely overwhelming. But despite her self-centeredness—*and face it, Noelle, you've been just as bad lately*—there wasn't a mean bone in Cassie's body.

Kevin arranged the balls in the triangular frame, then carefully removed it. "You can break."

Shaking off her thoughts, she set the cue ball on the opposite end of the table and lined up a shot. The white ball cracked against the others and sent them scattering. The seven-ball disappeared into the corner pocket. "What are we playing, anyway?"

"Straight-Eight. Know that one?"

"Sure. I'll take one through seven, obviously." She leaned over the table and balanced the cue stick in the valley between her left thumb and forefinger. With a smack, the two-ball glanced off the cue ball into the side pocket.

"Dude! You're pretty good. Did Dad teach you?"

Noelle balanced the end of the cue stick on the toe of her sneaker while considering her next shot. "No, he never had time. Warren taught me."

She missed and Kevin took over. He made three neat shots, then accidentally knocked in one of Noelle's balls. "Aw, rats."

"Hey, I need all the help I can get."

Kevin was the first to sink all seven of his balls. He called his next shot for the eight-ball, but missed. Noelle finished off hers on her next turn but missed her eight-ball shot. The position of the cue ball made a difficult shot for Kevin, but he called it accurately and the black ball skidded into a corner pocket. "Game!" He reached across the table to slap Noelle's palm.

"You are too good, my man. You give me no choice but to demand a rematch." She racked the balls and gave Kevin the break.

As Kevin knocked in one after another, Noelle leaned on her cue stick and shook her head. "You hustled me."

Kevin grinned as he aimed his cue. "Didn't want you quitting on me before we even got started." An orange ball banked off the edge, glanced off the eight-ball, and sank into the corner pocket.

Noelle gave an exaggerated groan. "I may as well give up now."

"Not so fast," came a familiar voice. "Maybe we can team up against him."

Noelle spun around to see Warren standing in the doorway. "What are you doing here?"

"You said you'd be playing pool with Kevin. Thought I'd join you—that is, if nobody minds." He sauntered over and selected a cue stick from the rack.

"Hey, great." Kevin balanced on one toe and leaned across the edge of the table. "Now, let's see. Eight-ball, off the edge with a roll-back and into the corner pocket."

When Kevin's shot came off perfectly, Warren gave a low whistle.

Noelle wrinkled her nose. "He never gave me a chance."

"I'll see if I can make it up for you. Rack 'em, Kevin." Warren chalked the end of his cue and then blew off the residue in a puff of green dust.

"I'll get us some drinks." Noelle started for the kitchen. "Let him have it, Warren."

She found Rebecca at the kitchen table checking email on her laptop. Rebecca looked up with a smile. "How's the game going?"

Noelle took three cans of soda from the refrigerator. "Kevin's been practicing. He cleaned my clock." She set the cans on a tray and filled three glasses with ice. "Warren just came over. He's in there right now defending my honor."

"Oh, is he?" One eyebrow shot up as a funny smile flickered across Rebecca's face. Her gaze softened. "It means a lot to Kevin that you're spending time with him. He misses Gary—your dad—when he has to be away."

Noelle faced her stepmother. It was hard to think of Rebecca that way—stepmother, replacement mother, substitute for the real thing. No one could ever take Mom's place. That gaping emptiness would never be filled again. And yet . . . here was Rebecca, being nice, sounding sincere. All this time, Noelle had worked so hard to keep from liking the woman and her son, keep from letting either one of them into her heart. But they persisted. And somehow it mattered.

"Kevin's a nice kid," Noelle said at last. "Besides, none of this . . . other stuff . . . is his fault."

Rebecca lowered her gaze. "It isn't entirely mine, either."

Noelle arranged and rearranged the glasses on the tray. "I know, Rebecca, I promise I do. I'm trying. I really am."

"And I'm grateful. I just wish you'd give your father half a chance, too." Rebecca rose and laid a gentle hand on Noelle's arm. "You didn't see how hurt he was when you didn't tell him goodbye before he left for Tokyo."

Noelle jerked her arm away. Years of tearful goodbyes drowned the seeds of forgiveness so close to breaking through. "Well, for your information, he didn't notice the *hundreds* of times I was hurt when he left Mom and me to go on another stupid business trip. He never cared how disappointed I was when he had to miss my recitals and my school programs and my plays. And did you know he didn't even show up when Mom got her master's degree? None of it mattered to him. And it still doesn't. My play opens one week from tonight. And where is my father? Clear across the ocean. He might as well be on Mars."

She spun around, almost knocking the tray off the edge of the counter. She grabbed it and turned to rush from the kitchen, but Rebecca stepped in front of her. "If you'd only spoken to your dad before he left, he would have told you. He's coming home for the weekend. He'll be here to see your play."

Noelle's eyes narrowed. This had to be a trick, another of his lies. "I don't believe it."

"Returning for opening night was the deal he made with his boss, or he wouldn't go to Tokyo at all—even if it meant he could lose his job."

A tiny explosion of hope rose in Noelle's chest, and just as quickly, she extinguished it. "I've heard those kinds of promises before. You just wait. Come next Thursday, he'll phone to say there's been an emergency and he can't leave. He won't get here. Just wait and see."

Oh, Gary, please don't let her down. With a tired moan, Rebecca returned to her computer. Retrieving the email she'd been composing to Gary, she continued typing:

> We've had a pretty good day here. Noelle has been playing pool with Kevin tonight, and Warren just came over to join them.

As she debated whether or not to mention Noelle's disbelieving response just now, a tinny bell sounded from her computer speakers and the instant-messaging window popped up.

> GTownsend: Hey, sweetie, nice to find you online. How are things in Dallas?

In happy surprise she typed back:

> RMTownsend: Not too bad. Was just emailing you. What time is it over there, anyway?

> GTownsend: Almost noon, and it's already Saturday here. About to go to lunch with the Numata bigwigs. Flying west is like fast-forwarding through time!

> RMTownsend: Fun. Wish I could zap myself over there so I could skip right through this lonely weekend without you.

> GTownsend: Wish you could, too! How was work today? Matt giving you a hard time about demanding your clients back?

> RMTownsend: Matt, I can handle. He's not as tough as he acts. It's just that . . .

Her fingers hovered over the keyboard. He needed to understand returning for Noelle's play was one promise he could not afford to break.

RMTownsend: Gary, promise me you won't let ANYTHING keep you from coming home next weekend.

GTownsend: From your lips—er, fingers—to God's ear. Hey, my lunch appointment just walked in. Gotta go. Will call tomorrow. Love you!

Closing the instant-message window, Rebecca pondered Gary's last post. It almost sounded as if he were praying. Dare she hope?

Noelle sat on the sofa sipping her soft drink while Warren systematically defeated Kevin three quick games in a row.

"No more—I'm done!" Kevin raised his hands in surrender, grinning at Noelle. "This guy's almost better than Dad."

"Terrific." Noelle's remark held no enthusiasm. Her conversation with Rebecca had reminded her all over again why things would never be right between Noelle and her father. She plunked her glass on the end table and drew her legs up under her.

"Hey, you were in a good mood when I got here." Warren plopped down beside her. "What gives?"

She waved a hand. "Nothing."

"Nothing. Right. It's just your usual 'Dr. Jekyll and Ms. Hyde' routine." He reached for his soft drink.

"Please don't start," she said with a groan. "What are you doing here, anyway? Why aren't you over at Cassie's nursing her back to health?"

Warren set his glass down with a thud. Seizing her arm, he pulled her roughly from the sofa. "Excuse us, Kevin. Noelle and I have to discuss something." Tightening his grip, he dragged her through the side door to the sunroom and yanked the door closed behind them.

"Hey, it's cold out here." Worse, she could feel a lecture coming on. More of Warren's big-brother routine, and she was so done with it. She reached for the doorknob.

"So suffer." He blocked her exit. "Seems to be what you do best lately."

"What's that supposed to mean?"

"It means I'm sick and tired of the way you've been acting."

Red warning lights flickered at the corners of her mind. She should keep her mouth shut, before Warren's irritation goaded her into saying something she'd later regret. But the anger won out. "If you don't like it, you can leave. Like I said, you ought to be with Cassie, anyway."

"Will you shut up about Cassie, for crying out loud!"

"Why? She's your girlfriend, isn't she?"

Warren sighed, and his tone softened. "I like Cassie, sure—for the airhead she is. But give me a break. *Girlfriend*? No way!"

"But I thought—"

"You thought what? That you'd do us both a favor by playing matchmaker? And you were so obvious about it, right from the first time when you made me sit next to Cassie at the movie."

She twisted her shirttail. "But I could tell how much Cassie likes you, and I realized how unfair it was for you to be stuck babysitting me all the time. I'm a big girl now."

Warren stood in front of her, trapping her face between his strong hands. "Then act like one. Start using your head, will you?"

"I—I don't understand—" She took hold of his wrists and struggled to free herself.

"I finally figured that out." Easing her onto the yellow padded loveseat, he took her hands in his. "Somewhere in your twisted brain you decided you knew what was best for me and Cassie. You really set us up good, didn't you? Every time I'd make a suggestion for something for us to do, you'd wriggle out of it and I'd be stuck taking her."

"But the homecoming dance. You invited her."

"It's what you wanted, wasn't it?" He snorted. "I can't believe you think I'm such a loser that I couldn't find my own girlfriend."

"I don't think that at all! You could have your pick of any girl at school."

"You crazy, mixed-up kid." Chin lowered, he stared at the floor. "Don't you have any idea why I've never seriously dated anyone else?"

Noelle searched her thoughts. Surely she hadn't totally misread what was going on between Warren and Cassie. Then she recalled all those times she'd chalked it up to his embarrassment whenever he'd flinch or pull away when Cassie tried to get affectionate.

How could she be so dense?

Her chest swelled like an overfilled helium balloon. Trying to breathe, she focused on the way his hair swirled around the crown in soft, ash-brown waves.

He lifted his eyes to meet hers and fixed her with a cockeyed grin. "You really don't know what's going on here, do you?"

She shook her head, biting her lip.

"Noelle Townsend," he began gently, "I quit thinking of you as the little girl next door a long time ago." He lifted her hands to his lips, pressing them with a tender kiss. "Getting the message yet?"

Noelle shivered, but not from the cold. *It's me! Warren loves me!*

21

Numata Kenji—Ken, as his American colleagues called him —passed a serving dish to Gary. "More shrimp? You have not eaten much, my friend."

Food was the last thing on Gary's mind, but he politely accepted a small portion so as not to offend his hosts. "It's all delicious, but I think my system is still adjusting to the time difference." The haunting strains of a Japanese melody created a soothing aura in the small, private dining room of one of Tokyo's finest restaurants. Almost too soothing. Gary could barely resist the temptation to rest his head on the table and close his eyes for a quick nap.

"We should not have pressed you to join us so soon after your arrival." Juro, Ken's older brother and co-owner of Numata, Ltd., deftly maneuvered a pair of chopsticks. A young woman wearing the traditional Japanese kimono and coiffure shuffled over with a decanter of sake, but the slightly balding businessman gently shook his head. "*Mou, kekkou desu,*" he said. "But perhaps our companion would care for more."

The woman inclined her head toward Gary with a questioning look.

He nodded toward his still full cup, which he should never have accepted in the first place. "No, thank you. But some coffee, perhaps?"

As the woman disappeared behind an ornately painted rice-paper screen, Ken elbowed his brother. "Is this the same man we met with last year in San Francisco? The one who enthusiastically consumed five cups—"

"It was seven by my count." Juro wiggled his eyebrows.

"Indeed. *Seven* cups of sake without so much as crossed eyes or slurred speech."

He gave an embarrassed chuckle. "That was another lifetime."

The brothers exchanged puzzled glances, and Ken said, "You surprise us, Gary-san."

Gary could only shrug. "I've kind of surprised myself." Their server returned with a coffee carafe and three delicate porcelain cups. Ken and Juro accepted some along with Gary. He took a thoughtful sip. "To be honest, I found myself depending too much on alcohol to escape the problems in my personal life."

Ken stirred cream into his coffee. "Yes, strong drink offers false comfort."

Juro rested one elbow on the table, a concerned look creasing his forehead. "Things are better now?"

So much for the Japanese custom of keeping personal concerns private. "I'm . . . hopeful."

Juro laced his fingers together and leaned closer. "Ken and I would be honored to pray with you."

Gary snatched up a spoon and stirred his coffee, even though he'd added nothing to it. "I'm still feeling my way in the God department."

Another inscrutable glance passed between Ken and Juro. "But you are a believer, Gary-san?" Juro asked.

Do I believe? Do I want to believe? For weeks now, he'd tried to grasp what difference faith had made for Rebecca. God obviously hadn't made all her problems disappear, or both he and Noelle would surely have been excised from her life long ago for all the grief they'd brought her. Yet how could he fail to notice how much more at peace she seemed lately? Could God really do that for a person?

Maybe it was time to quit dabbling in this thing called faith and go all in.

He cleared his throat. "I'd very much appreciate it if you'd say some prayers for me. Heaven knows I could use them."

Ken smiled warmly. "Heaven does indeed know. Tell us, how can we pray for you?"

At the first light of dawn Saturday morning, Noelle's eyes popped open. In the quiet moments as the sun's pink rays filtered through her mini-blinds, she realized something was different about today. Very, very different.

Then it hit her. For the first time since Mom got sick, Noelle hadn't awakened angry. Instead, a quiet joy washed over her. She hadn't felt this content—this *loved*—in forever.

Warren. All this time, and she hadn't known. What an idiot! The harder she'd pushed him into Cassie's arms, the more confused he must have felt.

She crept to the window and gazed through the trees at the cotton-candy sky. A movement caught her eye in the direction of Warren's backyard. Kneeling on the edge of the deck, he zipped up his fleece hoodie and adjusted the laces of his running shoes.

If she hurried, she could catch him before he started his run. She tore off her nightshirt and jammed her legs and arms into a jogging suit. She grabbed socks and shoes and ran barefoot out her patio door, the frosty grass chilling her toes. "Warren, wait for me!"

Halfway to the creek, he looked back and grinned. "You're crazy! You'll freeze to death."

"I won't if you give me five seconds to finish getting ready. Now wait up!" She plopped down on the cold lawn and jerked on her socks and shoes. With her fingers already growing numb, she fumbled to tie the laces.

"Here, let me." Warren tucked his gloves into his pocket and knelt in front of her. After tying her shoes, he pulled Noelle to her feet and shoved his gloves onto her trembling fingers. "You actually look happy this morning. Nice change." His grin melted her heart like butter in the microwave. "Any special reason?"

She glanced away with a shy smile, savoring the feel of her fingers inside the gloves already warmed by his hands. "If you tell me I only dreamed what happened last night, I'll never speak to you again."

He tweaked her chin and then shoved his bare hands into his pockets. "If it was a dream, don't wake me up. Now let's get moving before my blood freezes!"

They jogged along the path side by side, their feet hitting the hard ground in a steady rhythm, their breath coming out in misty white puffs. The path led to a park several blocks away, and by then Noelle was winded.

"I haven't—done this—in a long time." She slowed near a bench and hoped Warren would take the hint.

"Okay, okay, we'll rest." Warren jogged in place as Noelle fell onto the bench, her sides heaving. After a couple of minutes, he motioned for her to get up. "Sit there too long and you'll never get moving again. Come on, I'll race you back home."

Still gasping for air, she waved him away. "I'll catch a taxi."

He burst out laughing. "Where are you going to find a taxi in Arden Park at seven thirty in the morning?"

"I'm patient. I can wait."

Warren stopped jogging. He stared at her for a long moment, then sank onto the bench next to her. "Well, I can't." He drew her into his arms and kissed her long and passionately, a kiss like Noelle had never had before.

Tingling from head to toe, she touched a gloved finger to her lips, still burning with the heat his kiss had left behind. She sighed and gazed into his warm, tender eyes. "You really do love me."

"You sure made it hard for me to let you know."

She swallowed and searched for the courage to say the words herself, words she knew she'd always wanted to say, words she'd buried under too many months of anger and confusion and fear. "Warren, I love you, too."

He kissed her again, this time with a deep yet gentle urgency.

As they drifted apart and her skittering heartbeat settled, a troubling thought filled her mind. She pushed off the bench and marched several steps down the path.

He caught up and grabbed her hand. "Hey. What's wrong now?"

"Cassie. What are we going to do about Cassie?"

Looping his arm around her shoulder, Warren answered, "I think Cassie is going to understand."

In the sunroom, Rebecca wrapped her hands around a steaming mug of Ethiopian dark roast and gazed across the back lawn as rose-gold fingers of morning light broke through the trees. In moments like these, when the world seemed at peace, she missed Gary more than ever.

Oh, God, why can't he know You the way I do?

The first time she'd suggested to Gary that maybe they could attend church together, he'd brushed off the suggestion with barely concealed distaste. "God never did anything for me, and I have no use for Him now." She'd learned enough about Gary's past to realize his bitterness toward God stemmed from his hard life growing up and his parents' early deaths. More times than she could count, she'd heard the saying, "God never gives us more than we can handle." It sounded good, but if it were true, how could a loving God allow so much adversity into Gary's life that he'd turn away from the Lord?

Immediately the words of Romans 8:28 filled her thoughts: *And we know that in all things God works for the good of those who love him, who have been called according to his purpose.*

Here was the real truth—not that God intentionally permits "just enough" misfortune to test and strengthen His children's faith, but that God can be counted on to bring about a higher good from every trial.

She could only trust that the Lord would soon reveal His "higher good" for Gary, for Noelle, and for all of them as a family.

She took another sip of coffee and was about to turn away from the tranquil view when she glimpsed Noelle and Warren crossing the lawn. Warren swung his arms and moved freely, while Noelle trudged up the small slope as if she were about to collapse. Had they already been out for a run? Rebecca could believe it of Warren, but how in the world had he dragged Noelle out of her hermit cave and convinced her to go jogging with him?

Warren reached for Noelle's hand and pulled her into his arms. When he lowered his mouth to kiss her, Rebecca felt a blush rise in her cheeks. She backed away from the sunroom glass and hoped they wouldn't notice her watching. Her astonishment grew as Noelle melted into Warren's embrace, fervently returning the kiss. The two finally parted, and at the sight of Noelle's beaming face, Rebecca's breath caught in her throat. The girl's smile turned to rippling laughter as the pair made their way toward the house.

Rebecca ducked into the den, her own heart thudding with a strange mixture of emotions—elation for Noelle's happiness, wistful yearning for the sweet days of courtship when Rebecca and Gary had first fallen in love. Hearing the outer door slide open, she scurried to the recliner and feigned a casual expression.

Noelle entered alone, pausing to wave a cheery goodbye to Warren. Seeing Rebecca in the den, she gave a startled "Oh!"

"Out jogging already?" Rebecca grabbed up the morning paper. "Wish I had your energy."

"My legs feel like rubber." Noelle bent down and untied her sneakers, her tangled ponytail falling across her shoulder. She started to rise, but suddenly sank onto the carpet as if her legs had given out. Leaning back on her elbows, she lifted sparkling eyes to meet Rebecca's. "You saw me with Warren, didn't you?"

Rebecca nodded, unable to suppress a knowing smile. "I had a feeling about you two."

A pensive look shadowed Noelle's gaze. "I can't believe how blind I was. I can't believe I shut him out for so long."

"Oh, Noelle, honey—" Rebecca checked herself. Her heart was bursting with everything she wanted to say to the girl, but if she forced her way through this tiny crack in Noelle's fragile veneer, it could shatter any chances of a lasting breakthrough. She sat forward, choosing her words with care. "I'm very, very glad for you. I hope you know I've always only wanted your happiness."

Noelle pushed off the floor and locked her arms across her chest. A sharp sigh sliced the air between them, and she looked as if she couldn't decide between a sarcastic retort and a simple *thank you*.

Rebecca laid the newspaper aside. "I can understand why you wouldn't believe me, but it's true. I care about you, Noelle."

"I, um . . ." The girl sucked in her bottom lip. "I need a shower. I should—"

"Please don't go yet. I've been hoping for so long that we could talk. You must know I'd never try to take your mother's place. I only want to be your friend." Rebecca ignored the subtle flattening of Noelle's lips. "Actually, we have more in common than you might think. Did you know my father was killed in a car accident when I was just a year or so younger than you?"

Noelle's sideways glance reflected a hint of curiosity.

"It was an awful time in my life," Rebecca went on, grateful for an opening. "My dad was dead, my mother had to go to work to pay the bills, my friends deserted me because I was stuck home after school taking care of my little brother."

Noelle sank onto the sofa, her hands clasped between her knees. "Wow. I had no idea."

"It felt as if the whole world had abandoned me. All I wanted was to put things back the way they were." Rebecca's throat tightened. She flicked a tear off her cheek. "I think I've been trying to ever since."

"I hear what you're saying." Resignation echoed in Noelle's tone. "My mom is dead and things will never be the same."

"No, they won't be." Rebecca edged closer, wanting so badly to take Noelle's hand, but the wounded look in the girl's eyes made her hold back. "But maybe, with time and trust, things will get better."

"Maybe . . ." A muffled chirping noise drew Noelle's attention. She groped in the pocket of her jacket and pulled out her cell phone. As she read the caller ID, a smile stole across her face. "It's Warren." With a quick "Excuse me," she darted down the hall to her room.

In the silent den, Rebecca sank into the recliner and closed her eyes. Had she pushed too hard, said too much? Or would Noelle finally come to see that she wasn't so alone after all?

22

I t was Monday before Noelle and Warren found their chance
to talk to Cassie. She'd been too sick all weekend even to
make it for her costume fitting. Until Cassie felt better, Noelle
hadn't the heart to break the news about her and Warren.

As the three of them sat at their usual lunch table, forcing
down more of the school cafeteria's infamous soggy tacos, Cassie
glanced toward the next table, her eyes brightening. "Look,
there's Bruce Thatcher, from the Daystar band." She giggled
through her stuffy nose. "Smart guy. He brought lunch from
home."

Noelle winked at Warren. "Smile, Cassie! I think Bruce is
looking at you."

"Oh, no—is he?" Cassie dabbed her mouth with a napkin.
"And here I am with taco juice running down my chin."

"I doubt he's looking at your chin. Who could resist those big
blue eyes of yours?"

"Stop it, Noelle!" Cassie blinked furiously and shifted in her
chair to face away from the Daystar drummer. In a raspy whisper
directed at Noelle, she said, "Besides, I'd never flirt with
somebody else in front of Warren."

Warren chuckled. "How about behind my back?"

"No! I mean—" Cassie made a growling noise in her throat.

"Cassie, it's okay." Warren slid his tray to one side. "Noelle, would you mind if I talked to Cassie alone for a few minutes?"

"Oh. Sure." Better if Warren broke things off gently. Spying an empty seat a few tables over, Noelle pushed back her chair.

Glancing between Warren and Noelle, Cassie narrowed one eye. "Okay, what's up? I saw the look you two just shared."

Noelle gulped. "Warren should tell you."

"No, I think you both should. Because . . ." A smile played at Cassie's lips and slowly spread into a wide grin. "Uh-huh, I knew it. About time, you two."

Shoulders sagging, Noelle collapsed into her chair. "You *know*? But how—"

"Are you kidding? I've known all along you and Warren were meant for each other." Looking smug, Cassie rested her chin on her hands. "I just can't believe how long it took for you both to figure it out."

Warren smirked. "I wasn't the one who had to figure anything out."

"You never fooled me for a minute." Cassie patted Warren's arm, then reached across the table for Noelle's hand. "Couldn't be happier for the two of you."

With a grateful sigh, Noelle tugged at a stubborn bite of chewy taco shell. For a change, school cafeteria food didn't seem so bad after all.

For a change, everything felt right.

"Rebecca? I can barely hear you."

"Hi, honey! How's it going over there?"

Gary closed the door to the small office he'd been using as a base of operations at Numata. "Hectic. A real madhouse."

"Please don't tell me you can't make it home this weekend."

"I'll be there if I have to break my neck trying." He needed to get home now more than ever. So much to tell his wife, so much he needed to explain to his daughter.

"Good." Rebecca blew out a long breath. "You know what it will do to Noelle if you aren't at the play Friday night."

"Is she there? Maybe if I told her myself—"

"She's at rehearsal. She'll have another late night, I'm afraid."

Gary rubbed his throbbing temple. "Just keep assuring her. I'm not letting her down this time."

"I'm doing my best, but Noelle still has a long way to go before she'll fully trust either one of us."

A groan rumbled from Gary's throat. *Lord, we'll only get through this with Your help.* Praying still felt awkward, but each time got a little easier. Ken and Juro had invited him to an English-speaking worship service last Sunday, and afterward he'd spent a good two hours talking with the pastor. Would he ever be able to reverse the effects of relying only on himself, or had he wasted too many years striving to prove his worth through success?

"Gary?"

"Sorry, my mind was wandering. And believe it or not, I wasn't thinking about work."

A pause. "Dare I ask what, then?"

"Just that I'm sorry you're stuck there trying to hold down the fort." He'd wait to tell her the rest until he could hold her in his arms. "How's everything else going? The family still coming for Noelle's play?"

"Looks like it's all going to work out. David and Susan get to the airport around the same time as Irene, so David is renting a car for all of them."

Through the partially open mini-blinds, Gary glimpsed Juro's frantic wave. The new network server had been giving them problems all morning. Gary lifted a hand to signal he'd be out in a moment. Regret darkening his tone, he said, "I guess we'll be moving back to the condo for the weekend." Two short days at home, and he'd have to spend a good chunk of the time miles away from the daughter he so needed to reconnect with.

"Actually," Rebecca said slowly, "Noelle had a better idea."

"Huh?"

"I emailed you that Warren and Noelle are, um, seeing each other in a different way these days."

"Yeah, terrific news. But what does it have to do with this weekend?"

"Nothing, except for having a positive effect on Noelle's attitude in general. Rather than making us give up our room, she suggested David and Susan could stay next door at the Ameses', and I've already talked to Debby about the arrangements. Noelle will share her room with her grandmother. So you and Kevin and I can stay right where we are."

Thank you, Lord! Maybe God was looking out for him and Noelle after all. Then he thought about how Rebecca might feel about the plan. "Are you okay with it? I mean, I thought you might be looking forward to a weekend away from all the tension."

"I think we'll be fine," she stated, and the tone of her voice said she meant it.

"In that case, I'd better get back to this nightmare so I can leave it for a couple of days. My flight is supposed to land in plenty of time for me to get to the auditorium. In case I miss you beforehand, leave my ticket with an usher and save me a seat."

"Okay. I love you."

"I love you too. And give Kevin a hug for me."

Gary hung up, wishing he could have asked Rebecca to pass his love to Noelle as well. No, he'd have to tell her—better yet, *show* her—in person. It was the only way she'd ever believe in it.

Juro met him on his way out of the office, a grimace

contorting his face. "Gary, we need your expertise. None of the Ethernet connections on floors six and ten are responding."

He shrugged off his suit coat and prepared to do battle with a buggy network server. If he didn't get these glitches worked out quickly, he'd be hard pressed to make his flight.

One hand deftly maneuvering her computer mouse, Rebecca studied the monitor as she tested various aspects of the interactive website she and her staff were designing for one of DataTech's biggest clients. It was among her most challenging projects to date—and one of her most innovative designs. She couldn't help feeling just a tiny bit proud, especially after Matt reluctantly admitted he'd made the right decision reinstating her corporate accounts.

"Marbach would have fumbled this one big-time," he'd said after reviewing her progress reports. "Thanks to you, Hammond and Sons has signed a long-term service contract with us."

Feeling valued and productive again, not to mention being back in Matt's good graces, made Rebecca's heart lift. Even so, she constantly had to tamp down her worries about the coming weekend. It was Thursday afternoon, and she hadn't heard from Gary in two days. No phone calls, no email, no instant messages, nothing. His flight was supposed to leave Tokyo around midnight tonight, Dallas time. She prayed this wasn't a bad sign and hoped he was merely concentrating on the job at hand so he could make the flight home.

The images on her computer screen blurred as her mind drifted. She still had so much to do before everyone arrived tomorrow. The housekeeper had come this morning to do the cleaning, thank goodness. After work, Rebecca planned to stop at Costco to pick up a selection of family-size entrees. A salad here, a takeout dinner there, and their mealtimes should be covered.

Not exactly home cooking, but who besides Laurence cared much for Rebecca's culinary attempts anyway?

Her gaze drifted across the ornate façade of the Hotel Adolphus. The vivid contrast between the hotel's historic baroque architecture and the surrounding ultra-modern high-rise office buildings always took her by surprise, reminding her once again of the distinct yet interconnected facets of her own life. She was as much a career person as she was a wife and mother. All she could do was continue to give her utmost in each area.

But she wasn't Superwoman. And she didn't have to be. From now on, she'd measure success according to her own scale, not DataTech's or her mother's or even the late Kate Townsend's.

That's fine as far as it goes, Rebecca. If she was truly serious about moving forward in her marriage with Gary, if she had any hopes of finding her footing in this new role as stepmother, she needed to take her attitude adjustment one step further. Gary, Kevin, and Noelle all deserved the assurance that she had no intention of deserting them. Not for a day, not for a weekend, not for a lifetime.

She pressed the intercom button on her phone. "Craig, I need to get hold of a good real estate agent."

Gary had been up since 4:00 a.m. battling software bugs, network failures, and encryption errors. Thanks to the combined efforts of his technical staff, the initial stages of bringing Numata's expansive interdepartmental network online had been completed. Sweat staining his shirt, he hauled himself off the swivel chair where he'd been working at a terminal. A sharp pain shot through his back between his shoulder blades.

"We've got it under control, boss," his chief tech said. "Go catch your flight."

Gary checked his watch and whistled through his teeth. He needed to be at the airport in less than two hours. "Man, I hate cutting things this close." Groaning, he bent over to pick up his coat, then stuffed some papers into his briefcase. "If anything falls apart while I'm gone, *don't* call me, okay?"

Freshening up at the hotel temporarily revived him—even more so, the thought that in a matter of hours he'd be enjoying his daughter's opening-night performance and proving he really could keep a promise. He dressed casually, leaving his business suits hanging in the hotel closet, and stuffed his pajamas and shaving kit into a roll-aboard. Bad enough he hadn't been able to get a reservation on a nonstop flight. He didn't need to add time by checking luggage.

After negotiating airport security, he stopped at a kiosk for a sandwich, bottled water, and a San Francisco newspaper. He'd barely situated himself in the waiting area at his gate when an announcement blared first in Japanese, then in English: "Flight 730 to San Francisco has been delayed. Boarding expected in approximately one hour."

Gary's stomach cramped. If nothing else went wrong, he could hurry through customs in San Francisco and still make his connection to Dallas. Maybe this would be an appropriate time to try prayer again. *Are You with me, Big Guy? I don't need anything messing up this trip home, okay?*

When boarding finally began, Gary whooshed out a relieved sigh. As soon as they were airborne, he tilted his seat back and closed his eyes. The nine-hour flight to San Francisco would be his best chance to get some sleep and attempt to catch up to Dallas time. His physical presence at Noelle's play wouldn't count for much if she caught him dozing halfway through the first act.

The plane set down in San Francisco only a few minutes behind schedule. Gary breezed through customs and then had a couple of hours to stretch his legs before the next flight. As he ambled toward the departure gate, another delay was announced.

He tried to maintain his cool as he approached the check-in counter. "Excuse me, what's the problem with the Dallas flight?"

A curly-haired man looked up from a computer terminal. "It's a continuing flight from Seattle. Takeoff was delayed because of heavy rains."

Gary paced back and forth in front of the windows, his eyes focused on the maze of runways. Thirty minutes passed, then an hour. He marched to the counter. "Any updates?"

"Your plane should be landing any minute, sir."

Ten minutes later the plane still was not on the ground. Gary joined an increasingly exasperated group of travelers storming the counter. "What's going on here?" an elderly woman demanded. "If I miss my granddaughter's wedding—" Others joined the fray with urgent business and family matters of their own.

The young flight agent lifted his hands helplessly. "We've got a lot of air traffic and weather problems today. Please be patient, everyone."

Gary elbowed his way to the front of the line. "Look here"— his gaze fell to the agent's name badge—"Stan, I need you to get me on the next available flight to Dallas, any airline, any price."

"I would if I could, sir, but I've already checked. With weekend travel picking up, the next several flights to Dallas are already overbooked. You'll be much better off sticking with what you've got."

Gary bunched his fists and returned to the waiting area. Running some mental calculations, he figured if the plane landed right this minute, and if absolutely nothing else went wrong, he *might* be able to arrive at the auditorium by curtain time. *Is this a test, Lord? To see if I'm serious about trusting You?*

More likely, it was God's payback for all the years Gary had denied him. *Turn your back on Me, will you?* God was probably saying. *And you expect Me to forgive and forget and make things magically run smoothly for you?*

No, God didn't operate that way. God always forgives and forgets. That much, Gary remembered learning in his childhood Sunday-school classes. Snatches of Bible verses flitted through his mind, words about God remembering His children's sins no more, casting them as far away as east is from west.

East from west, about as far as Dallas from Tokyo. *The irony is not lost on me, Lord. Just get me home on time, okay?*

At last the plane came into view. Within twenty minutes, the long-awaited announcement to board finally came. When the plane lifted off and Gary saw the San Francisco airport receding in the haze, he let himself relax into his seat. Just over three hours later, the plane pulled up to the terminal in Dallas. Gary pushed ahead of the other passengers in the jetway, excusing himself several times as he bumped them with his travel bag. His head was pounding when he finally made it to the exit and hailed a taxi.

Sinking into the backseat, he checked his watch. Seven twenty-two—eight minutes away from opening curtain. And he was on the verge of breaking yet another promise to his daughter. *Come on, Lord, I could use some help here.* Maybe he could still arrive in time to catch the second half. At least Noelle would know he tried.

He leveled his eyes at the driver through the rearview mirror. "Get me to Arden Heights High School Auditorium in thirty minutes or less, and you'll earn yourself a hundred-dollar tip."

The driver grinned and sped away.

23

Noelle fussed with the buttons on her costume, an ankle-length muslin dress with lace trim and mutton sleeves. Looking over her shoulder into the mirror, she tied the wide blue sash in a floppy bow. She checked her makeup one more time and jabbed in extra bobby pins to secure the two braids wrapped around her head. In a few minutes the lights would dim and she would step onstage to begin her opening lines as Katrin.

Cassie burst into the room. "Where's Laurence? Is he in his basket?" She lifted boxes and bags searching for the cat.

"He's right here under my feet." Noelle shifted to one side. With a mew, Laurence ambled out from beneath her skirt.

Lifting the old cat, Cassie buried her nose in his fur and hauled in a deep breath. "Good old Laurence. He's the most relaxed member of the cast."

Mrs. Sanchez peeked into the dressing room, her eyes sparkling. "Let's go, ladies. It's show time."

The cast members bustled across the hardwood floor and found their places for the opening scene. Noelle tiptoed behind the curtain at stage right, ready to step out and take a seat at the writing desk for her opening monologue. Peering around the edge of the curtain, she scanned the dimly lit auditorium in search of her family.

She spotted them in the third row—Gran, Uncle David, Aunt Susan. And next to them were Rebecca and Kevin, with an empty seat between them. Disappointment curdled in the pit of her stomach. She tried her best to shrug it off. *You really didn't expect him to show up, did you?*

But Rebecca said he promised!

Her eyes burned. She let the curtain fall back into place. Well. Now they'd all see what a consummate actress she really was. She took a big breath to steady her nerves, pulled herself erect, and became Katrin. She slipped through the folds of the curtain and seated herself at the writing desk, gracefully adjusting the folds of her skirt. As her spot came on and the audience responded with applause, Noelle took up a pen and pretended to write. She laid the pen aside, then lifted several sheets of paper, eyeing them appraisingly. She began to read:

"'For as long as I could remember, the house on Steiner Street had been home. . . .'"

As she finished her monologue, the curtain parted to reveal a kitchen scene with Mama in an armchair and Papa standing above her. Shortly, Cassie entered as Dagmar, hugging Laurence. The docile cat looked out at the audience, his big green eyes reflecting the stage lights. His loud "Meeooooow" brought a spontaneous round of applause. Laurence seemed to smile in acknowledgment as he let Cassie haul him over to a chest, where she sat down to stroke him.

Oh, Laurence, you ham! Stifling an admiring chuckle, Noelle could barely stay in character.

The rest of act one continued smoothly, and the curtain closed for intermission. Noelle fanned herself with the hem of her skirt. Under the hot lights, her temples had begun to perspire.

Warren handed her a cup of water. "You did great."

"It went by so fast."

"I saw your family in the audience, but I never spotted my folks. Did you see them?"

"Your mom and dad are about ten rows back, dead center." She smiled up at him. It wouldn't do any good to dwell on her own disappointment—something she should be used to by now. "Your parents must be so proud of your sets."

Warren drained his cup and angled her a sad smile. "I know you were counting on your dad being here."

She shrugged, turning away. "No big deal. No big surprise either." But it didn't make it hurt any less.

"Five minutes, crew." Mrs. Sanchez bustled across the stage. "Places for act two, pronto!"

Warren caught Noelle's elbow. "Don't give up on him. Whatever held him up was probably out of his control. He could still get here for tomorrow night."

She started to shake off his hand, but his warm eyes held hers. She relaxed into his arms, the only place she wanted to be at this moment. Except the faded double-breasted suit still reeked mothballs. Stifling a sneeze, she jerked away. "Come on. We've got a play to do."

As the house lights faded, she took her place once more at the writing desk. Under the spotlight illuminating her corner of the stage, she pretended to write, then lifted the manuscript to read.

"' . . . which was very, very seldom. I don't think I can ever remember seeing Mama unoccupied.'" Here, Noelle was to lay the paper aside and look out at the audience to say her next line. "'I do remember one'—"

A motion caught her eye, someone rushing down the darkened side aisle, straight toward her. A tall man in a tan jacket and turtleneck.

Dad!

He paused at the end of the third row, cast her a sheepish grin, then excused himself as he worked his way down the row to his seat. Rebecca looked up at him with a relieved smile and squeezed his arm.

"Noelle?" came a frantic whisper from backstage. "Do you need your line?"

She swallowed, her gaze shooting laser beams at her father.

"Noelle!"

She forced herself back into character. "'I—I do remember one occasion, though. It was the day before Dagmar came home from the hospital . . . .'"

The rest of the performance floated by in a haze. The moments Noelle had most looked forward to—Warren's fake cat's howl, Laurence's wag of his tail when he supposedly awoke from a chloroform-induced sleep—left her feeling disconnected, like she'd stepped into an alternate universe.

After the play, the entire cast stepped onstage for their curtain call, and then the individual actors took their bows one by one. As Noelle approached the footlights, she stared into the third row for the hundredth time that night. Yes! Her dad was still there. She hadn't dreamed the whole thing. As she bent into her curtsy, she saw Dad rise to his feet in a standing ovation, the entire audience joining him. She bowed again, feeling numb and dazed.

The curtain drew shut for the last time, and Noelle sank into the armchair onstage. Her fingertips tingled. She couldn't catch a full breath.

"What is it, babe?" Warren knelt in front of her. "You're white as a sheet."

Mrs. Sanchez hurried over, placing a hand on Noelle's back. "You're hyperventilating. Probably all the excitement. Try breathing into your cupped hands."

Noelle obeyed and soon felt better. She waved away the cast members hovering around her. "I'm okay. Quit staring."

Cassie plopped the old cat in Noelle's lap. "Here, hug Laurence. He earned it. Did you hear all the applause he got?"

"The star of the show!" Noelle rubbed her chin across the top of Laurence's head.

Cassie offered a hand up. "Let's go get changed. I'll help you out of your costume."

Noelle took her time changing into her street clothes. Every time she pictured her father rushing down the aisle, her stomach did a nosedive. The idea of facing him, of making herself listen to his excuses for showing up late, of deciding whether to forgive him or go on resenting him—she had no idea how she should feel or what she would say.

After stalling as long as she dared, she gathered up Laurence and his basket and went in search of Warren. She found him waiting with his parents in front of the stage.

"Great performance, Noelle." Mr. Ames patted her on the shoulder.

"Outstanding." Mrs. Ames pulled Noelle close for a quick hug. "I think we'll have to come back tomorrow night and see the play all over again."

Noelle smiled her thanks. She swung a nervous glance around the almost empty auditorium. "Did my family already leave?"

Warren shuffled his feet. "Your grandmother said to tell you they'd see you at the house. I'm taking you home."

"Oh." A bitter taste filled her mouth. Maybe it was her own fault for taking so long to change, but it still hurt to realize Dad hadn't even waited around to congratulate her. So much for thinking she really mattered to him. To any of them.

Rebecca parked near the entrance of an all-night pancake restaurant and shut off the engine. A glance at her husband's red eyes and drooping shoulders told her he wouldn't hold up much longer.

"We should have waited for her." Gary rubbed his forehead. "I'm not that hungry."

"Honey, you're running on empty. Noelle will have to understand." She unbuckled her seatbelt and reach for the door handle. "The minute we get home, you can hug her and tell her how wonderful she was."

"Hug her. Right." He heaved himself out of the car, weaving drunkenly. If Rebecca hadn't been convinced it was only fatigue, she would have thought the worst.

Even so, something about Gary was different tonight. They hadn't had time to talk yet, but as he'd held her hand during the play, she'd sensed a subtle change . . . a serenity that hadn't been there when they'd said their goodbyes at the airport just over a week ago.

The hostess seated them in a quiet booth near the back of the restaurant. Finally admitting his exhaustion, Gary rested his head in his hands and asked Rebecca to order for him. She perused the menu for something nourishing but not too heavy, settling on scrambled eggs, fruit, and an English muffin. As Gary ate, clearly more famished than he'd realized, she sipped herbal tea and studied his face.

After several minutes she asked softly, "Gary, is . . . is everything okay?"

He pushed his empty plate aside. With one arm folded along the edge of the table, he crumpled his napkin in his other hand. "I don't even know if I can find the words to tell you."

A quiver began in her stomach, old fears threatening to choke her. *This is awkward, Becky. Not sure I can find the right words.* She'd never forget Rob's fateful ship-to-shore call nine years ago.

No, God wouldn't do this to her again. She loved Gary, and he loved her—she believed it with all her heart. If only he'd just tell her, stop fidgeting with his napkin, stop looking at everything in the restaurant but her, stop working his Adam's apple and *just tell her.*

The knuckles of her clasped hands whitened. "Please, if it's something I've done or said, if I've hassled you too much about Noelle—whatever's wrong—"

His sudden chortle made her jump. "Wrong? Honey, nothing is wrong. It's the opposite, in fact." He laughed again, a shaky, embarrassed laugh. Reaching across the table for her hand, he ran his thumb across the shimmering diamonds in her wedding ring. "I'm sorry if I worried you. What did you think I was going to say?"

She looked up, her lips parted in bewilderment. Her husband's eyes spoke only love and tenderness, and the fear in her heart subsided. "Maybe you'd better just say it before I put my foot in my mouth."

With difficulty, Gary described his recent feeble attempts at prayer, then the encouragement he'd received from the Numata brothers and their pastor. "I'm sorry I put you off for so long about going to church. From now on, I want us to go as a family."

Tears filled her eyes. She slid from her side of the booth and squeezed in beside him, sobbing her gratitude into the soft folds of his collar as he held her close and stroked her hair.

Whatever happened with Noelle, whether or not the girl ever came to accept her stepfamily, Rebecca finally had full confidence her marriage would survive.

Noelle handed Laurence's basket to Warren, then fished for her house key in the depths of her suede hobo bag.

"Good ol' kitty." Warren reached inside the opening and scratched Laurence behind the ears. "You stole the show, fella."

"He was great. Nothing fazes him." Noelle stabbed the key into the lock. She envied the old cat, oblivious to the dramas playing out in her real-life world.

The door swung open on the darkened entry hall. Warren set

the basket inside the door, and the cat jumped out and darted toward the kitchen. Noelle bit her lip. "Guess I'll see you tomorrow. Good night."

"Hey, not so fast." He turned her face toward his and kissed her lightly on the lips. "That's for Noelle Townsend, leading lady." He kissed her again, a toe-curling kiss that made her senses reel. "And that one is for Noelle Townsend, girl of my dreams."

Love for Warren crowded out the stinging disappointment about her father. She gazed after him until he disappeared through his own front door before she slipped quietly into the house. Noticing a light in the kitchen, she found Uncle David, Aunt Susan, and Gran sitting around the table sipping cocoa.

"There's our superstar." Uncle David pushed his chair back and came around to give her a hug. "The play was great. Sure glad we could make it."

"How about some cocoa?" Aunt Susan rose to get another mug from the cupboard.

Noelle caught sight of the apothecary jar. A pain shot through her temples. "No, thanks. I'll make myself some tea."

She filled a mug from the electric kettle, then plopped in an apple-cinnamon teabag and carried the mug to the table. Might as well ask the question burning a hole in her brain. "So where is . . . everybody else?"

Gran looked at Uncle David. Uncle David glanced at Aunt Susan. Finally Gran answered. "Kevin's in the game room getting ready for bed. Rebecca took your father to a restaurant to get him something to eat. He was utterly exhausted after the flight—hadn't eaten for hours."

Noelle's eyes stung. An aching lump climbed into her throat. *Nothing's changed! Nothing's changed at all!*

Aunt Susan drew her chair closer to Noelle's and placed an arm around her shoulder. "Sweetie, it's not what you're thinking."

She knotted her fists and pounded the edge of the table,

rattling the cups. "My father stood me up again. What's so different about this time?"

"Everything, honey." Aunt Susan covered Noelle's hands with her own. "Your dad really tried to get there—tried his best. You wouldn't believe the problems he had—all the flight delays, then his taxi getting caught in traffic—"

Noelle jerked her hand away. "*Wouldn't believe* is right. I bet he had his alibi memorized before his plane ever landed. And why did he bother to show up at all if he was just going to take off again as soon as the curtain fell?"

"You're being completely unfair, Noelle." Gran hiked her chin. "It was obvious to all of us he wouldn't hold up another minute. They should be home soon. Your father made us promise we'd ask you to wait up."

Noelle collapsed against the table, knuckles pressed into her burning eyes. Whether any of it was true or not, she didn't have the energy to face her father tonight. She didn't have the strength to listen to more of his excuses and try to sort fact from fiction.

"Tell him I was just *too tired*." Sarcasm laced her tone. Jaw set, she poured the rest of her tea down the drain and trudged to her room.

The next morning, everyone but Gary, who'd hardly stirred since Rebecca had gotten him into bed last night, walked next door for breakfast with the Ameses. All through Debby's buffet offerings of whole-grain waffles, fresh berries, scrambled egg casserole, and sausage links, Noelle remained silent and sullen. When the rest of the family returned home, Noelle stayed behind with Warren, and Rebecca had the sense there would be nothing romantic about their conversation.

Awhile later, Rebecca emerged from the laundry room to see Noelle traipse through the back door, just now returning from

Warren's. The girl took one glance around the den, and the hurt in her eyes deepened. She started toward her bedroom without a word.

"Wait, Noelle, please." Rebecca dropped her laundry basket. She caught up and lightly touched Noelle's arm. "You can't still be angry with your dad. He tried, honey, honestly he did."

"Oh, yeah? Well—"

"There's my favorite niece!" David came around the corner from the kitchen, Susan right behind him. He tugged on Noelle's braid. "We don't want to monopolize your time, but we did come to see *you*, after all."

Rebecca backed away. Since she wasn't making headway with Noelle, maybe David and Susan could try. Retrieving her laundry basket, she set it on the sofa and began folding clothes.

"It's a great day," David said. "What would you say to spending a few hours at the zoo. I promise we'd have you home in time to rest up and shower before tonight."

Noelle shrugged. "Who all is going?"

"Gran said she was interested, and Kevin might go along." He turned to Rebecca. "If Gary's up soon, we could make it a family outing."

The offer touched Rebecca more deeply than she dared let on in front of Noelle. "I think we'd better pass. Last time I looked in on Gary, he was still dead to the world. But thanks for including Kevin."

"Come with us, Noelle." Susan stretched an arm around the girl's waist and squeezed. "We'll have fun."

"There could be traffic, or . . ." Noelle edged toward the piano and fingered the keys. "It's just not a good idea." She plunked a few notes on the piano, then hammered out a chord.

The sound set Rebecca's teeth on edge, and whatever trace of understanding she felt for Noelle dissolved. She spun around and gave the girl a cold stare. "Show some consideration, please. Gary's still sleeping."

Noelle slammed her palm down on the keys. The ugly sound echoed off the paneled walls. "Well, if *Gary* wants to sleep, then *Gary* certainly may. I wouldn't want to disturb his precious rest."

"Noelle!"

She ignored her uncle's stern protest and charged through the sunroom, heading back across the lawn toward the Ameses'.

Rebecca heaved a pained breath and shook her head. "I'm sorry. I'm sure I handled that all wrong."

David shoved his hands into his pockets. "In her frame of mind, whatever anyone said would have been the wrong thing."

Susan offered Rebecca a sad smile and came to stand beside her. She lifted a red polo shirt from the basket and neatly folded it. "Honestly, Rebecca, I admire you so much for the way you've handled this whole situation. Anyone else would have thrown up her hands and walked out."

"You don't walk out on people you love," Rebecca said softly. *And I want to love Noelle. I really do, Lord. Help me.*

"Back already?" Warren held the door for Noelle. "Did you talk to your dad?"

"*Gary* is sleeping and cannot be disturbed." She mimicked Rebecca's slightly nasal voice. "Can I stay over here for a while? Everybody at my house is mad at me."

"Yeah, I'm sure they are." Warren's eye roll suggested he didn't believe her. He planted a kiss on her forehead and led her into the sunlit living room.

She sank onto the sofa. "Why is it you always take the other person's side?"

"I'm always on your side. But somebody has to protect you from yourself."

"What's *that* supposed to mean?"

Warren sat sideways beside her, propping his elbow on the

back of the sofa. His warm brown eyes bored holes through her. "Sometimes you're your own worst enemy. You'd rather believe the worst than give people a chance to do the right thing."

"There you go again, talking down to me like a big brother . . . or my father."

He moved closer, wrapping her in his arms. "I thought you understood, the last thing I want to be to you is a brother. As for your father, if you'd just once let him be a father to you—"

She pulled away. "Give me one good reason why I should let him back into my life."

"Because he loves you. And you love him."

Old memories swam to the surface, leaving her choked and breathless. "I used to love him. I used to trust him and believe in him. I used to look forward to spending time with him when he got home from his trips." Her voice cracked. "I used to love to snuggle up with him in the big chair in the den and smell his aftershave."

She closed her eyes for a moment, her heart swelling with the memories, how some of the scent always rubbed off on her after she hugged him, how she used to go to sleep with her sleeve pressed to her cheek so she could keep on smelling him. When she knew he was packing for another trip, she'd sneak into his bathroom and sprinkle his aftershave onto her pillow so she could have him close all the while he was gone. She'd never let Mom change her pillowcase until after he came home again.

She pushed off the sofa and stared out the window, hugging herself. Emotions engulfed her until she thought she would drown. "If only he hadn't left us when we needed him the most!"

"That's it, isn't it?" Warren moved beside her. "You could have forgiven him for all the other times, but not for staying away when your mother was dying."

"Please, just stop," Noelle begged, her voice ragged. "Nothing is going to change what he did."

Warren took a few steps away, looping his thumbs in his belt loops. "Tried, convicted, and sentenced, by a judge and jury of one."

She shot him an icy glare. "And the condemned man ate a hearty meal and went to bed." She grabbed her jacket off the arm of a chair. "I think things were better at my house after all."

Outside, she stormed past the shrubbery and burst through the French door to her room, slamming it so hard that the glass panes threatened to shatter. Love and anger and bitterness twisted together inside her, an ugly, painful knot in her belly. Why was she always getting hurt by the people she cared the most about?

24

G ary turned his head, a distant thud disturbing his sleep. Squinting, he peered at the bedside clock. Almost noon? Great, he'd slept half the day away.

Thoughts rushing to Noelle, he bolted upright. He stumbled out of bed and shoved his legs into the trousers he'd discarded across a chair last night. By the time he and Rebecca had made it home after his late supper, David and Susan had already gone next door to spend the night at the Ameses'. Irene had stayed up only long enough to assure him they'd all done their best to convince Noelle how hard Gary had tried to get to the auditorium on time, but she'd refused to listen and had gone straight to bed.

What did it matter? No explanation would have been good enough for letting his daughter down again.

And now he'd slept much later than he'd intended. Noelle was probably off doing her own thing by now, avoiding him as usual.

"Rebecca?" He tramped into the den. "Rebecca? Anybody home?"

She appeared in the doorway from the game room. "In here, sweetie. Just putting away Kevin's laundry."

"Why'd you let me sleep so late?"

"You were exhausted. You needed to sleep."

"What I really need is to talk to Noelle." For all the good it would do. He shoved past Rebecca and sank onto the game room sofa. "Where is everybody, anyway?"

"Everyone except Noelle has gone to the zoo. They'll be back in time for an early supper before the performance tonight."

"And Noelle?"

Rebecca glanced away. "She was over at Warren's for a while, but I think she's in her room now."

Gary paced to the window and gazed across the patio. The curtain was drawn on the French door to Noelle's bedroom. He rubbed a hand along his whiskery jaw. "We're back to square one, aren't we?"

Rebecca hooked her arm through his. "Why don't you go talk to her, explain to her yourself about yesterday?"

"She'll only accuse me of making up more excuses—if she listens at all." His chest ached. Could things get any worse? His last hope to prove himself to his daughter, and he'd failed. "It's no use. Maybe I can arrange an earlier flight back to Tokyo."

"Oh, no, you don't." Rebecca seized his arm and forced him to look at her. "This weekend isn't only about Noelle. Kevin and I need some time with you, too."

He hung his head. "I wasn't thinking. It's just—" A choked sob caught in his throat.

She wrapped her arms around him, and her love was almost unbearable. He didn't deserve it, never would. But he clung to her anyway and let the wet, silent tears trickle down his cheeks.

"Enough feeling sorry for yourself," Rebecca said roughly. She took a step back and wiped away his tears with her palm. He saw moisture in her eyes as well. "Don't you ever forget how much Kevin and I love you. We are your family, and we always will be, whether Noelle ever comes around or not. Sure, you've made mistakes, but haven't we all? It's who you are now that counts."

A new creation in Christ—that's what the Japanese pastor had told him. He wanted to believe it, to accept the total forgiveness God offered. "But how can I forgive myself for the way things have turned out for Noelle? What if she's completely lost to me?"

Rebecca stretched up on tiptoe and clasped her hands behind his neck. Pulling him gently forward, she pressed her cheek to his and spoke softly into his ear. "You've done everything you can do, and God knows it. Now you have to trust Him to work on Noelle's heart."

Gary had never loved Rebecca more than he did at that moment. He had failed her so many times—just like he'd failed Noelle, just like he'd failed Kate. And yet here she was, offering him strength and hope. God willing, he'd make it all up to her.

"You must be hungry," she said at last. "You had 'breakfast' last night. Could you eat a sandwich?"

"Sounds good. Let me go wash my face."

In the guest bathroom, he leaned over the sink and splashed handfuls of cold water across his eyes. In the stillness after he turned off the faucet, he pictured Noelle, only a few feet away in her room. He longed to put his arms around his little girl again, to make her believe her daddy was back in her life to stay.

Watching Gary mope around all afternoon, Rebecca ached for her husband. At every sound from the far end of the house, he glanced hopefully in the direction of Noelle's room, but the girl never made an appearance. Rebecca was tempted to storm down the hall and physically drag Noelle out of hibernation—anything to get her to quit hiding and face her father. But no, force wasn't the answer. Over and over, Rebecca reminded herself the situation was best left in God's hands.

The rest of the family returned from the zoo shortly before five. Kevin set plates around the table while Gary filled iced-tea glasses. As Rebecca mixed vinaigrette dressing into the salad, Irene entered the kitchen, followed by Susan and David.

"What can we do, dear?" Irene asked.

"There's a plate of cold cuts in the fridge," Rebecca said. "If you'd set that out along with the sandwich rolls and condiments, please." She carried the salad bowl to the table, then turned to Irene with a hesitant look. "Did you happen to talk to Noelle after you got home?"

Irene skewed her lips. "She said she's not hungry and will get something to eat after the play."

"I don't like it." Rebecca frowned. "Even if she doesn't want to be with the family, she should eat something nourishing before she performs tonight."

Susan looked at Gary and shook her head. "This mulish behavior of hers has dragged on way too long. She owes you better than this, Gary."

He sank into a chair. "She doesn't owe me anything."

"But you're her father. It's time she grew up and accepted that things don't always go as planned." Exhaling sharply, Susan turned to leave. "I'm going to try to talk some sense into the girl."

Rebecca stopped her. "Susan, don't. If we start anything now, it'll ruin the whole evening. This play means everything to her."

Susan paused, hands lifted in resignation. "You're right, this is not the time." She fixed Gary with a resolute stare. "But don't you leave here this weekend without resolving things."

When supper was over, David and Susan returned to the Ameses' to dress for the play, and Irene excused herself to change in Noelle's room. When she returned to the kitchen later, she told Rebecca and Gary that Noelle hadn't spoken more than five words to her. "She was out the back door and gone before I finished dressing."

Arms folded atop the table, Gary glanced away and sighed.

"Come on, honey." Rebecca pushed the start button on the dishwasher. "We'd better get ready."

In the privacy of their bedroom, she wrapped her arms around her husband. He'd been gloomy enough before Susan's ultimatum, but all through supper Rebecca had watched every remaining fragment of hope drain from his spirit. If not for the play, she wouldn't have been able to stop herself from barging into Noelle's room and shake some sense into the girl. Gary's daughter needed to understand exactly how much her father loved her and how much he was willing to sacrifice to prove it.

Wait. Wait. The command, spoken in the depths of her heart, was unmistakable.

She pressed her cheek against the rough cotton of Gary's polo shirt. God's timing was perfect. She would force herself to wait and follow God's lead.

After a hot shower and a much-needed shave, Gary pulled on a pair of slacks and tucked in the tail of his undershirt. Susan's words still rang in his mind. Only one more day before he had to return to Tokyo. A breakthrough with Noelle in so short a time? Not likely. Rebecca kept insisting that God could at this very moment be designing a miracle to bring Gary's daughter back to him, but he couldn't find the strength to believe it.

"But I believe in *You*, God," he said aloud, eyes toward the ceiling. He believed—he was *trying* to believe—that whatever happened, God loved him and would always be with him. He would live in the strength of that promise, and he would go forward. He would ask God every day for the power and wisdom to be the husband and father he was meant to be.

It surprised him once more, the calm assurance resting in the Lord could bring to his soul. Taking a long, cleansing breath, he reached for his aftershave and started to shake some into his palm. Something made him stop short, a gentle tug at his memory, something about Noelle . . .

With a clatter, he dropped the bottle on the counter and then rummaged through the cupboard. His old British Sterling—there had to be some still stashed away somewhere. He used to keep travel-sized toiletries in this bathroom, for the times Kate had the master bath so steamed up that he could barely see through the fog.

Aspirin bottles, miniature shampoos and hand creams, packages of cold tablets, a box of Band-aids . . . Yes! A half-used sample bottle of British Sterling. He unscrewed the cap and held the bottle under his nose, breathing in the almost forgotten scent. He cupped his palm and poured some of the silvery-clear liquid into it, then rubbed both hands together and slapped them against his face. The alcohol made his freshly shaven skin tingle, sending a shiver down his spine as the woodsy fragrance filled his nostrils.

Please, God, just let me get close enough for Noelle to notice!

25

Noelle had spent the afternoon huddled on her bed, curled into a miserable knot. Not even Warren understood—and he claimed he loved her? It didn't help that Uncle David, Aunt Susan, and Gran all sided with Warren. Like she should simply blow off the last decade of her father's broken promises. Like she could just snap her fingers and forgive him.

Like she would *ever* give him another chance to hurt her again.

While Gran was in the bathroom getting ready for the play, Warren had phoned Noelle's cell. "Are you too mad at me to let me drive you to the auditorium?"

The gentleness in his voice had almost undone her. She'd been so mean to him, but he stuck by her, kept right on forgiving her. She clutched the phone. "I'm sorry about earlier, I really am." She'd wanted to say so much more but could barely speak over the suffocating tightness in her chest.

"Can you be ready in ten minutes?"

"Meet you at your car." She hung up. *I love you.*

She only had to keep her focus for one more night—for the play's sake, for Mom's sake—and then she'd think about falling apart. She sensed it coming, the biggest crash of her life. So much for courage. So much for dignity. She didn't have any left.

She gathered up Laurence, set him in his basket, and slipped out to the patio. Seconds later, she stood shivering in the cold next to Warren's Mazda.

Stepping out his front door, he grinned as he punched the remote to unlock the car. "Wow, you look great."

"Thanks." Before he could get her door for her, she jerked it open and dropped into the seat. Polite gestures weren't anything she could endure right now.

At seven twenty-nine, she took her position onstage, ready for her opening lines. She made quick note of where her family sat —fourth row, her father in the aisle seat. Good. Now all she had to do was avoid looking toward their section for the rest of the performance.

Tonight the play seemed to go on forever, dull and flat and lifeless. She'd lost the emotional spark, the excitement that had carried her all through the tedium of rehearsals and the tension of opening night. She felt leaden as she moved across the stage, each scene dragging out like a slo-mo replay. She hoped it was all inside her head and that the audience wouldn't notice.

When the last scene drew to a close, she took her bows along with the other cast members and joined Lynn Larson to present Mrs. Sanchez with the traditional bouquet of red roses. More applause, another round of thank-yous. Then the excited whoop of victory backstage after the curtain closed for the final time. Another of Mrs. Sanchez's group hugs. "Great job, gang! You've made me so proud."

"And don't forget," Lynn Larson chimed in. "The cast party begins at my house in thirty minutes!"

The hug broke apart. With Laurence snuggled under one arm, Noelle followed the girls into the dressing room.

"You feeling okay, Noelle?" Cassie slipped out of her ruffled skirt. "You've really seemed out of it tonight. I hope you're not catching my cold."

"Guess I'm just tired." She grimaced. "I hope it didn't show in my performance."

"You were great, as always. But between scenes you were avoiding everyone. Did you and Warren have a fight or something?"

Noelle bristled. Why did Cassie have to be so nosy?

A wave of guilt washed over her. *Get over yourself, Noelle.* Would she ever stop being so angry, taking offense at every little thing? She eased out of her dress and hung it on the wardrobe rack. "It's nothing," she said at last, smoothing the skirt. "I'll be fine after I catch up on some rest."

"Okay," Cassie drawled, not sounding convinced. She pulled on a pair of skinny black jeans and a tunic-length sweatshirt appliquéd with neon-bright comedy/tragedy masks. "You are coming to the cast party, aren't you?"

Going to a party was the last thing Noelle felt like doing, but it would be easier to show up than give reasons why she couldn't—and tons easier than going home to face her family. She wished she'd never have to lay eyes on her father again, wished she'd given up her life in Arden Heights when she'd had the chance and gone to Nebraska to live on the farm with her grandmother.

"Noelle, did you hear me?"

"What? Oh, the party. Yeah, I'm going." She turned away, avoiding her reflection in the mirror as she undid her "Katrin" braids. She didn't want to look at herself just now, afraid of the ugliness she would see. She pulled a black Angora sweater over her head, then lifted her long waves from underneath. Static-charged strands flew out, crackling in her ears. Smoothing them down, she cursed the cold, dry weather.

"What's with Noelle?" one of her castmates murmured.

Cassie glanced in Noelle's direction and shrugged. "Just leave her alone, okay?"

Scooping up Laurence in his basket, Noelle darted out the door and made her way around the furniture and props that had been moved to the side of the stage.

"There you are." Warren met her at the bottom of the proscenium steps. "Ready to party?"

"Sure." Time to pull out the acting skills again. She faked a smile.

"What about Laurence? Do we need to drop him off at your house?"

"No way!" Lynn Larson breezed over. "Laurence can't miss the party. He's an important member of the cast."

Noelle pursed her lips. "It's been a long night for him already. I don't know . . ."

"Please, Noelle? Everyone will be so disappointed. You *have* to bring Laurence."

Several other cast members peered over Lynn's shoulder and added their pleas. Noelle reached inside the basket and rubbed Laurence under the chin. "What do you say, fella? Up to a party?"

"Great!" Lynn shifted the strap of her tote. "See you at my house in a few minutes."

As Noelle watched Lynn and the others jog up the aisle, she caught sight of her father waiting just inside the double doors. When he started toward her, the muscles in her legs bunched like coiled springs. It took every ounce of willpower not to escape back to the dressing room.

Too late. He stood right in front of her. She froze and stared at the collar of his leather jacket.

"Honey, the play was wonderful. *You* were wonderful." When she didn't answer, he stuffed his hands into his pockets. "Warren, great job on the sets."

"Thanks, Mr. Townsend." Warren gave a polite nod.

Noelle adjusted her hold on Laurence's basket. He squirmed inside, his shifting weight throwing her off balance—or was it her father's nearness?

Dad rocked on his heels. "You must be starving by now. Could I take you out for a late supper somewhere? Anywhere you want."

The hopefulness in his voice only fed her resentment. "I'm going with Warren to the cast party."

"Right. I should have realized." His shoulders sagged. He took two steps backwards. "Then I'll see you in the morning, I guess."

"I'll probably sleep in."

"Well . . . enjoy yourselves at the party." The corners of his mouth twitched upward briefly before he turned and trudged toward the lobby.

Disapproval shone in Warren's narrowed eyes. "Did you have to be so cold to him?"

Her moment of self-righteous satisfaction melted into a puddle of guilt. She swallowed and looked away. Nothing she could say would make Warren understand. "Let's just go to Lynn's, okay?"

By the time they arrived at the Larson house, the party was in full swing. In a quiet corner of the spacious game room, Noelle curled her legs under her and sank onto the Berber carpet next to Laurence's basket. Warren headed straight to the refreshment table, where he refilled his plastic cup three times as he stood there chatting with friends.

Creep. Did you forget I'm your date? How could he say he loved her one minute and then completely ignore her the next? Okay, so it was her own fault for being grouchy all the time, but it didn't lessen the sting.

About the time her self-pity meter reached the red zone, Laurence mewed and stretched his body through the basket opening. He placed a paw on Noelle's knee, the other poised in a furry crook.

"Hey, Laurence. You feeling neglected too?" As she stroked his head, she remembered the litter box she'd left beneath an unused counter in the auditorium dressing room. The custodian would find a nasty surprise next time he came in to clean. "Sorry, kitty, do you need to go potty? Well, there's no litter box here, and I don't think Mrs. Larson would like any messes on this fancy new carpet."

Two choices—either interrupt Warren's conversation and ask him to drive them home, or take Laurence outside and see if he would take care of business in the Larsons' flowerbed. Since Warren had barely glanced her way all evening, why bug him now? With a groan, she lifted the heavy cat and carried him out the front door.

As she set him down under a nearby hedge, a chill north wind whipped her hair across her face. She pushed it out of her eyes in time to spot Laurence before he sniffed his way around the corner of the house, his white patches shimmering under the glow of the street lamp. She followed, hugging herself against the cold and wishing he'd hurry up and take care of business so they could go back inside.

"Laurence, come on, kitty." He'd disappeared behind the prickly holly bushes. "Where are you? It's freezing out here."

She was almost to the Larsons' back fence when a low, menacing growl came from the other side of the cedar gate, then a sudden, ferocious bark. The startled cat leapt from behind the bushes and dashed past her.

"Laurence!" Noelle spun around and chased after him.

Tires screeched. Noelle jerked to a halt at the edge of the lawn. A scream caught in her throat as a man in a trench coat barged from his car in the middle of the street and knelt beside a limp, motionless body—*Laurence!*

The man looked up. "Oh, no, I'm so sorry. Is this your cat?"

She pressed a hand to her mouth, nodding.

"He's still alive. Do you have a vet you can call?"

The question didn't have any meaning for her. She couldn't think, couldn't understand what she needed to do. With a sickening shudder, all the air left her body. She stumbled between the parked cars toward her beloved Laurence. Falling to her knees, she cradled the cat's head, his shining green eyes fluttering open in a helpless, unseeing stare.

"I'm sorry, I'm so sorry," the man repeated. "I never even saw him until it was too late. I can call my vet if you—"

"Laurence," Noelle moaned, huddling over the cat. Panic rising in her chest, she glanced up at the man. "Please get help. *Please!*"

Moments later several from the party stood at the curb, their mouths gaping. Noelle waited for someone to do something, but they all seemed as confused and helpless as she.

Then Warren pushed through the crowd. "Here, babe, let me see him." He bent over the cat, stroking him gently. "Dr. Hays is your vet, isn't he?"

Noelle gave a shaky nod.

"He's our vet too," Lynn Larson called out. "I'll get Mom to phone him."

"Tell him to meet us at his clinic." Roughly, Warren thrust his car keys at Noelle. "Here, get the door open. I'll carry Laurence."

She struggled to her feet, reeling toward Warren's car at the end of the block. She stabbed the button on the key fob, then jerked the passenger door open and fell into the seat. She held out her arms for Laurence, oblivious to the blood oozing from his wounds onto her jeans. An instant later Warren climbed behind the steering wheel. The engine roared, and they sped away, squealing around corners and cruising through yellow lights until they reached the Hays Animal Clinic.

After changing into pajamas and robes, Rebecca and Irene sat at the kitchen table sipping chamomile tea. Everyone else had gone to bed. After several minutes of silence, Rebecca asked, "How do you think it's going?"

Irene leaned back and shook her head. "I wouldn't venture a guess."

"I've been praying about this so hard, asking God to soften Noelle's heart, asking Him to give Gary the right words."

"So have I."

Rebecca reached for the older woman's hand, her throat tightening. "Irene, there's something else I've been praying for, and I hope your kindness toward me this weekend is my answer. Do you . . . *can* you forgive me for taking Gary away from your daughter?"

"Oh, honey, you bear no responsibility whatsoever for what happened between Kate and Gary." Irene's gentle gaze conveyed her sincerity. "From the day those two announced they wanted to get married, I had a feeling they were headed for trouble. Gary always had such big ambitions, and all my daughter wanted was love and family. Kate had a lot of growing up to do, herself, before it was over."

"Gary did love her, still does," Rebecca said softly. "He regrets so much now. He isn't the same man he was a year ago."

Irene smiled. "I can see that. It helps more than you know."

The phone rang, and Rebecca rose to answer it. An unfamiliar voice greeted her in anxious tones. "Mrs. Townsend? This is Deb Larson. My daughter Lynn was in the play with Noelle."

Rebecca gripped the receiver, dread curdling her stomach. She remembered something about a cast party at the Larson home following tonight's performance. "Is it Noelle? Has something happened?"

"Noelle's okay. I mean, she's not hurt or anything." Silence. "I'm afraid it's her cat. He's been hit by a car."

"Oh, no!" Rebecca collapsed onto a barstool as a sob escaped from her throat.

Irene hurried to her side, her face ashen. "What is it? What's happened to Noelle?"

Rebecca covered the mouthpiece. "It's Laurence. A car hit him."

"Oh, the poor thing! Poor Noelle!"

Mrs. Larson continued in Rebecca's ear, "I've already called Dr. Hays. He's meeting the kids at the animal clinic. I thought you'd want to know so someone could go over and be with them. Noelle looked very shaken. I couldn't see how badly the cat was hurt, but . . . I'm sorry, it doesn't look good."

"Thank you. I—" She didn't know what else to say. "Thank you," she said again, and hung up.

Then it occurred to her that if Noelle went to the party, obviously she wasn't with Gary. And since Gary hadn't come home yet . . .

Rebecca pressed a hand to her throat. Her gaze met Irene's. "I've got to find Gary."

Irene rubbed her temples. "Does he have his cell phone?"

Rebecca grabbed up the phone again and stabbed Gary's speed-dial code into the keypad. Before his phone even had a chance to ring, the call was transferred to his voicemail, suggesting his phone must be turned off. She used the few seconds listening to the recorded greeting to gather her thoughts, then spoke after the tone. "Gary, please, please check your messages. You need to go to Noelle. She's at the vet clinic with Laurence. He's been hit by a car. Call my cell when you get this."

Rebecca's thoughts raced as she hung up the receiver. Whether the girl could admit it or not, Noelle needed a parent tonight. She needed a strong shoulder to lean on. Even more, she might very well need an adult's loving support in making a very painful decision.

Gary, where are you? If he couldn't be found, someone else would have to go. But did Noelle have enough respect yet for Rebecca? True, they'd come a long way in their relationship, but they still had miles to go. The last thing Rebecca wanted was to make matters even more difficult.

She turned to Irene. "I have no idea where Gary is, and Noelle needs someone she trusts with her. Let's get dressed. I'll drive you to the vet's."

"But what about Kevin? Someone should be here with him."

Rebecca massaged her forehead. "Maybe David or Susan can come over. I'll call next door." She reached for the phone again, but Irene stopped her.

"It's nearly midnight. They're probably sound asleep." Irene lifted Rebecca's hand and pressed it between her own. "You go, dear. I'll stay with Kevin. You be there for Noelle."

"But I—"

"Listen to me. It's you and Gary she must learn to depend on, not her grandmother or uncle or even her best friend. Most of all, Noelle needs"—her voice broke—"a mother."

I can't, Lord, I can't!

But she knew Irene was right. She needed to do this. Each breath grating through her lungs like sandpaper, she ran to the bedroom to pull on a sweatshirt, jeans, and sneakers. *Oh, God, help me. Help me do the right thing!*

The clinic lights blinked on moments after Warren and Noelle arrived. Dr. Hays held the door as Warren carried Laurence into the examining room. Laying the cat on the stainless-steel table, he said to Noelle, "Maybe you should wait outside."

"No, I have to be here." She touched Laurence's head with a bloodied hand. Though Warren tried to shield her with his arm, she didn't take her eyes off the cat all the while the veterinarian worked.

Long minutes later, Dr. Hays sighed and stepped away from the table. He pulled off blood-smeared latex gloves and dropped them into a waste receptacle. "He's in very bad shape. I've given him an injection to ease the pain, but there's little else I can do."

Noelle's fists clenched. Fear and anger knotted her stomach. "You can't let him die!"

Warren stroked her arm. "Exactly how bad is it, sir?"

"To be certain, I'd have to take some x-rays, but I'm pretty sure he's got a broken pelvis and severe internal injuries." The vet bit his lip and spoke softly, more to Warren than to Noelle. "Have you called her dad? A parent should be here to make this decision."

Decision? Panic strangled her. "You want to put him to sleep? No!"

Warren tried to soothe her, but she beat her fists against him and broke away, hovering over Laurence's broken body.

Behind her, Warren murmured, "Then there's nothing you can do?"

She glanced up to see Dr. Hays sadly shake his head. "Even if I could patch him up, it would be cruel to keep him alive this way. He'd lose every scrap of dignity."

There was that word again, *dignity*. It grated against Noelle's senses like a fingernail on a chalkboard. Images flashed across her memory, images of her mother's shrunken form, face pale against the bed covers, the catheter, the morphine, the shadow of death drawing closer and closer, waiting to suck the last breath from her body . . .

She straightened, her chest heaving. "Who cares about dignity? What matters is *life*. If you can save his life, you have to try!"

"You don't understand, Noelle." The doctor spoke slowly, patiently. "Even if Laurence survives, he's likely to be partially paralyzed and lose all control of his bodily functions. After the long and healthy life he's lived, it would be the ultimate humiliation for him. You wouldn't want him alive like that, would you?"

Her face crumpled. She let out a long sigh that shook her entire body. How could she be so selfish? She had fought so hard against her mother's decision to face death with courage, but now, could she give Laurence the dignified end he deserved?

Dear God in heaven, if You're there, help me do the right thing.

Her heart breaking, she leaned over her beloved Laurence. She brought her face close to his, feeling his soft fur against her cheek. Her ear picked up a strained, muted rumbling. Laurence was purring! As she cradled his head in her palm, he rolled his big green eyes toward her and mewed, a sound as gentle and timid as when he was a kitten. His feline features seemed to smile at her. His eyes glazed, and the purring stopped.

A swelling lump of agony closed Noelle's throat, and she pressed her face against the cat's lifeless head. A choking sound wrenched from her trembling lips. It was followed by another, and another, and she realized with a strange kind of relief that she was crying, sobbing uncontrollably, releasing all the pent-up grief she'd been storing up since her mother's death.

She felt a hand on her shoulder, arms lifting her up, enfolding her. Eyes swimming with tears, she allowed herself to be led away, out of the pain-filled room. She reached out blindly for someone to hold on to, and felt strong arms hug her close. She buried her face in a solid shoulder and let the tears flow.

A familiar masculine scent filled her nostrils, blocking out the gory memory of blood and death. "Daddy."

"I'm here, honey, I'm here."

26

It was literally by the grace of God that Gary had gotten the message about Noelle and made it to the veterinary clinic in time. He'd turned off his cell phone before the play started, then never thought to switch it on again, especially after Noelle's rebuff had stolen away his last remnants of hope. He couldn't face going home and explaining to Rebecca and everyone else that he'd lost yet another chance to make things right with his daughter, so he'd gotten into his car and started driving.

His first impulse had been to find the nearest bar and drink himself into oblivion. He had tried so hard to believe God really could bring good out of any situation, even the death of a marriage, the estrangement of a child. Maybe God wasn't so powerful after all.

Or maybe God simply didn't care.

Then Gary found himself pulling in not at a bar but a church parking lot. He didn't have the guts to actually go inside, but he sat shivering in his SUV and laid on God every accusation, every regret, every demoralizing instance of failure festering within him. He beat the steering wheel until his palms felt bruised. *Why,*

God? I've promised to change, and I've tried so hard. I asked You for this one thing—my daughter's love and forgiveness.

With the front of his leather jacket damp from a flood of unmanly tears, he'd suddenly remembered his cell phone. *Check your messages, Gary. What if you missed an important call?* The prompting seemed more habit than God-directed. Six months ago, he would never have turned off his phone for something like a play or concert, just set it to vibrate in case he had to step out and deal with some work issue. But tonight he hadn't wanted anything to distract him from his reason for being in the school auditorium: his daughter, the star of the show, the pride and joy of his life.

He almost didn't activate the phone even then. He was certainly in no mood to deal with any problems that may have come up across the ocean. He'd be returning to Tokyo soon enough, and not with the jubilant bounce in his step he'd imagined after reconnecting with his daughter.

Reluctantly he'd pressed the on button and then cringed when the phone flashed the *new voicemail* message. With resignation he tapped the icon to listen to the recording.

Rebecca's words sliced through his self-pity with more bite than the icy winds of a blue norther. He tossed the phone on the passenger seat and sped toward Hays Animal Hospital. Minutes later he found himself holding his sobbing daughter in his arms.

"Daddy," she murmured, and his heart ripped in two. Fresh tears mingled with Noelle's as he kissed her forehead and held her trembling body.

Someone burst through the entrance. He looked up to see Rebecca, her face scrubbed and shiny, her soft curls windblown. She froze, holding the door, and put a hand to her mouth. Her eyes sang out love, grief, and thanksgiving all at once, the very emotions melting his insides. Silently she backed out the door. Through the glass he watched her return to her car and drive away.

Dr. Hays and Warren came into the waiting area, and Gary stroked his daughter's hair while the doctor gently explained that Laurence had died from his injuries. Gary freed an arm to reach toward his back pocket, but the vet shook his head. "Later."

Gary nodded his thanks. "Sweetie, let me take you home."

"No, not without Laurence. We can't leave him here."

Gary turned to the vet. "Can we take him home to bury him?"

The man nodded and returned to the examination room. A few minutes later, he carried out a small cardboard box. Warren held out his hands for it. "You go on. I'll bring Laurence in my car," he said, and followed them outside.

Between their two cars, Noelle paused, looking dazed, uncertain. Gary pushed a strand of damp hair from her eyes. "Would you rather ride home with Warren?"

She trembled and reached for him, tucking her cold hands beneath his jacket. "No, Daddy, I want you."

Noelle awoke to the sudden dizzying sensation that she was falling. She gripped the edge of her bed and flung her eyes open, relieved to find herself in her own room. Had last night really happened? *Oh, please, God, let it be a horrible dream!*

Then in slow motion she mentally relived the awful sound of tires screeching, the blood on her clothes and hands, the crushing realization that Laurence had died.

But there was more—Daddy holding and comforting her, drying her tears over and over again. Daddy had brought her home and tucked her in bed, caressing her hand, talking to her through the long night of endless tears. Her sobs had been purging, cleansing.

All night her father had sat with her in the darkened bedroom, telling her again and again how much he loved her, how much he cared. He talked of her mother, and the past, and how things used to be, reminding her of happy memories long forgotten. The summer before Noelle turned five when they'd spent a week at the Whitney farm in Nebraska, and Daddy had shown her the cows and the chickens, even helped her gather eggs early in the morning. The Christmas they'd spent at Vail, and he'd taught Noelle, eight then, how to ski. A trip to Estes Park and feeding peanuts to the chipmunks along Trail Ridge Road. The time Laurence fell into the pool, and she screamed until her father dove in with his clothes on and fished him out, while she stood on the side shouting, "Save him, Daddy! Save him!"

And then she'd fallen asleep, a sound, still, dreamless sleep in which she felt safe and secure, and more loved than she could remember.

Thoughts of Laurence returned, and she bolted upright. The hollow feeling of loss threatened to engulf her, as powerful and terrifying as the day last summer when she'd stood at the foot of her mother's empty bed. It was grief, yes, and it hurt like crazy. But something about it was different. Somewhere beneath the pain, a tiny spark of life still glowed, a piece of lint under a magnifying glass, catching the sun's rays, igniting. The warmth spread, fingers of flame clawing away at the cold emptiness around her heart.

She pulled on her robe, stuffed her feet into her fuzzy bear-claw slippers, and stepped into the hallway. The house was silent except for the burbling of the coffeemaker in the kitchen. Not even Kevin's video games or the *thwack* of billiard balls disturbed the stillness. Noelle trudged through the empty den, then into the kitchen. The house appeared to be deserted.

"Noelle?" Her father's voice startled her.

She spun around. "Where is everyone?"

"We're all outside, down by the creek. Get a jacket and come with me."

Confused, she glanced down at her robe and slippers. "But I'm not dressed."

"Doesn't matter." Her father went to the hall closet and got a coat for her, guiding her arms into the down-filled sleeves. Taking her hand, he led her through the sunroom and out into the cold, clear air.

The sun shone brightly in a cloudless azure sky, filtering through the naked tree branches, making crisscrossing shadows on the path along the creek. Warren huddled with the rest of Noelle's family near one of the oak trees by the creek. A shovel leaned against the trunk next to a cardboard box. Nestled between two exposed roots Noelle glimpsed a rectangular hole, and beside it a moist, brown mound of dirt.

She shivered as a gust of wind bit at her cheeks. She knelt beside the box and folded back the lid. Wrapped in a remnant of sky-blue satin, Laurence lay curled up inside. He seemed so peaceful, almost as if he might lift his head and mew, just as he had as Uncle Elizabeth in the play the morning after Papa had given him a dose of chloroform.

Noelle sighed and choked back a sob. If only life were so simple. If only a good night's sleep could make everything all right again.

Warren took her elbow, lifting her to her feet. She held her breath as her father carefully lowered the box into the hole. He handed her the shovel, and she scooped up some of the dirt and let it fall over the box. One by one, the shovel went around the circle, until each of them had added a spadeful of dirt to the grave. Noelle's father finished off the pile, tamping the mound with the back of the shovel.

"I made a marker." Kevin reached for a stone from behind the tree. It was a smooth, round rock, about a foot across, on which Kevin had used a black marker to print the words:

LAURENCE TOWNSEND
FRIEND AND COMPANION TO NOELLE
MAY HE REST IN PEACE

With Warren's help, Kevin placed the stone at the head of the grave.

No one moved or spoke for several minutes. Noelle listened to the soft sniffles going on around her, her own breath squeezing in and out of her lungs as if they'd forgotten how to work.

Rebecca was the first to break the silence. "I'll miss the old fellow," she said with a sniff. "He was the only one who appreciated my tuna casserole."

Noelle glanced up to see Rebecca blow her nose and dab at her cheeks with a damp tissue. Their eyes met, and the briefest of smiles fluttered across Noelle's lips, a smile that spoke both gratitude and apology. The look in Rebecca's eyes told her she understood.

Rebecca held back as Gary picked up the shovel and started toward the house with the others. She glanced down at the little grave, her eyes brimming at the loss of the sweet old cat, her heart aching for Noelle. And yet somehow—*oh, thank You, God!*—the hate inside Noelle seemed to have died as well.

Looking up, she saw Noelle pause and turn toward her. Lips trembling, throat working, the girl reached for Rebecca's hand. Sensing her struggle for words, Rebecca took her hand and squeezed. "You don't have to say anything, honey. It's okay."

"Yes, I do. I've been horrible to you, and I'm so, so sorry." She swallowed and brushed away a tear. "I haven't acted very . . . *dignified*, I guess, not like my mom would have wanted. I didn't understand what she meant until now. When she talked about dying with dignity, I thought it meant she was giving up the fight. And I never wanted that. I never wanted her to just give up and die."

"Of course you didn't. And she didn't want to leave you. She would never have left you if she'd had a choice."

Noelle sank to her knees next to the mound of dirt covering Laurence's body. "I finally get it, though. Dignity comes from believing you've done your best, even when it's hard. It means never giving up trying, or hoping, or caring—never losing faith." She stroked the headstone. "But it also means being strong when it's time to say goodbye."

Rebecca knelt beside the girl and touched her shoulder. "Warren told me how strong you were last night, how you were ready to make the right decision for Laurence."

"I'm glad I didn't have to." Fresh sobs shook her. "At least I was there."

Leaning close, Rebecca couldn't refrain from bestowing a soft kiss on the girl's cheek. "That's what families are for, honey. That's what families are for."

Uncle David and Aunt Susan had to leave at noon to catch their flight back to Phoenix, but thank goodness Gran could stay another couple of days. Too many goodbyes in one day had Noelle tearing up over and over again. As David backed the rental car out of the driveway and turned up the street, she put her arm around Warren and rested her head on his shoulder.

Gran started for the door. "Noelle, honey, don't forget your father is leaving soon, too."

A fresh wave of grief made her suck in her breath. She glanced up at Warren. "I need to spend some time with my dad before he goes. Will you come over later?"

He kissed her on the forehead and gave her a gentle shove toward the house. "I'll be around."

She found her father in the guest room packing his travel bag. He looked up and smiled. "Come on in, honey."

She didn't know where to begin. It was one thing to make peace with Rebecca, whose patience and understanding had opened the door to friendship. But so much pain had passed between Noelle and her father. How could one weekend heal the years that had separated them?

Dad reached for her hand. "I was hoping we'd have a little time together before my flight. There's a lot I need to tell you—things about myself, about why I couldn't be the father you needed."

They sat together on the side of the bed while he delved into his past. The things he told her—all the disappointments and hardships from his childhood, his parents' financial struggles, his need to prove himself and do better for his own family—so much made sense now. She tried not to blame him for never sharing these things before, for keeping his anger and bitterness bottled up inside. Look what bitterness had done to her.

"It doesn't excuse how I failed you and your mother," Dad said. "Nothing can erase those hurts. But I see now where I went wrong, and I know God is helping me to change."

Noelle looked up, surprised. "I thought you didn't believe in God. You stopped going to church with Mom and me years ago."

"I think I've always believed there is a God, but it was easier to trust myself and my own abilities. I didn't want to need God or anyone else." He gave a rueful laugh. "At least, not until I realized what I had to lose."

This was her dad speaking? It was like he'd climbed inside her head and read her thoughts. The change in her father was certainly a miracle—the change in her own heart too.

When the time came for Dad to leave, Noelle stood back as he kissed Gran on the cheek, then leaned down to hug Kevin. "I'll be back in two weeks," he told the boy. "Just don't make any plans that will be messed up if my flights are delayed again."

"Don't worry." Rebecca tousled Kevin's hair. "The only plans we're making are for you to get home safe and sound."

Dad opened the passenger door for Rebecca, then paused to cast Noelle an expectant glance. She went to him, timidly reaching her arms around his neck, inhaling his cologne, making a memory. The same words she'd spoken so often as a little girl sprang to her lips. "Come back safe, Daddy. Come back home."

Her father kissed her on both cheeks and gave her a warm, tender hug. "I could stand here hugging you all day long. But if I don't get moving, I'll miss my plane. Promise me we can do this again when I get back in two weeks."

Noelle gave him an extra squeeze. "Count on it."

She waved from the end of the sidewalk until her dad's car turned at the end of the block. Heaving a wrenching sigh, she traipsed inside, only to be overwhelmed by the emptiness. It felt odd, and yet somehow natural and right, to miss Dad so much. She wished she could run to her mother's arms just like she used to. *"Tell me again how long Daddy will be gone this time. When is he coming home, Mommy?"*

"Two weeks, sugar. Daddy will be back in two weeks."

She paused at the closed door to the master bedroom. If only she could open it and find her mother waiting on the other side! Mom would be reclining on the chaise with a novel, or in the bathroom brushing her beautiful brown hair. Noelle whispered out a long, slow breath and opened the door.

Everything was the same—the damask bedspread, the lace curtains, the family portraits on the wall. What would Mom think if she knew her room and her possessions had become a cold, neglected shrine, frozen in time on the day she died?

Fingering a silk lampshade on the dresser, she recalled something her grandmother had mentioned on the phone a few weeks ago.

She went to the door and leaned into the hallway. "Gran?"

"In here, honey," her grandmother called from the kitchen.

"It's time, Gran. Time to go through Mom's things, like you said."

Gran came toward her, her lips pressed together in a sad smile. "Are you sure you're ready?"

"If we're going to keep living here, I need to make room for Dad and Rebecca to have their own stuff and feel like it's their home too."

"Is that what you want, for all of you to stay in this house?"

"Yeah, I think it is. For now, anyway." A sharp sigh raked Noelle's lungs. "But I was thinking maybe I'd move my things into Mom's room and give Dad and Rebecca my old room. It's not much smaller than this one. And then Kevin can have the guest room. Do you think it would be okay with them?"

Gran's eyes sparkled. "What a perfectly lovely idea." She pulled Noelle close for a kiss on the cheek. "I'll get some boxes from the garage."

The task was both easier and harder than Noelle had expected. Each piece of jewelry, each article of clothing, each book and photograph and knickknack on the dresser held a special memory, a happy memory. She chose some treasures to keep, while Gran put aside a few things for herself, Uncle David, and Aunt Susan. They boxed the rest to pass along to a local charity.

In the bathroom, Noelle sorted through tubes of lipstick, eye shadow palettes, a curling iron, hair dryer, brushes and combs. On a gilded tray with a mirrored base, she found her mother's English Rose cologne. She'd touched so many of Mom's things today, relived so many memories. Did she have the courage to immerse herself in just one more?

Gingerly she lifted the silver cap, touched her finger to the opening, and tilted the bottle. She dabbed her wrist with the pink-tinged liquid and then pressed her arm to her face and breathed in the delicate fragrance.

She tilted her head. Her eyelids fell shut. She could almost hear her mother speaking.

"I'm proud of you, Noelle. You survived. You came through with courage, love, and dignity, just as I always knew you would."

It had taken all of Gary's willpower to tear himself away from his family's embrace and drive away. For the first time in his career, anywhere was too far to travel, any length of time too long to be separated from the family he cherished. Maybe he couldn't do anything about the past and all the lost years with his daughter, but he could do something about the future.

On the drive to the airport, his mind spun with the possibilities. He'd earned a respectable level of seniority at DataTech, not to mention invaluable knowledge and skill. He'd use these as bargaining chips, negotiate for an advisory or consultant position that would keep him closer to home.

And if that didn't work out? His lips quirked in a smug smile. With the investments he'd made, his family could live comfortably for as long as it took for him to find new employment. Maybe he'd even teach computer science at SMU or one of the community colleges.

Arriving at the busy terminal, Gary edged into a vacant spot by the curb. He leaned across the console and pulled his wife close, embracing her roughly. "Dear God, I don't want to go!" A more heartfelt prayer he'd never voiced.

"Two weeks will pass before you know it." Rebecca coiled her fingers through his hair. "And before long the project will be finished and you'll be home to stay."

He crushed her lips with a lingering kiss and had to tear himself away before he decided not to leave at all. "When I get back next time, I've got some ideas I want to talk over with you."

"Oh?" She gave him a sly smile, color rising in her cheeks. "I may have a few ideas of my own, and they don't necessarily involve conversation."

He grinned. "I can't wait."

Aiming the car toward the airport exit, Rebecca realized she'd never had a chance to talk to Gary about putting the condo on the market. Yes, it was definitely time. Settling into Kate's house still felt awkward, but over the last few weeks she'd come to realize she and Kate were not so different. They both cherished their family above all else. They were both women of faith, doing their best to seek God's purpose and live in His will.

Merging onto I-35, Rebecca pictured Kate Townsend that day outside Gary's service anniversary party. A smile of admiration spread across her lips. Nothing subtle about the woman—a lady of poise, wisdom, and courage in every sense. When Kate had set her plans in motion before she died, she must have had some idea of the maelstrom she'd be unleashing. But in the end, what had seemed like Kate's reckless gamble with others' lives and emotions had turned out to be a legacy of love, truly a family inheritance that had changed all their lives for the better.

"I wish I could have known you as a friend, Kate," she whispered as she turned into the driveway and shut off the engine. "I'll do my best to be one to your daughter."

Entering through the front door, Rebecca paused in the entryway. From down the hall came Noelle's and Irene's muted voices. Rumblings from the game room suggested Kevin was slaying monsters in one of his video games.

With a contented sigh, Rebecca closed the door behind her and strode into the den. "Hey, kids, I'm home!"

I hope you enjoyed
THE SOFT WHISPER OF ROSES

If you did, please spread the word among your reader friends and wherever you share about books on Facebook, Twitter, Instagram, or other social media.

I'd also be most grateful if you'd post a review on Goodreads, your blog, and/or your favorite online bookstore. A review doesn't have to be lengthy or eloquent, just a few brief words sharing your honest impressions. Reviews and personal recommendations are the best ways to help authors get discovered by new readers.

To receive regular updates about my books and special events, be sure to subscribe to my newsletter (signup form on my website).

Visit Myra online:
www.myrajohnson.com

AUTHOR'S NOTE

This novel has gone through many iterations since the idea first began germinating more than thirty years ago. The earliest version was told entirely through Noelle's point of view, a teenage girl coming to grips with her mother's death, her father's estrangement, and the unwanted stepfamily she'd been thrust into. But as I delved deeper into Rebecca's and Gary's pasts and their resulting emotional and spiritual struggles, I knew their love story would become central to the Townsend family's journey toward restoration.

I have many to thank for advice and suggestions so generously given during the creation and evolution of this story. Attempting to acknowledge each person who contributed over the past thirty years will certainly mean inadvertently omitting someone, so I won't even try.

However, it is with deepest gratitude that I mention my most recent advisors: author Melissa Jagears for her spot-on critiques and untiring assistance with cover design, and for sharing her abundance of publishing and marketing wisdom; editor Teresa Lynn for helping me further refine the plot and characters; author Walt Mussell, who made sure my Japanese phrases were accurate; and, as always, my amazingly wise and ever encouraging agent, Natasha Kern.

On the home front, my eternal gratitude to my sweet and supportive husband, who doesn't mind doing the grocery shopping, running the vacuum, or tossing in a load of laundry so I can keep working on the book. You are the best, honey!

Abundant thanks to you, my readers, because without you, the stories are incomplete. I love hearing from you and hope you'll stay in touch! You can always reach me through my website, www.MyraJohnson.com, where you can learn more about my books, meet my alter ego The Grammar Queen, and subscribe to my newsletter.

And just for fun, here's a photo of me playing "Aunt Trina" in my high school production of *I Remember Mama*. The dress once belonged to my grandmother!

Thanks for coming along on this journey, and may God always watch over you!

— *Myra Johnson*

I Remember Mama was first produced by Messrs. Richard Rodgers and Oscar Hammerstein II at the Shubert Theatre, New Haven, Connecticut on September 28, 1944 and subsequently at the Music Box Theatre, New York City, on October 19, 1944.

ABOUT THE AUTHOR

Native Texan Myra Johnson is a three-time Maggie Awards finalist, two-time finalist for the prestigious ACFW Carol Awards, winner of Christian Retailing's Best for historical fiction, and winner in the Inspirational category of the National Excellence in Romance Fiction Awards. After a five-year sojourn in Oklahoma, then eight years in the beautiful Carolinas, Myra and her husband are thrilled to be home once again in the Lone Star State enjoying wildflowers, Tex-Mex, and real Texas barbecue!

Married since 1972, Myra and her husband have two beautiful daughters married to wonderful Christian men, plus seven amazing grandchildren and a delightful granddaughter-in-law. The Johnsons share their home with two pampered rescue dogs and a snobby but lovable cat they inherited from their younger daughter when the family was living overseas.

Find Myra online:
www.myrajohnson.com

f facebook.com/MyraJohnsonAuthor

y twitter.com/MyraJohnson

instagram.com/mjwrites

BB bookbub.com/authors/myra-johnson

g goodreads.com/MyraJohnsonAuthor

pinterest.com/mjwrites

BOOKS BY MYRA JOHNSON

CONTEMPORARY INSPIRATIONAL ROMANCE

Autumn Rains

Romance by the Book

Where the Dogwoods Bloom

Rancher for the Holidays

Worth the Risk

Her Hill Country Cowboy

Hill Country Reunion

The Rancher's Redemption

Their Christmas Prayer

The Rancher's Family Secret

CONTEMPORARY ROMANCE COLLECTION

The Horsemen of Cross Roads Farm

Three full-length novels:

A Horseman's Heart

A Horseman's Gift

A Horseman's Hope

FLOWERS OF EDEN HISTORICAL SERIES

The Sweetest Rain

Castles in the Clouds

A Rose So Fair

TILL WE MEET AGAIN HISTORICAL SERIES

When the Clouds Roll By

Whisper Goodbye

Every Tear a Memory

CONTEMPORARY WOMEN'S FICTION

All She Sought[1]

One Imperfect Christmas

The Soft Whisper of Roses

NOVELLAS

The Oregon Trail Romance Collection: Settled Hearts

Designs on Love

Lifetime Investment

---

1. Previously published as *Pearl of Great Price*; see author website for details

CPSIA information can be obtained
at www.ICGtesting.com
Printed in the USA
LVHW031623090321
680995LV00007B/1028

9 781735 610702